Corruption

Isaac Diaz

Corruption

First edition.

ISBN 978-069 2703939

Pure Publications.

To Shawna, Ben, Riley, and Asia

Prologue

I stared aimlessly at my palms. They were covered in the leather-like material that had to be secured and tightly strapped to the rest of the suit. A light amount of metal was placed at the top of my hands, just enough to not be a hassle to simply raise my hand. I liked the weight. It made me feel more secure even though I knew the armor would do nothing against bullets.

I tried my best to do anything to keep my mind off my mission while I could. The moment I stepped out of the vehicle I'd be bombarded with everything. I was the main part of the mission. If I screwed up, everything we've done, all the sacrifices people made, they'd all be for nothing. It was all up to me and I hated it. There'd be no one to blame but me.

"Violet."

I didn't hear my name called the first time. Rylan would say my focus was one of the best, and I knew it was

1

too, but right now I was completely out of it. I wasn't myself and it was the worst of times to be happening.

"Violet," Rylan called out once more.

I picked my head up just enough to let my eyes ease on him. Despite the bumpiness of the terrain, I was able to steady in on him. I allowed the calmness he gave off to try and aid me.

"You okay?" he asked.

His expression was more solemn than I've ever seen from him. Surely he knew how important this was too. Heck. He was the one who started everything. Of course he knew.

I wanted to lie. I wanted to tell him I was fine but there'd be no point. One, he could read through any of my lies and two, I needed to show as much confidence as I could right now. Lying would do nothing to help that.

"Yeah."

The lie stung. I waited to see his disappointment in me through his eyes. He was always one to be slick in every situation. There were times where he was almost dead and he still held his smug smile. Right now, that was all lost. His face didn't change and he gave a small nod.

"Good." He knew I was lying. "We'll go over things one more time. No point in not being over prepared."

I threw my eyes to the left of me, expecting a snobby comeback from Scarlett. Her natural red hair was hanging over her eyes as she held her head down. The sight nearly made me jump. The more and more I saw everyone morbid, the more things were closing in on me. Realization was horrible.

Her red armor mixed with her hair perfectly. A brief feeling of nostalgia coursed through me. I remembered perfectly the night we got those. I remember how close I was to killing Scarlett and the bullet Rylan shot in my knife to knock it out of my hands. I could blame it on my hormones, and it may have been partially the reason, but either way, I made the decision, almost killing her when the Palace Guards invaded, leaving her helpless on the beach.

It was because of that night they made me the leader over Scarlett and Aqua. I asserted my dominance and my anger, showing to what extent I wanted justice to whoever deserved it. I let out a sigh before I caught myself and halted it in its tracks. Why couldn't I be as strong as I was then, or anytime for that matter? I had missions that put my life and others on the line as well but nothing near the point of affecting the future as significantly.

I was 18 at the time as well as Scarlett and Aqua. We were mature and had experienced the effects of war first hand. But it was just the start. We'd witness something far more magnificent.

Rylan sat up just a bit to talk.

"Violet, you'll be kidnapping the Princess. Again, we don't know much of the layout inside the palace. You'll have to pretty much search everywhere for her. Obviously a nursery. You should have it somewhat easy. Well, let's say easier than it should be. Aqua, Scarlett and I are gonna join the diversion at the front of the Palace, taking all the guards attention."

I gave a nod.

"And Violet," he said, trying to find firmness in his voice, "there's no extraction. You'll have to find your own way back to the lab for the final tests before transport."

"I know."

"Hey." Aqua placed a hand on my shoulder. Being the softer of all of us, she could have a way with words. "You'll do good."

"It doesn't matter if I do good or not, Aqua. If I die, they take the Princess. If the Princess dies, we all lose. Good isn't gonna cut it. Perfection. Just like always."

3

"And you'll be perfect just like always then," she said with a smile.

I finally turned my head towards her and took in her blonde hair. It lusciously flowed over her shoulders on top of her blue suit. The light hue of LEDs that emitted from the cracks of it threw some blue on her and made the ends of her hair just as her name calls her.

All three of us were here including Rylan, our leader and the creator of Equilibrium Headquarters. All of us were here except one person. A person I loved. A person I hated. A person I envied at some times, thinking Rylan loved her. We were missing Purity. With her not being there, I didn't know how to feel. She was often gone, off doing whatever the heck someone like her, someone with powers like her, would do.

Rylan looked over his shoulder to yell over the sound of the engine into the cabin.

"Ed, how much longer?!"

"We're coming up on it! I'd say about a mile!"

"You get me as close as you can, you got it?!" I yelled at Ed.

He gave a chuckle that was loud enough to hear.

"When have I let you down sweetheart?"

"Just about every time," I said sarcastically, surprising myself that I was the one doing it instead of Scarlett.

I saw my entrance coming up fast. I went ahead and threw my helmet on with my brain using the suits neurotransmitter attached to my spine. The HUD wasted no time and came up instantly, scanning all the faces in the vehicle. A display of information on them threw itself at me just before I chucked it aside with my mind.

"Hey."

The voice was jagged at first, coming out of a state of not talking for quite some time now. It cleared up after the first few words and instantly found a place in my memory. Scarlett lifted her head and let her green eyes focus on me.

Her eyebrows tugged in to the point of showing sincere frustration. There was no remains of sarcasm and joy. Malice found its way to her look to demonstrate pure hatred.

"You hurt Zalus where it hurts the most."

"He doesn't love his daughter that much," I said.

She gave a nasty chuckle.

"Of course I know that. It's power he loves. Take it." The far left of her mouth twitched up. "Take it all."

I wished I would've taken off my helmet to allow her to see my smile.

I'm not one to reminisce over memories or special moments such as the last ones you'd know you'd have with someone. Without ever saying bye or giving them a heads up, I jumped out of the vehicle and rolled onto the asphalt to keep up with the momentum. Not once did I think to look back at them leaving. No. They were busy with their mission and I was busy with mine.

I was left with the task of kidnapping the Princess. A crime that was held highest of all. That didn't bother me though. I was one of the top criminals in Novus next to Rylan, Purity, Scarlett, and Aqua. I was used to the opposition. I wasn't bothered by that one bit. It was something far worse.

What was to happen next would determine the future. Not only mine.

But hers.

*   *   *

My state of mind was constant anger once I stepped foot inside the Palace. Just the thought that I was standing inside it was disgusting. It was the filth's house. His abode. I wanted no part of him. I spent all my years fighting him. Why would I ever want to be this close to him?

I flicked my helmet off and it folded back into its pocket. I threw my hand behind my hair to throw it out and allow it to fall to its position.

I wasted no time and started with a bold pace. My head was constantly searching. It wasn't the nursery I was looking for. I knew she wouldn't be this low to the ground. I was waiting for the moment I'd be jumped with hundreds of Palace Guards. I waited for the sea of black that I fought way too often to make their way towards me.

I knew the rest of us were fighting out in front of the Palace in a firefight but I didn't think they'd fall for it. How flawed could you be Zalus? Why would we ever fight you head on? We know your weakness. But I guess not knowing what we were coming for was a factor.

There would be the occasional rumble from an explosion that would absorb into my suit. I knew if I wasn't where I was at that moment, I would've been in the front lines right now firing away at people in black, aiming for heads and a quick shot. Instead, I was subject to the silent ambience of the large expanse of useless space.

He really liked white. It wasn't the kind of white that was hard to look at, though. He had the lights that hung above in vibrant chandeliers dimmed, giving an offset of grey.

Before I stepped into the open, I activated my EMP inside my suit that pulsed in a radius. All the cameras were maimed useless. If no one was even walking around here I doubted there was anyone at the cameras and would notice that some were offline.

Annoyed at their flaws, I finally stepped out and made my way towards a staircase, trying to ignore as much of the Palace as I could. The delicacies here was the complete opposite of home. Equilibrium Headquarters was mostly underground. I was used to the rust and the smell of metal. I grew to love it and now this was just absolutely horrid. Who would ever find the smell of artificial flowers pleasing?

We hardly had colorful plants anymore. You were lucky if you found a hint of yellow in a stray flower that sprouted out in a weed that made its home in a crack. I was just happy that there was still some type of plant life alive. Hundreds of bombs being dropped wasn't helping in any way. But as people say I guess: life finds a way.

Once my metal boots made contact with the first step, my heartbeat started to increase. I heard the thumping in my ears but I ignored it. I told myself I wasn't nervous.

When I made it to about halfway up the first floor, I heard a humming coming down from above me. I watched as four Palace Guards stepped out of the elevator and ran out towards the entrance to the Palace, hoping to somehow aid in the bloodbath they wouldn't win.

As they faded out of vision and ran behind a wall, I noticed my hand automatically went to my gun. The fact that they were too distracted made me feel a little more comfortable but I shook my head, still trying to keep my stance on my confidence.

I let out a grunt and unlatched my gun and activated the magnet in my glove to let it fly into my hand. I loved the hiss that it spit out and the clank that it made when it whacked my hand.

Nothing was like the feeling of my gun. I knew the power and the force it provided. With it in my hand, a pit of fire was ignited inside my chest.

Find your anger Violet. Show them what we're capable of. What you're capable of.

They knew we were notorious for fighting their Guards and halting his crappy campaigns. This time we'd watch him burn. That's right. We got a plan this time. One that's gonna make him squirm. One that's gonna make him cringe. You think were just a bunch of people with guns fighting for something we can't ever obtain. But no. You're wrong. This time we have something that's worth every life that falls for him. You'll truly know the pain of the Equilibrium. You'll truly know *his* pain.

I recited all the fueled flames that got me burning as I made my way up the stairs. Oh how I'd love to see my face at a time like this. I adored the way my anger burned and whenever I'd see my reflection at HQ, it'd push me harder. It assured me of who I was and I needed every drop of it.

Once I made it to somewhere around the tenth floor I started to hear movement of people. I was making my way to the core of the Palace. But this was nowhere close to the bustle that it must've had when there wasn't an attack on it. Everyone was hiding or in some type of secure location, all the important people at least.

I raised an eyebrow as I hid myself between pillars, waiting for two people in white coats to wander on by. Did that mean that the Princess was with the King in some type of bunker? Would he even do that? Without a doubt he had one when the war started out, but now that this is the only country left, he'd have no one to fear. Heck, we'd never get our hands on a bomb and if we did, we'd never hurt innocent people to kill him.

My confusion turned to frustration. Of course he wouldn't be hiding. That cocky idiot. He thinks he's gonna win. He was probably watching the fight from his balcony and despite the Princess being the only bloodline of the

Exon family left besides him, she was probably just in her normal room.

I thought about how much he was gonna regret letting his guard down when we attacked after finding out his daughter was taken as I was drawing closer and closer to the top.

And then I found it. A room with the sign on the side of it.

Princess Exon

I released my gun into my hand and whirred it up. I thought about it for a second but decided to leave my helmet off. It'd startle them even more, but not like it mattered.

I raised my gun and held it firmly in both my hands, the leather making a clean grip with it. I kept my eyes focused on everything. Step by step, I put one foot in front of the other and stealthily made my way inside the nursery.

The first thing I noticed was two women standing with their backs to me in outfits designed specifically for caring for the Princess. I immediately noticed they both had neuro transmitters on their spines. With one tick of the mind, they can speak and transmit their voice to the big guys pretty much.

The counter to the side of them had utensils and tools along with the normal care for a baby. In front of them was a crib with the Princess inside. I noticed there was light coming in from the window behind her, illuminating what I came for.

I stood for a good few seconds and thought of how I was gonna go about this since I had an edge over them. Grab one of their necks and put one to sleep while dealing with the other?

I wanted to let out a sigh but they would've heard me. It wasn't that easy. They could let the whole Palace know of my presence with simply their voice. But there was no running around the fact that I had to act regardless. I went ahead and braced myself for whatever they'd and spoke up.

"I want both of you to turn around with your hands up and not speak a word," I demanded in a calm voice.

Both of them straightened their backs at the sound of my voice and froze. They did as I told and turned. My eyes darted for the gun they had strapped to the front of their waist. There'd be no way they'd use it. Would they?

I made the most concerned face I could to express my sincerity.

"Please, for the love of God, don't use your transmitter." I gave a small shake of my head. "I don't want to have to kill you."

We all stood without saying a word or moving a muscle, waiting for something to happen. Catching me off guard, one of them spoke.

"Zalus, we have an intruder in the Princess's room. I need backup imme-"

I pulled my finger back making her drop to the floor. Without moving my attention elsewhere, I kept my eyes on the other one. She kept her hands up and she had her eyes widened because of the death of her colleague.

"Don't shoot," she said. I was surprised that I couldn't hear fear in her voice. I was so used to it that when I finally found someone who wasn't afraid, I almost instantly wanted to let my guard down. "Let me just ask what you're doing?"

"I'm taking the Princess."

"Violet, right?" she asked.

I nodded. God, was I that known?

She stepped out of my way and watched as I walked up to the King's last hope. With one hand on my gun and another free, I reached in for her. When I started to cup her in my hand, my hand was tapped and moved just a bit. Startled, I turned and saw that the woman who was still alive was moving me away from her. With a sense of confrontation, I raised my gun at her.

She continued what she was doing but held a smile on her face.

"Don't need to shoot. I'm only helping you."

I thought of it as a lie immediately but when she brought the Princess over to me wrapped in a blanket, it slowly dissolved.

She read my face and let out a small laugh.

"You're from Equilibrium right?"

"Yeah," I said, barely lowering my gun.

"That's what I figured. I see you all the time on the news. Something new and crazy. Something that ticks Zalus off even more than the previous time. We all see it. And to be honest, I can't help but feel happy when I watch that."

She held the baby ever so carefully. She fixed the bend of the blanket that came around and covered her cheek. If I'd never known anything about the Princess, I'd think she was her mother. But I knew that wasn't the case at all. The Queen was dead and for only one reason. Her dying face flashed in my head when I saw the resemblance in her daughter.

"I only want the best for the Princess. She didn't deserve to be born into this awful mess of a world." She returned her attention towards me and I focused in on my reflection in the browns of her eyes. "That's why I'm gonna help you."

"What?" I said silently.

"Yeah, and I suggest we get going because she actually sent in a transmission. They're probably right around the corner."

Still not really getting what she was trying to do, I let out a firm frown.

"Then I hold her," I ordered.

"My pleasure," she said, handing her to me.

She let out a big breath and gave a good stretch. Her hand reached down towards her gun and readied it in her hand.

"Ready?" she asked with a smile.

I stood with a blank face, completely hopeless for words.

"Oh right, my name. Don't really trust me without it, huh?" She gave a look I'd never forget. It was a look that would haunt me for years to come, slowly corroding my mind. Making me beg for answers, asking whose face that was. "Name's Penn."

I watched her for a few moments, making myself look stupid.

"C'mon. We stand around here any longer and we're dead," Penn said. She placed a hand behind me and slightly pushed me forward to get my feet working. I never took my eyes off of her when we started to leave the room. Was I really gonna let her help me; a member of the King's Palace? I didn't realize it at first but apparently the Princess was slipping out of my hands. Penn turned around and ran towards me. "No. You're holding her wrong."

She fixed the Princess's head in the crevice of my underarm, using it as a pocket. She then moved my arm downwards to snake against her backside.

"You wanted to use your gun, right? This is the only way. Now you hold her tight and don't let go. C'mon, I'll show you fastest way outta here."

12

She took the lead and held her gun downward as she ran. I didn't know much about the procedures of the Palace but it seemed like they trained their people to use weapons. Everything about her holding it and her run told of her training.

I eventually had to reassure myself that I was trusting this girl with everything. It wasn't just the life of the Princess and mine but also all the work that's gone into this.

Once we left the nursery, we ran out into a long corridor. With every corner we would pass she would lift her weapon up, ready to fire at whoever was there. The fact that this girl was willing to simply betray the people she worked for scared me. Her head whipped back every other second to make sure I was right on her tail.

Just when I thought maybe the transmission didn't go through, a bullet flew over my head from behind and flung itself into a pillar, making pieces of it fly out and litter the floor. I hunched over and readied my gun. Before I could do anything to deal with the people behind me, I was pushed forward by Penn. She swapped positions with me and made sure she would be the first to be shot, willing to give her life for the protection of the Princess.

I didn't expect them to stop firing, and as I assumed, they didn't. They were persistent on stopping us from leaving with her. As I was focusing on sprinting to some sort of salvation, I heard the sound of a bullet tearing through flesh. Right as the sound entered my ear and my brain registered it, I felt something pull on me. I took it as a sight of hostility and readied myself for whoever it was that was pulling me through a doorway.

After entering the doorway and gathering my bearings, I turned to see Penn out of breath with a look that I once expressed. Only once. She looked up at me, almost confused, and gave a chuckle that was not meant for laughter.

"I just shot someone," she said. I could tell her smile was still trying to press through despite what happened.

I nodded my head, remembering that I felt the same way.

"Yup. And you're gonna have to do it again. Feels disgusting but you're gonna have to get used to it if you want to live."

She examined her gun in detail and even put her eye down the barrel, making me roll my eyes at her carelessness.

"Never really knew how powerful this thing was."

The abrupt sound of the door sliding open behind her sounded through the room. Standing there was a Palace Guard with a weapon of his own. I raised my gun and pulled the trigger, barely missing Penn's head.

She pivoted her head just enough so she could see me with her peripheral vision.

"You're pretty quick."

I let out a sigh and stormed out of the room. I didn't have time for her remarks.

"The exit. Now!"

"Right. Right," she said, jogging to catch up to me.

I checked to see if the Princess was still in my arms and to my surprise, she was still asleep.

Penn moved back in front to take the lead and I watched as her hair flowed around as if it was happy.

"You're lucky you got me ya know," she said with a smile. "Being the caretaker for the Princess, I pretty much have access all over the Palace, including the ones no one's supposed to know about."

We walked up to a bare wall and she placed a hand over the smooth surface. After a few seconds, a computer voice spoke.

"What are you doing Penn?"

The voice was strange. It had a presence that of a human. The way it slurred after every word made me realize just how smart this thing was despite the few words I barely heard.

"None of your concern ALIS," Penn said, still trying to access a panel that appeared on the wall.

"King's orders that no one leaves the Palace besides the Guards."

"Don't give me this right now ALIS. I'm here to escort the Princess to a secure location."

"And her nursery wasn't secure?"

Penn let out a sigh.

"ALIS."

"It's in my coding that I obey the King's orders above any other."

"And it's in my directions that I protect the Princess in any way possible."

There was a short pause before the computer spoke again.

"This person with you. Who is sh-. Oh. Hello Violet."

I felt my eyebrows fold down.

"How do you know who I am?" I asked.

"It's quite simple. I have records for every person living on Novus."

"I'm not on the records."

"Exactly. I couldn't read you. It was obvious who you were. I have to say, I thought humans were smarter. If anything were obvious to *you*, you'd know of my stalling. Sorry Penn. Access denied."

The panel Penn was using disappeared, making her step back from the wall. I watched her, hoping that her look of shock would dissolve. She had to get it back up. It's not like we could just waltz out of the entrance to the Palace.

"Penn. You get that panel back up!" I demanded in a firm voice, using the same tone I would use on Scarlett and Aqua.

She turned her head towards me and focused on me for a brief second before I noticed her eyes switched to something behind me. She shook her head as footsteps sounded through the hallway, letting out a chuckle.

"Oh you're gonna get it ALIS."

I tightened my grip around the Princess and ran forwards in front of Penn. I was so used to everything about the Palace Guards that I didn't need to turn around to know what idiots were there.

Just when I turned a corner to another corridor and didn't feel the presence of Penn behind me did I noticed my training and instinct kick in. She was risking everything for me and I left her like she was nothing. But now wasn't the time to be caring about people I didn't know. When everything was resting on my shoulders, it wasn't an option on who would be the first to go.

Gunshots were fired. The sound didn't surprise me in any way. I wasn't quick to doubt what happened to her and pushed even harder, knowing I was next.

I kept making turns I had no clue where they'd lead me to. I eventually made it to a dead end. It was an elevator that required a hand print and my access to this means of escape was now dead. I cursed in my head about how careless she was. She should've been here.

Although the elevator was glass, it was no doubt bullet proof just like everything else in here so there was no point in trying to break into it.

"Don't worry! I got it!"

I turned and saw Penn out of breath and sprinting towards me. Her gun was held in her hand and sweat dripped down her forehead.

"You're not dead?"

I didn't realize what I said until I saw her reaction towards it.

"Nope. Pretty good aren't I? I'd say give me a few more months and I'd be just as good as you." She walked up to the panel and placed her hand on it, causing it to open. "I don't know. Maybe even a little better."

She turned and gave me a wink.

What's wrong with this girl? Why the heck was she so kind? What could she be wanting to gain? It only meant one thing for her. Either she goes into hiding or dies for treason.

I noticed she did the same thing with her eyes as earlier. It shifted to something behind me after looking into my own eyes. Despite what was coming for us, her smile still held. If anything, it was even brighter.

She bobbed her head at the elevator.

"Don't wanna miss your ride do ya?"

"Wait, what?"

I was terribly confused. I could read situations quite well. It was extremely important to my missions. But her smile. It was too hard to read through.

She walked forward towards the Palace Guards as they ran down the corridor.

"Do me a favor will ya. Take care of her. Oh. And by the way, she has no name. At least not yet. Just make sure it's a pretty one."

Out of nowhere, two clear glass panels closed in front of me. I looked down and saw that she actually placed me in the elevator. I shot my head back up just when the lift shot down. Right before my vision was cut off by the floor, I witnessed blood color the top of the elevator as she was bombarded with bullets. It happened all too fast that I never saw her hit the floor.

I was left with myself, speechless. I didn't know why, though. I've seen so many people die that I couldn't even begin to think of even numbering them. It was common. An everyday thing, especially in a world like this. Why couldn't I get over what she did for me? Was it any different from what people did in EQ Headquarters? They often risked their lives for us. If I was ever sentimental, it should be over them, not her.

The elevator kept falling down its shaft, dropping a floor every second. All I could do was watch the light in the elevator go from a flash of light to pitch black. From a flash of light to pitch black. Light. Black. Light. Black. In every flash, I saw one thing.

Penn.

I looked down at the key to the mission.

Are you really worth all this much? You're just a little girl.

The floors that I was passing through faded and I was met with the view of the city. The bright orange hue of the evening sky painted a stroke of itself across all the buildings. I could see the smoke from where I was at. It billowed up and darkened the sky. I'd never seen this side of the Palace. Usually all I saw was the front but this was a secret exit so it was obvious I would've never seen it.

With the light from the sky, I looked back down at the Princess. I folded back the blanket that was covering the top of her head to make sure it was really the Princess. There was a mark, something that specifically marked one a royal. For males, red eyes. For females, red eyes and hair.

The small amount of red hair on the child was curly and stuck up. Just to make sure, I carefully lifted an eyelid to see her eyes. Just as expected, her iris was the same shade as her hair.

With me touching her eyelid, she turned in my hands and I felt her move for the first time. The feeling of holding a baby, a small human, in your arms was something extraordinary. You could feel the potential resonating from all parts of them.

She opened her eyes in a daze from the sleep just for a second. During that time, I gazed into her eyes. This was royal blood. Her eyes spoke of it. This child was clearly marked as a Princess. But she wasn't that at all.

With the shortsighted view I had, I could never have known what she would do to me. I would've never known.

Thoughts of doubt litter my mind. What if I never kidnapped her? What would become of our future? What would become of our world? What would become of The Equilibrium?

I watched her eyes close again as she went back to sleep. Just the few seconds I saw her marvelous eyes made me want to see more.

See the Blood Red.
See the Beauty.

Oh, but little did I know what lurked in those eyes.

See the Corruption.

Chapter 1

You know, I should've expected this coming. Granted, it was kinda impossible to figure out what the heck she meant without someone telling you, but still, after everything that's happened it should've been seen from miles away.

Psh. Says the one who was desperate for any sort of explanation.

The girl's smile held and she refused to let me out of her sight. I stared right back at them, unaware I was even doing so. My mind wasn't focused on the fact that she was staring at me when I'd normally consider something like that creepy. It was fully focused on trying to discern her words.

The shared feeling that I got from them and they got from me was something I was experienced with. But never did I think that confusion was one of the things that connected us. Well, maybe it wasn't exactly confusion.

There's so many other emotions that link with it. Anger, frustration, anxiety, desperation. Must I continue? Whatever the heck we were feeling, it forced itself down my chest.

I could see the others in my peripheral vision. They were all frozen and assumed the same position as me. I noticed Wendy's pigtails were flowing in the wind, blowing around every time a gust came by. To be completely honest, I have no idea how long we stood there. After all, we just finished a fight. Rest was desired by our bodies. Especially for my wound that I completely forgot about.

"So, I don't really know about you guys, but I don't think you're pretty enough for me to be staring at you all day. If you guys were a little cuter than maybe."

Her voice made my mind go insane and wrestle with what I was hearing. Why did she sound so familiar?

The girl stood about my height and had long brown hair. The definition of her cheeks weren't as defined as people's tend to be. They had a soft presence that followed down to her jaw line. She was wearing a black coat that appeared light in weight; something she could move freely in. Around her neck was a scarf that looked rigid. Nothing about it yelled comforting. The ends that would usually flare out were tucked in her coat that she had zipped up.

"Even then. I can't really stay around for that long. Time isn't a luxury I have."

She turned her head to the left of her. All of our heads moved along with hers and immediately caught sight of long lights that threw themselves in the air and on the surrounding buildings in the distance. The tattered structures reflected the light and revealed that they were getting closer.

"Yeah. Palace Guards are no fun." She looked back at us. "Especially when they're trying to kill you."

It's funny. The words that should've scared me didn't have much of an effect on me. I've been there done that. Death was always a factor and now that didn't really matter. All I wanted was answers.

Wendy dipped down just a bit as if she was a toddler giving a tantrum.

"Oh come on! Are you serious?!" She pointed a finger at the girl. "Looky here Missy. Me and my friends have been busting our butts for the past couple of hours fighting. Now, you're telling me that there's more idiots trying to kill us?"

I agreed with every word Wendy was saying. After all, I could feel her frustration quite well.

"Well, you're quite the buzz these days. Hard to not get attention when you got a buddy like yours here."

She bobbed her head at me and they turned to make me the center of attention.

"So, Wendy," she smiled, almost like she wanted to make her more upset, "do you wanna stand here and complain some more or do you wanna get outta here alive?"

Wendy confronted her with a nasty sneer, not caring one bit that she was pretty. She didn't realize that doing so was against any sort of code of honor to pretty faces.

"You don't know who you're messing with, so I suggest you watch what you say."

She gave a remark of her own with a smile. No amount of anger makes Wendy upset. It's when she's upset and someone is still happy that aggravates her to no end. Yet, she does it all the time. You can't ever have your way with this girl.

"Oh, I know very well who I'm dealing with." She switched her attention to Charlotte. "Charlotte, I'm gonna need your help. You see that ledge over there? That's where we're headed. Granted, it's not the best place to hide but it's all we have right now."

"And what do you need my help for?" Charlotte asked.

"Don't play stupid here. How else do you think they're not gonna see us." She let out a sigh before she continued. "We need your invisibility."

Charlotte's lips scrunched up. Seeing her after that fight gave me a feeling I couldn't describe. Every time she fought showed how much she could handle herself. I felt like in a lot of ways that I was leading them. Now, how could that be the case when my fighting capabilities were far lower than any of theirs were? I felt the need to protect Charlotte the most out of all of them, yet, she could do that on her own and far exceed what I could ever do. Her whole figure spoke of her strength that she always kept hidden.

"That's gonna be a problem," Charlotte said. The girl never asked why. She simply pulled her eyebrows in as she looked on at Charlotte. "We have limits to our powers. Mine happens to be that I can't make others invisible along with myself. Well...I can. It just hurts like crazy."

The girl let out a scoff. The more she talked the more she sounded like the girl in white that saved our lives.

"Well then, that's not gonna help now is it? How about impressing me then, Wendy? Hm? You're up."

"Psh. You stupid or something? I was gonna get us outta this mess anyways," Wendy said as she crossed her arms.

"Then what are you waiting for?"

Wendy rolled her eyes before she reached out and grabbed our hands. When I reached out just a bit to grab hold of Charlotte's hand, my shoulder screamed. The pain was becoming self-aware that it needed to be cared for. I held it in as much as I could and waited for Wendy's jump. I closed my eyes as the other girl joined hands with Wendy. I took one more deep breath before we went through Wendy's quiet world to take us out of the building.

When I opened my eyes, I noticed we were higher than we were before. Just below us was the room we were standing in. With the wall torn down, you could see inside with ease with the help of the moonlight. I didn't get a chance to see what was in there when I was standing in it. From what I could tell, it held some type of machinery that looked like it was beyond its years of performing. That may have been the case but the technology looked way more advanced than anything I've seen. What stood out the most was a broken circle that was attached to the wall that was behind us.

"Who are they?" Will asked, bringing my attention back to what was happening.

"Like I said. Palace Guards. King Exon's very own." She shook her head with the same smile she's kept. "Idiots do anything he says."

"King Exon?" I asked.

The girl let a laugh out. It was almost out of complete pity of our cluelessness. I was about to frown when I noticed I already was. How long was I like this? If it was a thing, my forehead's probably gonna be sore in the morning.

"I'll explain what I can when we get out of this. Agreed?"

"Don't lie," Monica said ever so quietly.

"Lie?" the girl said, raising an eyebrow.

"Someone's already told us that same thing before. What'd we get?"

"N-o-t-h-i-n-g," Wendy said, finishing Monica's point.

"Don't worry guys. We don't keep lies."

Do you know how much I hate the word "we" now? It means only one thing. A group. But what does that matter?

Easy. It means people I don't know. And in turn, that means more things they know that I don't. I don't care what kind of people we've met or ran into, they always seem to know something. BloodLip. The mysterious group of people that saved us before coming here, which by the way, still didn't know where *here* was. They all knew something and they didn't tell us one thing. Can you answer me this before you say I'm too desperate, even though it's the truth. Why the heck haven't they?!

"If I gotta give one thing to the Guards, it's that they're persistent. Either that or they don't know when to give up. So, let's have some fun with your powers. And uh," she tucked her head in a little, "Wendy, love the teleportation by the way."

"Oh please. Don't try to kiss up to me."

The girl rolled her eyes before she got up and walked over to the wall behind us. She sized it up and started to look for something. I was watching from behind before Wendy punched me in the arm. I swear to God if she hit me any higher I would've strangled her. She hit just below my shoulder but it still allowed the pain to ripple up towards it.

"What!" I yelled, quickly turning to her.

"I saw what you were doing." Her face held a nasty smile. I knew from it that she wasn't being serious at all.

"What the heck are you talking about?!"

"Them apple bottom jeans." She raised both of her eyebrows and gave me a wink.

"Do you mean what I think you mean?"

"Come on Mark. You know you were staring."

I was about to push her but the girl called out.

"Will. See if u can get me that piece of metal."

He let out a sigh before getting up. Even after a fight and coming to this place where people already want us dead, he still didn't care about anything. It's like he just wanted to get home and lay down on his bed. And even then, he probably would be annoyed of that and want to do something else.

Every time I saw him stand at his full length, it ticked me off a little. He was naturally tall. I wasn't really known for height. To be completely honest, I was usually the shortest. I was just thankful that out of all of us, I was the second tallest. I was grateful for having a short growth spurt before my sophomore year. But even if I was shorter than Charlotte, it wouldn't matter. As long as she liked me for who I was, it wouldn't even be brought to mind. Right?

When he got up to where she was standing, he pushed the stray hairs that he had in front of his eyes away despite the wind's constant persistence to keep messing it up.

"That one right there," she said, pointing up towards a piece of metal that stuck out from a broken window.

It was clear to me now that the whole city we were in was abandoned. There wasn't a soul in sight besides us and the people chasing us. Who knew what happened to this place. Whatever happened, it obviously wasn't pretty. You could see marks from explosions and bullet holes all over the place. Glass along with other debris was thrown on the floor like it was a common thing.

Will extended his arms and used his Telekinesis to lift the metal out from the window and gave it to her.

"You better have a plan for this thing and not make me throw it at them," he said as he gave her an annoyed stare.

"C'mon. I didn't come here without knowing that we'd be chased. Of course I have a plan."

She held the piece of metal and walked up to where Monica was crouching.

"Hi," the girl said. Her smile seemed special this time, made specifically for Monica. What I didn't like, though, was that she was treating her like a child. So what she didn't talk much. She was way smarter than any of us were. She stayed crouched, waiting for a response from Monica. As expected, there was none. Monica just stared coldly back at her, making her uncomfortable.

"You can trust me. Like I said, we don't lie."

"You already did." Again, the girl raised an eyebrow. "Everyone lies."

"Well, yeah, of course. But you know what I mean. Anyways, Monica could you—"

"My name. How do you know it?" Monica interrupted.

She brought up a valid point. How did she know our names? She said we were quite the buzz. But what the heck did that mean? How did people know about us?

The girl's smile returned quickly.

"Everyone knows about you guys." She looked up and around at all of us as she spoke. "The Equilibrium. I mean, who doesn't know who you guys are? People hate you. People love you. For the past couple years you've been what's on the minds of everyone in Novus."

"Novus?" I asked.

The girl stood and stomped her feet and stuck out her arm like a lady from the Price Is Right.

"You're standing on it. It's our world. I'll make it simple for you. You were on Earth. Now you're on Novus. Easy right?"

"Are you saying we're on another planet?"

"Another planet. Another dimension. Yeah. How the heck do you think you got here? There was a dimensional door you guys went through. Right?"

So that's what it was. A dimensional door. It's what opened up right above our heads in the mall, sending me through a transport ten times worse than Wendy's. But when she said dimensional door, I turned my head back to the room we were standing in. Is that what the circle was?

I was about to ask her but a light flashed over us and blinded me.

"Get down!" she ordered.

All of us fell to the ground. At the time, we were on what looked like a broken piece of a building that fell. There was a piece of concrete that allowed some cover but it wasn't enough to provide a haven forever.

"Monica, light it up," she whispered as she slid the piece of metal towards her.

Monica grabbed the metal and slowly threw her electricity into it. It seemed like any sort of exhaustion from her trying to kill me in the slip space was gone. I watched as a small area around her glowed purple. She was trying her best to suppress the crackling noise that came with her power and contorted her face because of the heat from the scorched metal.

Once she was done, she scooted back and looked at the girl for further instructions.

"Will. You're gonna pick it up and pretend like this metal is us. Keep it at a pace that we'd normally run at and throw it in a different direction."

"Ugh! I told you I was gonna have to throw it!" he loudly whispered, snapping at the girl.

She gave a pitiful grin and showed her teeth as she shrugged her shoulders.

He threw his eyes to the back of his head and kept his head down as he crouched, just barely allowing his head to see over the concrete. I peeked over the side to see what he was doing, getting close to Charlotte. Despite us being on the disgusting floor, she still smelled godly. She was doing the same as I was and got even closer than we were.

Once Will got the metal close to the floor and started running it along on it, the Guards were quick to notice there was something there. They quickly chased after with their lights and shouted at what they thought was their targets. They let bullets fly out of their guns into it and followed right behind. After sending them away from us by a good distance, he let go of the metal.

The girl got up quickly and threw a hand up to signal us to do the same. Without even seeing if we were doing what was told of us, she took off into the city, the back of her jacket flaring up with her speed.

"What's with all these prissy girls," Will muttered as he got up.

"I think you got a thing for them," Wendy said.

Will stuck out his hands and jabbed them into her back, pushing her forward.

Even though I was using my feet, my shoulder suffered with every step. I examined it for the first time and saw just how deep Penn stabbed me. The blood flow seemed to go down for the moment but that meant nothing for me. It was still there and I was losing blood ever so slowly.

After we ran for a few minutes, we eased up on our pace. Charlotte hadn't said much in a while but she made sure to stay close to me. I got a little upset that she chose to stay close at a time like this when normally she wouldn't care at all as to where she'd be, leaving me to my struggles of trying to get close to her. I tried to alleviate some pain in my shoulder but nothing was really helping.

Without saying anything, Charlotte kneeled down for a second and pulled on something. I tried not to look and somehow make myself look cool by not caring but my curiosity got the better of me. When my eyes met with her hands, I noticed that she was pulling on her skirt. The fabric tore after a hard tug. She held the cloth in the air and pulled it to its length.

"Should be long enough. Come here."

I obeyed her and walked closer to her. She held the cloth firmly in her hands and placed it over my wound. She then went on to get the other ends and tie it around my underarm.

"Thanks."

"Mhm," she said quietly.

The unusualness of her response forced me to look at her head on, taking her in fully. Her face had some marks on it from the fight. Nothing major like what I had but scratches nonetheless.

"You alright?" I asked.

"I—I don't know. I just can't stop thinking about what happened in that abandoned building. And then we come here. It's just a lot to take in."

"Tell me about it."

"I guess looking on the bright side, Wendy's still her usual self."

"Who says that's a good thing?"

I gave her the most heartwarming smile I could give at the time, hoping that it'd comfort her in any way. I don't really know if it worked all that much. She was doing her best to look like she was doing okay. I know for a fact that she wasn't. None of us were. We needed to be honest with ourselves; we were scared out of our minds. And then we had to stumble upon this place and have another load thrown on us.

I could only wish that we'd get our answers. That'd be the only way I could—no, we could get any sort of satisfaction.

I used the time to look around at the war stained city. I wasn't all that sure if indeed there was a war. I could only assume from what I saw. There were some cases of whole buildings the size of the Penthouse toppled over. But despite all of the trash and debris, you could see that this place was once thriving. How could there be skyscrapers every other foot and there not be people here? If this girl was right about us being on another planet, it could only be proven, if it was true, from the things I saw.

Take for example the stuff I saw inside the first building we were in. This was technology that I've never seen before. And then now the city we were walking through. The buildings were made out of shapes and materials that weren't in Springfield.

There were also pathways that connected everything inside the city. The best way to describe everything was an organized mess.

Out of all of us, Monica was the one doing the most looking around. She was touching every surface we'd come close to only to hold her hand in place for a second and then do the same to another surface. For sure, she had to be trying to connect to whatever tech there was. All the while, the girl that welcomed us "home" was walking in front of us not saying a word.

Why were people even helping us? Was it just because of me? Just because I was this special person?

"Alright. We got out of what we were in. Now do you care to explain some things to us?" I asked.

She turned her head around and started walking backwards. She seemed overly happy, especially for being chased down. I bet letting her smile simmer in someone's face was something that she must've liked doing. It let her take control. After not saying anything and looking at us, she spoke.

"Ask away."

"Where are we?"

31

She shook her head.

"Why are you gonna ask the same kinda questions? Out of everything you'd want to know, you ask something I've already told you?"

"But what the heck *is* Novus?" Wendy asked.

"I thought I already put it simply. To be honest, I thought you guys would be smarter."

"Look, we just came through a freaking dimensional whatchamacallit. This stuff isn't common! Intelligence has nothing to do with this!" Will said.

"That could be argued. But beside the point, Novus is our planet. The one you were on was Earth. But now you're back to your birth home."

"You implying we were born here?" Charlotte asked. The girl gave a big nod. "No we weren't."

"How do you know that?"

"We have proof."

Her smile moved towards the right and she raised an eyebrow, clearly trying to prove Charlotte wrong.

"Yeah?"

"There's pictures of when I was born. We even have videos of our mothers giving birth."

"Really. Have they showed you?" I stopped to think. She was asking all of us. "Every time you ask them about your birth they get kinda weird, don't they. They change the story—try to change the topic. But "why" is the question."

She said this all with a smile. I wanted to claim what she was saying to be false but I couldn't deny the fact that what she said was true. If my birth was brought up, my mom would get exactly how she said. It would mainly be changing the subject.

"You think that's all the proof you need to clarify to yourselves that you were born on Earth? How do you know that was really you?"

"What kind of question's that?!" Wendy yelled. "Of course it's us! Who else would it be?"

"Then answer me this. Why do you all have the same birthday?"

As much as what she was saying had validation to it, I ignored all of it. So what we all had the same birthday. That was because we all had powers. It had to do with that, not with where we were born.

But. But what if. What if what she was saying was true? What if all I knew was wrong? What if this was really my home? I knew nothing after all. I didn't know why we had powers, let alone my own, or why BloodLip wanted me dead in the first place. All I could think of is what Violet said. Why was I so dangerous? Even if I did have such a dangerous power, I'd never use it to harm anyone.

I think everyone else was thinking the exact thing because no one spoke a word after her question. Not even Wendy.

"Then why? Why do we even have powers? If you claim we were born here, why the heck were we on Earth?"

"So you believe me?"

"No. But at least answer me that."

"Well, believe me. I'd like to. But there are some things that I'm not exactly supposed to say yet. Terra could go off on me is she knew I said something I wasn't supposed to. It's sorta her job to do all the big talk and do all the explaining to you guys."

Great. Another person I didn't know.

She noticed we were all looking at her, waiting for her to explain who Terra was.

"Oh, Terra's the leader of Equilibrium Headquarters."

"Headquarters?" I asked.

She gave a chuckle.

"Ready to find out who you really are?" She took my silence as a yes. "Good. Terra along with everyone else has been waiting for this day for 16 years. It's time to bring the Equilibrium home."

*   *   *

I was completely exhausted. I wanted to stop. But every step was now mechanical. I couldn't even if I wanted to. We've been walking for about three hours now. Three hours through this mess of a city.

My shoulder still ached immensely but it was suppressed to a degree because of Charlotte skirt around it. No, it wasn't because of the fact that it was stopping the blood from coming out, although that was probably a big reason. It was because it smelled like her. It was right next to my face and surprisingly, it overpowered the smell of my blood. From that, you probably think that she pours a whole container of perfume on her everyday but that's not the case.

Charlotte's distinct scent was something that couldn't be recreated. It was a smell that was combined with the scent of her house along with her shampoo and a tad bit of perfume. All of that formed the thing that defined Charlotte besides her hair and never ending kindness.

The girl, which I was still confused about why we never asked for her name, told us that we were going to meet up with Terra, the leader of Equilibrium Headquarters.

How'd I feel about that? Okay, let's see. One, I finally found something that was about the Equilibrium that wasn't specifically directed towards me. I was allowed to look at this annoying term from a different angle when I finally find out what it means. And two, I knew I was bound to be more confused than I was when I got here. Why? Why else? Because no one seems to care when this "important" individual doesn't know a thing about himself.

"We're here!" the girl shouted out in excitement.

The moment she said that, all of our heads picked up, searching for where exactly we were.

She pointed out in front of us.

"This is it. The last of Novus. Or in other words, as the King puts it, Exon. Arrogant fool names it after himself. People inside the city say that, but we, on the other hand, like to think he was just too stupid to come up with a name for the city."

As we took more steps, the toppled building that was covering it started to reveal this city. It was a stark contrast to what we were walking through these past few hours. You could tell in an instant that this place was full of people. The hum of the city could barely be heard. With the sun rising now, it reflected the fresh sunlight off and directed it at us. What seemed to take control of the whole city, setting everything lower than itself, was a huge pointed building that I could barely see. It was almost like a backdrop for the whole place.

I noticed our pace was a lot faster now, trying to see the city as a whole. I was all too focused on doing just that that I didn't see her in front of me.

"Wow."

The voice caught me off guard and my eyes quickly searched for the source of the sound. She was standing not that far from us.

Terra.

She stood at a reasonable height. Probably somewhere along Will's height. For a woman, she was tall. She had brown hair that was similar to Charlotte's but just a tad longer. From where I stood, I could see her green eyes perfectly. I hardly ever saw that color eye, and when I did, it made itself present, forcing you to know of its uniqueness. She was standing with her hands behind her back as a soldier would. Her attire consisted of a pressed military jacket of some sort. Usually you'd see some badges that would take up a large spot on there but there was none of that. The only thing I was able to find on her was the letter "E" behind an upside down triangle on the left side her chest and on top of her shoulders.

"It's a real pleasure to welcome you guys back," she said with a smile.

The girl dropped her jaw and looked back and forth between Terra and us.

"What?! Okay. First thing you need to know about Terra. She's never like this. You know, all smiley and stuff. You really have to be someone special to do this to her."

Terra gave a scoff but never dropped her smile.

"I hope Kerren escorted you properly and in a safe manner."

"So that's what your name is," Wendy said. "Kerren is an ugly name. I think I liked her better when I didn't know it."

"No one asked you if it was a pretty name or not!"

"I don't need to be asked!"

"So this is The Equilibrium then. All grown up I see," Terra said, doing her best to ignore Kerren and Wendy arguing. "You don't know how long we've been waiting for this day."

"Yeah I do," Wendy said. "Kerren said 16 years."

"No. For me, a lot longer." She returned her sight towards me. "How you feeling Mark?"

"Not so good," I said, looking at Penn's work.

"Don't worry about that. We'll have that taken care of when we get back."

36

"It's a pleasure to meet you Terra," Charlotte said. "Now can you please explain to us why we're here?"

"We have a job to do. All of us. But besides that, you're home now."

"This isn't home," Monica said quietly, disgust filling her voice, hatred for the thought of some foreign land being home.

"Nice to see you Monica. Whether you like it or not, you can't deny that you were born here."

"Doesn't mean it's home," she said with a glare.

"So should we get going?" Kerren said, breaking the conversation early.

"Yeah. We should head out."

"Good! And by the way guys, Terra never leaves Headquarters. She'd only leave for you guys. The King doesn't necessarily like her. Hence, why the Palace Guards were out looking for us. But..." She walked over towards where a street seemed to start and break away from the torn city, "when you're bringing the Equilibrium home, you have to tell the world. After all, everyone on Novus is celebrating."

There was a vehicle that I wouldn't necessarily call a car. It was more bulky, obviously made for some sort of combat. On it was the same symbol on Terra's jacket. It was the letter "E".

"Well doesn't this scream to the world who's riding in it," Will said.

"Like I said, it's meant for that," Kerren said, opening the doors and taking off her coat to reveal her slim figure. "Trust me. We live underground in a secure location and we're very picky about our security and privacy. But when you guys come back we can't help but to be a little festive. Plus, it's a big slap in the King's face."

Terra got in the driver's seat with an even bigger smile and she turned on the vehicle.

"Don't worry. I drive pretty well," she said, signaling us to get in.

I looked at the others to see if they were willing. If we didn't get in then what? We couldn't just go wandering around in this place we knew nothing about. We had no other choice, just like all the other times, but to listen to them.

We all got inside and sat comfortably in the seats. For the most part, it was all leather. As for the color? Well, let's put it this way, Monica would love it.

It reminded me of a limousine. It sat us in a circle in the back. In between every seat there was a border that stuck out just a bit.

Despite all that was happening, I was surprised that we weren't asking much or speaking just in general. We were just along for the ride, quite literally this time.

"Where's the seat belts?" Charlotte asked, looking around her waist.

Terra and Kerren gave a laugh.

"Who the heck needs seat belts in a bike?" Kerren said, looking back at us from the passenger seat.

"A bike?" Wendy asked. "You guys stupid or something?"

Kerren met eyes with Terra and gave a playful smile. She then turned around and sat straight in her seat.

"Stupid? No. Crazy? Yes."

With that, Terra stepped on the gas and sent the vehicle flying forward. When I almost bumped heads with Will I started to think why we were letting someone that we knew nothing about drive us to who knows where. I was about to ask another question when a sight that was beyond anything I've ever seen filled my view.

The city was so gosh darn huge. It must've been twice, maybe three times bigger than Springfield. The size made my chest pound. If downtown scared me sometimes for being so huge then this place was surely to make me pass out again. I ignored everything for a little bit and just stared out the window, letting Monica's blanket of hair act as a curtain.

If I could describe it in one word it'd be "future". You know in those sci-fi movies where everything is fancy looking and it's almost all shiny? Yeah. That.

There were little rivers that ran through the buildings and illuminated the bottom of them. In what looked like the middle was a large pool the size of a lake with little man made islands in them. And of course, they were occupied with buildings.

"What the heck is this place?"

"Ok Wendy," Kerren said. "If you ever want to claim that someone's stupid you need to take a good look at yourself. I've already explained it to you."

"Shut it Kerren!"

"Oh you're saying my name now? I thought you said you hated it."

"You girls sure will have a good time together," Terra said.

"And what the heck is wrong with *you*?" Kerren said, punching Terra in the arm. "Is part of Mark's powers to change people? Why the heck are you being sarcastic!?"

She shrugged her shoulders.

"I don't know. I guess he has a way of bringing out my old self."

"You were a different person?" I asked, intrigued at what I heard.

"Yup!" Kerren shouted. "Word has it she used to be as annoying as Wendy."

Terra let out a chuckle. I noticed the bottom of her hair bounced just like Charlotte's does. For some reason that ticked me off. That was part of Charlotte. No one else can just take that and have it as part of themselves.

"Annoying as Wendy? I hate to break it to you but that's not possible," Charlotte said. I could tell she was trying to ease everything up. Not for everyone else, but for me. I know that sounds selfish on so many levels but I know for a fact Will would be annoyed either way. Monica could manage any situation given to her. As for Wendy, I don't need to explain that. You know her well enough. But I was the one that needed help. Everything always seemed to be about me and she wanted to take that away by being a little more loose.

A small smile found its way to my face. Thanks Charlotte. I guess I shouldn't be so selfish.

"You'd think so, but I promise you I was. Maybe a little worse."

"How bout you just shut up! I'm not the worst person in here! I mean c'mon. You have Mark here," she said pointing at me.

I gave her a look. Not one of annoyance, even though it could probably have been read that way, but me taking on her words.

"I'm the worst one in here?" I asked her, clearly sure that she would say yes regardless.

"Yeah. Maybe just underneath Kerren but still the worst under my standards," she said with a sure nod, making her pigtails fly up and down quickly.

"You guys are cute," Terra said.

"What! Did you seriously say that?!"

"What? Is Mark dating someone else?"

"What the heck does that matter?"

"Well, I mean, why else would you tease him like you do?"

I could see Wendy's face turned to as if she ate something poisonous. Her whole body shook with a shiver and she refused to look me in the eye.

"I don't tease him!"

"Then what the heck do you call what you do to him?"

Wendy froze. Now that's what scared me. She always has something to say. Regardless if she had something to say or not, her mouth was constantly moving even if it didn't make sense. Not only was her mouth frozen but her body was glued to the place in the world where movement was forbidden.

The sun was coming up at the time so everything was the same hue as the bright orangish red. It reflected onto all our faces but something about Wendy's was different. I may have been just trying to run around the fact that she was blushing. Even now I hate the fact that I hear myself say that.

Her chin moved ever so slightly over towards my direction but stopped the second it started. The soft brown of her eyes tried their best to unlatch their position and meet mine. They wanted to see what would be looking back at them.

That's when all of us looked over at her. She was stuck. Even Monica was phased by it. Her eyebrows knelt down just a touch at the ends, expressing all that was needed for the situation at hand.

Will went ahead and made her feel even more uncomfortable by leaning over to get a closer look at her face since he was sitting right beside her. He raised an eyebrow to get her to reveal whatever the heck she was trying to say.

Wendy's head picked up ever so slightly to meet eyes with Charlotte. This is the type of interaction that

41

scared the heck out of me. You could have Will fight me all dang day. You could make Wendy yell all the curses ever put on any human being. You could have Monica be annoyed at my actions. But when you have Charlotte look at you head on without a trace of happiness, you know you've tread on grounds that release monsters never seen by any soul before.

Wendy looked back down.

"He deserves every ounce of hatred I give him."

Terra, thankfully reading the situation correctly, gave a nod to settle things.

"Understood."

I was glad whatever the heck that was was now over. It let me settle down a bit but to someone it never did. Charlotte still was looking at Wendy with the same face. As I stared at Charlotte and gazed into her dark brown eyes, I brought up the image of Wendy being completely frozen. The blush on her face.

Why couldn't she say anything? Why the heck was she blushing? Anything like that would never cause that reaction. We've teased her to no end and Will especially about her body size. Even when that comes up I know she is actually affected by that but this was nowhere close to what was expected. Something was happening between the two of them that I knew nothing about. And this? This was just the start of it.

*   *   *

The speed of the car was fast enough to make what just happened fly out of my mind and get left behind in the trail of exhaust. I noticed Terra and Kerren were getting all giddy with Kerren letting out tiny, almost inaudible, squeals and Terra constantly tightening her grip around the wheel.

We were going farther and farther into the heart of the city. Roads crisscrossed all over each other and made a mess of a maze. They traveled around, inside, and under buildings. Already this early in the morning it was bustling with people.

"You guys ready for something you've never experienced?" Terra said.

"Is that people on that street?" Charlotte asked, sticking her face in the window.

I searched for what she called out and noticed that on one of the highways similar to the one we were on was full of people. From here, little specs.

There was a faint subtle noise that was continuous. It was loud enough to reign alongside the roar of the vehicle. It kept going, not letting up.

"What the heck are they doing?" Will asked.

"How bout you find out yourself?" Terra said. She pressed a button and instantly all the windows fell. Wind from outside blasted our ears but the sound was still the runner up.

My heart started pounding when I realized what the sound actually was. It started to spread all over my body and make me squirm in my seat. It made me remember that I was in a car with the letter "E" on it. There was a Headquarters that was known as Equilibrium. And what person was inside? The Equilibrium.

"They're cheering," Monica said softly, realization of what was happening filling her voice.

"Why?" I asked, surprised by the sounds of my voice being shaken.

"Why else would they? They're welcoming you home. They've been waiting for their savior to return."

Savior?

Terra was somehow able to speed the car up even more, zipping by all the people. The whole highway was covered end to end with hundreds of people cheering for us. Chills started to spread and that's when we exchanged looks. All five of us. Was this what Penn was talking about? Was I this loved?

"Woah! That's my name on a sign!" Wendy shouted, pointing out towards someone in the crowd. "Look Charlotte. Yours is there too! Ooh and Monica! What the heck? Why would someone ever put Will on a sign?"

Why? Why were they doing this? They knew nothing about me and I knew nothing about them.

"It gets to you huh?" Kerren said, looking back at me and giving me a huge smile.

My cheeks hurt and I knew the reason. I was smiling. The whole time I had no idea that I was. These were hundreds of people. A mass all dedicated to one thing at the time. One thing that they've apparently have been waiting for for years. This was one of the first times I was ever happy that I was the Equilibrium.

As I've mentioned before. I can get a little susceptive to things that I never would've done before if it involves one thing. A crowd. If there was a mass of people there you'd bet I'd do anything to show off. And right now I was put on high.

Wendy turned around and looked at all of us.

"Guys. We're famous!"

I wanted to claim that we weren't and I know Charlotte did too. It didn't help when we turned the bend on the road that we saw people in the streets running below us to get a closer look. We were stopping everything to grab everyone's attention.

It took a while but I noticed all of our faces shared the same expression now. Who wouldn't feel an insurmountable feeling of joy when you're driving through an unknown city that has tons of people cheering for you— welcoming you home?

I was lost to everything. The chills just wouldn't stop. I knew what it was like to be the main focus of a crowd. This is what it was like to be the Equilibrium and boy did it give me a high unlike anything else.

I felt a punch in my rib. I turned to see Will with a smile I've never seen from him before. His eyes were full and they looked at me with happiness expressing itself freely.

"You had to go and make us popular, huh?"

I sat up in my seat and let my back slide up along it. My eyes lit up at the sight of all these people standing on top of buildings, running along streets, looking out windows, and going to the point of even filling an entire highway with people to just get one chance to say that they saw us.

With the windows open, it wasn't hard at all to hear the helicopter above us. It flew over us and pressed forward to get ahead of us.

We're even getting on the news?

"Looks like they finally decide to show up," Kerren said.

I looked back behind me out the window where there wasn't as many people and saw two motorized bikes hugging close to the car. They were both dressed in black and had helmets that seemed to attach itself to their clothes. One looked at me and kept its gaze. All I was able to do was stare back at the darkness and see the warped image of me looking out the window.

I noticed something on his hip. It blended in well enough that you couldn't see it from a certain distance and considering how close he was to me, I should've seen it from the start.

The gun looked a lot more advanced and fancier than any of our guns were like on Earth. The tip pointed out a bit and had a lot more mechanics on it. He apparently noticed me staring at it because his head dipped down just enough to put it in his view without ever letting me leave his sight. With that, ever so calmly and smoothly, he returned his head back to its original position and looked forward.

"Uh, I don't think these guys are fans of us," Charlotte said, becoming anxious.

"They're not. You already know that," Terra said. "They already tried killing you once and they never finished their job."

So these were what the Palace Guards looked like. All I was able to see of them earlier that morning was an outline. Even then it was hard to see with them throwing their lights around at us. But they looked trained beyond compare. The man that was in the bike next to me had shoulders as wide as boulders. You could see his arms just as clearly as you could if he wasn't wearing any clothes.

"They're not gonna try to take him in front of everyone, are they?" Kerren asked Terra.

"Who knows. It's all up to Zalus. Now he has to pretty much make the right choices if he wants to please everyone. Either try to hurt us out in public or deal with the Equilibrium accordingly in a polite manner."

"So which one is it?"

"Hard to say."

"Then why the heck did he send the Guards out if he wasn't going to do anything?"

"Send a message to the crowds that he's aware of their arrival maybe. But it's not gonna go down like that at all," Terra said as Kerren smiled and took out a weapon of her own. A handgun similar to the one the Palace Guard had. She loaded it and took a firm hold of it. "He wants to assert his dominance just like always."

"But we're gonna make it backfire, just like always," Kerren said, finishing off with a laugh followed by a smile of approval from Terra.

That's when I notice the Guard reach for the gun on his waist. It was the same causal movement as his did with his head. All the excitement from the crowd cheering for us was gone from within me and was now replaced with fear.

Kerren stepped out of her seat and climbed to the back of the vehicle to the circle we were sitting in. She all gave us a look with a smile similar to one of waiting for someone to trip your trap and dump a bucket of water on them. This was her time to show off and she's been waiting to do it.

The bikers saw that she came to the back and threw their hands to their weapons. I felt the car jerk forward and scream as it changed gears at a moment's notice. Terra stepped on it to get a lead over them, to put Kerren in a good position.

She pushed Wendy out of the way and sat next to me. Wendy tried to yell out something to her but was cut short.

"So how's your welcoming party so far?" Kerren asked, getting pretty close to my face. Her giddiness seemed to be derived from somewhere far beyond my comprehension. She gave me a wink and stuck her head out the window with her face looking up towards the sky. Her shirt lifted up and I could see her stomach full on. It was what you'd expect from someone who was dealing with combat. Slim stomach that could run right alongside the top models. Her figure is what a lot of guys would consider perfect. Not an ounce of flab. Wendy gave me another punch for staring even though we all were.

Once half of her body was out the window, she positioned herself to just the right posture. Her core flexed, exposing more of her stomach to us as she held herself up. She tightened both her arms around the gun and aimed at the bikers.

All of it looked a little too fantastical to me. Her perfect figure. Her stance as she stuck half her body out the window. Her hands holding the gun, flexing the little amount of muscle she had on her. The way her hair was thrown about because of the wind. Then again, I had to remember that I just came through a dang portal to a whole other dimension.

Shots fired and the recoil was absorbed with perfection. She never let the gun jerk back at her. The sounds of the gun was nowhere close to what a bullet being fired sounded like. It still had the clank to it but it had a whole other element that wasn't there on Earth.

I whipped my head back to see if she was hitting her targets. Just as I was about to check, I threw my head back to looking inside the car. Did I really want to see what another dead body looked like? Did I want another episode of Violet's face to bombard my memory?

Regardless if I wanted to see or not, I saw in the rearview mirror the bikers weaving about and firing their own shots. This didn't bother Kerren in the slightest but probably made her more determined to make one of them topple.

That's when the cheers reached a peak that I never heard before. All of us looked back over at them and saw them going crazy. This was a show for them. They got to see the Equilibrium fight the King's Guards even thought I was doing absolutely nothing. It was all because of Terra and Kerren that we've gotten this far.

I felt the ground rumble as I heard an explosion following a shot. A wave of heat pushed itself towards the car. Kerren hit one of the Guard's engine for sure.

"Woo! Got one!"

"Keep em coming girl!" Terra shouted.

She gave a nod and her smile finally faded as her determination infused her bones to fulfill Terra's command.

Something caught my attention out of the corner of my eye. I saw Will fiddling with something. I looked over to see him looking at his hands, examining them closely. He took in a deep breath and shook his head.

He scoot along the line of cushion to get to the other side of the car opposite of Kerren. He stuck his head out and using an incredible amount of force, threw his hand to the side while letting out a hearty grunt. The Guard on the bike tumbled the second Will took control of his position, grabbing him with his whole body.

Kerren looked over at Will and gave a squeal.

"Gosh your guy's powers are amazing!"

"Watch your six Kerren!" Terra yelled, snapping her back to reality.

Five more Palace Guards on bikes showed up. They rode an off ramp down to get onto the street. This just made the crowd go even more wild. Kerren took a few more shots before coming back in the car.

"Can't take that many by myself. We have to split."

"Split?" I asked.

Terra turned her head around.

"You guys ever ride a motorized bike before on Earth?"

"Uh...," we all said, looking at each other.

"Well it's never too late to learn."

Kerren climbed over us to get back to her seat. She gave Terra a nod and pressed a button on the console in front of them. The pressing of the button triggered something underneath us. I could feel something moving inside the car.

The center of the ring we were sitting in popped up. It was divided into five different sections with a handle pointing out towards all of us.

"Everyone grab one!"

A handle came up in front of Terra and Kerren as well. They had no hesitation and pulled one. I did the same and instantly regretted my decision.

The middle section that was dedicated to me lifted up and pulled over my head. It wrapped around me and threw me back into my seat. The seat lifted up. Out of nowhere sunlight became abundant. My heart was trying to keep up with the adrenaline that it was pouring out into my body. It was when I realized that the vehicle was tearing itself apart that I wanted out of the situation.

When it finished, I was all by myself out in the middle of the street but was still sitting. I had nothing to rest my back on and fell forwards, forced to grab the handles. What handles? Good question. I was thinking the same before I looked down and saw I was on a bike just like the Palace Guards. But there was something on my neck. It clung tightly to me and kinda hurt to be honest. It was cold so it must've been some type of metal. There was a beep and then a glass screen lifted itself over my face, darkening my vision just as sunglasses would do.

A panel at the bottom of my screen came up and showed audio lines.

"All of you follow the map on your visors. We're making our way to Headquarters. It's not that hard, trust me," Terra said.

"I don't need your dang trust," I heard Monica mutter, making another set of audio lines come up.

"Monica?" Charlotte said, surprised she could hear her voice.

"You can hear me?"

"You're all linked to each other. All the blue dots on your map are you guys. Any red is obvious," Kerren said.

I searched for mine, surprised that I was still somehow on the bike and didn't fall off like an idiot. It was only a matter of time. On the map I saw seven blue dots and five red ones coming in fast behind us.

On my side was Charlotte and Will. Monica and Wendy were farther ahead closer to Terra and Kerren.

"How the heck do you work this thing!?" Charlotte yelled, being completely flustered.

"Figure it out yourself," Wendy said. "I'm too busy feeling awesome. Who gets to legally speed on a bike?"

She sat up on her bike and lifted her hands in the air and gave a fist pump. This was her dream. She already sped once in a Corvette. Doing this was just adding to her list of things she's wanted to do.

I could already start to feel her excitement burn through my chest. I let out a little chuckle through my nose, creating a small amount of fog on my visor.

There was an overpass that was coming up and inside was a dark tunnel with a small amount of lights.

"Once you get out of the tunnel, follow the paths on your map. You each have a different one but they all lead to the same place. And for God's sake don't get lost."

There was a burst of anger as I saw Terra and Kerren take off after that. They sped up and left us in their dust. I wasn't upset because they left us to fend for ourselves but because of the way they looked. Sounds stupid, I know. But the way they hunched over just before they sped off made something tick. I wasn't envious of something. But I had to be. It was the same feeling I'd get when I saw people with friends before I made the ones right beside me. But if it was envy. Why?

Envy for what?

I made Charlotte's head turn and look back at me as she felt my anger burn. This was probably the only time envy was helpful. I got so caught up in the spotlight that we were put in. I forgot all about what I wanted. I wanted answers. I hated the way they could just act so casually when we knew absolutely nothing. I should've been asking the whole time and not sit idly by like an idiot.

There's something that's going on Mark. Remember. There's someone that's coming for you. Be ready for her wrath.

*　　　*　　　*

All the heads that I saw on the highway next to me turned to a blur as I sped past them. Once we made it out of the tunnel, the road split up into five different parts. According to my map, I was supposed to follow the one I was on at the moment. I was hesitant to leave all the rest especially in a place that I knew nothing about but I just made myself sulk in my anger towards everything and pushed on without a hint of regret.

As I listened to the noise that was a crowd cheering along with the sound of my engine, I felt incredibly focused. How I must've looked to the hundreds besides me was kinda crazy to think about. Here he was. The Equilibrium. The person they've been waiting years for. He's on a dang advanced motorcycle with a whole black helmet on his head that hid any sign of emotion. To them, I looked like Will. You know what I mean by that. Don't care about anything. The cheesy super cool guy.

The map eventually led me out of the city. It wasn't something gradual like Springfield either. It was a direct cut off. Right at this line it opened up into a dirt road with what looked like a more degraded version of the torn city we walked through earlier. After driving about twenty minutes straight, I noticed what looked like clumps of buildings from where I was.

"What are those?" Will asked.

"What? The cities?" Kerren said.

"Those are cities?" Charlotte asked.

"Yeah. The one behind us was the King's. Pretty much the main one. Just outside of the fog are some more. They aren't that big as his but they're for the different races. It's his way of looking like he isn't impartial even though it screams it to the world," Kerren said.

"Headquarters is stationed in Ashillon. It's the largest out of the others," Terra said.

"I thought you said that Exon was the last of Novus," I said.

"That's true, but he set these up for them specifically. I'll explain more when we get there."

Why did it always involve some more to it? Why not now? I decided to shut up and let her do what she wanted. I figured I'd get my answers eventually. Why keep pestering the person who knew the answers when she could choose not to say them at all?

The map kept leading me towards one of those clumps just like Terra explained. The first thing I noticed about this was that it wasn't anywhere close to as fancy as Exon. The buildings still had the crazy futuristic look to them but they weren't shiny or polished. A lot of them looked like they were run down with sandpaper. But looking at it without Exon in mind, it was still pretty big. I could very well see myself getting lost in it even if I knew the whereabouts of the place.

Unlike the cutoff of Exon, Ashillon was a gradual buildup into it as it did back home. There were a few houses here and there and they started to become more abundant the closer you got to the center.

I still remember when people first saw me for the first time. There were two small kids, maybe in third grade and there was a group of teenagers that were hanging out in what looked like a park. I slightly turned my head towards them and I watched as they went crazy. It made me chuckle as they realized who they were looking at.

The little kids froze on the jungle gym and held their mouths open. The group of teenagers stopped talking and I immediately picked out the "cool" one. The one that probably controlled the rest of them. Even he dropped his front and started to freak out and run towards the street. All of them started yelling and screaming at the top of their lungs in the happiest form.

"He's here!" one of the teenagers screamed.

"The Equilibrium!" the little girl shouted.

I watched in my mirrors as they kept running towards me, their voices getting lost to the strength of the engine. But it wasn't long until they were joined by other people. Adults on the sidewalks started freaking out in the same way as the kids.

I felt a chill go down my spine and start to spread.

Oh my gosh. Was I really this well-known? Everyone on Earth that knew I was the Equilibrium treated me special but I never knew why. I still don't but now I see how much people do see me as special. I was pretty much a celebrity here. Violet said I was too dangerous to live. Was this too dangerous? Was this what you were talking about? Cause I look like anything but. Here I was treated like a god.

"Uh...are you guys seeing this too?" Monica said.

"Let me guess, there's a crowd following you too?" I asked.

"Crowd's an understatement."

"I wasn't kidding when I said we were waiting for you," Kerren said. She let out a giggle before she screamed. "Long live the Equilibrium!"

I could imagine what she was doing. Raising a hand to the world, expressing a joy that shouted and moved through the very presence of everyone.

But those very words made a picture of the girl in white flash in front of my eyes. I never found out her name. She gave her life for all us of. For me. Just so she could have us go to the mall and—

Wait. Did she mean for us to go to the mall and meet BloodLip there to go through the portal? Were they involved with these people? Who *are* they?!

A rumbling rising ever so slowly, building power with every instance, raised over the buildings. A chant. I tried making out what was being said. But I was too stupid to realize what she started. Kerren was still shouting in my ear but I drowned her out with my thinking instantly. It kept getting closer and closer. Stronger and stronger.

All the people in shops and on the sidewalk. In the windows. They all looked out towards me with eyes wide. The chant traveled towards them and the rumble spread underneath my tires into my body. Through the air to shake my helmet.

"Long live the Equilibrium!"

I was making cars stop in the middle of the street. People were getting out of their cars, whole families, to get a clear look at me.

I looked down one of the streets and saw a bike just like mine on the left of me. Blonde pigtails stuck out the back of the helmet. When I made it to where the block started, buildings covered my sight of her, clearing after a couple seconds where the street continued. This time she was looking at me. I was surprised she wasn't as stoked as she was when we were getting shot at. But this time she never said a word.

The street she was on merged with mine and she rode right beside me. Her head was facing me as the helmet folded back into her neck where the metal pocket was that snaked to the bottom of the bike. I was waiting for a smile but got a blank face. It looked almost as if she was depressed. Her eyes mimicked the crowd with their shock.

I stared right back at her as we rode to our destination. The moment she took her helmet off, the crowd immediately recognized her and started to shout her name.

"It's Wendy!" someone shouted from behind her.

But not once did it move her to take her eyes off of me. It finally hit her. As the chant ensued she realized something. She realized who I was to these people as did I.

*   *   *

Steel doors were held shut. This was the destination on our maps. Once Wendy and I got to the double doors, we met Terra and Kerren. There was no sign of the others yet. I parked my bike and got off of it, taking off my helmet with nearly the thought of it. After a few seconds, I turned at the sound of motors coming towards us and watched the other three roll on in.

"Can't say I've ever experienced that before," Charlotte said.

"Neither have I," Kerren said with a smile a mile wide.

"No one would cheer for you anyways," Wendy said, glaring Kerren down.

"The cheering didn't matter," Terra said. "What mattered is what they saw."

"A guy on a bike doesn't mean anything," I told her.

"You're right. It doesn't. But what does is what was in him that he gave others."

"My powers?"

She shook her head as she signaled to a camera above us.

"Hope."

There was a creak as the metal hinges turned to the direction of the wiring. It was a slow process but the doors were wide enough that we could walk in before they were even halfway done opening up.

Once we got inside, the only thing I could see was black. There wasn't a source of light. I didn't want to take any steps inside. I didn't want to be consumed by what I didn't know despite that being my whole life. Darkness. But why? Why all this darkness? Why all the secrecy with me and my powers? Who was the one who thought of the idea to make my powers unknown, especially to me? If that was the case with people like Superman, he'd be nothing but an ordinary dude with huge biceps and massive calves. Nothing more, nothing less.

But darkness is what leads people to the pit of despair. Despair leads to thinking which in turn leads to more questions. I hated it. All of it. Again, the universe was out to make my life miserable.

I turned to give the others a look. Monica, for once, had wide eyes as she stared at the emptiness. I could tell from the instant I looked at them that they had no fear in them. Why would she be scared in the first place? She was used to this color. It just wasn't the color of the atmosphere, it was her curiosity. In the "fog", as Kerren called it, she was touching all kinds of things to see if she could connect with their tech. This place? A feeding ground for her. I guess "welcome home" had a lot more meaning for her.

Two people came from the side of the doors and walked up to Terra. They gave her a nod and locked eyes with me. I could tell one of them was new to his position. He naturally looked a lot younger and didn't have any markings on his face. His blue pretty boy eyes showed pure cleanliness. The one next to him had pitch black eyes that held all kinds of horrors. It was seen clearly. If he was to be one to guard the doors he had to be unshakable and as tough as any concrete rock would be.

"Welcome back sir," the older one said, looking at me straight on.

"Y—yeah. Welcome home," chimed in the younger one with fear in his voice.

I scoffed and rolled my eyes, heading off into the darkness. Once I was well in my steps, I realized what I just did. I was never one to be disrespectful to people older than me. I knew better unlike Will and Wendy. But gosh was I tired of hearing that stupid phrase. So what if I was back home. Who the heck cares? Deal with it quietly. You don't need to rub it in my dang face. And what about the other four? Why don't they get hassled about it?

Kerren, joined by Terra, hurried up to run in front of us.

"Wait here please," Kerren said. "They're closing the doors now. Don't want anyone wandering off without any lights."

As she was saying the last few words, the smidgen of light that was coming in through the entrance was dissipating and was soon lost to the darkness. I waited in our little huddle for the reawakening of light. It wasn't long before Kerren took out a flashlight of sorts and aimed it in front of her. She took the lead in taking us through the enormous corridor.

"So this is your secure location?" I asked.

"Who said it was?" Kerren said, not looking back.

"Just figured that we drove all that way here to get to-"

"To what? Your answers?"

I furrowed my eyebrows.

"Okay Kerren," Charlotte said. "Do us a favor. Why don't you go ahead and put yourself in our shoes? We don't know jack squat. We watched our city fall to terrorists. Watched people risk their lives for us. We then come here and have to deal with all of this," she said, gesturing to everything around her.

I could see that she was taking on my frustration. She was tired just like I was.

"All of this?" Kerren said, sounding legitimately upset for the first time.

"A King we know nothing about wants us dead. There's a *world* we didn't have a clue that it existed! You just come out and claim that we weren't born on Earth! How the heck do want us to feel?!"

I let a smile form. It was rare for Charlotte to get irritated like this. She was speaking every word I would've said.

"I never expected you to feel any way. Okay? I never told you that you were supposed to take this simply. But you don't disrespect my home by calling it "all this", Kerren said, mimicking the same gesture Charlotte used.

I heard Terra let out a sigh. She walked forward and took hold of the flashlight form Kerren. Kerren looked at her with confusion, wondering why she took it. But it was clear. Clear to me at least. In this case, the flashlight had to be shown in front of everyone, meaning that the one holding it had to be in front—the leader. Terra taking the light meant that she would be the one to take the lead from here on out. Although a lot of people wouldn't consider a simple flashlight to be a symbol of dominance, it meant everything here.

She turned her head just enough to eye Kerren.

"In a broader spectrum, yes. We are heading to Headquarters. This place used to be a famous building for business. It was a Trade Center for interaction between other countries when there was such a thing. Building got a hard beating in the war but it's still standing. We just use this as our main entrance into the underground facility."

"So what's with the whole no light dealio?" Will asked.

"You really want your enemies to know how to move around if they ever get in?"

I turned to watch his face scrunch up as he thought. He seemed to be a lot more relaxed which scared me a bit.

"I guess not, but why use such a huge building in the first place?"

"Easy," Kerren said. "If you're as big as the King with the whole world to yourself, you think big. When you take us into mind when you're at his stature, he thinks small." She turned around and squinted as she showed the small length with her fingers. "Very small."

"Hiding in plain sight," Charlotte said to herself.

"Well, kinda," Kerren said. "Headquarters is still underground, but you know."

The walking continued for a few more minutes until we reached two metal plates that reflected us back, making the light from the flashlight blind us. Terra walked up to the panel and pressed a button. Usually back at home, elevator buttons were simply up or down. This in front of me was something else. Who knew what all those commands were for?

Without a delay, the doors opened and revealed one more guard standing inside. Something about him seemed different though. It felt like he belonged there. Not just to be stationary inside the elevator, but rather, to be with these two girls I met today.

He was tall and stocky with a chest that stuck out farther than any yard stick. His muscles were enormous and made Eli look like a joke. He had dark skin with a bald head. From what I could tell, he appeared to be somewhere around his late forties.

"Howdy there kids," he said with a deep voice, as expected.

"How many times do people keep gotta calling me a kid?!" Wendy yelled.

He gave a hearty laugh that I felt vibrate through my chest.

"When you hear how old I am and what I've been through then you'll know how much of a kid you really are."

"What's your name mister?" she said as she walked up to him and put her size into perspective, making all of us snicker.

"Names Ed little girl," he said, giving her a good rub on her head.

Wendy jumped back at his greeting and desperately tried to fix her hair.

"Okay, *Ed*. One, you *never* do that again! And two, I'm no little girl!"

"Uh-huh. Sure," he said as he signaled us with his head to get in.

I watched as Wendy stepped into the elevator. She gave me a quick look but the second she saw I was looking right back, she jerked her head in an unnatural way, avoiding eye contact.

Hm?

Once we all stepped inside, Ed closed the doors. He stood in front of us with his chest sticking out towards the doors. I guess it was some sort of safety precaution. It seemed like the most logical thing. I mean, he was a giant for crying out loud. He was born to protect others.

"So how you guys like it here?" Ed asked us as I felt my stomach fall to the descent of the elevator.

"This place is a mess," I said, shocked at what I blurted out. I widened my eyes and straightened my back, hoping that I didn't step on one of Kerren's landmines.

He gave another hearty laugh.

"You're right about that Mark. It seems like I can hardly remember when it wasn't like this. It's been only a few decades but boy does it feel like a lot longer."

"You've been working here that whole time?" Charlotte asked.

"Don't really consider it work, but yeah. More or less. I've known Terra here since she was a little girl. Gotta say. She was a lot cuter back then," he said, giving her a wink.

A sincere smile, one that I could clearly decipher as different from the rest I've seen from her today, spread across her face as she looked at him.

Wendy squirmed as she took what he said in a completely different way.

I noticed Monica had her hand up against the wall and was in some sort of trance as she stared blankly into it. I slowly inched up behind her and rested my head on her shoulder to ease up on her in a playful way.

I surprised myself, once again, about how I was acting. One second I was frustrated while the next I was like this. It had to be something about this place.

Instantly I was filled with Monica's perfume. I took in a nose full and slowly let it out to not annoy her being that I was close to her ear.

"I don't get it," she said softly. "It's completely different."

"Hm?" I asked, making her shiver, my voice no doubt vibrating through her.

I stepped back from resting my head on her shoulder and took her view in as a whole.

"Your circuit system. It's completely rewired differently. It's not even on the same level as Earth."

I turned to see Kerren having a mini freak out as she watched Monica inspect the wiring of the place. Monica slowly took her hand off the wall and clenched it in a fist, frustrated at not knowing. She turned around and met eyes with Terra, gazing her down with her black pearls.

The elevator came to a jolt and made my shoulder sting with the weight pressing down on it.

"If you were confused about that, wait until you see Headquarters," Terra said.

We all shifted our attention to the doors as they opened up. Upon opening, we were met with people standing in two lines along each side of the elevator. At first, no one spoke. There were a few whispers here and there but mainly silence. They all stared at us with eyes full.

And then the smiles came along. Again, it was slow. Gradual. Once Terra took the first step out of the elevator, everyone went crazy. They were cheering, clapping, shouting our names, pointing. Terra was well along in her strides when she turned around and gestures us with her hand to follow her.

So there we were. Terra leading us into Headquarters with the five of us following behind. Behind us was Kerren and Ed following right along. I did the same thing that I did with the crowd on the highway and thought of what they must've been seeing.

Here Terra, their leader, was returning after never leaving Headquarters with the Equilibrium and his friends. I immediately thought of the girls and how they looked to everyone. Slender legs. Monica's long luscious hair. Charlotte's bob to her hair when she would take a step. Wendy's swaying pigtails. Will looking cool and everything. And then good old boring me with someone's skirt wrapped around my shoulder. Pathetic. To them? Probably one of the most amazing sights they've ever seen.

It seemed like all the people there wore the same thing. Same uniform. They all had the same symbol with the letter "E" on it like Terra had as well as the car that split.

She led us deeper into the facility that eventually opened up into a wide space. Here there were control panels upon control panels. This was what Terra had to be telling Monica about. On the opposite wall was the same symbol etched into the wall.

As she said, all of headquarters was underground. The walls reminded me a lot of what a sewer would look like. Heck, maybe this was a sewer once.

"Welcome to Equilibrium Headquarters," Terra said with a smile, this time aiming her words at all of us. With the crowd that followed us to what seemed like the main area of the place, it made Terra's words more remarkable. "But more importantly, welcome home."

The crowd started to cheer and made my natural inclination of anger upon hearing those words subside.

"Now," she said, straightening her back even more than it already was, "I'm not one to be completely formal. I'd like to think that in some cases I am, but normally, I'm known to give things straight to people."

Yeah. Sure. Cause you've been giving everything straight to me.

"Basically, this is where everything happens. Where we all prepared for you," she said focusing on me.

"So what, you got a bunch of random people working for you all cooped up in here?" Wendy asked.

"They aren't working for me. They're working for a cause. To fix what's been torn from this world."

"Okay that's great and all, but this is all the people you got in here?" she asked as she looked around the room. "I mean, this is a lot of people. But when you put them into perspective with the city, it's kinda pathetic."

What is with this girl?! I was rude too but come on Wendy!

"All but three. Rouge's coming in soon. They're finishing up a scout. They were probably there when we were on the highway."

"Rouge?" I asked.

"Yeah. Speaking of," Kerren said, "they're here. Need your clearance."

"They're clear. Let em in. They deserve to see who's here."

I looked on the screen that Kerren was showing Terra. There were three people that were walking towards the same elevator door we just came through. I couldn't read much from their faces on the camera but I could tell that I wasn't going to like them.

Terra returned her attention back to us.

"Rouge is our covert group. They consist of three people a little older than you but not by much. Basically their main job is to tell me what's going on in the city along with if the King has any plans."

The two doors flung open as the three came out of the shaft. Everyone turned to watch them walk into

Headquarters. Within seconds they were in front of me, almost like they were eager to meet us but not in any friendly way.

The one in front was what a lot of people would consider fit. Not too bulky. Not anywhere near skinny. His hair was similar to mine but was a lot messier. His eyebrows were held down by some weight as he looked into my eyes before he sized me up.

All three of them were wearing some fancy battle material. Seemed really comfortable and allowed for a lot of movement.

"Alex, meet Mark, the Equilibrium," Terra said.

"I know who he is," he scoffed. He rammed a finger in my chest making me wobble on my heels. "Look buddy, don't think for a second that just because everyone here is crazy for you that you're needed. We can get by just fine without you and your popular high school clique."

I threw his arm out of the way and gave him a glare of my own.

"Like you're not in some fancy click of your own."

A girl behind him sighed as she put a hand on her forehead.

"Were not a clique," she said. Her body was something that I noticed instantly. Talk about good looking. Her hair came down to a normal length, but one thing that made her unique was her thick use of eyeshadow. For someone to go out and do fieldwork with makeup sounds absurd.

"Then what do you suppose you are?" Monica said, making all of their attention shift to her. "A clique is defined as a group of people with shared interests but don't allow people to join them. So I have a question. Will you let me join you guys?"

"Of course not!" Alex yelled.

"You're a clique," Monica confirmed.

"Beside the point," the last one said, "it's nice to finally meet you guys."

"Oh, so you're a kiss up just like Kerren then," Wendy said.

The last member of Rouge raised an eyebrow and let out an awkward laugh.

"Kerren's a kiss up?"

"I am not!" she yelled.

All it took for Terra to get the attention back was to scoot forward just a tad with her feet. She had so much presence that all it took was a simple shuffle of the feet.

"Alex, you know well how much we need them. And don't act like you haven't been working for this outcome anyways."

He crossed his arms and took Terra on.

"I haven't been working for these idiots. I've been working for the people out there. But are you kidding me Terra. These guys? They're all weak." He shifted his attention back to me. "Why the heck do you think you have powers? You can't even care for yourself if you didn't have them."

Oh boy. Just then I felt a huge wave of adrenaline. I didn't need to think twice about who it was coming from.

Wendy reached out and grabbed hold of his collar, squeezing it harder than she needed to. Her other hand punched him square in the face making him tumble back. Without hesitation, she teleported behind him and grabbed him by his neck, throwing him down to the floor. She stood over him and put a foot on his chest.

"What the heck did you just say?"

"Enough!" Terra shouted, getting tired of our useless bickering. "Rebecca, help him up. I still need your info from your scout."

Rebecca reached down and helped Alex up. As he tried desperately to not rub his face that was already turning red, he explained to Terra that the King was doing nothing but his usual things. The only thing different was that he was trying to keep everything calm with my arrival.

"Hm. Seems a little too good to be true. Why the heck would he not do anything but send a small squad out to try and kill us?" Kerren said, thinking out loud.

"Unless he got what he wanted." Kerren looked up at Terra keeping an arm on her chin. "His attention span is short. He gets distracted easily. You all know that. So what's the only logical reason for him not to go crazy about these guys?"

"He got her back," Kerren said with wide eyes.

Terra nodded her head.

"Got who back?" Charlotte asked.

"The Princess."

"Wait who?" I asked, echoing Charlotte.

"I'm sure you've met her. It's been years since I've seen her but you can't ever forget her. Red hair. Red eyes."

"What?!" all of us shouted.

"Penn?!" I yelled.

"So that's what they named her. Then yes. Penn."

"She's a Princess?"

"Yup. The King's very own daughter. It's a thing the Exon family does. They've done it for who knows how many generations. They genetically engineered their bloodline. Males have red eyes and females have both red hair and red eyes. So every time someone comes into the royal bloodline through marriage that wasn't beforehand has to go through that genetic engineering process."

"Then why the heck was she on Earth?!"

"Well, it's best we start at the beginning if you want to know. Basically, Novus used to be a prosperous planet.

Countries that were advancing in technology at a rate faster than we've ever experienced before were abundant. Everything was perfect. But something was slowly going wrong behind the scenes and a man named Rylan knew that.

"He was no one special. Just an ordinary guy. But someone came to him one day and convinced him that there was a world war to soon erupt. He never met her before but together with her they started what was known as Equilibrium. They didn't come up with the name but they took it from something everyone was used to hearing. It's a long time legend here on Novus that was told. It never died out because some people actually believed in it.

"Basically, what the legend told was that when a civilization such as a human race on a planet was on the brink of extinction from itself, an Equilibrium would be born. He would then grow up and when he was of age, he would help stop the impending doom from coming about by doing one thing. It's in the definition of his title. Equilibrium: A state in which opposing forces or influences are balanced. They pretty much cancel each other out.

"So Rylan and the girl went to an orphanage to start up their group. There they met three girls with names that make you think things were planned. Funny enough, there were three different orphans all at the same age of thirteen named Scarlett, Aqua, and Violet."

"Wait! Violet?" I asked.

"Yeah. I'm guessing you met her as well. Rumor has it that she was taken on their last mission of kidnapping the Princess and was brainwashed, having her memory wiped to think that she was working for the King all along. So you met her then?"

I took a quick look at Charlotte and held my head down.

"She's dead," I said quietly.

"What do you mean she's dead?!" Terra yelled.

"I killed her."

She gave a scoff.

"You didn't kill her."

My heart skipped a beat when I heard her. What the heck do you mean I didn't kill her?! Do you have the audacity to claim that I never did what has held me down?

"Yeah I did," I said, raising my voice.

She shook her head.

"I knew Violet personally. She was the best fighter we had. There's no way you could've killed her."

"I killed her!" I screamed, straining all the neck muscles in my body. "Don't you dare claim that I didn't! Are you telling me that I didn't watch her bleed out?!" Terra's face changed instantly. She scrunched up her forehead and stared me down. "She had a knife to Charlotte's neck! Don't act like you wouldn't shoot!"

The top of her lip flared up as well as her nostrils. She clenched her fists and took a step forward before Kerren reached out to grab her arm. Kerren gave her a good tug on her and forced her back to her spot. Terra looked back to give her a look and Kerren followed with shaking her head, looking into her eyes.

She let out a large sigh before continuing.

"These three weren't just any girls, Mark. They were trained by the two to be the most agile and best fighters on Novus. And that's just what they turned out to be. Covert soldiers that fought for the Equilibrium. I grew up with these girls. I've been friends with them for years when I joined the Equilibrium.

"And then the war broke out. It started with one of the King's airships hovering over one of Ashillon's cities. It dropped a bomb over it and killed millions. From there, things broke out and it wasn't pretty. At the time of the outbreak, Rylan, the girl, and the three along with the others that joined them started to revolt against the King in his own kingdom.

"Over time, people began to learn of the group known as Equilibrium and mainly the faces of the three. People feared them. People loved them. Hated them. Wanted them dead. Wanted them to be praised. There were tons of mixed emotions towards the face of Equilibrium.

"They carried out mission that couldn't be done by anyone else such as executing the Queen after she gave birth to the Princess. She was just as vile as the King. She was known to put on lipstick made from the blood of bodies from the battles that would be held on someone else's country. Everyone would call her BloodLip."

All five of us looked at each other, realizing how they got their name.

"That's what they're called," I said. "Penn and her friends. They're called BloodLip."

"Of course they are. The King probably made Violet call them that. Every time someone says their name he wants them to think of his beloved. She was part of this covert group where they went on missions. It was normal for them. They were used to it. But when they were eighteen, the science engineer they had at the time found an anomaly. He found an Equilibrium. There was one to be born from a young couple here in Exon. Their first child. We approached them and told them everything. We told them that their son was the Equilibrium and that he was going to change the world.

"They agreed to be part of our project that Rylan and the girl proposed. The project? Project Salvation. Salvage what was to save us and store it away until it was time to come back. We approached other families and asked if they'd be willing to let their child who was due around the same time as the Equilibrium to be part of our project.

"The main process of the project was quite simple. Once the Equilibrium was born, we'd take pieces of his DNA and manipulate it. We'd engineer it to whatever we wanted. In our case, we made this piece of DNA provide powers to whoever it was in. We'd take the DNA and place it inside the other participants of the project when they were born. This was intended to protect the Equilibrium while he was away. And that's how the plan would go.

"Just before the outbreak of the war, the science engineer we got was researching with other countries dimensional travel. He used that data and made a portal to the nearest dimension. That was your dimension. The one with Earth. We traveled there before we sent anyone in and studied it just enough to get a basic understanding of the place. We found the nearest hospital and found out what families were due for delivery along with what names they were going to name their child.

"It was brave on the families' part on Novus. They were going to give up their kids and take up ones that they knew nothing about. They weren't going to be related to them in any way. Pretty much they were gonna swap kids without the parents on Earth knowing. So when the time came for the swap to happen, we disguised people as nurses and when they gave birth, we used the excuse that there was a medical problem with the child and needed to be tended to right away, giving us time to swap babies.

"The plan was that you'd grow up on Earth. But just in case something wrong happened, you'd have your friends protect you with their powers. The science engineer told me that you guys would have a connection that would make you guys meet one way or another. He said you'd have a connection that would attach you to Mark and Mark to you since you are essentially a part of him."

So was that the reason why we've felt this way the whole time? We all exchanged looks and recalled the many times we've felt that way.

"But back on Novus that day we were planning on sending you through the portal, things went wrong. It was an all-out battle at the front of the King's Palace. It's the huge pointed building you saw when we were on the highway. It's way too big for any of you to have missed it. All of Equilibrium was fighting the Palace Guards to distract them as we sent Violet in to kidnap the Princess. We figured that she was the last bloodline of the King. If she was kept alive, she would grow up to be trained by Zalus and we would never kill an innocent child. So we decided to take her from him and put her in the portal as well.

"When we were in the process and sent the first five of you through and had the earthlings on Novus is when something I'll never forget happened. Aqua was shot in the head with a sniper rifle and dropped dead instantly. That's when the Palace Guards stormed our building and attacked us. We destroyed the portal and tried to erase the plans for it but unfortunately the engineer was shot before he could do so. Violet and Scarlett were fighting but Rylan gave the order to retreat. Rylan took one of the baby girls who we retrieved from Earth and left.

"Once we got back to Headquarters, we realized Violet never made it back. When Rylan came back with the baby, he was covered in bullets. We tried to help him recover and gave him all the medical attention we could but he was dying. It was then that he appointed me as leader of Equilibrium. He was planning on making Scarlett the leader, but infuriated at the loss over Project Salvation, she left, saying that she'd return to fight the King if The Equilibrium ever came back.

"The King took the three other children that we had for the project along with the Princess. The other children from Earth were killed along with your biological parents. The King went ahead and built another portal in another location and apparently sent brainwashed Violet along with them, telling her to make them kill the Equilibrium and not make him return home. He was scared of you Mark. He wanted you dead at all costs."

It was a lot to take in. All I could do was hold my frown from her upsetting me about not killing Violet. I looked into her eyes as she looked back, waiting for some type of response from us.

"Then explain to me what the heck we're supposed to do," Will said, crossing his arms. "If you sent us to Earth just to protect us for a short time and wanted us to come back, what are we supposed to do? We don't even know what the heck Mark's powers are."

"You don't?!"

Terra stared me down with the same look that Will and Monica gave me when they heard that I didn't have any in the computer lab.

"I thought *you* knew my powers!" I said, defending myself and disappointed at the fact that she didn't know either.

"What the heck! You were supposed to know them! Rylan said. He said you'd know them when you came back." She slammed her fist into the control panel. "Why the heck don't you?!"

"Don't ask such a stupid question," Monica said firmly. "You're the leader of all these people and have to make life threatening decisions daily, yet, you can't understand us when we tell you that we don't know his powers?" Monica tilted her head downwards and looked at Terra with complete dejection. "You're pathetic. Stuck inside your hopes and can't even compensate yourself when they aren't fulfilled."

The more we talked, the more ticked off Terra became. She hated hearing what the truth was it seemed. Monica was right. All she wanted to hear was what she expected and didn't want to accept what was reality.

"I'm pathetic?! You're the one who we worked so hard on and you don't even know your dang powers!"

"You're avoiding my question," Will said.

"What? You wanna know why you're here again? Simple. For one reason. To kill the King."

"Huh?" I said.

"You're all gonna storm that Palace and kill him. End the madness he's created."

"We are not killing anyone! Violet never should've died. It never should've happened and there's no way that someone is gonna fall again by my hands!"

"You think I care?!" Terra yelled in my face, making her chest rise with every word. "I had to fight when I was a little girl! I was fourteen when I first killed someone. You don't think it hurt? I still remember it to this day. I can't forget the face of the Palace Guard when he fell to the floor. How the heck do you think I felt?! It hurts. I know! But do you think that just because it traumatized me that I got sympathy and was let free with the thought that I didn't have to kill anyone else anymore? No! So you don't get a choice whether you want to help stop him or not!"

So she finally decided to show her real self. She finally let everything drop. Anger is all that was needed. I've seen this in the case of people faking a personality to get people to like them. With Terra, it was the complete opposite. When she first met us, she was excited to see us again, hence why Kerren mentioned the fact that she was acting different. But once her expectations were dropped along with the fact that her past companion was killed by the very person who stood in front of her, she was subject to her usual self.

Did I care one bit? Nope. Absolutely not. You could be as sincere as you wanted with us but nothing was gonna make me kill again. Nothing.

"Are you crazy Terra! We don't even know this place," Charlotte yelled with concern filling her voice. "We just got here hours ago and you tell us you want us to kill a King?!"

"Oh so you're thinking along the lines of morals now? Then if that's how you look at things, can you find somewhere in your *logical* thinking to tell me how I should be the only one to go through what I went through? How is that fair?" She stood even higher now and inhaled. "Everyone here is doing everything in their power to stop the King. People make sacrifices daily. People younger than I was are doing things that I could've never thought of. How do you think they feel? And for you guys to come and to simply say you aren't gonna help." She stared daggers into Monica. "I'm the pathetic one?"

"I don't know if you know this or not," Wendy said, "but on Earth, we aren't maniacs that make little kids kill people."

"You think we *make* them do it? Look around you. Everyone here is only here because they want to be here." I turned my head behind and ignored the look from Rouge that still stood behind us. Behind Rebecca's shoulder were two little kids that were looking at me with eyes as wide as you'd expect from someone of their age. "Now how do you think they feel when they hear you tell them loud and clear that you don't wanna help them? After all that they've done and waiting for you—waiting for your approval of all their work and they get "I'm not helping". What kind of person are you?"

Who am I? Who am *I*?! You decide to ask me this question? The one question that was gonna tick me off. I sure know what I *used* to be. I was a pathetic kid who had no friends. I hated everyone because of it and envy was my only companion. But something amazing happened and that was that these four people that are standing at my side are here because they want to. We may be connected because they have my DNA and are naturally drawn to me but it's only out of love that we've gotten this far. Trust was tested but we all ended up in the same place as always. Friends.

So, you're asking me who I am. I'm a friend to others. That's what I am. I make sure what I do is in line with them. We don't conform out of our standards and if someone dares try to make one of us, they were in for a world of pain.

I turned around and, out of complete anger now, stormed up towards where she stood. It took her off guard just a bit and forced her back a few steps. I got centimeters away from her face to the point where she could smell my breath.

"Who I am is something that's ever changing. But one thing's for sure. I'm no murderer and neither are they!" I said, pointing behind me.

She stared right back at me and that's when everything went silent. The whole room was quiet as they waited for Terra's response. I noticed that her shoulder jittered and I looked down to see that she already had her hand wrapped around the handle of her knife. She squeezed it, contemplating on what to do since every action of her was being watched by all the people that called her leader.

She used one arm and took hold of my neck. My heart jumped, thinking that she was actually going to hurt me with the knife, but instead, she leaned in even closer to whisper in my ear.

"You're home now. And when you're here you play by my rules. Rule number one, never humiliate me in front of others. And two, you're gonna be on the front lines," she whispered.

She threw me back like I was trash to the others. With her hand still secure on her knife, she looked at Ed.

"Take them away."

"What?" I heard Charlotte say silently next to me, backing up.

Ed along with a few other people walked towards us with their command set in their mind. I followed suit and started stepping back as well. They weren't gonna basically take hold of us and confine us in front of everyone were they?

"You can't make us fight!" I yelled. "You can't make us do anything!"

"Stop Terra!" Charlotte cried out.

"You dang cultists! Ugh—wha! Get the heck off me!" Will yelled, trying to force the guard back.

They took a good hold of him by his shoulders as he tried desperately to get free. I watched all of them get taken hold of. They were all being manhandled and Ed was coming for me. I let the rage build. I let it fill me. I made sure it was strong enough for them to feel it. If you wanted to mess with us, you bet you were gonna see us fight back.

All of a sudden, they looked at me. I knew they were able to read my anger and feel it deep seated now in their own hearts. What scared me the most was that I saw a smile from Will. A nasty one that told of his intent to take on my anger and further it. After his smirk of death, he threw his leg into the stomach of one guard and threw his hands forwards, sending all of them flying back.

Wendy teleported behind one of them and swept her feet to make him fall. Monica raised her shoulders and let her lighting burst from her hands. What was different this time was that it wrapped around her whole arm, acting as sleeves. It was as if she was letting the energy accumulate. The guards on the floor looked up in terror, frozen by what they've never seen before. A small teenage girl with dark encompassing her letting lightning create a show of lights soon to be thrown inside them.

"Monica!" Kerren yelled.

I looked up and saw Kerren strangely satisfied and scared at the same time with what she was witnessing. She no doubt didn't want her hurting them but she was so lured by her magnificent powers that she could only gaze on after her shout.

Monica didn't care but still charged up and got brighter, her face now contorting. The more she waited, the longer my anger grew and I wanted her to just throw it in them, make them squirm like I did in the mansion.

"You hurt them and you'll regret it," Terra said, holding a gun in her hand pointing it downwards.

Monica looked up at the sound of her voice and noticed immediately what she was holding. In that split second that she stopped, the guards got back up and rushed towards us, getting more of a firm hold of us this time. Ed placed a hand on my shoulder, making me scream with all my strength—a mixture of anger and pain. But it's not like he cared. He was given an order to take us away. To where? I didn't know.

They led us off with Terra staring us down with this new personality to us, but one that was probably always the same to everyone in the room. I gave her one last look, trying my best to get a good view of her before we turned the corner. But all those faces. Terra, Kerren, Rouge, and all the rest of the members of Equilibrium. Who did they think I was? They all must've thought the same thing. He's a selfish idiot. Which was probably true but despite whatever the heck they called me, I was used to it. I always used to think everyone thought bad of me no matter who they were so this would be no different.

They took us down so many different corridors. Doors seemed to be everywhere. No matter where you looked it was almost guaranteed that there would be a door there. It didn't take long though to get to where they were to take us to. It was a smaller hallway that ended, leading to nowhere but a wall, which seemed uncommon in this place. What was special about this hallway besides that it ended? It had five rooms.

They all threw us into a room and started to close the doors on us and pressing things on a panel outside of it. For some reason, Ed let me watch all of them get thrown into their rooms. There would be grunts from them and you could hear a shout before the door closed, especially the one from Wendy. After they finished, the guards gave me a look and walked off like they had something else urgent they needed to tend to.

Ed, still placing his stupid hand on my shoulder, gave a small smile as he opened the door.

"Look kid. This isn't anything personal. I'm just here to do my orders."

As he kept talking, I could hear running coming around the corner. Kerren ran up to us with a sincere look, which surprised me. From what I've seen of her, she was always happy, even when she was getting shot at.

Automatically, I looked at her with disgust. Not really directed towards her I guess but just everyone in this place.

"I'm sorry Mark. I—I…" she said, stumbling over her words. "I mean, I just wanted you guys to get your answers and—"

"I got my answers all right and I hate them," I interrupted.

"You can't deny them though."

"Who said I was denying it?" I shot back, glaring at her and giving her only the side of me.

"Look. I'm sorry."

I scoffed.

"I don't need your sympathy."

She let out a sigh and dropped her shoulders.

"Alright. Just trying to help."

With that she turned around and walked off. I tried to watch where she was to go but Ed nudged me in the room. Surprised that he placed me in the room, I looked up and waited for the door to close just like it did on the others. Ed let out a sigh of his own.

"She was just trying to help you Mark. But oh well," he said, shrugging his shoulders. "I guess that's one way to meet your sister."

"What?!"

With that, he shut the door.

Chapter 2

Sister? Sister?! What?!

I paced my room with my hands clenched around my skull. What the heck was Ed talking about? I never had a sister. I never heard of such a thing from my mom. But, she wasn't even my mom in the first place. No. What the heck am I saying? Of course she is. But, I wasn't born on Earth.

With legs shaky, I fell back and slumped against the wall. My chest was rising and falling quickly. It must've hated me for keeping it like this constantly now. But I had no choice. It wasn't because of me that these questions and things came up. I don't even know if I believe everything I was told. If it was true, though, that'd mean that I wasn't born on Earth and my mom wasn't actually my mom.

Just the thought made me quiver even more. It couldn't be true. It can't. I've lived with her all my life so nothing that these random people that I happened to meet tell me could be true.

But it has to be. I mean, think about it Mark. All that they told you holds true. You can't contradict a thing.

Gosh. This place was horrible. This whole planet. It was a complete mess and they expected me to fix it.

That's all I could think about as I sat in my room for hours. In there was a bed and a closet that I checked that had the same change of clothes. There was also a bathroom with a shower and that was it.

I walked around and examined it all as I thought about what Terra was saying about us and Novus. What came to mind a lot was what she said about Violet. To think that she was once on their side was hard to think. She tried to kill me because of the King's orders. It made a lot more sense now in accord to her actions towards us. But she must've been having some sort of flashbacks. When we were fighting in her classroom and Charlotte shot her knife out of her hand, she looked dazed and told something to get out of her head. It could be the only reason.

Even though I wanted to think that it wasn't true, the more I kept thinking about it the more true things started to become. Take for example what Penn said when we met them in the mall. She was yelling at me and telling me that if I joined them that I had a chance to live among royalty. And it's clear what she meant by that. So obviously that means that she knew that she was the King's daughter. It also explains why they knew so much in the first place. Violet was from here after all. The King told her to tell them all that she knew I guess, brainwashed or not.

Wait. The whole time they knew what my powers were. They knew all along. Meaning Violet knew as well. She was even telling me about them in the classroom when she had me tied to a chair. Then that could only mean one thing. The King knew what my powers were.

I bolted up from the floor and ran towards the door only to notice that there wasn't a doorknob. The only thing I could see that could lead it to being opened was the control panel next to it. When I tapped it nothing happened and seemed to be turned off. It was only logical. Terra wanted us to stay in here anyways.

I started endlessly tapping the panel as I zoned out thinking about the King. Who was he? Why did he start a war? Better yet, why did he want me dead? Why were my powers so dangerous that you needed to kill an infant?

Violet's words shined through once again and let anger fill me. I let out a yell and punched the panel, hurting my knuckles and leaving the panel the same. Frustrated, I stormed back towards the wall and leaned up against it to try and better my strained breathing.

I wondered if the others could've felt my anger just then. Could they have always felt it? No, I don't think so. The hormone was secreted during puberty. But were they really drawn towards me? Even if Brittany never burned down my old school, would I end up being friends with them or would they be just another person I'd pass by walking in downtown?

But they had my DNA. That means they were scientifically engineered. But me? I was the real deal. I had something in me that was not natural. No human being could emulate this. I slouched down again and looked at my hands. The hands I was looking at weren't the ones that came from the woman I knew at my house in Springfield. They belonged to a couple I never knew. Did they have a girl and that's who Kerren is?

Knock Knock

I looked up towards the door before I heard some beeps from the control panel on the other side. There was a hiss as the door slid open and in walked in a girl. The door closed behind her and she gave me a soft smile. She walked slowly towards me with her hands behind her back. As I watched her walk towards me, I knew instantly who she was—where she came from. She was never born on Novus. She was born on Earth, born to two parents who would get their kid taken from them and replaced with another. One bearing gifts withheld inside him. I knew now why she reminded me a lot of my mom. It was because she was her daughter.

Kerren took her place next to me on the floor with our backs to the wall. She let her knees raise up and wrapped her arms around them. I didn't bother to look at her in fear that I'd see my mom again, reminding me that she wasn't mine.

"Why are you here?" I asked, spite creeping in my voice.

"What? I can't come in here when I want? You are a guest after all."

"There'd be no need for you to come in here. After all, you said that I wasn't cute enough to stare at so why should you?"

She giggled and stretched out her back.

"I just wanted to come in and talk. I—I mean, Ed. He told me what he told you," she said, sneaking me a quick look.

"It's not true is it?"

"Yeah it is. Uh, partially that is." She thought for a second. "Well, not technically. Oh I don't know. It doesn't matter."

I nodded my head slowly.

"Yeah it does."

"I'm not biologically your sister. But technically half-brother and half-sister cause the mom you know is my biological mom and yours is…"

"Dead?"

After thinking whether to answer or not, she gave a nod.

"Yeah."

"So you were the one Rylan saved?" I asked.

"Yeah. I was the lucky one I guess."

"So what, you were raised here?"

"Yup. Been here at Headquarters all my life. I do go and visit Exon every once and awhile though. I'm a registered citizen there but I live here."

I sat next to her and didn't say a word. I thought I'd let her take over and do all the talking. She was the one who wanted to come in here in the first place. She looked at me nervously as I ignored her.

"U-uh. It's…"

She paused. And it wasn't no short one either. It was emotion taking over. I turned to finally give her my attention and instantly saw my mother. But that's not what frightened me. Kerren had somewhat of a smile and a frown on at the same time, battling with her inner emotions on which one to display. From the light of the room, I could easily see her eyes were getting watery. At the bottom they billowed up but she wouldn't allow them to fall.

"It's good to finally have you here Mark," she said in a shaky voice. "I've waited so long. Ever since I could remember they would tell me about you. It'd be special when someone would tell me stories as a kid about the siege of the Palace. How they protected you with their lives. And ever since then, I've always thought of you as my hero. They couldn't really explain it at the time because I was so small but they told me straight that you were my brother." She let out a chuckle and sniffled. "And boy did I think I had the most amazing brother. I would have dreams about you coming back and helping us. I would be right next to you and I would just gaze you down, so proud of what you were to do. So proud of my brother being the hero he was.

"Me and the little girls in Headquarters and in Ashillon would play games about when you'd come back with Charlotte, Will, Wendy, and Monica. We'd storm the Palace again but this time we'd kill the King. It was so vivid but I couldn't help to get this euphoric feeling when I would think of you, always knowing that you would come back."

She put a palm on her forehead as she started to let the tears finally flow down.

"I know you're not my real brother Mark and I don't expect you to look at me as your sister, but I know one thing's for sure. Nothing's gonna stop me from looking at you as my brother." She looked at me straight on with tears smeared all over her cheeks. "The brother I've been waiting sixteen years for."

She wasn't my sister. She was right. But she always thought of me as her real brother. I know most people would see her as weird for thinking that but I could sympathize with her to an extent now that I knew my mom wasn't my real mother. Family is based by no means on blood. It's based on the connections you have with those people and the love you have for them. Just in the same way as Penn and Violet.

"Well," I said, "I always wondered what it'd be like to have a sibling."

She started to laugh as she wiped her tears. I moved myself to face her full on. As I watched her try to control her hand from not shaking as she would wipe the tears and laugh, it gave a new feeling.

This girl. This girl I never knew. She's always thought of me as her brother and I could do the same as looking at her as my sister. Just then something sparked inside me. A feeling of deep seated sentiment. I realized I had the chance at another family member. One who I could truly care for as

I did my mom. One who was my age. One who had a past similar to mine.

"I'm sorry. I don't usually get like this," she said wiping her nose with her arm.

"It's only natural right?"

"Of course it's not Mark. Nothing's natural about what's happened. Seriously, who the heck gets to say that they traveled dimensions when they were just born?"

"Ten people if you wanna be exact."

"Yeah. I guess you're right." She hit my arm and yanked it back quickly remembering about my shoulder wound. "Hey, Terra wants to show you guys something."

"I couldn't care less about what she wants to show me."

"Don't be like that Mark. She gets upset quickly. That's why I was telling you that she was acting differently. She was just excited to see you. But how she was now, that's her all the time."

"I liked her better when she was nice."

"I don't." I looked at her in confusion. "I know it might sound weird but I'm too used to her as she is. And plus, when she's upset, she's more focused. It's rare to see her out of focus but when she is it's a real mess. And because I'm second in command here, I gotta pretty much take over when that happens."

"You're second in command?"

"Yeah. Terra's been training me all my life. I've always been by her side. It's a funny experience cause you get to see her in a different light being with her all the time."

"So what, when she dies she's gonna hand things down to you?"

"Mark! Don't say stuff like that!"

"What?! I'm being honest here."

"Well...yeah, then technically."

"Fine then. What the heck does she wanna show us?"

"Terra tells me that on Earth you guys have things called superheroes. Humans that have special powers that make them incredibly strong and that little kids and sometimes even adults almost seem to worship them in a way. They make them celebrities even though they don't exist."

"Your point?"

"We have that here on Novus but they aren't called superheroes. They're referred to as five teenagers called The Equilibrium.

*   *   *

Yes! Finally people I know! I was being overdramatic but it felt like I was locked up in my room for hours. It ended up only being for one before Kerren walked in. She went ahead and unlocked the rest of the doors and let the others out. Wendy tried to punch her and we had to hold her back before she could do so.

We met up with Terra again and took a car out of Headquarters. Once I saw Terra, I gave her a nasty look as much as I could, trying to uphold what I set up for myself. But it seemed like it was stuck. Her face now always had a frown on it. It always looked like she was thinking about something incredibly important that was stressing her out. I didn't care whether or not she actually was worried about something and went along for the ride.

In the car I explained with Kerren how she was my sister. Partly that is. And of course, Wendy and Will both had to say something about it. Charlotte was glad that we were able to meet again and that her dreams were fulfilled. Monica, well, Monica stayed Monica.

We drove out into the street and I realized that it was about afternoon now. To think that I found out so much in the short amount of hours we were here made it feel like it's been so long.

I stuck my head out the window as we drove along and Kerren, being extra close to me, kept pointing out different things. Restaurants that were her favorite, places where she would play as a kid, and her favorite hangout spots. Every time we would come up on a place that made her really excited, she would grasp my arm and squeeze it. Her face would light up and she'd go on and on about it.

She did really see me as her brother. I could see it in her eyes and in the way she would ecstatically show me everything like she's been waiting to go to these places with me. I let out a smile and started to ease up a bit despite being in the car with Terra.

Ed was driving the car through the streets and people seemed to move out of the way for us. It didn't seem like it was obligated but people here held high respects for Equilibrium.

"Where we going Ed?" I asked.

"We're goin—"

"We're going to a park," Terra said, cutting him off. "The school schedule on Novus is the same as on Earth but since today is technically a holiday of sorts, there's no school. Everyone's too excited about you."

"So what's with the park?" Charlotte asked.

"There's a park right outside one of the Elementary Schools here and the kids were gonna come with their families there to have sort of a barbeque. You're gonna show up and greet them."

"What, so this is just some publicity stunt?" Will asked with his arms crossed.

"No. You're going there to learn."

"Learn what exactly?" Monica asked.

"That's what you'll have to find out for yourselves."

The car turned on a street and the school was right in sight. It didn't look like any traditional school like on Earth but you could tell right away that it was one. In front of it was the park. What was unique about it was that the trees weren't as large as they'd normally be in a park. Also, the grass seemed to be struggling a lot to keep some sort of color. But the whole place was filled. There were people out in the street and the whole place was cut off and allowed the kids to walk in the streets. We parked right outside of the whole district and got out of the car.

One of the little kids that was out in the street stopped playing with his friends and his eyes widened at the sight of the car and the symbol on the side of it. When he saw us get out of the car his eyes were quick to meet each one of us. He turned around and tried to tell his friends that The Equilibrium was here. They didn't believe him, telling him that we'd never show up.

Charlotte giggled at their childness and walked up to them. She kneeled down hugging her knees, keeping her skirt close to her skin. Looking at her from behind made my heart jump. No matter how many times I've seen her, the pure sight of Charlotte always made me get excited like that. It told of all her happiness and her kindness.

"Hi," she said with sweetness filling her voice.

The two other little kids that were with him looked up at Charlotte confused at why she was talking to them.

"Uh, hi," one of them said, turning back around to pick up one of his toys off the floor.

"Do you know who I am?"

"No," the two said all the while the one was in a trance looking at her. I know kid. She was drop dead gorgeous. But you gotta be careful. You try to get any closer and you'll have to deal with me.

Charlotte giggled once again and faded away. The two kids' eyes turned to mimic the other kid's and they started to immediately search for her.

"What are you guys looking around for? I'm still right here."

"What?!" one of them shouted.

Charlotte reappeared in the same position and gave them another hearty smile.

"Charlotte?" they all simultaneously said.

"Yup!"

They went crazy. They started to jump around and to be honest, they looked like maniacs. The first kid that initially saw us grabbed Charlotte's hand and started to pull her towards the park, telling her all about the people he wanted her to meet. She hesitantly agreed and trotted on with him while she held his hand.

"Well she's quick to get things started," Kerren said.

Terra shook her head.

"No. She's just good with kids."

I watched from behind as we all started to make our way towards the park, following a good distance from Charlotte. There were fancy looking grills that had smoke coming out from some sort of exhaust. Whatever they were cooking made me hungry. The atmosphere was perfect though. Although it was a different planet, it still smelled, looked, and felt just like a regular barbeque.

It wasn't quick for the atmosphere to take over inside me. I didn't want to feel upset and irritated the whole time. I deserved some sort of stress free time and it wasn't hard to do that with a crowd in front of me. Not to mention that there were skyscrapers in the same street I was walking. It was just like Springfield. Once I was subject to this type of area, something would change inside me. My natural inclination was to show off and ease up.

I nudged Wendy's shoulder.

"You're disappointing," I told her, excitement filling me.

"What?! You're already complaining and I didn't even do anything this time! You're the one who's disappointing!"

"C'mon Wendy," I said, noticing that she was reading me quite well, making her smile to the extent of showing her teeth, "we're in a crowd of who knows how many people. Here you're a celebrity. Why aren't you taking advantage of that?"

The left side of her mouth lifted in her devilish sneer as she raised an eyebrow.

"Oh yeah? So what do you want me to do?"

"I don't know. Something flashy."

"Don't need to tell me twice!"

She instantly grabbed my hand along with Monica's. Since I was being dragged into this I thought I might as well have Will suffer as well so I went ahead and yanked his hand. Will yelled out trying to tell her not to do what was inevitable but she wasn't going to listen. Heck, I could even see it coming from a mile away when I instigated it but it still caught me off guard.

Wendy teleported the four of us right in the middle of the whole park, making the sound of us coming out of her silent world drag everyone's attention towards us. Before anyone could realize who we were, Wendy stepped on top of a table and looked around for Charlotte.

"Charlotte! Where the heck that little kid take you?! If he's with you any longer and not with Mark he's gonna start to get bratty! Oh! There you are!"

Swoosh

Everyone's face started to change as they witnessed Wendy disappear in front of their faces. All of their heads turned to swivels as they searched for where she went including me. But it was quick to pinpoint her location. All you needed to do was one thing. Listen.

"C'mon Charlotte! We have to go look cool!"

"But he was gonna introduce me to his parents," Charlotte said.

"I don't care. He can show you his parents later. So come on!"

"Fine. I'll come with you to meet your parents after I deal with this girl okay? Woah! Hey—Wendy!"

Swoosh

Wendy appeared just fine with Charlotte looking discombobulated. Wendy started yanking us up to get on top of the table with them. Being as I wanted to let loose for a little bit, I agreed and got on even though I felt extremely out of place.

"Do we really have to get on top of the dang table?" Will complained.

"Come on!"

Wendy reached to grab hold of Monica but she snatched her wrist before she could touch her.

"Don't teleport me again. Not unless it's needed or I tell you," Monica said, glaring at her.

"Oh come on that's no fun! Just get up here."

Terra, Kerren, and Ed, walked up and stood at the back of the crowd that stood around us.

Wendy walked to the front of the table and addressed the shock stricken crowd.

"Hiya!" she waved.

Just like it's always been here, our faces were met with screams and shouts. I remember in particular that a father picked up his kid and put him on his shoulders to get a better look at us. But what were we worth looking at? Just a bunch of teenagers with nothing but egos wasn't something special. If anything, the ones who should be cheering are us. Gosh, that sounds like I'm selfish. That's true, but we should be the ones cheering in the aspect of being saved. We all could've been dead many times now but it was only because of the people that helped us that we got out.

What struck me was that there were kids pointing out towards us and distinctly identifying us. One would call out to Wendy, pointing straight at her. Another to Monica. So on and so forth.

I looked towards the back of the crowd to where Terra was standing. She had a faint smile on her face as she watched the crowd's excitement. What'd she think of me? Psh. She probably thought of me just the same way I thought of myself. I was useless. I didn't know my powers. She was right in that aspect. But what I hated is that she expected us to kill a King that we never heard of.

I only killed once and I never planned on it. And now this King that wants me dead so badly has his only daughter that also wants me dead for revenge. As all the little kids rushed us, I thought of what BloodLip was doing at a time like this. Did they know everything there was to know?

Heck, maybe they've been back here once before. I didn't have a clue. But I did know one thing, putting two people together who hated me wasn't a good combination. And I was going to find out just that.

*   *   *

"So how old are you?"
"Sixteen."
"You're so old!"

I snorted.

"Yeah right. You don't know old." I leaned down really close to the kids to whisper. "But if you want a glimpse of what an old person looks like, Wendy's starting to get those ugly wrinkles around the eyes."

All the kids looked over at Wendy who was dancing with one of the little girls.

"Go tell her she looks like an old lady," I told them.

Without any hesitation, they agreed and ran over. I leaned up against the scrawny tree and watched the madness play out. One of them tugged on her shirt and told it square to her face that she looked like an old lady.

"What?! I do not!"

"Yeah you do." He reached up to point at her face. "You have the ugly wrinkles next to your eyes."

Her smile of the devil smeared over her face and made the kids take a step back. She put her hands behind her back and leaned in really low without bending her knees. Without raising her voice, she spoke calmly.

"You all have five seconds to run before I chase you."

Just like that all of them took off laughing and flailing their arms. Keeping her word, Wendy counted to five and teleported after them, making others look on as she put on a show for them.

With Wendy now out of the area and her loud mouth nowhere to be heard, things settled down on our side of the park. The small chatter of the kids was still present but you could tell they were taking on someone's quietness. These kids weren't naturally quiet. They were subconsciously mimicking the Queen of Silence herself.

Monica stood in front of four little girls. From behind I could instantly tell something was wrong. She was standing even more rigid than she ever does. It was like someone pushed her into a corner and forced her to stay there and not move or it meant her life. Nothing here would be that drastic but with Monica the simplest thing could be the most profound in the situation.

I walked up behind her and stood there without her knowing. The four girls didn't even notice me. Immediately, I noticed the girls all had something in common. Their hair was the exact same image as the one who stood in front of them. They may have been wigs or involved some type of technology I didn't know about. Either way, they were trying their best to do one thing to Monica. Impress her.

I finally walked in front of her and joined the little girls. Monica was quick to take notice of my presence and stare me down. She refused to look away and look back at the girls. All the while, they kept rambling on about how they saw her in the news on the highway. It started to make some more sense. Of course this place would have some sort of media. They must've dissected us and broke down who was who. It was the reason why some of the girls had their hair up in two pigtails just like the brat herself. Some had the lovely cut of Charlotte and hardly any had Monica's. These were the only four. And respecting Monica, they all had a black bow in the exact spot it needed to be in.

"I kept telling Riley that your powers were way more powerful than any of the others. Can we see it?" the little girl said, clasping her hands together as she bounced on her toes and waited in anticipation if Monica would give in to her demands.

There was a pause before there was any sort of muscle movement from Monica.

"You mean my lightning?" she said timidly.

"Yeah!" they all shouted.

Her eyes seeked my approval and desperately begged for an answer. Almost being entertained by

Monica's submissive state, I smiled and nodded for her to do it.

She awkwardly drew her hands up to her face and, with fidgety fingers, clenched her hands into fists. The crackle was a lot softer than normal as the power started to increase. As I watched the kids look on in amazement, I couldn't help but notice the stark contrast from earlier when I saw something that I've never seen from her. The lightning was crawling up her arms and the light was way brighter than it's ever been before. It made me wonder, could what she had charging up kill them? To think that all of that was instigated by my own anger. Boy was our connection strong.

"Don't get too close. That stuff hurts like crazy," I said.

They looked up at me.

"You've felt it before?"

"Yeah. Once," I said, thinking back to when fake Charlotte told her to force it into my head. The way it made me convulse on the floor. The way my vision started to darken. It was horrible.

They looked back towards Monica, probably thinking about why she would ever hurt me. But that didn't stop them from smiling like crazy as they witnessed something never to be seen before. I watched Monica intently as she continued to let the spark crackle in her hands. But that got me thinking. Why was she still doing it? I mean, sure, she was showing the kids, but she didn't want to in the first place. She was never forced to be in this uncomfortable position but all they needed to see was one quick little snippet of her powers. What they were seeing now was even confusing me.

Monica kept staring at her hands in confusion. Her eyebrows were bent down as if she was trying to solve something in her head.

"Gosh that's so awesome! I was telling my mom that I wanted to grow up to be just like you when we saw you on the news this morning."

"Like me?" she asked, perplexed while she still stared on at her hands.

"Yeah. Mark and Charlotte were cool. Oh and also when Will threw the Palace Guard's bike. But you looked the coolest. You're so pretty and strong looking. So we all went out and got our hair done before the barbeque. I didn't even think that you'd guys would come here."

The ends of Monica's mouth dipped down and her eyes started to billow up at the bottom.

"I'm not strong," she said faintly, barely allowing any of them to hear.

It was my cue to intervene and save her. I quickly blocked the kids' view with my body and turned them around.

"Alright, that's enough girls. I know you like Monica but she's feeling a little tired from this morning. Why don't you go annoy Will for a bit, okay?"

I didn't let them answer and pushed on their shoulders. I turned to look for Monica but she was already wandering off, pretty quick actually. She was fast walking away from me, hugging the sidewalk close to the buildings where there were less people. Bent on helping her, I ran towards her.

"Monica!"

She sped up at the sound of my voice. I reached out and grabbed hold of her arm. We were next to an alleyway when I caught up to her so I used that to my advantage.

"Come on," I said, dragging her in. "What's wrong?"

Her face was already covered in tears. It scrunched up and she took a good look at me, trying to decide what to express. Then she let go. She let it all go. She burst into more tears and let out sobs as she fell on my shoulder. I know it sounds bad, but I felt a little happy that I was seeing her like this. It was only me that was allowed to see her in this state. We agreed on it at the party when I helped put her bow back on. I was the one to protect her from anyone seeing her cry.

I placed a hand on the back of her head and the other around her back.

"I'm scared, Mark," she sobbed. "All these kids think I'm special. They think that I'm gonna save them." She hugged me even tighter, letting everything out. "Maya was telling me that she can't wait to see me in front of the Palace with you by my side as we storm it. She said that I was gonna save her. I was gonna help her mom stop having anxiety attacks because she works so hard for her. But—but, I'm not the person they think I am. I can't save them."

I rested my chin on her head and took a deep breath of her shampoo.

"I know they don't know. Hardly anyone knows the real you. But believe me, Monica. I'm scared too. I'm not gonna let any of these people tell us who to kill."

"No!" she yelled, hitting my chest with her fist. "No, Mark. We need to help them. We need to." Her sobs started to increase. "We can't let them live like this anymore. They're under constant oppression from the King. We were bred for this for crying out loud!" But did we really need to help them? We just found out about this place hours ago and now we have to put our lives on the line for millions of people? "I'm not letting them suffer anymore. I may not be strong, but I'm gonna try everything in my power to do so."

I stood there with her head underneath my chin laying her head on my chest. I never knew of this determination from Monica. It was rare that she ever spoke out so determined about something and usually let us do the deciding. What was I to say at a time like this? I didn't know, but I kept my place at that time and enjoyed our moment. Well, at least until someone ruined it.

"Monica?"

Monica picked her head up at the sound of her voice. At the sight of Wendy, she pulled away from me and quickly wiped the tears from her face. Her head went back to its normal position of looking downwards ever so slightly so she would be frowning. She didn't bother to acknowledge Wendy at all and walked past her.

Wendy watched her leave the alley. Once she was gone, her head slung back towards me. Her face was full of rage. Not the usual from Wendy, but actually legit anger.

"What the heck was that?" she said firmly.

"Nothing," I said, hoping to protect Monica's softer side.

"Oh don't give me that! You guys were hugging!"

"Don't you think for a second that it was like that," I said, letting firmness take hold of my voice as well.

"Then what the heck *was* that?!"

"One of the kids made her feel sorry for her. That's all."

"You're gonna need a better story when I tell Charlotte."

"Tell her what, that I was caring for a friend who was feeling out of it?!"

She searched for words as her face contorted into the same face I saw in the car. Her eyes refused to look me in the eye, reminding me of the time I complimented her at the party.

"Just think of other's feelings before you go and do something like that." Her eyes dashed towards mine really quick to look back down in defeat. "Charlotte's feelings that is."

"What? How is this gonna affect her feelings?"

She let out a sigh.

"Please don't do that again. You're gonna end up hurting someone."

Yeah? Like who? Explain that to me. I was doing what any of you guys would've done. I couldn't believe Wendy at that time. What the heck was she even talking about? I liked Charlotte but this was no sign of affection. This was me showing empathy towards Monica? Now, if you could find some place to tell me where I went wrong here I'd desperately like an explanation.

I stepped out of the alley a few minutes after Wendy. What Monica said really made my head take a beating. It's funny how that was usually the case with whatever she said. It wasn't often that she spoke out as she did so whenever she does, it hits like a truck.

My first few steps were heavy with her furious pounding on my chest as she objected my proposition. I rubbed the area she hit me, feeling the extent of her punch.

"Mark!"

I looked up to see Will running towards me. The urgency of his run made my thoughts of Wendy's stupid reaction get thrown out the window. Immediately my mind went on the track of thinking of the most horrible possibilities. The person I thought who was associated with this was Monica. As unstable as she got, anything could've happened and only the worse was coming to mind.

The only reason I thought it could've been associated with someone we knew was because of the concern on Will's face. But who could've affected Will that much?

"It's Penn," he said, stopping a ways from me, almost like he was scared of my reaction to his words.

"Where?" I said, my heart picking up its pace as well as my feet.

"She's not here. She's on one of the screens on the building."

He took me over to where all the people from the park were standing now. Everyone was huddled up against one of the scrappers that had a jumbo screen on it that played the usual ads. What was different was that it had five people standing in it facing the camera.

"Good afternoon everyone," the man standing in front of the four said. "I hope you're having a pleasant day. This marks a remarkable day in Novus's history. As you all know, this is the day that everyone's been waiting for. The return of The Equilibrium." Everyone turned to look at me really quick before returning their attention to the man on screen. "That may be the case but this day is also significant in another way." He took a step back to show everyone who was standing behind him. "The return of my daughter, the Princess."

My eyes were quick to notice Penn. She was standing with Eli, Sarah, and Brittany by her side. They all shared the same expression of anger. Everything from her frown to her hips told of her constant hatred for me. And it was all for me. The way her fists clenched every other second and her very presence on the screen let this cruel world know that she was out for my blood.

Eli was standing next to Penn and his sister. Their duo reminded me of when they kidnapped me from my very own bed and took me to my death. That matched with Penn's newfound personality would spawn a tremendous wrath.

The King was a tall man that was in his forties. He was wearing a suit that was somehow futuristic looking just like how everything else in this world found a way to look.

But around his nose was something that looked familiar. No, not an object itself but I was finally able to see Penn in her father. That way their jaw lines both came down to the same length and how their eyes were both painted with blood. Royalty. It may have been looked at upon everyone here as a sign of respect to show to these high people, but to me, every time I saw the red within her eyes, it reminded me of the spilled blood I was laying in when Wendy stabbed me in the stomach.

"I'd like all of you to meet BloodLip. Penn, Eli, Sarah, and Brittany." When the King mentioned their names, they all squirmed. "It's wonderful to have them back and I expect all of you to treat them just as you'd treat me. They're royalty just as much as I am so you listen to their commands. But that's that. Let's get onto the fun part. Each of them is equipped with unique abilities. Would you guys like to demonstrate them?"

How the circumstances have changed. Penn was the very one to tell them the same thing when she was showing their powers to us. Gosh was she a different person back then. The smile she had the whole time she was talking. But the second that Trent Willis walked into the alley and took that picture, the person in front of me now appeared. All it took was just me to unlock it permanently with a single bullet.

Penn eyed her dad with disgust as he waited for her to show everyone their powers. He spoke like they were some kind of machines. Equipped? Really?

Just like last time, they all showed their powers. The only thing was that I was waiting for Brittany to shoot Sarah again but it never happened. Eli turned into a rock, Brittany turned into a ball of flames, and Penn took out her sword, this time holding it with the tip behind her pointed upwards.

"All of their abilities are all pretty self-explanatory. Eli can turn into any type of material he touches. Brittany can control fire and Penn can use her natural form of energy to create the very sword in her hand. Sarah, well, Sarah has a wonderful gift of regeneration. It's difficult to show that, but if the time comes, she won't need to worry about her own health."

He gave Penn a smile before he faced the camera once again. I didn't realize but my hands were getting sweaty at the time. I tried rubbing it off as Charlotte came closer to me with the little kid holding her hand, clenching it and holding on for dear life as he watched the orders of the King himself.

"These people you see in front of you are the future of Novus. They'll all be aiding me in my new upcoming project. It's quite marvelous I have to say, but, you'll all be able to see that for yourselves in a short time. Now, in regards to the Equilibrium and his friends, I welcome you. Rumors have it that he's in Terra's hands and rumors tend to be true around here. So, Terra, I expect you to comply formally to my request to speak with all of them. I'll be hearing from you soon. And if not, no matter. Everything will be fixed in its due time. After all, the Equilibrium is alive, isn't he? His purpose will be fulfilled one way or another. Preferably, the one I intend. But all things aside, I wish you a "welcome home" from the House of Exon."

He turned on his heel and walked off with his hands behind his back, letting the ends of his suit jacket flare up. Penn and the rest of them stood there with their frowns growing by the second. Brittany's hands grew and grew with flames, never ending her spur of heat. Penn's face kept contorting and her mouth moved. With her father gone, the mic that was attached to his jacket was meant for only his voice to be heard. But whatever she said had to be directed towards me. It had to. She let the sword dissolve and in her hands she created the same bow that was aimed at my heart earlier. She pulled it back, but this time she didn't let it hold. Without hesitating she let it fly straight into the camera and ended the broadcast.

No doubt, it was a sign for me. Her last words burning into my skull, reiterating it nonstop.

Be ready. We're coming for you.

With everyone now anxious and confused about what he was talking about, the noise of the crowd increased once again, but I stayed in the same place looking at the screen that soon returned to the long running show of ads. Will came up to me along with Monica and Wendy. All four of them were looking at me, almost waiting for a reaction. But what was I supposed to feel? What was this project he was talking about? And more importantly, what did he mean by "my purpose being fulfilled"?

"I need to talk to him," I said.

"Sounds good and all but what's that gonna accomplish? Who knows what he'd do to you if he got a hold of you," Will said.

"It's gonna accomplish everything. He's the only person on this planet besides BloodLip that knows my powers. And if I know what they are we can fix everything. The fake Charlotte in my slip space told me that my powers can make something horrible or beautiful. I don't know what that means, but it obviously means something."

"That you can fix whatever problem that's gonna cause this human race to become extinct," Monica said.

"Exactly. And I need to find out what it is."

"Well you're not gonna go alone that's for sure," Charlotte said. "We're all coming with you." The King already gave me an invite of sorts so I was good to come over I guess. But how I'd go about doing it I didn't know.

"We need to leave. Now," Terra said firmly as she stormed over towards us with Ed and Kerren. "Get in the car."

"Why? I was actually starting to have fun with these kids," Wendy said.

"Cause he never reveals what he's doing. It's only for a reason why he did that. We need to get to headquarters right away."

"To do what?" I asked as Kerren ran up to the car to turn in on.

"You're gonna tell me everything you know about BloodLip."

Chapter 3

The hallway was quiet. Not a sound entered the area, and if one thought to even dare to, it would've been killed instantly. The whitish grey walls sapped any sort of emotion that could be displayed and threw it away, not even using it for itself. I don't know who designed the Palace but it no doubt was made by someone with no sort of thought to color.

The six of us were walking through the King's Palace as one of the Palace Guards was guiding us through a hallway, after stripping us of any sort of items of course. Kerren was the only one to come along with us from Headquarters.

When we got back from the park, I told Terra all I knew about BloodLip just as she wanted. Everything, not withholding any information. She wanted to know what he was planning but from what I told her, nothing sparked. Because she was desperate to get any information, she was willing to send me in, knowing for a fact that he wouldn't hurt me. That was her thought but it was nowhere close to what I thought. He sent a group of people to kill me after all. Who could say what his actions were gonna be?

Ed drove us over to the front of Exon and the six of us got off. Palace Guards were already waiting there for us, armed for any chance that we'd attack. From there, we were taken all the way through the city. Kerren paid no attention to the Guards in the car and spoke just like she did when we were driving to the park.

Terra was telling me that Kerren was the only one in Headquarters who was a citizen in Exon. They made sure when she was a little girl that they registered her so she could have easy access inside the city. So as we drove through, she was, once again, pointing out places she liked. She would answer our question about certain places and how the city worked in terms of how people got around.

When we reached the Palace, I was finally able to see it in full. It reminded me a lot of a castle but if it was modernized. Metal points stuck up from the top in different places but in the middle was a tall point that extended above all the others. I had to admit, it was beautiful. The only thing that made it gross was all the Palace Guards that littered it. They wore the same black suits that I saw on the highway minus the helmet. But with the whole place in mind, it had to be bigger than three football stadiums combined.

Since we were to be talking to the King, I expected some grand throne, but instead, they led us to a casual room. The Guard opened the door and gave us a look and we all entered the room. All but one.

"You're not allowed to enter," one of the Guards said to Kerren. Kerren looked up at him as if he offended her. She put her hands on her hips and didn't care for any sort of social cues as she burned into his eyes.

"Excuse me?"

"The King's not interested in you. He wants to speak to The Equilibrium, not anyone from your little rebellion."

With all of us in the room and looking back into the hallway, we watched her arguing with the Guard as if she did it on a regular basis.

"Hello there," said a voice behind us. We all turned to see a man in his forties sitting comfortably in a chair behind a desk. His arms were held together by his fingers on top of the glass in front of him. The desk alone looked to be worth millions. He smiled at all of us and extended his head out over the table to see who was arguing behind us.

"ALIS?" he said, speaking out loud.

"Yes my Lord?" a voice said, coming from the ceiling. No, I wouldn't necessarily say the ceiling, but rather, it had a presence from within the whole area. It was the voice of a computer that spoke in a monotone pitch that also found a way to display emotion with three simple words.

"Who's the girl?"

"Kerren Anderson, sir. Sixteen years of age."

Hearing the same last name as mine associated with hers made a cold feeling run down my chest. It was her real last name after all, not mine. She gave me a look to see my reaction towards what the computer said.

"From Equilibrium I presume?" Kerren stood there waiting for an answer from ALIS before she realized that Zalus was talking to her.

"What does it matter?" she said in disgust.

"Answer my question," he said in a soft voice, still holding his smile.

"Yeah, and?"

"You're a registered citizen when you don't live in Exon. You know that's not allowed Kerren. ALIS, delete her information."

"Done."

"I bet it was nice meeting your brother for the first time." She glared him down with a sneer. "Oh don't be like that. I'm being honest here. I can sympathize with you. I finally got Penn back after not seeing her for sixteen years. To see her all grown up is an amazing feeling."

He nodded at the Guard and he took Kerren away. The door closed behind us, leaving only us and the King in the room. There had to be more people in the room, right? It was the King after all. Monica had the capability to kill him if she wanted to. There had to be more protection for the King.

"Please, take a seat," he said, pointing to the five seats in front of the desk. Each of them matched the style of the desk and were quite comfortable. I sat in the middle with the others on my side.

"What is it?" Monica asked, already in a fixed position and not allowing the movement of her spine. It was the way she always sat—completely rigid.

"What is what?" he asked.

"ALIS? What does it stand for?"

"Ah, that. ALIS is our very own Artificial Living Intelligence System."

"Why not just call it Artificial Intelligence? What makes it living?"

"She used to be a real human being. She gave up her life for the sake of science and we found a way to take someone's thinking brain that acts for itself and transfer that into an artificial intelligence."

"What was her name before?" Charlotte asked.

The King gave a snicker.

"Alice."

"Alright cut it out," I said. "Why did you want us here?"

"Why wouldn't I want you here? You're the Equilibrium after all. Everyone's been talking about you for years and here you are."

"You sent a group named after the Queen to kill me," I said, leaning out of my seat to get closer to him.

"That's true. Those times called for desperate measures."

"You calling dropping a bomb on a city desperate measures?" Charlotte said.

"You think I did that? That cult that Terra leads claims that they know the "truth" to everything. Answer me this, how do you know that I did that?" He waited for the pause that was us thinking. "Exactly. I never commanded a ship to drop a bomb over Ashillon. One of my ships was stolen and suddenly all the blame was shifted over to me."

"That still doesn't answer why you sent Violet to kill us," I said.

"Let me put it simply Mark. You're dangerous. Extremely dangerous. If you were given the knowledge to what your powers are, there's no telling what you'd do. I had to protect my people. If you were capable of destroying everything then I needed to make sure that'd never happen, even if that meant killing you."

"So you're able to tell us straight to our faces that you were willing to kill us?" Will asked, leering his head down. With the sight of him sitting next to the stiff Monica with her hands placed calmly in her lap sure made a sight for the King.

"I'm being honest with you. There's no need to lie here. Terra doesn't have those sort of morals."

"You claiming she's lied to us?" Wendy asked.

"Who knows what she's lied about but I can guarantee you that she has. Look, I've been dealing with these people for years. They've tried to inflict as much damage and chaos as they can. I know exactly who they are. They're nothing but vile cultists who try to make their popularity spread like fire."

Will sighed.

"Are you seriously trying to persuade us to go against them when they're named after the guy for crying out loud?" he said pointing at me.

Zalus dodged the question and went on.

"You don't know what plans I have; plans that are going to change the world. If you were able to help me then we'd finally be able to help the planet." He waited for our interest to raise. "So sometime really soon we can start expanding again. We have rules that make sure everyone is confiding in the boundaries of Exon and if not, you're part of another race in the outer cities. But we can only contain so much. If we finally take part in this new project we'll be able to go out into the fog and start rebuilding; start expanding."

"Why can't you start right now?" I asked.

"The land out there isn't the cleanest."

"Toxins?" Charlotte asked.

"Something more. If you help me, you'll be abl—"

"We aren't helping you."

The interruption came from Monica. Her body stood in its strict form but her eyes were the only things that moved, focusing on him. I felt in her the determination that I felt when she was crying. It was a force that I really started to like in her. Next to her I felt Will's joy peak. A smile that he couldn't contain revealed itself. Boy did he like what he was seeing in Monica, as we all would.

"Not willing to join me are you?"

"Of course not," she said.

"Very well."

His hand moved to a drawer that we couldn't see and it slid open. With his face still keeping its smile, he pulled out a handgun and placed it in front of him. All of our eyes darted over to it. Its shape was exactly like the one the Palace Guard had on his waist.

"That supposed to scare us?" Will scoffed.

"No. Not at all. It was meant to get a reaction. What you'd do when you saw it would tell me a lot about who you are. Anger. Fear. Frustration." He raised his eyes towards mine. "Nothing. That alone told me all I needed to know. Thank you for your cooperation."

Are you kidding me! Come on Mark! You couldn't see that coming. Before when I didn't have these people with me, I felt that everyone was always talking bad about me in their mind. To counter that, I made sure I wasn't who they thought I was. But when Charlotte, Wendy, Monica, and Will came along, there was no need to hide who I was. Even though it felt good to not constantly hide, it hindered me. People were able to read me again, something I absolutely hated.

My anger spiked as he slid the gun towards us, making sure the chamber pointed out towards him and the handle was towards us. Did this idiot think I was really gonna pick up the gun? I'd never make that mistake again. The first time I touched a gun, there was a fight that followed. The next time followed the deadly consequences that a bullet to the head possesses.

But he wanted a reaction. If he sees that I don't pick up the gun, it shows I don't fight. I don't take an advantage. It shows something I'm not all the while telling him of my fear. What if I did pick it up? Would he find reason to kill me for it and end everything just like that?

Just when I was coming to a conclusion, I felt it again. Oh no. Will don't you even dare.

The gun lifted in front of me without anyone touching it. With his head still dipping as it was and the adopted Wendy smile persisting, Will lifted and aimed the gun at the King. With the gun still in front of me, it made the same picture of that night reappear. Me holding a gun pointed at the head of my homeroom teacher.

The King's smile grew.

"Wonderful," he said. "Please, by all means, continue." Thanks Will. You idiot, you just told him everything about us. But even if I wanted to grab the gun out of the air and put it back on the table, it'd show even more than we needed to show.

The bottom of the gun dropped and was pulled out of the handle. Once the magazine was out of it, Will threw the gun to the side, making it hit the wall. Carefully, all the bullets were pulled out of the magazine, and once again, he threw the magazine. Ironically, five bullet were placed in the magazine. He separated the bullets and put one lying flat in front of each of us. We were all confused at what he was doing but then he went and slid his bullet that was in front of him forwards and pointed it at the King.

"My bullet's been expended," Will said. He moved his head to look down the row of seats. "They've yet to use theirs. Notice where they're pointed Zalus." Will stood and crossed his arms. "All at you. Now, I'm just the least out of all us. You could tick me off for days but I'd pretty much stay mad at you just the same as before. But when you mess with them, then you're in for a world of pain. And let me tell you, their bullets hurt more than mine ever will."

Monica stood and took the bullet that was in front of her and clenched it in her hand. Her fist sparked as the bullet crackled in her palm. Charlotte and Wendy soon followed, taking their own bullet. I felt all of their determination pull together and grow with every second. With me still sitting, I watched the male version of Penn wait for a reaction in me.

Monica wanted this. She told me. It was the reason for her following Will and taking the bullet. She wanted to use it. Her mark that she's gonna fight him. She's gonna make things right. Not for her own sake but for the sake of those kids. For the lives on Novus. For our past home. For the members that had fallen for our sake. For peace. For the freedom of others. For the Equilibrium.

I stood with fire burning in my chest and took the bullet in front of me. I was gonna fight. Fight by the side of my friends to stop this madness. To stop what started all of this.

All of us turned towards the door and opened it, ready to just get the heck out of there. Just as we were about to leave, Zalus stopped us.

"Hey Mark. Penn wanted me to tell you she says hi."

Liar. She didn't have a clue about us getting together like this. She would've been here the instant she heard it to execute her judgement.

His smile changed and that's when I remember really looking at him with that pure hatred I used to have for everybody. It was all because of him that everything started. That I was even born. The reason I killed Violet. The disgusting look that he killed someone and loved every second of it. I saw the murderer he really was, just like I was, but he embraced it. And that's why I hated him.

Chapter 4

Would you call it a vacation? I don't know. If you were in my position I don't think you would. But, I would be lying if I said I didn't have some sort of fun. I mean, come on, I was with my friends the whole time. If I were to go to any place, the only thing that would ever make it fun would be who was there.

Was it all fun? Not really. It was part of it but it still had all that stress put over it. Once we got back from talking with Zalus, we had all determined for ourselves that we'd fight him. The first step was training. And let me tell you, it's a long one. The first week of us being on Novus was us starting our training. With Terra, there wasn't any time to be wasted.

Kerren would come and wake us every morning telling us that Terra wanted us in the mess hall within ten minutes. Once we'd put on the clothes that was hanging in the closet for us and in a drawer on the side of the bed, we'd meet each other in the hall to wait to walk together. I remember the first morning that we started training, Wendy was complaining about how long the shorts were.

"If they're shorts then why the heck make them this long?!" she said.

What did I see the next morning? When we met out in the hall her shorts were severed at the bottom. She noticed I was staring at them, wondering why they looked like that, but when I noticed that I could see her whole thigh, I knew exactly why they looked like that.

"Did you cut your shorts shorter?" I asked.

"Yeah. And?"

"They practically look like underwear," Charlotte said.

"Better than what they looked like before."

All five of us would go down to the mess hall and meet up with Kerren to have some breakfast. Even though I saw everyone the first time I stepped into Headquarters, I didn't see everyone doing their own thing. When we'd get there, there were people already eating breakfast, some already finished, and some just getting there like us. People like Terra probably already ate way earlier than us since she had to run things around here. And I thought when we woke up as being early.

The first day, Kerren took us through the process on how to get the food even though it was self-explanatory. It was basically a buffet line and we'd just take whatever we wanted. It's what we've been doing for years at school whenever we bought lunch. Charlotte was kinda confused by her explaining it.

"Uh, we kinda know how to serve ourselves food," she told Kerren.

Kerren looked at her, sorta embarrassed, but tried to keep her composure as she kept explaining.

The food was quite interesting but a lot of it was similar to Earth's food. They had the usual eggs, bread, oatmeal but what was the interesting part was seeing what they made for themselves that we found strange. Yet they found some of our food to be foreign and almost taboo. How could Kerren not understand cereal?

Once we got our food, we sat in a table that was empty and was in the prime position to look at Rouge. When Rebecca made eye contact with me, she let a sly smile accompany her thick eyeshadow eyes. She leaned over and whispered in Alex's ear. He looked up and noticed that we were sitting down. He disregarded me quickly but he was looking for his target. Wendy. Since she completely mocked him in front of all the people here, he wanted at her. He was able to get eye contact with her and gave the most disgusting frown he could give without having to get up and punch her in the face. Wendy gave a smile and waved at him before blowing him a kiss. Alex quickly looked away in disgust, scrunching up his nose, not being able to bare to look at her.

It was perfect. Wendy knew how to push people's buttons. When they were upset, make them squirm by being as happy and perky as you could be. Naturally, we all laughed, making everything at our table so much more comfortable. Once again, just rely on Wendy to do that. There was nothing this girl couldn't accomplish with her way of manipulating a social situation.

The other member of Rouge, which I found out later that his name was Ethan, gave a simple wave, making Alex frustrated and yanked his hand down, not wanting him to address us.

After we ate, all of us headed down to the training chamber. And when I say chamber, yes, I mean it's an actual chamber. There was a glass case around this pit that extended down, almost as if it was an empty pool that went down more than twenty feet. Its length was longer, extending for quite a bit. On the outside of it was a few sets of control panels that contained monitors of inside the chamber and dials that I hadn't a clue to what they controlled.

From what I could see on the outside, it was all white, not mentioning that huge white lights were suspended from the ceiling, enhancing the lack of color.

Kerren explained how this was where everyone in Headquarters that does field work trains. She also went on to explain how Violet, Scarlett, and Aqua were the first to train here. They set records that no one has ever beaten. On the wall next to the control panels was three cases. Each one had a small emission of a specific color, one according to their name to be exact. Inside each one was a black suit that had bits of metal attached to it. These were the very suits that they wore as they would go on their black ops.

Terra came along and greeted us. Her face was no different though. It still had the same look of anger to it. Her frown just couldn't seem to go away. She took us through the stairs to the room before the chamber. There, fake guns were hung on racks and there were various items such as armor plates with targets on it. It was all for the training. In front, there were two doors that opened up into the white world. Without saying anything else, she nudged us in the chamber. She stepped in with us really quick and pressed a button next to the double doors then slammed them shut on us.

We all searched around for what was to come up but the white just filled our eyes.

"All right guys. Get ready. I know it's gonna look kinda creepy at first since you've probably never seen something like this, but the area around you is gonna change. It's gonna look extremely realistic, but it's all just a simulation," Kerren said over speakers.

I looked up for her through the glass but when I went to go look, a black film put itself over the glass.

"Test number one. A.K.A. the Three's first test. It's quite simple to be completely honest." There was a hiss as a white column came out of the ground with a red button on top. It was placed on the very opposite end of the chamber. "Just press the button."

Okay. Doesn't seem so bad. Right? Alright Mark. If you keep assuming things are gonna be how you envision them to be, you're gonna really end up screwing yourself over. Of course it's not gonna be easy. The second she finished talking, the ground changed to a battle torn city. It reminded me of the city we walked through when we first got here but if we were there when everything was happening. Buildings pushed through the ground and suddenly the whole chamber was gone. I looked up to see the white lights that were shining down a second ago and those were gone as well. The only thing shining down on my face was the sun.

Suddenly, the button that we were to press was getting farther and farther away. This may have been a crazy moment for us to witness, with the atmosphere taking shape right before our eyes and stuff, but what freaked us out the most was what Monica did.

Still standing there like she would've normally been doing, she took a black rubber band out of her pocket. She put her five fingers in it and extended it out. Raising her hand to her hair, she pulled all of her thick blanket back and put her hair into a ponytail. Now, I've known Monica for a while now. The whole time I've known her, been to her house, seen her in her dang pajamas, witnessed her in her most comfortable and in the hottest conditions, she never conforms to putting her hair in a ponytail. Her eyes were glued to the button that was mocking her, telling her that it was gonna be impossible to get to.

Palace Guards came out from behind buildings and were holding firearms to protect this button. As we were still standing there, more Guards spread out amongst the buildings. They were ready to fire at whatever they saw.

"By the way," Kerren said, "you're being timed. Might wanna get a move on. Things get harder the longer you wait."

"Noted," Wendy said as she burst into a sprint. I wanted to wait a little and think logically about what we should do, but with the time matter on our hands, we had to do that on the fly. All five of us ran forward and started to step on the tattered streets that had various potholes around.

"Three Guards to your left," Will said, already looking around for more.

I looked up at the window of one of the buildings. The glass was broken and they had their weapons at the ready. When they made eye contact with me and noticed all of us running through the streets, they aimed at us. Will quickly picked up one of the stray pieces of metal and covered the window long enough for us to get across the street.

But of course things weren't gonna be that simple. Sure, you deal with one group of people, but you'll still have another one chasing after you. Bullets whizzed by us from behind to carry that notion and prove it true. We all lifted our hands and covered our heads as we scattered not having any sort of order. Charlotte disappeared right from my sight and Wendy teleported out leaving the three of us to be shot to death.

A door to one of the buildings opened on its own. I knew it to be Charlotte so I grabbed Monica's hand and ran for the building. Will followed right behind us as he threw another piece of debris at the Guards.

"Lock the door!" I yelled when we got in.

"It's not gonna matter!" Will yelled at me, slamming the door behind him. "There's more on the way."

"We just need a vantage point," Charlotte said, already walking up the stairs of what seemed to be this apartment.

Since we really didn't know what to do, we followed Charlotte. I noticed Monica was gliding her hands along the wall as we ran up the stairs to get to the roof. Every time she would touch it she would shake her head in confusion and create that same frown.

"Then what the heck do you expect us to do after we get to the roof?! Jump off?!" Will yelled in frustration at Charlotte.

"Of course!" Wendy answered. "You have me you idiot."

The roof wasn't any help. In fact, it just made things harder. We saw from up there that the button was covered and guarded by two high powered cannons. If they even saw us for a second they'd tear us to shreds, simulation or not.

"Well great, how are we gonna get passed that?" I asked.

All of us immediately started brainstorming. Charlotte was the one to come up with the cleverest ideas. We all kept thinking, but the one who I thought would've gave the most logical and simplest one would've been Monica, but she wasn't talking at all. She had her head turned in the opposite direction, looking back at where we started out near the door.

"I think I know what—" she tried saying before she was cut off by Wendy and Will arguing. She turned to furrow her brows and walked towards us. "Guys they all moved by the door."

Once again, her quiet voice was overlooked. I heard her, but to be honest, I wasn't even listening. I was too focused on what they were arguing about since it involved what we could do to get to the button.

Without saying anything, she turned around and stormed down the stairs. What knocked me out of the conversation was her frustration that I felt. I called out to her as I ran back down stairs and the others stayed arguing over what to do. When I made it out to the street, she was already a ways away running straight for the door. What she said was right. All the Guards shifted over to where we originally were and not guarding the button.

As she was running towards them, she started to charge up her lightning. Her arms crackled and an aura of light was created around her. The Guards raised their guns and aimed at her. It made my heart jump before I remembered it was a simulation. Before they could shoot, she let out the lightning into all of them, making them convulse as they fell to the floor.

When she made it to the door, she simply raised her hand and pressed on the wall. When she did that, the whole world that was made around us fell apart and reverted back to the white chamber, reminding us that it was all fake.

So, apparently, the real button that we were to press wasn't the one that she showed us but the one Terra pressed before she locked us in here. Of course, Monica was the only one to figure that out. And we didn't even bother to listen to her, being all caught up in our little world of argument.

We all walked up back to above the chamber and we saw that there was a small crowd that gathered to watch our performance. But I didn't care about that. What I saw was that Terra was upset, not like the normal upset she's been but legitimate frustration. Kerren behind her had a look of shock on her face.

"The record set for this test was set by the Three," Terra said, glaring me down.

"How long was that?" Wendy asked.

Terra's mouth ticked before she spoke, hating what she was saying.

"One hour and forty-two minutes."

"Yours was five minutes and twenty-three seconds," Kerren said, not moving anything but her mouth.

So if I thought things might get better in the future with Terra, this offset that even farther than I ever hoped. The Three that she knew so well, the ones that she knew to be the best just got outsmarted by a sixteen year old girl. The whole training simulation was given to people who were to go in the chamber for the first time to see if they can think abstractly. Terra later told me, after her fit of anger of course, that Rylan was extremely adamant on that sort of thinking. It was the only one that was gonna help you win a war.

But that test helped us a lot. It showed that if we were gonna keep working things out like we were, we'd just end up arguing over and over again about what to do. Sure, Monica was still able to figure out the test within seconds of getting her bearings, but imagine how fast we would've gone if we actually listened to her and worked together.

So, that's the very thing we did. When we'd wake up every morning, Terra would have us train. There weren't that many simulations but only at certain benchmarks. Basic training included hand to hand combat. She also taught us how to find people's weak spots when she'd have us fight each other. And of course, every time I had to fight with Wendy she would go straight for my stab wound. Because of her abusing that every single dang time, I bet the healing process of it was reduced tremendously.

You'd think that when we were told to fight each other that it was to be fair, or, at least I did. Not the case at all. Terra told them to abuse their powers as much as they can. It's what they were made for anyways. So, me being the only one who didn't know what my powers were, had to deal with a constant barrage of what felt like misused power. I was finally able to see it through other people's eyes.

Gosh was it annoying! Wendy would jump all over the place and I'd be constantly spinning around looking for her and all I'd hear was *swoosh swoosh swoosh*, just barely being able to see her pigtails before they disappeared from my eyes.

Will was just as annoying. It wasn't really his powers all that much that ticked me off but it was his face. At least I was allowed to actually hit it this time with valid reason, though, I never really got close. He'd always push me back. With time, I was finally able to a few times but not as hard as I wanted.

Then there was Monica. When I was told that I had to fight Monica for the first time I was so timid. I didn't want to lay a hand on her soft image. But boy was that thinking wrong. Monica completely destroyed me, not holding back at all. She would throw bolts of lightning into me and make me reminisce over the ordeal in the mansion. You'd think that maybe she'd show some sort of compassion, but there was nothing. She would do so in a straight face like everything else she did. Overtime, I learned that I needed to drop the caring act when we were training and went after her. She'd still beat me most of the time but I was getting better.

Charlotte. If there was anyone I would never hurt it'd be her. I know I said that I didn't want to hurt Monica, but as bad as it sounds, I'd sooner want to hurt Monica than Charlotte. As you can probably tell, that thinking was the kind of thinking I had when we first started training. When I'd get frustrated when she'd randomly disappear from my sight, I'd find a way to vent that through my combat, holding onto her so she wouldn't disappear. If she were to do it while I was holding onto her then I'd be transformed just like her. So every time it'd be me tackling her and we'd fall on the floor.

I gotta say, I loved when I was told to fight Charlotte. Because I had to go and tackle her before she could disappear, it'd make for some close encounters. I remember the first couple of times I'd do that, it'd surprise her. She would fall back and sometimes even whack her head on the floor, but her eyes would lock with mine. Sounds all lovely dovey. I know. But let me tell you, things changed. Like I said, I loved when she'd look at me like that, but over the next couple of weeks of our training and us being there in Headquarters, something happened and I hated every second of it.

Let's see. What's the best way to go about explaining this? Alright, well I'll start off with my thoughts on Charlotte. You know how much I appreciated her. You can take that in any way you want. It applies all the same. Her looks, her simplicity, her kindness, her humbleness. Whatever it is, I liked all of it. Now, I thought that I'd be the one to have that for myself. I always had the mentality that she'd always have these feelings for me and it'd be this way until the time when I'd want to date. Pretty much, I thought I had my future set out for me. Was that thinking flawed?

Apparently.

When we'd have relaxing evenings or on the weekends when Terra would allow us to go out into the city, Rouge would occasionally join us. That occasionally turned into consistency and it was now a regular thing. I never thought of this as being a big deal but boy was it now.

I was busy one day talking with Wendy, Monica, and Kerren. I was so engrossed in our conversation that I'd forgotten all about Charlotte. Wanting to include her in the conversation, I looked around for her, hoping that she'd be close by. Instead, she was quite a distance away talking with someone. Who was it? Take a guess. She was chatting it up with Alex. I wouldn't have normally cared cause why should I, but the thing was, no other member of Rouge was there with him. Rebecca and Ethan were ordering some sort of dessert from a stand at the time.

My immediate reaction was anger. I know I didn't have a right over who Charlotte talked to, but gosh did that infuriate me. It wasn't just the act of talking, Alex was making her laugh. She was smiling like crazy when she was looking at him. I was the one who was supposed to make her laugh like that! The very sight disgusted me but I kept looking. I wanted to do something about it but there was nothing to do.

Kerren asked me a question and I turned back towards them and answered, keeping my face as happy looking as I could get it, probably making it look fake. Monica gave me a silent look, of course being the only one to notice I was disgruntled.

Okay. So that was one time. Whatever. But when it happened again and again, explain to me how I was supposed to feel. Whenever we would eat, they'd always end up talking somehow and she'd be away from us. It was starting to get to me. For the first time in almost a whole year, that deep seated anger that I had for everyone came back up, but this time only for two people. Yes, that includes Charlotte. And I hated myself for that reason.

It led me to do every sort of desperate move on her to somehow gain back her attraction for me. When we'd talk, I'd just make things awkward as if I was rushing to spit something out when in reality, I was just buying time so she wouldn't be talking with Alex.

And how could she even like a jerk like that?! He was ruthless with the way he treated us. He even called us out and said that we'd be nothing without our powers. How could she go and talk to him like nothing's happened, no less like him?

Monica could notice my desperate state. She never fully acknowledged it with any words but she would always give me that look like she knew what I was going through. But I didn't understand. She doesn't like anyone.

Right?

Anyways, that was an ordeal. But I was able to cope with myself somehow, for the time being at least. So like always, train, eat, sleep, repeat. It was our whole lives. I was tired of it. To be honest, I missed home too. We all did. I missed seeing my mom, regardless if she was my biological mother or not.

Terra would always make sure that we knew how to fight against someone with a sword for obvious reasons. It was pretty quick for me to learn the basics and I learned to fight with one of my own.

For the others, they got some special training. They all had to try and extend their limits with their powers. For Charlotte, she had to try and make other people turn invisible with her for long periods of time. She also had to make all of us invisible once. Her neck strained with every sort of stress as she screamed out because of the pain. It was the same for Wendy. Try to teleport through thicker walls and longer distances. Will had to try and pick up heavier objects like cars. He also practiced to pick heavier things up with only his mind, not using any of his hands to aid him. Lastly, Monica had to see how many much wattage she could shoot out. When she tried her hardest, she blew out all the power in Headquarters for a few hours, even shutting down the backup generator.

If there was any day that was significant during our training, it was a simulation that signified that you were ready for field work. In other words, it meant for us that we could aid in combating Zalus in whatever he planned to do. It's not like we really needed it though. I already agreed with Monica and the others that we were gonna help fight. It would just mean that I would help fight, I didn't need to kill anyone. The execution of the King would be up to Terra.

I didn't really dwell on what would happen that day but just focused on what was happening now. You know, the training and the whole ordeal with Charlotte.

On this day that we passed this simulation, I was crazy tired. People would watch like normal and once we finished they cheered for us. It was the equivalent of sporting events on Novus. Because of the extensiveness of the physical activity in this one, I rushed back to my room to shower and get on a fresh change of clothes. My stomach was still empty since we had to perform this one of an empty stomach and it took somewhere close to two hours to complete, not to mention that we broke the record again.

Gotta say, we were a powerhouse there at Headquarters. When we'd walk in a group as five, people would stop in their tracks and stare at us whether they realized it or not. It felt godly. Power just resonated from inside when we'd walk around the place like that and even within the city as well.

The simulation we finished was in the early evening so it was just in time for dinner. I made my way down the hallways that I'd come to know to the mess hall. But as I drew closer something became apparent with each step.

"Is that music?" I asked myself.

My curiosity peaked and when I entered the mess hall my question was answered. Usually, there were people sitting calmly at the tables that were spread around. Now? Well, they were thrown about in weird position to make room for dancing. Yes. Dancing.

Wendy?! What the heck are you doing?! She was on top of one of the tables and had a microphone to her mouth as more lyrics were sounded. Amps and speakers were on the side of her and blasted the music out to the whole place. She was the one responsible for the voice that sung.

It's stupid. Completely stupid. I don't know how much I've heard this girl's voice. She always complains to me anyways so I've heard various pitches of it, and heck, I've heard her sing before, but I guess you can't compare it with the music she was singing now since she usually raps. But now, her voice was almost heavenly dare I say. She was so immersed in the music with her eyes closed and leaning over to draw out her voice as much as possible.

Will waved me over to where they were sitting, watching the show. When I made it to the table, there was food thrown around. It was mainly half eaten and dripping on the table. There was a plate next to Monica who sat quietly looking at a glass panel. It was a sandwich that only had a few bites in it. She peeked her eyes up from her tablet and noticed that I was looking at the plate of food. Her hand slowly lifted and shifted the plate over to me.

I took the sandwich from the plate and leaned over her to see what she was reading. She didn't bother to lean back at me being completely nosy. From what I could tell, she was reading some of the history books that they make the kids read in schools. If any of us were to really delve into the history of Novus it'd be Monica. For me, I just relied on what people told me.

Monica's been doing a lot here lately in her free time. She finally figured out the circuit work of Novus. It took a while but when she got it she jumped out of her shell for a split second. We were finished with a day of training and were relaxing before we went to bed. All of us, including Kerren, were sitting together and talking. Monica was the only who wasn't with us at the time. She was running around in between hallways and running from control back to her room. She had a computer set up next to us where she was sitting previously. She would run back and forth between these places and move with incredible speed. In between her sprints, she would occasionally touch the wall and look around. It was quite a sight to watch but once she figured it out—

"Yes!" she yelled as she jumped up in joy. "I got it!"

Our faces shared the same expression of shock. She read our faces and shot us a look like we were idiots, changing her face back to the expressionless sheet. The lights spontaneously shut off in the whole facility before she turned it back on and apologized. She blushed a bit as she went back to her computer and silently tapped on the keyboard like nothing happened. She was later telling us how different the mechanics of wiring and electrical outputs were compared to Earth. She said that looking at this, it made humans on Earth look stupid for not thinking of this earlier.

I smiled as I thought back to her true self.

"What do you think?" Will asked as he nudged me.

"About what?" I asked.

"Wendy you idiot."

"Why the heck is she even singing? Who planned this?"

"You're listening to her right now," he said. I let out a sigh. "She thought that since we pretty much graduated from training we should have a party."

"Makes sense if it's coming from her. You're not bothered by the music?" I asked Monica.

She gave a small shake, still scanning her eyes over the words.

"No. I like her voice. If anything it helps me read better."

"Am I going deaf or something or did I just hear that right?" Will said. "You like her voice?!"

"You know you do too. Hiding her passion is her thing. She's always sung, just when we're not there."

"But she would've sung in front of me," Charlotte said, sitting over the lip of the table.

Monica shook her head.

"You don't get it do you. She still wants some sort of privacy just like we all do. We're all good friends but that doesn't mean we don't withhold some things from each other. You can't just randomly sing like this. She's been practicing, waiting for this exact moment."

Monica was right. This was her enjoyment of sorts. She liked singing. I always knew that. But this was her true singing that required the amount of effort unseen by her before.

I kept feeling uncomfortable but decided to just go with what Wendy was doing and enjoy her singing and the dancing of the people. Kerren was constantly on what was considered the dance floor, moving to the melodies of the songs.

I didn't think Wendy was gonna stay at this level of music and I was right. She moved on to more party music that had lyrics only she could say without a doubt of a conscious matter. I didn't bother dancing and neither did any of us. We were completely beaten by the simulation earlier that we wanted to simply relax to the tunes.

From where I was sitting, I watched Charlotte intently. She had her hands placed on the edge of the table to support her swinging her legs. Her smile was abundant and her hair bounced around in the way I liked. Why couldn't she be like this when I was talking to her like it's always been? Was she tired of me now?

"What the heck is this?!"

The voice made my newly developed muscles tense. It didn't surprise me but I was awaiting what action she'd take. Wendy stopped singing and looked up from her mic. With my back to the voice, I watched everyone else stop and look on, knowing they were doing wrong. The music still played out of the speakers. Considering how loud they were, it must've taken a lot for her to yell that and have everyone hear her. But it's not like it's something new for her.

I ever so slowly turned around, guessing what exactly her face was gonna look like. I was met with a snarl and clenched fists. It was completely different from what she looked like when we finished our last simulation. This was her just being mad. Horns protruded from her skull and the steam came out of her nostrils.

"I said what the heck is going on here?!" Terra yelled.

No one wanted to speak a word. Each and every one of them was guilty. We all knew that she wouldn't like this but we just didn't care, at the time at least.

"You blind? We're dancing to music," Wendy said through the mic with the music still playing.

"Don't you act smart with me girl!"

"So what, should I act stupid, cause it's kinda hard to change my appearance to look like you."

I placed my head in between my knees to hide myself from what was to come. Why couldn't she just shut up and answer her normally?

Kerren ran up from the dance floor and scurried over to Terra. It's what stopped her from running towards the table Wendy was standing on and yanking her off of it to strangle her. I've witnessed firsthand how much she hated being humiliated in front of people.

"And what are *you* doing?!" Terra said, beating into Kerren.

Kerren didn't shrink down. She stood at her full length but submitted to her wrongdoing.

"I'm sorry. Wendy wanted to have some dancing and I joined in," Kerren said.

"Obviously." Terra leaned in to whisper something to her as she did to me. I watched Kerren contort her face to her words. Whatever she was telling her, it wasn't good.

Terra walked over to where we were sitting and looked around at the whole mess hall to address everyone.

"Each and every one of you know that this is never allowed. You know what I allow and what I don't. You can have fun all you want when your duties are finished for the day and you're dismissed. But this chaos? Never!"

When she spoke, the very weight of the room became heavier with everyone shrinking down. If someone told me that she was the person she was being right now when I first saw her, I'd think they're the stupidest person ever.

"Turn the music off," she ordered Wendy.

Wendy scoffed and put on a promiscuous smile. The very smile of hers scared the heck out of me all the while making me proud of her. It was strictly vile and almost suggestive. But it just fit the moment so perfectly. Her stark defiance to Terra was completely optimized on her smile. The way her eyes viewed her from the side, displaying her light brown passion for objection. I loved it.

I might have loved it but it infuriated Terra, as expected. She turned to Monica and without hesitation, ordered her to do the same, knowing that she could do it in an instant.

"Shut it off."

Monica was still holding the clear tablet that she was reading. Without even moving her head, she shifted her eyes to focus on what was interrupting her precious atmosphere. She stared daggers into Terra. Her black pearls combated her in every way possible. After some time of looking at her, Monica resumed reading.

"Turn it off!"

She ignored her to every extent. Her eyes scanned the words that I could see from behind it. With that, Terra had enough and took the tablet from Monica.

"You listen to me when I'm talking to you!"

Monica darted up from her seat and slammed her hand on the table as she shot up. At that moment, a burning sensation of absolute anger filled the center of my chest. It was clearly Monica's, but it was so strong. Stronger than anything I've felt from them. The sudden burst of emotion from Monica startled Terra and she stepped back. Realizing it was a sign of weakness, she went back to her original spot, getting close to Monica's personal space.

"I'm tired of your stupid act. You think that just because you lead some resistance from the King that you're automatically supposed to be obeyed in every instance? I've told you once and I'll tell you again; you're pathetic. You try to portray yourself as some high and mighty person, but in reality, you're one of the weakest. You can't order us to do anything. You don't own us," Monica said.

"Oh yes I do. We *made* you!"

"And that's where you made a grave mistake. You may have made us but it means nothing. We're the powerful people that we are because of you, but it's also because of you that we have the confidence we have. Something you need to know about us, Terra, is that we're all connected. We feel every single thing each other feels. When someone's happy, I'm happy. When someone's sad, I'm sad. And when someone's ticks off Wendy, you tick me off!"

Terra salvaged together a terrible smirk.

"You don't think I know that? It's exactly the reason why all three of you girls are madly in love with Mark."

"What?!" all three of them said simultaneously, including Monica.

Each of them had their cheeks flushed with blood and they all looked at me to see what reaction I'd have. I was just as surprised to hear what Terra said as they were. It wasn't true though. It would never be true. Monica doesn't feel like that for anyone. Wendy, never in a million years would she ever consider me as attractive in any way. She had to be saying that to irritate Monica as much as possible. Hit her where it hurts the most. Her friends.

"What the heck are you talking about?! You think I like him?" Wendy shouted from the mic.

"You'd all be lying to yourselves, not only yourselves, but also to Mark if you said it wasn't true."

Wendy was looking at the floor with her eyebrows scrunched up like she was desperately searching for an answer to life's big questions. She would again do that thing that she'd do every once in a while; look up just barely to see if I was looking at her and look back down in defeat. All those times, they couldn't possibly be because she liked me.

Charlotte was lost in her stare at me. It reminded me so much of when she first stared at me like that back on the first day of school. Her mouth opened in some sort of unsuspended awe. The sole absorption in what she was looking at. Her whole embodiment of herself. It was majestic.

Monica gave me a quick look and without even playing our game of stare off, she disqualified herself by averting her eyes.

"If you wanna mess with us then you got yourself a real problem," Monica said. "Push us again and see what happens. I'll tell you right now you're not gonna like it."

Monica gave her one last punch in the face with her eyes before she cranked up the music louder than it ever was. I could feel the joy inside Wendy resonate inside me. She started to move to the music and jumped on the lyrics at the next verse, singing away Terra's demands.

Charlotte was still taking part with Will at putting Terra in her place. They were slowly pushing her away with just their constant pressure of their looks. Charlotte had a tilt to her head that reminded me a lot of Eris, her creepiness filling her whole existence added onto her death stare of emptiness.

Terra didn't bother to try and speak over the music and took her leave. I'm sure our punishment and the punishment for all the people that joined in the dancing wasn't going to be good. But to be honest, I didn't really care. We deserved this. Monica put everything as perfectly as she always did. We were one. You mess with one of us, you're messing with all of us. Quite physically actually.

I enjoyed the setting for the time being and laughed at Wendy's singing when she'd get into a song. Let me tell you, this girl can sing. Her range of pitches was crazy. As I watched her, I multitasked and watched Charlotte. I would make her face change back to the same gaze that she had a while ago and wonder what the heck that meant. That lead me back to arguing over and over again with myself if she liked Alex or not. Then I thought about how much I hated Alex because of it. Then I was sulking in heat, ruining everything.

I decided that it wouldn't do any good, me sitting there upset, so I said my goodbyes to them and was dragged on stage before I left. Wendy was still singing and had me do a little dance that I complied to really quick before she finished off with giving me a playful wink. Of course, that didn't help in making me think that Terra's claim was false.

With my head all hurt and me upset, I headed back to my room to just forget about everything and fall asleep. My whole body was aching and it desperately called for the firm mattress I laid on every night so it was well needed.

As I was getting in my bed, I looked on the table that was besides my bed. The silver bullet that belonged to Zalus sat with the point lifted up. I was halfway in the sheets already but held myself up with my shoulder as I watched it.

What was my bullet? What did it contain? Will's act of defiance to Zalus was started with taking the gun and stealing the bullets, showing that we were gonna fight. But the rest of us, what did ours mean? Monica was surely determined to use it to protect the girl that admired her so much. It was her wish to help the people here. Charlotte and Wendy, I wasn't so sure. As much as I wanted to know what their intentions were, I really needed to find out my own. If I was gonna fight him, how was I gonna go about it?

I hid myself under my sheets as soon as the bullet changed in my eyes to contain blood on the top. Not just any blood, but the blood of Violet. What would it be like if she made it through with Penn? Would Penn still have tried to kill me? Of course not, she would've been the same girl I met walking to school. The pretty faced redhead with a perky personality, always looking to ease things up.

What was gonna happen was gonna be hard. I just needed to make sure of one thing. Don't change someone again. Never.

*   *   *

"*Aaaaaaaaah!*"

The scream was horrible. The very feminine aspect to the voice made my heart pound. It was rare that I ever heard any of them scream. It may have been out of excitement before, but this time it was complete fear.

It's funny how my brain prioritizes things. It puts only one person in front of anyone else.

"Charlotte!"

I leaped out of the bed, getting caught in my own sheets. The sheets were dragging me back to the bed telling me to go back to sleep. With the pull, my face flung to the floor and my body slumped up against the side of the bed. Did you really have to choose this time to fight me?!

"What the heck?!"

Stupid thing. If I wasn't in a hurry I would've burned you at that very moment and spread your ashes in the place you fear most. Of course, there wasn't time for that. I yanked on all of it, completely pulling it off the bed and made a sprint for the door. I mashed the panel and ran down the dead end hall to Charlotte's room.

The dim lights fell upon the control panel as I tapped it franticly to get it open. It wasn't surprising that her door was locked but at a time like that it was. I guess surprised wouldn't be the right word. It simply added to my frustration for halting me in finding out what was wrong with her.

"Charlotte open the door!" I yelled as I pounded on the door.

Visions of what happened to Monica in the bathroom formed in my head. Would I see something horrible when the door opened? Would I hate myself for seeing what I was about to see? Or would she even open the door?

I heard sobs that drew close to the door. Why did she sound like that? Don't. Please. Don't ever do that again. You're aren't supposed to be like that Charlotte. I never want you sad.

The door opened and appeared a Charlotte that had tears down her cheeks that she was wiping with her sleeve. Her night clothes that draped over shoulders made her look completely innocent and vulnerable.

"I'm sorry. It was ju—"

"What's wrong?!" I yelled.

Idiot. She was gonna explain if you just listened for once!

"Bad dream. It's all it was," she said as she shook her head, trying to get the thoughts out of it.

"What was it about?"

In the moment, I badly wanted to slap myself in the face. You don't just go and ask people what their nightmares are about! You're practically invading their mind if you do that, intruding on every fear they have. I had no place, despite my closeness with Charlotte, to even be asking what was tormenting her.

She crossed her arms and held herself tightly, making me want to hold her close. Her head was still held aloft the whole time, peering down at the lines in the concrete floor.

"Uh, just…"

She paused and let out a sigh.

"You wanna go get some fresh air?" I asked her, trying my best not to just comfort her by hugging her. That'd just be the most selfish thing to do.

She gave a small nod like that of Monica. Glad that she accepted, I led the way out of our hallway to the elevator as I wiped all the junk out of my eyes so I could properly see her.

At the very top of Headquarters was the roof of the building we saw when we first came here. It was nowhere close to being the tallest but it was up there. I did know that it far exceeded the length of the Penthouse. When I'd walk around the city and look up, I could easily picture the height of the Penthouse when it was on fire. This building made my neck hurt, clearly indicating that it was far larger.

I always wanted to take Charlotte up here. After all, she was asking how much it would take to live on the top floor of the Penthouse. Now, I know for a fact that she wasn't just saying that out of curiosity. She had to have said it because she loved the idea of living up there. She's always loved heights. Heck, why do you think she loves that ridge on the mountain that we went to. It overlooked the whole area of Springfield, even reaching heights higher than the Penthouse.

As we waited for the long climb up the elevator shaft, we stood in silence. She hadn't moved a bit, keeping her form that she had when she opened the door. I hated every second of it. Why did she need to look this way? Why?! She didn't deserve anything to get to this point.

I lifted a hand to set it on her shoulder or her back but stopped before I did. We were close, but, what if she didn't feel the same way about me anymore? It'd be uncalled for and would make me look desperate.

Anger started to rise within but I had to do my best to subside it before it'd get to me and ruin any type of

142

conversation with her. She had her own right to whoever she was attracted to after all. I had no influence whatsoever.

The doors opened up to the cool air and rushed our faces. The initial blast was the only harsh touch it had. Once we stepped onto the rooftop, the slight breeze cared for us, doing my job in taking care of Charlotte.

The area that remained of Novus was really close to the ocean. Some of the outer cities that we've visited had the salty smell in the air that I loved so much. But with its location came the thick clouds that loomed so low. Almost every day was overcast here. I had to say, I loved it. It was a big change from the hot sun that beat down on us all day in Springfield. Now that it was far into the night, the clouds cleared, but on the horizon, you could make out the other batch of clouds that were rolling in for the morning.

I let Charlotte lead us to where she wanted. It seemed she had the same thing in mind with putting a large gap between us as she hurried over to the edge of the building. Of course she'd choose to sit that close to the edge—that close to our demise. I complied and took my seat close to her. She was shivering a little with the night air. With her thin shirt on, she hugged it close to her body.

It was my perfect opportunity. I took off the long sleeved shirt I had on and stayed in the thin shirt I had on underneath. I peeked over to see her face and handed her the shirt. Her eyes took it in view and she slowly grabbed it and put it on.

"Thanks. Aren't you cold now?"

"You kidding me? We just left one of the hottest cities in the United States. I love this weather."

It was my first step at success. She smiled and let out a puff of air from her nose. That alone was enough to tell me that she still cared for me. Maybe not in the sense that she did before but it was enough.

"I'm sorry for waking you up."

"Why are you apologizing? You had a nightmare. You can't control that."

"I know I can't. But I just can't make them stop." She scrunched up even more, pressing her crossed arms into her stomach. "They've been happening every day now. Ever since we got here. I think that it won't happen again but it never fails to return. And it's always about the same thing. I'm held up with a knife to my neck and you're standing in front of me with a gun in your hand."

I let out a sigh and ran my hands through my hair. Her explaining it from her standpoint made everything so much worse, bringing guilt back in heavy loads.

"Mark, I keep reliving that day over and over again. It ends different ways each time. Some good. Some bad. Some much worse than anything that's happened."

She stopped talking and looked over at me. I had my hands wrapped around the back of my neck with my head down. The cause of what I did is making her have the nightmares. If only I accepted Penn's request. If only I didn't shoot Violet. If only. That's all it ever is.

"I'm sorry for bringing it up. Shouldn't have told you," she said.

"Don't apologize. Okay? Just don't ever apologize. There's nothing you could do that would make you need to."

"What are you talking about? Of course I'm gonna need to apologize. That's the thing about being friends, Mark. You mess up sometimes and do something that hurts them, but because you're friends you make sure that you make things straight. It's gonna happen and it already has. But because I like us being friends I'm gonna keep apologizing."

Just like you've hurt me when I see you laughing it up with Alex? What about then? Why don't you apologize for that? Can't you feel my anger whenever you do?

Her eyes were still watching me as I looked out over the edge in thought. She raised an eyebrow and leaned in a little.

"Why are you upset? And don't say you aren't. I felt it."

"You said that friends make things straight right?"

"Yeah. Why?"

"Make this straight for me then. Do you like Alex?"

Her face completely changed. It almost looked like it took on a form of anger itself.

"What?"

"You're always talking to him and laughing. I even see you blush sometimes. No matter where we are, you always seem to end up talking with him. Just admit it. You do."

She stood in frustration and raised her voice.

"What are you even talking about?! I like you!"

She froze. Her eyes widened and she completely locked up. I had the perfect view. Charlotte was standing above me with a starry night backdrop behind her. She was wearing my shirt and her hair blew around with the light breeze. Her whole being made my heart skip a beat, not to mention at what she said.

The feeling itself was beyond compare. It was a white stinging that cooled with fire. Sounds completely stupid and out of whack, but believe me, when the girl you like tells you that she likes you, there's no way to describe the feeling with any sense.

"Uh...I—I..."

Charlotte stopped talking and slowly sat back down, holding her head in. Even though the sun was nowhere to be found and the night's companion, the moon, was missing as well, I was still able to notice the color change in her cheeks. It made my heart all squishy. I was almost scared for a second. Could the others wake from this strong of a feeling? If it woke them when I was taken by Sarah and Eli, it had to.

I really wanted to break the silence, but instead, we both sat there for a few minutes in silence, side by side. Our bodies were creating heat being as close as we were. The feeling of joy replaced the excited feeling but I could tell this one was from Charlotte. Same exact one I felt on the mountain.

"I always thought you knew," she said softly, holding the bottom of her thighs and pulling her body into her legs.

"I did. But there would always be times when I felt like you didn't even care for me. I felt outcast and alone, hoping that maybe the next day you'd look at me with the same look you gave me when you first saw me."

"I can be a little careless sometimes. I'm sorry."

Her head lifted at the sound of her apology and made us both laugh.

"Wait so that means that..." she said, pausing, hoping that I'd answer her question.

I gave a shyful nod.

"I thought *you* knew," I said.

"I did," she said with a giggle, making her smile.

Before the conversation led to anywhere awkward, she saved us.

"Thanks for bringing me up here. I liked the view."

"Yeah. I just feel bad for not being able to help you with your nightmares."

"I bet you when it comes time for us to do something about Zalus, they're gonna get worse."

"I don't even want that day to come."

"I know how you feel. Neither do I. Kinda crazy to think that we're gonna stop a whole Kingdom. But whatever happens, it'll be for the best."

"And if something bad happens? That gonna be for the best?"

She shrugged her shoulders.

"It'll better us just like everything else has." She stood and took off my shirt before handing it back. "And with whatever happens, we'll be stronger. Stronger than any force in this whole universe. All five of us." Her face changed to a smile that would mimic a crescent moon if it was in the sky. "Thanks again. I'll see you in the morning."

I said my goodbye to her as I held my shirt that smelled just like her now. I was expecting her to look back before she hopped in the elevator, but instead, she simply got in and closed the doors.

That alone said a lot about her. She's always been one to have heaps upon heaps of confidence. This was another show of it. Despite her getting all fuzzy just a second ago, she shifted to address a matter that affected both of us. It brought back all the times she hurt me when she'd talk to Alex. All the carelessness she would throw out, almost like she was doing it on purpose. As I heard the whirring of the elevator, I put her face in my head one more time.

That was the day I learned that angels could be bad.

Chapter 5

If you could take one moment from your life and change it, what would it be? Hard question, I know. But think about it, what would that even include? Maybe it was something you said. Something you did. Something you didn't do. The possibilities are kinda up to how much you screwed up. Now, if I had this, well, I'd save it for something very valuable. Maybe the death of a loved one. I'd use that one chance to change their very fate.

How about doing that for hundreds of lives. I wanted to. I really did. And gosh darn it that's an understatement. You'd bet I'd do anything to help all those people.

And to be honest, it's kinda stupid. Back when I was an idiot, not that I'm not anymore, I always wanted to be in some crazy situation. Maybe something like a hostage situation. I don't really know my intentions but I think it was to show off. You know, look cool confronting the person holding everyone hostage. Or it was maybe for the adrenaline rush. Now that I was actually put in those situations, I regretted ever wishing for it. You got your wish now Mark. You happy now?

Why does this even matter? Well, let's start off with Wendy running me over again.

Her whole body was moving at a speed that I hated looking at. I woke up not that long ago and she was already sprinting down the halls of Headquarters. I saw her heading towards me but I didn't bother to move. If she was smart she would've learned what to do in a situation like this since it's happened before. Thing was, she wasn't looking up. She was looking at a watch on her arm.

Why the heck are you so anxious? I could read it all over her face and the way she ran. Even the pigtails at the back of her head bobbed differently, like they were telling everyone they weren't messing around, which was hard to believe, let alone see.

So I let her hit me. I didn't fall this time. I guess the training was actually helping me physically or the reason could be that I actually saw her coming this time. She ran into my chest and her arms scrunched up into herself.

"Ah what the—"

She looked up at me and stared me in the eyes for a couple seconds before backing off.

"You were in my way again," she said, looking down in defeat, doing her shyful game once again.

"Yeah, sure," I said sarcastically.

"Uh...anyways, I wanted to tell you something." She placed a hand on her hip and spread her middle finger and thumb over her eyebrows. "You idiot. You made me forget! Ugh! What was it?!"

"Seemed pretty important with you running like a maniac like that."

"It was," she uttered with irritation filling her voice.

"Did it involve me?"

She stopped her thinking and glared me down.

"What are you implying?"

I was taken aback by her sudden anger at me thinking it had to do with me. But that alone started to put everything together for me. I didn't want to admit it to myself. In fact, I hated even the very thought of it. Like Terra said, I couldn't deny it. *She* couldn't deny it.

What did it all mean, huh? The look Wendy gave when we were driving to Headquarters and Terra claimed that she liked me. Sure, anyone would get all defensive like that over someone claiming such a thing, but for Wendy to do that was completely uncalled for.

Then there was the moment when she saw me hugging Monica. Her anger was turned to an all new high and spiked. Jealousy? Combine that with what Terra told us the day when Wendy was singing in the mess hall and you have a pretty obvious predicament.

She could see that all of this was running through my head as I looked at her, processing everything. Her cheeks were flooding with blood by the second and her whole face was burning.

"Wendy?" I asked.

"What!"

"Why'd you get so upset when you saw me hugging Monica?"

"I already told you! Do I really need to repeat myself? You're gonna hurt someone's feelings."

Something came over me. I don't know what, but it did. I took on her frustration and came outright and confronted her.

"What, like yourself? You'd be the one getting hurt feelings." Her mouth changed to a snarl and nostrils flared. "Aren't I right? You even got all flustered in the car on the way here and Terra even told all of us in the mess hall!"

"Yeah?! And so what! I do like you, okay!" Her arms were closing in closer to her sides as she squished herself in stress. She closed her eyes to stop the tears but they came out regardless. "Ever since I hit you at school. I thought I found a really nice guy. But with everything, Mark, with everything, I hide all my feelings. Then Charlotte started telling me how she liked you." She opened her eyes as it took everything for her to look me in the eye when she was like this. "Do you know how much that hurt me?! She's always been open like that. She had no trouble showing you that she did. And what did I have to do? I had to help her because I wanted the best for her. I want her to be happy! Do you think I got any compensation for the way I felt?"

Her tears dragged downwards on her eyelids and she hunched over in defeat. This was a side of Wendy that she never showed anyone. The fact that she was letting me see all of it told everything.

"This was the first time I really liked someone. I might've thought a guy was cute at school before but this was different. But no, it's just some stupid connection we have. It's all because we're made of your DNA. And on top of everything else, I find out that Monica has that same attraction for you! Why am I the one who gets crap for everything?! I saved your dang life twice because I loved you. I never wanted you to get hurt. And now, you ask me why I was upset when I saw you hugging Monica? You show some sort of affection and care for both of the other girls. You helped Monica at the party. You danced with her and then you danced with Charlotte. Was I ever in the realm of possibilities? Never! So don't you ever ask again why I was upset! You don't know what it feels like to get your feelings crushed day after day, but you're just grateful for having a friendship with him."

My heart hurt. Just as much as I could feel Charlotte's joy when she told me she liked me, I could feel exactly how Wendy was feeling. She threw her hand across her face to wipe the onslaught of tears and gave me a face full of anger.

"You never tell anyone what I told you," She let out a strained sigh, adding a hint of a groan to it. "That doesn't matter right now though. Kids are getting kidnapped. That's what I was gonna tell you. Report's come in and it's all over the news. You better be ready to fight whoever's taking them. If you don't then I'll really hate you."

*   *   *

I was really torn. I had two things that weighed heavy on my mind. Right after she tells me something that I never thought would ever be possible, she tells me that kids are being kidnapped from schools. Which one was I to think about?

My palms were all sweaty and I tried to rub them off on my pants but it'd keep coming back. Wendy sat across from me in the car and had her head down, resting her elbows on her knees. Her frown was still there and anyone who saw her knew she was beyond rage. This wasn't the Wendy they'd known for the past couple weeks.

When she got in the car, the others were raising eyebrows as they watched her enter. They all looked around at each other and then looked at me. I ignored their stares because of what was in my head at the time.

Before we even got in the car, Terra was briefing us on what was happening. Police reports have been made from various schools in the outer cities. Some were interrupted and cut short. Word is that kids are being abducted and teachers and staff are either killed or spared depending on the how the people felt. From the cameras, an unidentified ship is what's taking them away. No affiliation with any sort of party. Of course, that's not what Terra thinks.

"You're gonna need some type of experience. This is where it starts. God forbid you mess up on a mission like this. Kids are involved. Remember that. Also, this kind of thing hasn't happened for years. It's only started because of one thing." She pointed at us. "You guys. So there is no protocol here. It's called using common sense. Use it to the best of your ability."

Where we were headed, well, it was fitting that we were going to the very school that we visited. The moment Monica heard that we were going to be protecting that school, she straightened her back and widened her eyes. The very school of those four girls that meant so much to her—that had this lasting impact on her.

One thing that stood out was how Will was acting. He was sitting next to me and was acting weirder than I was. I could see how his hands were wobbling. He tried his best to hide them by placing them under his thighs, but it just went to show how bad it actually was. In all fairness, we were all nervous. The kind that I was feeling from him was completely different.

"We're a bunch of dang teenagers about to be sent into a school to protect kids," he said, almost in a daze. "When the heck did that happen?"

Sitting in the passenger seat, Kerren turned around to face Will.

"If it makes you feel any better, this is what people all over Novus, including the billions that died in the war were waiting for. Five teenagers that carried the name Equilibrium to protect them—their home."

"Doesn't matter if we were made for this. The fact that I went from living a normal life in Springfield to doing what I'm doing now was beyond all my thoughts."

"You think I ever thought I'd be fighting in a war when I was a kid?" Ed said from the driver seat. "I grew up just as normal as you did, but then when I got older, things got out of control. You know what I did? Fought to protect what was right. If I know anything, kidnapping kids isn't right at all. When I see you kids, I see myself. Strong people willing to do whatever they can to uphold that justice."

I looked around at us and tried envisioning it from his eyes. Our strength from the training had spiked. Mobility, strength, stamina. It was all tested and maximized. But that wasn't what he was talking about. He was referring to our spirit. Our determination.

We were dropped off a few streets away from the school for safety precautions. The few cops that were actually in the city were arriving at the same time as we were. One of them told us that he just spoke to Terra and they agreed on evacuating the kids. The kids were still in school and they were going about their business like normal. They didn't know about the danger that lurked.

Kerren handed each of us an earpiece that was similar to the one that was implanted in the helmets we wore. Upon attaching them, Ed was already going over the procedure with the cops. We were to go in carefully and quietly dismiss the classes one by one and bring them out into the park that we were in days ago. From there we'd give them off to their parents that were already being called.

Didn't seem too hard. It was a lot more mellow than I thought. I was just glad we weren't going to have to be putting anyone's lives on the line.

We started to head down the street and make our way to the school. As we made our way down, I noticed an extra noise. After listening for a few seconds, I realized that it was our collected heartbeats. It was tense to be in a situation like this. Of course we'd be somewhat antsy. But it didn't need to be as intense as it was just yet.

Out of nowhere, the sound of an engine roared from the sky. It pierced our ears and caught all of us off guard. We all assumed the worst and ran over to turn the corner onto the street with the park as the noise drew closer and closer. And there it was. A bulk of metal that was descending towards the school. We all stopped moving and watched as the ship set down in the middle of the school, right on top of the courtyard where the kids would play.

Out of all the times you had to come now. Right when we showed up. The ship's mass could be described with chaotic precision. The way it moved down into the courtyard and was cut off by the main building that encompassed it.

From where I stood, I could feel Ed, Kerren, and the cops behind us watching in fear the same way I was, wondering what could possibly happen next.

Before anyone else could react, Monica let out a huff from her nose. We turned to see her clenching her fists and gritting her teeth. Of course she'd get like this. What she loved was inside this very building.

She threw her feet in front of her as she ran forward in a sprint. Within microseconds, we all followed suit and sprinted along with her. This was our job. This is what we were made to do. Kids' lives were on the line now and that needed to be stopped. Ed called out behind us, telling us to stop. Most likely, they wanted to do things carefully and take extreme caution. But how could you even afford to stand around and think some more when you don't know how long until those kids inside that school were going to get taken.

There was no way I was gonna let that happen. No way *we* were gonna let that happen.

As we've done time and again, we all joined hands as we awaited transport by Goldilocks. One teleport to get closer. The second to get inside. That's all it took. She grunted each time she jumped, trying desperately to go farther than she normally does, making trees pass by us in the life drained park until eventually all life was missing.

All five of us stood in the hallway of the school phased by the sudden onset of the white walls. She didn't even need a second to recuperate like I always did. Monica went right ahead and started walking forwards.

"I overheard Ed talking to the cops. They already called the school and told them to go on lockdown. Everyone's inside the classrooms," she said as she glazed her fingertips across the walls. I saw a fleck of purple leave her fingers for just a split second. "We need to check to see if everyone's inside. Split up and look for any kids who aren't."

"Uh, and how do you think we're gonna do that? Never been inside this place," Will said.

"Neither have I." She lifted her hand from the wall and looked at it, letting her eyes get lost as she was focusing on her electricity. "The layout's quite simple. It's a square with the courtyard in the middle of it." She paused for a brief second and shifted her head just a pinch. "Two stories." She turned to look at each one of us. "Split up and search. The second you find one let Wendy know. You're gonna teleport in and take them to a classroom. Don't worry about being caught by the people in the ship. I'll make things a little easier for us."

Instantly, all the lights in the school went out. The artificial light that gave this very place its life was replaced by the presence of darkness. Just when she turned the lights off, there was a scream not that far from us. We all turned towards the sound.

"There's one," Charlotte said.

"I'll get him," Wendy said before teleporting in front of us.

Will took off in a sprint down the hallway, looking down every nook and cranny for a missing kid. His urgency sparked something in Monica. She looked up towards me, letting her bow come in full sight of my vision. After all this time, after all we've been through, she still hasn't let that thing go, not that I was expecting it.

"You know how you were asking if I liked holding your hand or if it was just coincidence?" She reached down and snatched my hand, holding onto it firmly. "I actually do like holding it."

I seriously don't know how she was expecting me to react to that. People in general were just bombarding me with countless amount of things that took me by surprise. It was the latest trend. Let's all shock Mark in the most extravagant ways.

Monica was leading the way, tugging on my hand, yanking me in the direction she was going. The view behind her told of her story. The dark hair that was only represented in that specific hue. The bow that I bought for her that showed my love for her and her love for me.

"You kidding me?" I said under my breath. Terra was actually right. How could she be? No. How could they even feel like that? So what they were part of me. So what they had my DNA. Did that really give valid reason for them to be feeling like that?

Well, if you wanna get technical with it, Monica's parents did tell me that when she came home from school that day I sat with her at lunch, she said that she met a nice boy. Nice boy huh? I did nothing nice to her. I irritated her. I made her get up in the middle of her lunch and walk away. But maybe, just maybe it was because she didn't want to show the way she was feeling in front of me. I mean, who really knows. This *is* Monica we're talking about.

"Where do you want me to take him? What classroom?" Wendy said in the earpiece.

Her voice was unsettling. It carried the conversation we had earlier in it. The anger. The unusual confrontation I put up. All of it. I could picture her clearly. The way her eyebrows must've been furrowed. Her jaw clenched. I loved when she was irritated just the same way she likes it with me, but this was different. She expressed the same thing, telling me that she doesn't like when I'm hurting. Why the heck you think she saved me those times?

"Oh my gosh. Wendy's practically hugging me," squealed the kid. I could only try and comprehend how he could see her as anything famous.

"Any. As long as it's locked."

Usually Wendy loved saying the last word in any conversation, even if it was a remark in the way of a sound or grunt of sorts. This time, nothing. That's what scared me the most.

As we ran through the hallway, we'd pass by windows that opened up into the courtyard in the middle of the school. The place where the kids would be playing during recess was replaced with the bulk of the ship. I tried my best to study the ship, how it worked down to who owned it. Despite how good I thought I was at reading things, I couldn't gather any information.

At the end of the ship was the hatch. A stepping platform threw itself out and made contact with the floor to stabilize itself. As we started to turn at the next corner, I got a better view of the ship. The door at the end slid up and opened itself to the playful scene of the grass and playground equipment. I saw a person, just for a second before Monica pulled me past the window and walked into a supply closet to check for kids. I almost wanted to let go of her hand to go see who was coming out of the ship and was responsible for taking all these kids but I remembered the surprise Monica gave me when she took my hand. For whatever reason, I held on and didn't have a chance to see what trouble was coming for me.

After checking the closet, Charlotte and Will met up with us since all the hallways connected.

"Done. No one down here," Charlotte said.

"Still haven't checked upstairs yet," I said.

"Wendy, you're not back yet?" Will asked.

"I'm talking to the teacher. Hold on," she said with irritation.

"Sheesh. Was only asking."

The sound of a handle caught our attention and the door to the bathroom opened up. A small boy turned and started to stroll down the hallway, probably not even realizing what was happening.

I was about to call out to him when another door opened up. This time it wasn't as calm as when the kid opened it. But who cares about the way someone opens a door. What mattered right now was what came out of it when it was opened, in this case, sunlight.

The light made us shrivel back and hurry over to hide in a corner, a part of the wall that stuck out from the hallway. A perfect little nook to hide ourselves in so the kidnappers didn't see us. But the kid.

Charlotte slowly stood and started to inch forward towards the kid before he was seen by the very person who was to take him.

"Alright I'm done talking to her. Where are you guys?" Wendy said in my ear.

Oh Wendy. Why? Why?! Can't you wait one more minute? You had to take that long now could you please stuff yourself back inside that classroom and just wait.

"Hello? Ugh! Is this stupid thing broken?"

Charlotte was inches away from grabbing him, but the second she saw the sign of a person, she left my vision. The boy stepped back in fear and let out a gasp.

"Oh would you look at this. Still wandering around when you're on lockdown? If you ask me, you're pretty much asking to get taken."

My heart dropped deeper than it has in a long time. Only a voice could do that. Not to mention when she came into vision did it confirm everything. Her brown hair that came down to the middle of her back. The smug look on her face. The way her hips stuck out as she wore tight fitting clothes. The knives that were clipped onto her waist.

Although Charlotte went invisible, I could make out the way she was reacting to seeing Sarah. How her eyes must've been just as wide as the kid, actually knowing what they were capable of.

"Where are you guys? Hello?!" Wendy kept shouting in our ears.

Swoosh

"Stupid thing, man. Why the heck does Terra even give these to us if they don't work?"

Oh boy. Wendy's voice carried in the hallways instead of through our ears this time. She had her earpiece in her hand as she stood in between Sarah and the kid. You know, something about Wendy was unique. She had the capability of either making something really good or screwing everything up. Let's start tallying up all the times she's screwed me over shall we?

Wendy turned slowly towards Sarah and within seconds realized what was going on. Despite seeing someone who was bent on hurting us, she was quite calm about it, as calm as you could get in a situation like this anyways. She dropped her shoulders and let out a sigh.

I could read Sarah's overwhelming confidence. What they've been wanting all this time was finally in front of her. She wanted it. She wanted it desperately. But with the sudden appearance, she was trying to find a way to express that. There was a short smile before it was replaced with a sneer, biting into Wendy's soul. The beast finally got what it's been craving. All she needed to do now was devour her meal. It was chow time and she was ready to eat.

Sarah reached for her knife. Her hands were shaking and missed the first time. It was all too much for her just as it was for us. So what they've killed someone. Just because they have doesn't mean that it makes them any less nervous. It brought the realness of their humanity back into my mind. These weren't any sort of machines that only runs on revenge. They're affected just as much by emotions as we are, and it was taking place this very moment.

Out of nowhere, Charlotte appeared and grabbed Wendy's arm. Charlotte let out a shaky breath that I could hear from where we were crouching. Then that's when it started happening. I know we've been training all this time. We've been trying to get better with our powers but nothing still compares to what happens in the heat of a moment.

Both of them were flickering. One second you could see them, the next you couldn't. It made complete sense to me why Charlotte couldn't make Wendy invisible at that moment when she did it to me days before. Sure, it still involved BloodLip but this caught us off guard. Her heart beat was pushing itself to keep up with the bounds of time. I could feel it.

We all stood and ran towards them, ready to help in whatever way. Sarah had the knife in her hand now, holding the end out towards us. With her overwhelming state, she didn't have a clue what to do but stand there and intimidate us.

Charlotte let out a scream as the pain was immense for her, trying to make Wendy invisible at a tense and stressful moment. They both revealed themselves as she fell on the floor. Monica ran up to her and helped her up before Sarah charged at us. Will stood in front of me and threw his hands out to throw her back. She flung back instantly and was knocked into the wall, whacking her head against it.

Charlotte gathered her composure as quickly as possible and ran over to the kid that watched everything in amazement.

"I'll take him to the class," she said in a hurried tone. "You guys get out of here."

"After you fell like that? No!" I objected. "Wendy can take him to the class."

"Penn! They're here!" Sarah yelled, getting up from the floor.

The very name of Penn made me shake. The red hair. The bloodthirsty eyes. It all burned through my head.

Revenge. Revenge. Revenge!

I threw my head to the window and saw three more figures standing there—three deadly figures. Penn made eye contact with me and simply watched me for a good two seconds before charging towards the door. She threw out her sword and sparked a chain of events. With Eli and Brittany following behind, they prepared themselves as well. Brittany ignited her hands and Eli took a piece of metal out of his pocket to quickly change form in the middle of his sprint.

Something about Brittany's fire was different this time. It seemed to be ignited not on the fact of having fire, but fed by sheer hatred. Passion for redemption.

Eli reached down and scooped her up, holding her as if she was a child. He had his hand cupped behind her knees and held her with his other arm on her back. He sped past Penn and wasn't coming for the door at all. The window was his target.

"Wendy!" Will yelled, hoping she'd get us out in time.

She reached out to grab hold of anyone but it was too late. Glass shattered as Eli ran through the window. Using the momentum, Brittany released herself from his arms and threw a wave of fire at us. Will threw down a panel from the roof to press the fire downwards and away from us. Just then, Penn burst through the door with sword in hand. Her eyes didn't take long at all to find mine and ran towards me.

"Go go go!" Wendy yelled as we ran in the opposite direction.

Charlotte was able to leave with herself camouflaging to the world. Wendy was going to reach for my hand but instead grabbed the kid and teleported in front of us and once again to go into a classroom.

I knew that it wouldn't be just a straight run. One of Penn's arrows whizzed by my head and flew into the wall, piercing the paintings of the kids they had hanging on the wall. The paper cringed when it got stabbed and made the wound visible when the arrow dissolved and another was thrown at us.

We turned the corner at the bend of the square and threw ourselves faster than we were running before. I kept looking as I was running to find something to stop them from chasing us, but when you think about it, what's stopping them? They're a group of superhumans bent on hurting us.

There's no way possible. Will thought of something in the moment but it didn't work out. When you put wood to metal, metal is usually always gonna win. He threw out a door in front of them but Eli smashed through it, sending the splinters flying everywhere. That was just wood. He even tried a thick metal door that was part of the office but to no avail.

Swoosh

The second I felt Wendy grab my hand, I latched onto Charlotte, her being my first person to ever save. We all linked together and BloodLip knew what was going to happen. With Penn's quick reflexes, she threw up a wall in front of us made out of her energy. The white came at us straight on all the while we were heading towards it.

"Who wants to bet we're gonna get stuck in a wall somewhere," Wendy said, out of breath.

"Better than what's behind us," Will said.

"True that."

Swoosh

The pressure in my chest from entering and leaving her world was short lived since I was in water. I mean, it's hardly ever really considered water since it's usually characterized by if you could drink it or not. Then I guess that'd mean that the ocean wouldn't be considered water, but whatever, you get my point. Point was that it reeked. My elbow was dipping into a toilet and my head slammed against the stall door.

There was a flushing of a toilet in the stall next to me as I heard gulping followed by a gasping. With my head as low as it was, I was able to notice whose shoes were in the stall next to me.

"Ewww!" Wendy gave a short pause before shouting even louder. "Ewww! My head was in that stupid toilet! What the hec—"

Her rant was cut short as she started to vomit out all the water she downed. All of it splashed on the ground and made its way into my stall, forcing me to rush to my feet. As I got up, I banged my head against something hard. I looked up to see Monica leaning over the wall of the stall with her stomach pressing into it. Her eyelids were shut over her dark eyes and let her eyelashes flare out. Her hair was let down and, with its length, it was practically touching the ground, the ground that Wendy was throwing up on.

How the heck did she get up there? Shouldn't we all still be holding hands when we teleport with her? It's always been like that so why'd we get disconnected like we did?

I reached up towards Monica to grab her by the arms and pull her down. It was when she started slumping down that I realized she was passed out. I know I'm stupid for not knowing beforehand since she didn't have her eyes open but I never thought of her to be a person that passes out. I guess even that thinking is stupid. What's that even supposed to mean? She's too strong to succumb to passing out?

Her whole body flumped down on top of me. I tried my best to grab her better but she slid down faster than I could react. Once her chest fell on my shoulders, I threw my arms around her back and hugged her tight so we wouldn't both fall. Thanks to Wendy, we did. Her vomit was all over the floor and made me lose my footing. I fell back head first onto the floor with Monica on top of me and screamed at the pain. The door to the stall jiggled and opened up, revealing Will. He smiled and raised an eyebrow, only letting me see one due to his hair.

"Am I interrupting something?" he said, gesturing to both of us on the floor.

"Don't be stupid," I said, trying to get up off of the disgusting floor as fast as I could.

"Well you are hugging her."

"What?!" I heard from the stall next to me. Wendy's voice sounded horrible. She spit out the residue of vomit in her mouth before opening the stall and storming over to the one we were in.

Gosh was she a mess. Her thick locks were dripping with whatever the heck it was called now. Vomit water? Her face was wet along with her shirt. But her face. She was glaring me down as I was forced to watch her. Well, I could've continued to get up and help Monica, but I wanted to show her what Will was trying to make sound like a crime.

She rolled her eyes and let out a groan before turning around and throwing her hands in the air.

"It's always bathrooms. Always!"

She walked up to the mirror that was lower than normal to accommodate for the kids but fit her short height just right. And then something amazing happened. She reached up to her rubber bands that held her hair in the classical position. I was expecting her to just fix their position like she'd usually do. But no, she yanked it out, letting her wet hair whip back down to slap her neck. She did the same with her other side then ran her fingers through her hair.

I rushed to my feet and helped Monica up, handing her over to Will. The whole time we were both watching in amazement as she did this. It was rarer than Halley's Comet. Rarer than an exploding of a sun. All the time we've known her we've never seen her take out her pigtails, even when we went swimming she kept it in.

Her eyes met with mine in the mirror and locked on them, shooting me a look.

"What, never seen a girl fixing her hair?" she said in disgust.

She stuck the rubber bands in her pocket and turned around to face us with her new look head on. Her blonde hair was now the same as Monica's, flowing downwards. Speaking of Monica, she was finally waking up now.

"Did you hit your head?" Will asked her as she moved in his hands.

"Where's Charlotte?" she asked, still somewhat dazed.

"Oh yeah. Where is Charlotte?"

As if on cue, there was a ding on the speaker in the school, signifying there was a message.

"Hello everyone. This is Charlotte Evans. For your safety if you could please file into the courtyard for further procedures. We are going to try and get you out as safely as possible."

"What?" I said. "What the heck is she doing? Penn's ship is out there."

"We need to get to her now," Monica said, pushing off of Will. She wobbled over to the door and yanked it open. The first thing I noticed when she opened it was there was a cool breeze that rushed into the bathroom. She squinted as the sunlight broke through and pressed into her eyes. "Huh?"

We were on the second story of the school. That wasn't the thing though. The wall to the hallway was ripped off and part of the floor was missing. Wires hung out of the concrete and there was a light that was dangling down.

"An explosion?" Wendy asked.

"Never heard one," I said.

"Guys?"

I turned to face the voice to the right of me. Charlotte was carefully inching towards us as if we were a pack of dogs that she didn't know whether to pet or run from. Her body was slightly leaning over and she had half of her body turned.

"Charlotte?" I said. "Why the heck did you tell all of them to head to the courtyard?"

"I didn't! I swear I didn't!" She broke eye contact with me and started to back up now. Her hands went up to her head as she started to shake. "It wasn't me. It wasn't me." She dipped her head down and clenched her hands over her head. "What's going on? Why is this happening?!"

"If anyone of you dares try to run you're gonna regret it!" The voice made Charlotte's head pick and focus intently on what she was hearing; Penn's voice. "You've been breathing in toxins all week long through your ventilation. They latch onto your cells and, if I want to, I can activate them. I think what happens next is pretty self-explanatory."

She was standing with the rest of BloodLip in the courtyard as classrooms were filing out into it. In her hand was the very thing that would activate those toxins. Teachers tried their best to huddle the kids together and have them stop crying, yet, the teachers were crying themselves. They were all being loaded onto the ship, coaxed in by the flames of Brittany that were on standby and the metal fist of Eli.

"How the heck do we get them out of the ship?" Will asked.

"I'll teleport them out," Wendy said.

"You can't," Charlotte said, still standing a ways away from us by the wall. "They'll see you and then who knows if they'll activate the toxins. We can't risk it."

"So you want them to get taken like all the other kids?" Monica forced, irritated at the thought of not doing anything.

As I looked at Monica, it reminded me of when she ran back from us in the first simulation. She solved this all on her own and because of that we set a record. We've completely demolished all of the Three's records, making a name for ourselves showing that we were able to think abstractly like Rylan wanted them to. If that's the case then why couldn't we do that now? Penn's trying to set everything according to what she wanted. It's how she gained her confidence after all. She knew what was gonna happen. Granted, she didn't know that we were gonna be here, but she did know what she was gonna do if she ever saw us again. That she was sure of.

Confidence isn't found, it's created.

Funny how I was using her own words at a time like this. It's because of that I found out what to do.

"One thing's for sure," I said, "we aren't doing this alone. If we try to go in somehow and take the kids out they're gonna activate the toxins. If we don't do anything then all the kids are taken. Monica, if we take out the controller Penn's holding for the toxins will it still activate?"

"Hard to say. It's like shooting a bomb. You're pretty much telling it to detonate. In my opinion, I don't think it will. Novus' technology is a lot more optimized than ours. It'll want things to be more sure before activating it."

"Well it's the only shot we have. But we need one more thing." I walked over to where Charlotte was and grabbed her delicate hand. I extended my other hand out in the direction of Wendy and bobbed my head over towards us. We all connected hands once again. "We're gonna need man power."

*   *   *

The park was completely full. Hundreds of people were all around to the point of not being able to see the ground anymore. Once Wendy teleported us out of the school everyone had wide eyes, hoping that we'd bear some good news.

What sparked my interest was that there were people holding huge cameras, one's you saw news stations holding. And it was exactly that. There was a vehicle that could be easily identified as a news station. I don't know how many cameras were shoved in our faces. Reporters threw black microphones at us, forcing us to talk about what we saw inside the school. Naturally, we didn't talk.

In the jumbo screen that played ads, the same one that showed the message Zalus played, had big letters at the bottom of the screen.

LIVE

My face was looking up and I was watching the back of my neck. We were all on the news and no doubt Zalus was watching himself. It was the first thing that came to mind. Make your words count Mark. Let's show off that shiny bullet of yours.

I stormed over to Ed who was talking with the cops still.

"We're gonna need help," I said.

"Of course you are. Why'd you run in there in the first place?"

"I'm not gonna argue about that."

"Yeah? Then what about Charlotte, hm?" He gestured to her with his head. "You don't direct the flow of kids especially when it's towards the enemy!"

"Look! It wasn't her alright!"

He leaned down towards me to whisper in my ear.

"Just because you have a thing for her doesn't mean you have to constantly defend her."

"It wasn't her! You don't know what we saw before we went through the dimensional portal. You don't have any idea what we've been through. This is something that involves us, not you!" I yelled as the sound of Charlotte's neck being snapped filled my ears again. "We're gonna need their help."

The parents were standing close by, some crying, some still phased by the fact that their kids had the possibility of being taken from them. A lot of them were confused just like I was. Why were they getting taken in the first place? Penn had no reason to hurt them. I was the only one that she needed to deal with, the only one that needed to pay for his crimes. These kids should've never been involved.

"Oh no. There's no way you're gonna put civilian lives at risk."

"There's already hundreds being risked as we speak!" Will said. "Having them help save their children's lives makes no difference of who's at risk."

"This isn't their fight."

"It's all theirs!" I said. "You guys are a resistance against Zalus. If you're planning on taking him off the throne than you can't expect it to be done by yourself. You need a revolution. You need people."

And I was gonna show him just that. I turned to face the eager parents and addressed them as a whole. I needed to force my words on them in a way that was gonna make them help no matter what.

"Listen up! You're kids are inside the school right now being forced inside a ship that's gonna take them to some place we don't know. All I do know is that the people who are taking them are bent on hurting others. Your children have toxins running inside their bodies as we speak. BloodLip has the capability of activating those toxins to end their lives. I'm not gonna let that happen and neither are you."

It was working. Their eyebrows went from being lifted to now being as close to their eyes as they could.

"Penn's holding a device that activates those toxins. If we deactivate that, we can run in and take over. We outnumber them massively so we'll use that to our advantage. Is anyone up for saving your kid's life?"

Will gave me a pat on the back as the crowd started shouting. This wasn't a cheer. It was a war cry. Their sign to combat BloodLip's wrath. I gave Ed a look before all of them started to follow me to the front of the school. The jumbo screen was capturing this all. I was leading them. I was making an impact on their decisions. It's gonna make two impacts. One on the citizens of Novus and one on Zalus. How does my bullet feel?

The five of us walked through the main doors of the school and told the parents to wait at the steps. From inside, I could see Penn still holding the device and watching as she was committing a crime. At least five whole classes were already inside the ship.

"Wait," Monica said. She was deep in thought and was watching the floor intently. "I could turn it off if I got my electricity inside it. We wouldn't need to gamble whether or not it'll turn on."

"So you'd just need to get close to it, right?" I asked.

"No," she shook her head. She reached inside her pocket and pulled out something we were all familiar with. It was silver and had a tip to it that could pierce human flesh at high speeds. It was her bullet. "Will, you think you can throw this into it?"

"I guess I can but if you're asking me to break it then I'm gonna have to throw it faster than a baseball."

She wrapped her whole hand around the bullet and let her hand fill with a bright purple light. She threw it up in front of his face before he caught it with his mind.

"It's light anyways. You can throw it fast enough. It's about aiming it right."

172

"Of course, give me all the hard work."

"You think you're the only one with hard work?" she said, still focusing on the ground. "I have to deactivate that thing the second my electricity touches it before the bullet breaks it completely. It has to be perfect. If I miss it who knows if it'll actually go off or not."

Wendy went ahead and dragged in about ten parents. She held their hands in a link and was crouching down a bit waiting for the signal Monica's gonna give.

"You better hit it," Monica said, still not moving her eyes from their stationary position.

Will rolled his eyes and scoffed at her even considering he couldn't. Using the spite he was festering, he started to rotate the bullet in place. The silver was revving up for its task, ready to impale the device. Without any moment of hesitation, he threw it forward, using a motion from his hand this time to send it farther and faster than he would normally make it go. Monica was tense. She had her shoulders scrunched in and her hands in fists. One second the bullet was there, the next it was next to Penn.

I was watching Monica at the time instead of the bullet like everyone else was. I was waiting for that moment to see if she was able to do it or not. She was the key, not Will. But there was a jump. A little hop in place that she did to make her hair bounce just at the end.

"Go!" she yelled.

Swoosh

I saw a mass of people linked together appear in the courtyard with Wendy. They broke apart just like we did when she took us inside the bathroom. Some of the parents were fumbling but got back up right away to sprint towards their kids.

Screams and yells sounded behind me in a clump, moving any air out of the way for their charge. I joined

Charlotte and rushed outside to the courtyard with her and joined Wendy. All of us were heading for Penn who had a shocked look on her face. Before anything else happened, I felt a spark of courage and hatred coming from Wendy ahead of me. She teleported once more to the air in front of Penn and came down with a fist flying towards her face. It made contact just as she intended it to and they both fell on the floor.

Eli and Sarah ran towards her but a lady jumped on his back. Still having the form of metal, it wasn't hard for him to simply grab her by the arm and throw her across the whole courtyard. But it wasn't going to be as simple as he thought it'd be. A man took her place on his back and another woman ran up towards him.

All the children who were waiting to get taken inside the ship scattered and ran with the teachers. It was unanimous how things were working out. I never heard parents assigning themselves to what they were going to do, yet, they split halfway, some helping the kids and the other half combating BloodLip.

Penn reached for the device that got knocked out of her hands as Wendy started to throw more punches in her face. Brittany ran forward and tackled Wendy, knocking her right off of her. As I drew closer to them with the whole army of parents behind me, I could see Penn's face as she realized there was a hole through the thing.

"Get in the ship!" she shouted.

A woman tried to throw a fist at her face but Penn snatched it almost immediately. She threw out her sword and the woman watched as Penn raised it, hopeless, knowing she couldn't do anything to stop her from cutting it clean off.

I sprinted faster than I already was, trying to get there in time to stop her but it was no use. I was too far away.

But she wasn't doing it. I was watching all of it, the whole time. Not once did she come down on her arm. Why? Why wasn't she doing it? She clearly had the opportunity.

Her face changed drastically. It went from that crazed look she adopted to frustrated confusion. Almost like when she stabbed me. She hesitated before Brittany called out to her and made me get the wound that was cared for now. What was going on inside that brain of hers?

The woman didn't do anything as this was happening other than hope she wouldn't do it. Penn held her brow down as she watched the situation as a whole. Eli, Brittany, and Sarah were all fighting innocent civilians, hurting them. She returned her gaze back at the woman and pushed her back, letting her sword dissolve.

"Get in the ship!" she reiterated to them.

Penn watched the woman who she let free search for her missing child. I saw what happened in Penn after that. The other three ran inside the ship as Penn was festering once again with rage. The short moment of mercy was snapped. Before she stepped in the ship, she reached out and grabbed a kid who was running by. Not just any kid.

"No!" Monica yelled. "Maya!"

The girl that Monica was talking to that day in the park, the one who said she wanted to be strong like her, was in the arms of Penn, screaming for anyone to help her. The second she stepped in the ship, it started to take off.

We all watched as the engine ignited with fumes and lifted off the ground, ascending to a place we could never go. Great. What the heck do I do now? There were still kids in the ship. I started to search for something to stop it with but my mind was fresh out of ideas. Once again, you never fail to disappoint brain.

Out of all the whole crowd one person burst out of it in a full sprint. She was shorter than the rest but because of that she was able to push herself faster than any other person here could run. There was only one person that I've seen run faster than her and that was Violet. But now, after all our training, I bet she could keep up with her no problem. Not to mention, she had ample reason to run even faster than before. It wasn't only the kids' lives on the line, but it was the anger, all the frustration she was expressing when she told me everything.

I heard a soft humming in my earpiece followed with muffled lyrics of some type of song. When the lyrics were starting to form, when everything was starting to come together, that's when I finally realized what was gonna happen and so did they. It was the same song she was singing back in Headquarters.

Both Will and I took a step forward, still trying to think of what to do, trying to prevent her from doing what she was planning on doing.

"Wendy!" I called out to her. I couldn't stop it. The pressure of all the zeal she had burned in us. Please Wendy, just stop. "Wendy!" I tried once more.

All of the hopes in my heart for her to hear me, they were all abandoned. Why did she have to be so confident?! Why did she have to be the one to go and try to do something like this? We all wanted to save them, I know, but why her? It had to be because of her trying to say something to me. She was trying to make something clear, that she wasn't getting the attention she wanted, but because of that, she would risk everything to get those kids back, to find out where they're going.

Despite my pleas, she still did it. She disappeared from the ground and was now hanging onto the hatch that was still open. Her hand gripped the metal bar that retracted to pull it in. Her other hand was flailing around with the force the ship was putting on her. With another burst of anger, she lifted her hand to it and dragged herself in the ship.

Will didn't hesitate to reach out to the ship. It was impossible. He knew that, but that didn't stop him at all from doing what he could do. Both his hands latched on from on far and he strained. Heck, strained is an understatement. He was screaming, yelling because of all the pain from trying to hold a ship full of people, not to mention that it was using fuel to push itself. He had to fight all of it. The tuft of hair that fell in front of his left eye was darkening his face of pain, making its appearance worse. But after all of that, he was holding it in place. He was really holding it.

This was my chance. It was held in the exact place needed for me. The roof of the school was right next to the hatch that Wendy was climbing into. It was a long shot but I needed to take it. She's saved my life a number of times now. This time it was my turn to return the favor.

Will knew I would want to do this even though the rest wouldn't. He gave me a split second of a look that I returned before bursting into a sprint to head into the school. When I whacked the doors open with my body to get into the hallway, I felt the despair in Monica and Charlotte. They were thrown into a corner now. Both of their friends were doing something they would've never wanted us to do. But the fact was, Wendy was right in what she was doing. We needed to find out what was happening. The only thing was that I wasn't going to let her be the one to find that out.

I found my way to the roof and step foot on top of the gravel floor. I kept my sprint and charged towards the ship. The gap made me want to take a second to evaluate the distance and see if I could actually make it but there was no time for that. I took a leap of faith and launched myself off of the roof towards the ship.

My stomach landed flat on the hatch and I started to slip off. I reached out to grab hold of the same thing Wendy used. She stood now and saw that I was in the same position as she was in.

"Mark! What the heck are you doing?!" she said over the cry of the strained engine.

What am I doing? Come on Wendy. Don't be so blind. I'm going to save you. You claimed that you've been hurt all this time, not by just some random person, but by me. I screw up all the time, I know. This time, I'm gonna try to make things better.

With a burst of everyone's adrenaline, I funneled it into my own and got up with ease and stood on high. Her face was solemn, like she was recalling the conversation earlier.

"I'm saving you."

I reached out for her hand and threw her out of the ship, sending her towards the ground. She reached out to grab me but her arms could only stay out like that as she watched me fade away, her face staying the same. She didn't want me to go, I know that. It could've been read by anyone. But it meant everything to me as her eyebrows curved upwards, something that was hardly ever seen from her.

Will let go of the ship and helped slow down Wendy as she fell towards the crowd of parents and students. I barely saw the act of them catching her before someone turned me around.

Red met me straight on. Her perfect nose and soft presence of her cheekbone still haven't changed. It's been awhile since I've seen her this close, the last being when she stabbed me. Behind her was Eli, regular form now. He slammed his fist into a button on the wall. I heard a whirring of mechanical wiring as the hatch closed. Both of their expression matched, carrying the same one they had on the screen in the park. Next all she needed to do was pull out a bow and send one of her arrows through my chest. With the adrenaline rushing through me still, fear didn't take hold like it usually did by now. I was just relieved that Wendy wasn't in this position right now.

"You can't get enough of us can you?" Penn said with disgust.

Her warm knuckles landed square in my face, making everything black. Her blood gems threw heaps of chaos at me, making it the last thing I saw before I fell back and landed on my head.

Chapter 6

"Stand over here. No! Not over there. Why would we ever wanna take a picture in front of a swing set?"

Who was saying that? Everything was dark as if I was locked inside my eyelids, suppressing any light that was trying to enter and immediately omitting it. I couldn't see anyone. But just at the bottom of the horizon, I saw a hint of something. It was hardly visible but because of all the darkness surrounding me, it stood out. A blurred figure was throwing out all kinds of happy vibes. Even with me hardly being able to see who it was, I was able to clearly tell that this person was happy.

It was a person so all I wanted to do was go towards them. I didn't know where I was so anyone in this place was better than me standing there alone. As soon as I took a step forward, the person would get even more faded. The edges around them blurred even more, the voice becoming more faded. I tried taking another step but the same thing happened again, this time even worse.

What sick place was this? I figured that since my steps were making everything worse that if I did the opposite and took some steps back, things would clear up. With confused anger filling me, I started creating more distance between us. As I thought, things did clear up. So I had two choices. Either get as close as I want but not be able to see anything, or get as far back as I could to get clearer vision but still not be able to see anything because of the length.

I could've been stuck in a labyrinth of some kind for all I knew. With nothing there but the person on the end, I was forced into the task of making a choice. For some dumb reason that I can't give, I gave in to the action it tempted me with.

I took some more steps back in hopes of hearing the voice again.

"Does it really matter if it's in front of a swing or not? It's just a picture."

I froze. The voice had the hint of angelic softness that I loved hearing so much. The dispersion of joy in her vocal cords made its way to my ears. The same hint of chirpiness that I was hearing then reminded me of when she was talking to me at the top of Headquarters. I couldn't just stand around. I needed to see what she was doing here and what she was talking about, not to mention that I was curious about who she was talking to.

"I know it doesn't matter but could we at least take it in front of something else?"

Her voice. I knew it from somewhere. School? A relative? I couldn't say from where. All I did know was that I knew it. It wasn't just a voice I heard on TV before. I had to have known her from somewhere. But the question was 'why couldn't I remember?'

"No. Now we have to take it in front of the swings. Just cause you said that,"

Usually I never heard this new voice that was added to the conversation despite hearing it every time I spoke. My ears would receive it but never process it as another voice. It was just the reverberation in my face that would be picked up by my ears every time I spoke. It almost made me want to gag when I heard it. Why was my voice so happy? No no no. Mark shut up. Why do you always ask the wrong question? Why was I even hearing my voice when I wasn't even talking?

"Fine. Then we have to shout my name when we take the picture. Wendy do you mind taking the picture?" said the unfamiliar voice.

"Of course I mind. It's Mark's camera." Okay. That was no doubt Wendy. Nothing different about her. "Let me use yours."

"Here."

She handed Wendy her camera and two other people came into the blurred vision of mine. One I could tell right away was me and the other was Charlotte. But this girl I couldn't recognize, she stood right next to me as we posed for a picture. I was in the middle and put my arms around both of them as both of the girls put their arms behind my back.

"One, two, three. Say ___!"

"___!"

All sound left when they tried saying her name. I couldn't hear a click from the camera, not even the white noise of the atmosphere, no less her name they were supposed to shout. The last blurred image of them I saw was all three of us smiling before they left completely.

"You trusted her once. Remember."

The voice was my own. It sounded throughout the whole dark world into my ears.

"You trusted her once. Remember," I echoed in a whisper to myself. I took a step back when I realized that I repeated what I heard myself say. I didn't even want to repeat what I was saying. I made myself.

I heard the giggle of the girl before the black disappeared.

*   *   *

"Ah!"

I woke up gasping for air and my chest rising significantly. My eyes were wide open yet they couldn't see much. Why did this always happen to me?! Why was I the one who was taken? I know Wendy was gonna do it but like I'd ever let her do that. You'd take me for a fool if you ever think I would. And it didn't even matter that she told me that she did like me beforehand. It made no difference. I still would've made sure that I was the one getting taken again. Better me than any of them.

I was half expecting Violet to be in front of me sitting on a desk, waiting for me to wake up. To be completely honest, I desperately wanted to see her there again. It'd mean another chance for me to fix things. It would've also been nice to see her relaxed face that she had on that day. Her solemn look of disappointment that showed she cared about something. Where was my covert teacher that I wanted to see?

Nothing looked like my classroom. This time I was on an incline with my face looking at the point in the room where the wall would meet with the ceiling. It extended quite a ways up, letting me know that this wasn't just an ordinary building. It had some significance to it.

When I started searching for Penn's red bundle of hair, I realized it was night. I could see a reflection in the glass of a tube of some sorts that there was a large window behind me towards the top of the wall. The moon was a lot closer than it was on Earth. It was shining with its full mass, the moonlight reflecting all of its surface area. Full moons were nice. I always loved it. But even when I was looking at it, it wasn't calming me at all. I was still awaiting the arrival of someone to come and try to end my life this time.

"You're awake. That's good," said a voice I just heard seconds ago in my dream.

"Charlotte?"

I turned my head to the left to try and see if she was actually standing there, waiting for me to wake up like in the nurse's office. Because of there not being any lights on in the building and only relying on the moonlight, there were dark patches of black all over the room. She was standing just at the end of one of those patches. Her back was facing me with the little bit of her neck exposing herself to me.

She was standing in front of a tube just like the one that was reflecting the moon through the window. Her head was looking up at it, examining it closely.

"Charlotte? Well, it depends on how you want to look at it," she said, adding a giggle at the end, making me want to think of it sounding cute but somehow couldn't.

Her head turned to face me and her body followed. As I looked her up and down, it was no doubt Charlotte. Every little thing I loved about Charlotte was there. If that was the case, then why the heck was she here and watching me strapped to an inclined seat like at a doctor's office? Her bubbly smile did its job as she walked towards me.

"Getting taken isn't fun, huh?" I didn't know how to respond to her. The more she spoke the more she sounded like…"I know this is the second time you got taken, but I just had to."

"What are you talking about, you didn't take me. Penn did."

She let out a small chuckle.

"Do you think what happened at that school was all you guys? Do you really think Will held that ship by himself? He's nowhere close to being able to hold anything of that size and propulsion no less when he's nervous."

"You're not Charlotte! Who are you?!"

She ignored my question and continued with her smile.

"I was actually quite interested to see the interaction between you and BloodLip after coming back to Novus. I needed to make sure that happened. So don't be surprised by her taking all these kids. When I found out what Penn was doing, I made my way over to the school. Lo and behold you guys were there." She paused and lifted a finger. "Oh, and you know that wall that was torn down? Yeah. Us too. Didn't want you to get stuck in a wall when Wendy teleported you guys out. You guys would've ended up in it. We had the means of moving it out of the way for you. Plus, I made sure we moved it in a way that it'd separate Charlotte. I did want to move things along my way after all. I couldn't possibly do that with you guys confused about how you were hearing her now could I?"

"What do you mean we?! What the heck do you want?!"

"It's simple. I wanted to see you. I did what I could to make sure you got on that ship. It was the only way we could get together like this. It wasn't the only reason though. I wanted to test something."

She tilted her head back a bit to show me what she was referring to. What she was looking at was those glass tubes that lined the room. Now that I was looking at them, I noticed there were tons, not just a few. Just behind the ones she was originally looking at was the hint at some more. There couldn't be that many could there? But the room didn't lie. When I checked to see how far down it went, the dark made it impossible, only making my guess at there being hundreds of these more and more plausible.

Charlotte turned and slowly walked back over to the tube she was looking at. Despite her villainous aura that she gave off, her walk was still the same. Her hips didn't sway more than they usually did. Her steps weren't longer. It was all the same.

"I couldn't pass up the opportunity of seeing if this will work. Cause if it does, then boy, do we got ourselves something."

She reached down and pressed something on the touch screen at the base of the tube. As she did so, the tube lit up, illuminating the water that was inside. But that wasn't all that was in there. No, why would there be hundreds of tubes of water? There was a mechanic string that hung down from the top and latched itself to the little girl's back, completely taking root in her body. She was suspended down from it as her hair flowed freely in the open water. Her neutral face resembled what she would've looked like if she were asleep.

"What the heck?" I said under my voice.

It was clear that this was where all the kids were ending up. Every last one of them that was taken. The ones I saw entering the ship and all the ones that I never saw get taken from all the other schools. With this tube lit up, the light entered some of the nearby tanks and revealed other kids, some older some younger, inside them suspended just like her.

Charlotte slowly and carefully lifted her hand and lightly tapped the glass. The second it made contact a dark purple essence left it and entered into the tank as if it was some type of dye. But it was moving at its own accord, almost as if it was alive. It slithered itself over towards the only life force inside there. The girl was completely clueless about what was happening, in a world of unconsciousness, as this thing made its way over to her.

The moment it touched the girl, the whole tank started to fill with this dark essence. But something else took place. Her hair instantly turned black along with her nails. Her body started to convulse but the mechanic string held her in place. There was a beeping that sounded from the panel that Charlotte had activated and the whole thing turned red.

Charlotte looked on in amazement as the little girl died. In the reflection of the glass, I witnessed her mouth grow to a smile. Her reaction doubled with the girl dying by something I knew nothing about made me speechless. I was so helpless and couldn't do anything to aid her. The convulsions got worse and her arms flailed in the tank. The only good thing was that she was still unconscious so she wasn't able to feel anything.

"Well that didn't work. It's synthetic then. Hm. Interesting choice."

"What did you do to her?!" I strained from my chair that I was attached to.

"It's something you need to be more familiar with," she said, turning around to come back to me. "It's gonna come one day, Mark, and it's gonna hit you hard."

She got the closest she has ever gotten to me and leaned in towards my face, bending down with keeping her back straight, letting her hands drop and clasping them together. All of it was the same as Charlotte but three things. Three horrible coincidences. She had pitch black hair darker than Monica's, black hole eyes that sucked me in, and tainted fingernails all just like the girl.

"Corruption hurts. Get used to it."

We both turned our heads to the sound of a door opening in the distance, somewhere not that far from where we were.

"Oh goodie. They're coming. Do me a favor will ya. Don't tell anyone I was here. Mkay? I just had to come see you though. It's impossible for me to stay away that long. After all," she leaned in to the point of letting the ends of her lips graze my ear, sending chills that spread down my spine, "you were my first kiss."

After my first initial shudder, I snapped my head around to look at her but she was gone. All that I saw was the tube of the little girl that was filled with this dark substance, the red monitor telling of her condition.

Two doors at the end of the room burst open and revealed the monsters that were taking these kids, the ugliest in front of them all. He wore luxurious clothes that draped behind him just like it did when I've seen him any time before. What upset me the most was that he held a smile as he approached.

"Welcome!" he said, raising his hands up. Penn and the rest of them followed behind with anger just at the sight of me. Good to see you too. "I hope everything's been well for you in the time we haven't seen each other."

I let out a scoff as loud as I could make.

"You're disgusting," I said, turning in my chair.

"Me?" He stopped to think for a second, looking up at the ceiling. "Yeah. I guess you're right. When you're able to think up something like this, then I guess you are considered disgusting. But compared to what you did, who knows. Have you heard of mud baths before, Mark? I'm sure they have that sort of thing on Earth as well. You lather yourself in the most vile thing, something that people step on, not even considering that it's precious. And being honest, it's not. Mud is gross, all mushy and horrid. Yet, people bathe in it. When they come out of the mud bath, they consider it the most clean they've ever been." Zalus paused and let his smile simmer into me. "I'd like to think the same applies now."

"You'll always be covered in filth."

"We'll see about that. When this is all over we'll see who's the cleanest. For now," he said, walking over to a panel that illuminated all the lights in the room, "I'd like to bathe in my mud."

I'm not kidding you. Hundreds and hundreds of kids were put in these tubes, hanging just like the girl.

"What are you doing to them?"

"It's no crime Mark. If it was, then you'd be part of it, your friends being the main victims of it. This is what I was telling you about. The project to clean the filth out of the land and start expanding. Wanna know something interesting about the whole deal after the kidnapping of Penn? After I had your place ambushed, I took my daughter back along with the rest of the kids. I had the data in their systems rummaged through and found schematics on the dimensional portal as well as how to manipulate the DNA in the Equilibrium. I handed that off to my engineer that specializes in manipulation of DNA, the same one that helped in giving us our mark of royalty."

Penn looked intently into the floor as her father talked about his plans. I couldn't help but read in her face that she hated what she was hearing.

"The reason we can't expand and rebuild is for one reason. Every city that's out there and has their own race is preventing that. Why do you think the war started in the first place? I may not have been the one who dropped the bomb but it opened the way for reason to start to rid of any other power, any other race besides my own. When things settled down and it was clear that I had the advantage, I made sure I kept it that way. I never wanted any of them to live, but it was a sign to my citizens, to my people that I loved, to put their trust in me just long enough that they could gain my trust before I killed the outer cities off completely. And I can't possibly waste all the young potential before I do that."

"Penn, you're helping this idiot?! What's wrong with you?!"

"Don't you even dare! You had to go and mock me! Mock all of us! Killing every little girl in Exon with the name Violet, really? And you said I was cruel!" Penn yelled.

"What?" I said, taken aback by what she said.

"It's not all there is to it Mark," Zalus said. "That manipulation of DNA they used to make your friends have powers, the same was used on them," he said, nodding towards the kids. "We couldn't use the same exact DNA since you'd have some form of control over them like you do with your friends. So we made it all synthetic. Each and every one of them have powers just like BloodLip and your friends."

Zalus took long steps over to one of the glass tubes. Inside it was a small boy that looked about eight. Just like his classmates, he was in an unconscious state, completely clueless about being next to the disgust of the planet, the so called King that everyone puts on high. He tapped at the panel that Charlotte did. As he was inputting commands, Brittany glared me down. The bottom of her lip was twitching as she watched me helpless in the chair, probably hating the sight, reminding her of when she had to make sure Penn never left her room when Violet was going to execute me.

"I have to give you credit though. Killing all those kids made this idea form in all our heads. It's what made these children the pinnacle of redemption."

Upon finishing his words, the water was flushed out the container instantly and the glass sunk down into the base of it. The metal string detached from the kid's spine and he flumped on the floor, wet and cold. Without wanting to, his body started to shiver due to the night temperature and the metal floor.

"Hello there Cadious. How you feeling?" Zalus said with a smile. He loomed over him and didn't bother to ever help him off the floor. "Come on. Why don't you get up so you can show Mark your powers?"

He put his hands underneath him to try and propel himself up, but to no avail. As much as I wanted him to get up off of the cold floor, I wanted him not to listen to Zalus and just lay there. He didn't need to. He wasn't obliged to follow the commands of this monster. But no matter what happened, he kept trying to get up. His arms shook with so much force that it made him look like he was having a seizure.

I heard sniffling as he crawled over to the base of the tube he was just in. He lifted his arms up towards it and yanked as hard as he could to lift his energy sapped body. No one bothered to do anything. No help from a single soul.

He finally made it up after trying again and again to climb up the base of the tube. Run little kid. Get out of here. He didn't deserve to be taken, tormented into something he wasn't. All the life that he knew, go to school and come back home to his parents, was suddenly disrupted by something that never involved him. If that was the case then why ever put them in this?

He stood with his back to me for what seemed like forever. I remember exactly what sound left his mouth as he looked on in complete fear, taking it all in, all the kids that showed what position he was in. It was a sob mixed with just a sound of despair. At that moment he didn't care about who he was standing next to. Who would ever care if they were awoken to a whole room full of contained children, people just like you?

His hands went up to his head and he started to scream, filling the whole building with his echoed shout. I shrunk back at the piercing sound of it, wishing I was never here.

Zalus let out a sigh and put a hand on his forehead, nodding his head in irritation.

"They didn't activate it yet. Do I really have to be the one to do it?"

He tapped on the panel once again, snapping the kid in a straight figure, stopping his shouting from leaving, stopping the fear from exiting his body. His body slowly turned around and faced me, revealing his blank face, not matching his previous screaming at all. This idiot even had the capacity to take control of them too?!

"Ah this one's interesting." He smiled at Penn as he firmly gripped the railing next to the monitor. "Might want to hold onto something."

The kid held his hands out and slowly lifted them, raising them to the heavens. With the blank face he held, everything that wasn't attached to something started to float up to the sky, completely ignoring gravity. Everything mimicked the mechanics if we were all in space.

The whole time I watched in amazement as this kid had the power in him to completely shut off gravity. We all had powers, including BloodLip, but with this new power alone, they were a lot stronger. Who knows what else he gave the other kids.

Zalus commanded the kid that it was enough. Without any delay he did as he commanded and let everything drop with the opposite movement of his previous action.

"You see Mark. You guys aren't special anymore. People could've been waiting for you for years but you can't even consider yourselves something significant. You've been of use, but I can't let you go back out and do whatever you want, especially when you have the capability of finding out your powers. If that happens, well, let's just say it'd end my mud bath. And lucky for Penn, I told her that once we were done with you she could have complete control over you." He paused for a second. "This is my handing you off to her."

He turned with his hands clasped behind his back and started to head out towards the door with the kid following close behind.

"Penn's not pleased with you Mark. None of them are. Remember that before they do what they do."

Penn's tilted head lifted ever so slightly to glare me in the eye. Her fire hair covered half of her matching eyes. The resemblance between her and her father was strikingly similar. Attitudes, not so much. I was just about to see more of that. I was too busy with looking at Penn's face to notice Eli run towards me. It was my last thought before I returned to that dark land and relived the same dream.

Chapter 7

"Did you check all the cameras?"

"Yes. But ALIS is giving me a hard time. She's starting to realize someone else is in the system."

The two voices serenaded me as my left shoulder was pushed. Being completely out of it, I let whoever was touching me do whatever the heck they wanted to me. I was way too tired to even bother with anything right now. If anything, I shouldn't even be alive. So whatever happened didn't matter.

A noise of a buckle being undone clanked and there was a loosening of pressure on my arm. Once the person touching me let go of me, I slumped back down on what I was laying on. Because of the footsteps, I was able to tell that they moved to the other side, my right shoulder. Once they touched it and pushed me up from there, the pain shot through me and traveled up my neck into my head. The wound's been dealt with but the residual pain was still there given the pressure.

I let out a yelp and flumped over my knees. Where was my strength now? Eli might've knocked me out but who knows how long ago that was. Who knows what's happened since?

"Sorry," said the voice.

The moment I heard the voice full on, I knew it was Charlotte. But after what happened, I didn't get phased by it at all, probably expecting something crazy to happen again.

I found all the strength I could to open up my eyelids and look into what horrible mess I was in now. To my surprise, it was only a room, a small one this time. There wasn't any light that came from the room but the only essence there was came from the hallway where the door was opened.

Still being completely drowsy, I looked at the four figures that stood around me. I already knew Charlotte was tending to me but I still looked at her anyways. What I saw was completely different from the one I let my eyes be infected with earlier. It was the same normal brown hair and unique smell that I wished I could take for myself.

In the doorway was an idiot. His tall demeanor reminded me of my short height, telling me silently that I couldn't get girls like him. Oh yeah, well so what. I didn't need your stupid girls, Will. I had one right here. Well, even though she's not exactly anything to me, she's still all I have, and anything I have can outmatch yours any day.

It was like he heard my train of thought since he turned his head just enough to let me into his peripheral vision. He was leaning against the doorframe with his back to me. Knowing where I was, he had to be watching for the very moment someone would come and object what they were trying to do.

"What the heck are you doing here?" I asked as Charlotte unstrapped my last arm.

"Helping you escape, obviously," Will said, being overly dramatic in his expressions, throwing his hands up in the air.

"But..." I said, confused about everything.

"I know you don't get much, but don't worry. We're just helping you out." Charlotte said unbuckling the last strap and lightly rubbing my shoulder. "We found out where Penn took you. To be honest it's not the best of locations but you have to do what you have to do."

"If we're planning on living then I suggest we leave now," Wendy said.

"Don't have to tell me twice!" Will said, waltzing out the door.

Charlotte helped me off the chair I was previously imprisoned on and gave Monica a look. She was blending into the dark room so well I didn't notice her. The black bow greeted me along with her eyes. Monica eyed Charlotte and gave a nod.

"Alright then. Can you walk?"

"Think so."

I took my first step after what seemed like forever. The last time I was standing was when I was looking into Penn's blood stained eyes as her fist flew into my face. Now that I think about it, I was never able to feel the pain of it. My face wasn't even bruised or sore when I woke up in the room full of kids. It had to have been days.

"How long has it been?" I asked.

"Since you got taken?" Charlotte said. "Six days."

"News travels quickly about you around the cities. Everyone knew you were gone," Wendy said, walking out into the hallway with us.

"Everyone was panicking so it spurred more of an incentive to search for you," the monotone voice said from behind me, closing the door to the room I was locked up in.

"Then how'd you find me?"

Charlotte turned around and started walking backwards. Her smile was way too big for a situation like this but I didn't care. I was glad just to see them again, her especially.

"How'd you think we found you when Violet took you? We felt you in danger then saved you."

"Yeah, like minutes afterwards."

Wendy let out a giggle that echoed through the white hallway.

"We couldn't just get here within minutes. You don't even know where *here* is. They took you to a mountain covered in snow far away from civilization."

"We're not in Exon?"

"You think Zalus is really gonna make his army of super children that close to the outer cities?" Will said from the front.

"Well it'd be closer to all of us. If he's planning on using them then it'd be a lot easier for him."

"You're avoiding the whole fact that Rouge makes their routine scouts. They can find things out like that easily. It makes sense for him to do this over here. Plus, this was the lab of the bio engineers back in old Exon."

Old Exon huh? The hallways were kept pretty clean considering that we were in the fog. Anywhere outside the known world of Novus was a wasteland. If this place was kept this clean than it had to have been rebuilt. Did they always know they were gonna do this to the kids?

"Then tell me why."

The unfamiliarity of the voice made me jump, instantly spiking my heart. Charlotte wasted no time and snatched my hand. The others linked together within a matter of seconds and held on firmly to the source that was gonna save us.

Charlotte's grip was stronger than the first time she saved me with invisibility like this. It was only weeks since the incident in the cafe. I was being held down by the Princess herself, having a metal pole that Brittany burned put close to my face. It was only because of them that I was alive. Wendy used the distraction of the cars to her advantage and got me out without any burns. We all worked in sync and everyone seemed to know what to do. As haughty as it sounds, I was the main priority. What difference was it now?

There was a turn coming up to the hallway that we were passing up, the direction the other voice was coming from.

"Hey, it's not my choice to use kids."

"Then why the heck are we?"

Standing there were two Palace Guards with their helmets off. It was a first. All the ones I've seen had their helmets on. We even made jokes about how they weren't even human or how they must've drilled them to their heads. There was one that was a lot younger than the other, somewhere probably in his twenties. Both of their faces shared a look of concern.

"You know exactly why. The Equilibrium and his friends killed off all the kids in Exon with the name Violet."

"So you're saying that they did that to piss off Penn?"

"Who knows why. But it did its work on BloodLip. It's what made them come up with the idea."

The Palace Guard that wasn't as set on the plan ran his hands through his hair and let out a deep sigh.

"This isn't right man."

"Hey, we don't make the rules, we just follow them."

I kept my eyes on both of them for as long as I could before the wall continued and covered my sight. The white from them made a perfect canvas for me to fill as the question poured in. Was he really claiming we did something like that? Why would we ever kill kids?! You'd have to be as cruel as Zalus to do something like that. All those children from Earth that were supposed to have a life here on Novus were taken to be nothing all because of his hand.

Charlotte unlatched from my hand. I was expecting sweat but she wasn't phased at all. There wasn't any sort of warmth in her hand and it wasn't just because of the cold of the altitude.

"Did you guys hear them?!" I whispered loudly.

The edge of Charlotte's hair was moved, revealing the side of her eyes as she was about to turn towards me. I could see her eyebrows from this position. I often relied on people's eyebrows to tell about their emotions. The way it embodied all of that was crippling to some people, especially to me since I hated when people could read me. If that was the case, why was it so dang impossible to read her at the moment.

"What are you doing?" a robotic voice said over our heads.

I shot my chin to the sky to look for the source of the voice even though I already knew it was ALIS. Nowhere on the ceiling were speakers. It just simply was there.

"You stupid?" Will said.

"Considering the word "intelligence" is in my name, I don't think I would say so."

"I thought you had a grip on her," Charlotte said, looking at Monica.

"I still do. She's not fully active right now. I still have a certain amount of control over her."

"Then why's she talking?" Wendy asked.

"I have the ability to talk whenever I please. That's not anything you disgusting humans could control."

"Oh you're calling us disgusting now?" Wendy said. "You forget you were a human once too."

"I never enjoyed my human form. Compared to what I can do now, I'd be considered a god in your society."

"If you're a god then why am I controlling you?" Monica said.

ALIS scoffed. You know, I don't think a robot could ever scoff. Yeah, I know she's not considered an actual robot, but you know what I mean. When you compare someone like her to humans it's not quite the same thing. Hearing her do that just reminded me how much her human traits were still there.

"You think you're controlling me? You think that just because you're connected to surveillance and shutting it down, merely giving the illusion that it's still going is controlling me? I knew the second you came here. I knew the second you walked into the room Mark was kept. I knew the second you decided to come here. Now what I'm admitting that I don't understand is how two things don't match up. You decided to meet up in Exon and come out by yourselves. Not once was there any from Equilibrium with you, yet, my cameras picked up movement from them making their way here."

"Monica," Charlotte ordered.

"Switched to binary mode."

"You can talk to her in binary?" I asked.

"Yes, and she's a lot more annoying in that mode. Think of it as her mother tongue." Monica stopped for a second as her eyebrows made a little hop "Oh. She just alerted the facility that we're here and we have Mark."

"Great!" Will shouted, throwing his hands up in the air. "What do we do now?"

"Stick with the plan," Charlotte said.

"We have a plan?" I asked.

Charlotte did her same little twist that made me jump. It sent a euphoric feeling through my whole body that they all could've certainly felt. Her soft smile that had the effect to pierce anything made for a really good oxymoron. She clasped her hands behind her back and bent down just a bit.

"Yup! And it starts with you holding my hand."

It took me by surprise, the soft skin that went through rigorous training, all the hard work and yet no callous, no dry skin considering we were in a moisture sapped terrain. I've touched her hand before, heck, I even danced with her once. Maybe if you want to count it, I even kissed her. I know the feeling of her but when you have someone that despite all that still gives you the little kid crush feeling, you know it's something else.

I gave her hand a good squeeze cause why the heck not. If I had the excuse to hold onto her hand I might as well. Because of our close grip she was able to maneuver us with ease, pulling me down another hallway.

"Monica found the circuit mainframe of the facility. She's gonna try and take control of it."

"Isn't she already?"

"No that's just ALIS. The one she wants is the system that links all the kids together. Take them from Zalus."

That's right. If he controlled that one kid who could manipulate gravity then there had to be a way Monica could take over his way of doing that, making her able to switch that off. These kids already had so much taken from them. If we could give them back whatever we could then you bet we were going to. I wasn't gonna let one of them be subject to Zalus anymore.

"Only problem is that we're getting closer to Penn," Wendy said, tightening her pigtail.

Oh boy. So you wake me up to take me closer to the person who wants me dead. Makes total sense. But I guess it actually did make sense. We'd show them our stand on them taking the kids even though I've clearly made my stand. And maybe if I got the chance I could clear up this rumor that we killed kids with the name Violet.

Violet. Wait. Violet. They don't know. Terra's told me all that there was to the Old Novus. How life was back then was nothing compared to how it was now. Thriving cities ten times larger than Springfield. That's something I could only imagine, especially since they're way more advanced in technology. But the Three that tried their best to save the very home they loved. Violet, Scarlett, and Aqua.

Violet was never one to kill people for mere duty. If she ever did it was to better the planet she grew up in, to prepare it for my arrival. It was Zalus who was the one to change her morals to turn into the monster she was, desperately trying to kill her student from homeroom. It was that Violet that convinced Penn and the rest of BloodLip to be as cruel as they are.

It made total sense. In fact, it was the only logical choice. If I were to talk to Penn, have the chance to get her alone without her killing me and tell her the truth about Violet, then maybe, just maybe I could get my redheaded girl back.

"Perfect. Where is she?"

Wendy whipped her tails to the wind and waited for an answer from Monica.

"She's sleeping right now. They all are."

"How late is it?"

"It's not late at all," Will said. "They're just spoiled and think they can do whatever they want. Since they don't gotta take any more kids they can relax all they want."

"That's not true," Charlotte corrected him, still holding onto my hand. "They were up late last night."

"Well where is it?"

They all turned their heads upon my spontaneous command to know their location.

"Do you actually want to die?" Wendy asked.

"They won't kill me. I know something they don't. We all do."

"Yeah? What's that?" Will asked.

"The reason why Violet was actually trying to kill us."

"We can't do something like that right now. We need to get to the mainframe for Monica and then get out of here," Charlotte said.

"They're this way!" someone shouted from the other end of the hall we just came from.

"And give up the chance of getting back the old Penn? Yeah right."

Whatever plan they had to get to the mainframe was gonna have to wait. I needed to talk to Penn and the rest of them. I know it sounds completely stupid considering that I was already taken once again and I could've told all of them, but this needed to be cleared up. I didn't know if this was gonna work but they needed to know despite whatever happens.

As much as I hated it, I yanked my hand from Charlotte and turned towards the direction the Palace Guards were coming from. If they were trying to save me then they had to come and help me. I trusted them to.

"Ugh! Mark wait!" Will shouted.

I ignored his stupid lady loving voice and kept running. I didn't know where was where but if it meant getting closer to Penn then I was all for it. Was it a wise choice to run towards the Palace Guards? Not really. I'll admit to that. But what can I say, I was fired up. A lost person had the chance for salvation. All kinds of endorphins were rushing in my blood. Why would being scared of the Palace Guards be brought up into my head at the time?

I burst through the corner and saw both of them with their weapons raised. From the way they were talking before it sounded like they were newer to serving the King in this fashion. It mean that they'd hesitate to shoot, at least I thought. The younger looking one panicked and tried to better his aim, only making it worse. He went ahead and fired, completely missing.

All the rigorous training I went through really never got put into practice. I was waiting for the time I could use it. I charged towards the younger one and firmly latched onto the wrist that was holding the firearm. With my other hand I yanked it out and used the blunt end to whack the other square in the nose. I used that one on Wendy a week before. She didn't take it as well as the Guard did.

He knew at this range that a gun wouldn't be of use. Keeping a hand on his nose to suppress the blood that spilled out, he threw out his knife, throwing his gun on the floor. The bulkier, more experienced one charged at me with his knife. With the split second I had, I pushed on the younger guy that I was still holding onto. I reached down and pulled out his knife that he still had concealed before I threw him to the floor.

I was never planning on using the knife. I wasn't going to cripple this guy. I knew what it felt like to have a knife enter into your body; twice actually. This man never did anything to me. He may be serving Zalus but who knows what the reasons could be.

He turned to face me as the other watched from the floor. Both of us held the knife with the blade away from our bodies, ready to combat each other. I wasn't gonna do that from the start. The only option I had was to evade any attack he would throw at me.

Being the one with rage running inside him for me breaking his nose, he threw the first attack. It was the one I waited for. I ducked since I saw he put all he had into the swing and went up on his hand, twisting his wrist to disable him. The second the knife clanked against the cold floor, I put the blade to his neck and pinned him against the wall. His eyes changed for the first time, mimicking the same look the other Guard still gave from the floor. For a second the scream Charlotte gave when Violet did the same blasted in my ears. No, get the heck out of my head. You're not stopping me. I needed to get to Penn *now*.

"Where's Penn?" I demanded with heavy breathing.

"The Princess?" he said, out of breath.

"No. The dang King. Of course the Princess! Where is she?!"

"Like I'd ever tell you."

"You'd be smart if you do."

He rolled his eyes.

"You might be able to take us both, but there's no way you swing that knife right now."

"What makes you think that?"

"For one, you're not even pressing it against my skin yet. It's distant and that's only because of you. You may have been trained but I've actually killed people."

"Guess what," I said, leaning into his face to make him smell the grogginess in my breath, "so have I."

"Oh my God," said the Guard on the floor. He started to crawl back with his widened eyes. "You actually did kill them."

I turned to look at him and raised an eyebrow, still keeping the other Guard pinned. He slowly got up and put his hands up.

"Don't hurt him. Please. She's in A-12. They all are. It's just down the hall to the left. You'll find it."

"Anders! You dang idiot! He's not gonna kill any of us!"

"You don't know that. If he killed all those girls then what's stopping him from killing us?"

Swoosh

All three of us turned our heads to see the others standing together watching the aftermath of a quarrel. Charlotte tilted her head as a dog would, curious how this all started out. I was just relieved that someone could deal with them as I looked for A-12.

I dropped the knife and ran the other way down the hall as the Guard told me. He initially thought I was running towards him and let out a yelp as he flinched, waiting for me to hurt him. Instead, I just ran past and let whatever happened back there happen.

I made the left and instantly my eyes searched for the letter A. The numbers started at 90 so I had a ways to go before I hit it. I looked down the hall and took a pretty good guess where the room was at. I put that in my mind and gave myself that time to think of what I was gonna say so they didn't kill me. No matter how hard I was thinking I decided to let it go. I was already running on adrenaline and pure heart. If it helped me get passed those Palace Guards than it had to help somehow when I would wake them up.

The further along I got, the more my heartbeat would gain in its speed. All those times Penn wanted me dead. It started from the moment she broke into my house and revealed to my mom what we really were. She chased me down the rooftops in my neighborhood. She ran me across downtown and got to the point of trying to kill me in front of people inside a cafe. What seriously would make you think, Mark, that she'd have a change of heart here? Pure hope to gain the old Penn that you loved? Whatever it was I needed that to be true.

I placed my feet in front of the door with "A-12" on it. The picture of them sleeping soundly couldn't get to my head. Peaceful isn't a word that could be associated with them. Maybe I was wrong. I took that thought and gave the panel a good look over. Even though I've been on Novus for well over a month I still forgot that the doors don't have doorknobs. It almost looked naked without it. The panel that was always placed next to the door had either a card you swipe or a hand that you place on it to read. I saw Kerren do it countless of times back at Headquarters.

"You gotta be kidding me," I said to myself.

What was I supposed to do now? I already tried breaking it back when got locked inside my room the first day we got here. Doesn't work. And if anything it seemed like these were bullet proof. There was no harm in trying my hand so with my desperation I went ahead and placed it on the cold surface. Instantly, the panel recognized there was a hand on the panel and started reading it. A white line scanned it just like a copy machine would. I waited for it to turn red and reject my hand. Almost immediately it should've done so but for some reason it was still scanning. After a few more seconds the line turned green.

"What?"

I took my hand off the panel and it read something I didn't understand.

Penn Exon

Access Granted

Penn? Why'd it think I was Penn? I couldn't answer my own questions in time. The door slid open. It was my calling to bring the truth to light. Still confused about the panel's reading, I slowly walked into the room. Once I stepped fully inside, the door clamped shut behind me, making a hissing noise. The lights suddenly switched on and revealed four beds that were scattered around the room. Blankets covered three despite it being considerably warm inside the room. The only one who wasn't covered was Brittany. She was wearing her brown tank with a pair of shorts, sprawled out if she were sweating.

Why'd they look so calm? None of them were trying to kill me. They were all in a state that no one could bring them in but slumber itself. I think this was probably the first time I saw them as normal people—just regular teenagers.

Red hair peeked out from the covers of a bed. Underneath she turned and threw her hand down to throw the blankets off her. I braced myself just like the Guard did, but she still had her eyes closed.

"What do you want Zalus?" she said with irritation filling her voice.

She thought I was Zalus? Wait. She doesn't call him dad?

"Penn," I said, cringing at the thought of her hearing my voice.

Just as I thought, the second she heard it, she opened her eyes. At first I thought it was the lighting of the room but it wasn't that at all. Her eyes weren't the red that I've always seen. Usually it's a shade brighter than blood but this time they looked purple. Even her hair. At the roots her hair was a shade darker. But what scared me the most was her nails. The hand that was still holding the covers had fingernails as black as Monica's hair. She noticed me looking at them and hid them from me, bringing her frown for the appropriate occasion.

The rest of them sat up in their beds. Despite the sleep filling their eyes, they tried their best to focus on me.

"What the heck are you doing here?" Penn asked.

"I know I should've been locked up but Charlotte and the others helped me escape." Me telling them straight up that I escaped made them raise an eyebrow, wondering if they were actually awake. "But I came back cause I needed to tell you something."

Once Penn stepped out of her bed, it signaled the rest of them to do the same.

"Well you made a mistake coming back," Penn said, revealing her sword. "We were supposed to return the pain when we woke up. I guess you really want it that bad huh?"

"Wait wait wait," I said, holding my hands up. "It's about Violet. Zalus isn't telling you everything. Look. I don't know what he's told you but I doubt it's the truth."

When I mentioned Violet, Penn's upper lip lifted in a snarl.

"And what makes you have the right to claim that?"

All of them pressed their glares into me. They could pounce on me at any second and the only thing stopping them was what I had to tell them. I had to get this right.

"She never was part of Exon. She was a covert agent for Equilibrium. There were three. Violet, Scarlett, and Aqua and each of them fought against the the King."

"You piece of crap! Who the heck do you think you are to say anything about her?! Why do even think she was doing what she was doing back on Earth?!" Eli yelled.

"Because she was lied to just like you were."

"Let me guess. Terra was telling you this," Sarah said, putting a hand on her hip.

"It's not her telling. It's in the dang news logs. There's a database of old news stories that Monica found in the old archives of Exon. It tells all about her, what she did, who she was. She was brainwashed after she kidnapped you."

"Kidnapped?"

Just then I saw her eyes change. Just like the sun setting, the purple from her eyes left and the bright red returned. It was a rare occurrence but for once in a little over a month I saw no sign of anger in her, just confusion. Was she actually believing me?

"There was a siege on the Palace before we were sent to Earth. Equilibrium hit Exon head on but it was a diversion for Violet to kidnap you."

"So what you're telling me is that Violet never served the King," Brittany said.

"That's right. Neither were you guys supposed to either. You were part of Project Salvation too."

"What?"

"He didn't tell you about that either?"

Out of nowhere, the purple rushed back into her eyes and her frown took place in its spot.

"What the heck does it matter to us anyways," Penn said with vile disgust. "The Violet Terra's told you about wasn't the Violet I knew. None of you know her like I ever did. She was the best person I knew. She's the reason I am who I am. No amount of persuasion you use on me, no matter how many facts you pull up is gonna make me go against the Violet I knew."

"And you don't think Terra's lied to you about who she is?" Sarah said, crossing her arms.

"Lied?" I said, stopping my train of thought at her words.

"The Queen, Reyna. You know much about her?" Penn asked.

"No."

"That's because Terra's never told you about her. She doesn't want you to know a single thing of who she was. My biological mother was said to be a "luxurious person", but she was just a common person before. She lived with her mom and stepdad and also had a stepsister. Her stepsister's name was Terra. Now, the only reason why Zalus took an interest in her was because her parents died. Get where this is going?"

"Terra's not right in the head, Mark," Eli said. "She killed her dad and stepmom for who knows what reason."

"Reyna was a lot older when this happened but her parents let her live at home with them. Terra was only eleven when this all started. Zalus ended up taking Reyna away from all the media ensemble that raised when the news heard about it. This went places and she became Queen. Terra was sent to a prison but somehow escaped." Penn let out a sigh and shook her head. "You claim that we're all murderers when you don't realize you're being led by one."

I looked down for a second to take all of this in. Terra told me that the Three killed the Queen before the siege. Her very friends were gonna kill her stepsister and she knew it.

"Now I have one question for you. What do you want from us?"

"Huh?"

"You killed all those kids in Exon with the name Violet for a reason. You wanted our attention and now you have it. What do you want?"

"I never killed any kids! You know I wouldn't!"

"Then why the heck do we have video of Charlotte, Wendy, Monica, and Will doing it?!"

"They were always with me! If they did something like that I would've known!"

Swoosh

Speak of the devil. All four of them placed themselves behind me, not needing to even say anything for me to know they were there. Charlotte took a step forward that made the other follow, taking their place at my side. None of them moved when they saw BloodLip, but stared at them. If anything they still all held somewhat of a smile.

"We got the mainframe," Charlotte said to me, still looking at them. "Monica's in now. I suggest we leave before more Guards get here."

Charlotte said all of this while looking at Penn. With her subtle smile that pierced her, it started to make her blood boil. I could tell. I didn't know why she was smiling but I wanted desperately to tell her to stop. It would break all social cues if I did so. Penn would realize that it was actually something that was pressuring her.

"Who's says you're allowed to leave?" Penn said, walking towards us with the rest of her confidence behind her.

"Penn," I said, trying to get her to realize what she was actually trying to do. I was desperately hoping it would have the same effect it did back in the shed. It saved someone's life momentarily but would it have the same effect now? "Violet wouldn't want you to do this."

"Don't say that!" she yelled, throwing her hands down. "Don't act like you know her!" Tears started to break through her eyes and her voice broke. "She was *my* mom. I knew what she liked, what she hated, I knew it all. And one thing that she wouldn't let up on is to end your life."

"You don't get it Penn! The Equilibrium is made to save races that are—"

"Gonna go extinct. I know," she said, finishing my sentence.

"I don't know what that is but it obviously has to do with your dad. Why do you think Equilibrium was made?"

"He's not my dad! I never had one. And did it ever cross your mind that Equilibrium is the very thing that brings about that future?"

"That's not possible. We're fighting against all the injustice that Zalus brings."

"What injustice? I don't see anyone oppressed in Exon. Do you realize who's leading you? It's the maniac who murdered her parents and escaped prison. What if she's merely fighting against Exon because of the position her sister was in? You said we were lied to but what about the lies she's telling you?"

Beeps stopped my awestruck state. I kept my eyes on her purple that took over the red as the door opened from behind me. The beep before it opened was the last thing I heard before my hearing was dulled. More questions than I could've ever asked for flooded my mind. Penn stared right back and I saw all her emotions that have been dragging her down reveal themselves. Ever since that one moment when she watched me send the bullet into Violet's head. Why? Why was all this happening?

Someone pulled on my arm and dragged me away before I was momentarily trapped by Wendy, set free the second my request popped in my head. I didn't want to be teleported out of there. I wasn't done. Penn didn't want to believe but she needed to. Who cares if there was Palace Guards there? I needed to convince her.

The bang from the gun of the Palace Guard that went off right next to my ear was what caused the dulled hearing. It started to clear a bit but just brought about ringing. I was teleported out into the hallway away to safety. I turned my head and watched as BloodLip burst out of the door, pushing all the Guards out of the way that were there.

Despite us being able to finally talk in a calm manner, it didn't stop her desire for revenge. I could clearly see that as the bloodthirsty pack started to chase down their prey through the corridors of the facility I've been in.

"We need to hurry," Charlotte said as she ran at my side.

The four of them were all there running with me, Monica leading the way.

"What about the kids?!" I yelled.

"Monica has control of them."

"So what! It doesn't mean that Zalus can't command a kill order on all of them. Why'd you even come here by yourselves?! Where's all of Headquarters?"

"All that matters is that we let Monica get access to it."

"They've made it through! All Palace Guards to the entrance!" the speakers said. Entrance? Who's here? "Your Majesty! We'll need your help," the Guard on the speaker said, regarding the only person who could hold the term "Majesty" here besides Zalus.

A streak of white whizzed by my head and landed in a Guard's arm that was running by, unintentionally taking the shot for me.

"How many times have I told you not to call me that?! I'm already on their tail!" Penn yelled from behind us.

"Will!" I yelled, intending him to throw them back.

"No! Wendy, take us to the next hall. We're not fighting this. Not yet," Charlotte said.

Why weren't you listening to me?! First you didn't want to help me explain to Penn what was happening and now you don't listen to me when I tell you one simple thing? I couldn't move away from Will fast enough before he grabbed my hand, linking me with Wendy's command.

Swoosh

I couldn't handle it anymore. I was out of breath from running after being strapped to a chair for so long, but now that she was constantly teleporting me out, my heart and lungs couldn't keep up with this rush. I wanted to stop for a second so I yanked my hand from Will as soon as I could see anything. Screw him too. Why'd he have to comply so much with her all of a sudden? I was all too caught up in my own pain and problems that I didn't even notice who was standing there. Once I heard the voice, it threw out all my intentions of caring for myself.

"Make sure you check everywhere. He's here. All of us felt it."

I froze when I heard the voice. I'd stack that one on top of all other times I've been shocked in this way. First you have the voice we heard back in the abandoned building and then you have the weird encounter I had with Charlotte when I was surrounded with kids in tanks. But this, this was something new. Why? Reason was is quite simple actually. There was two here.

The voice I heard was Charlotte's even though she was standing right next to me. And what was right in front of me confirmed pretty much everything. Charlotte, Wendy, Monica, and Will were standing in front of me with Kerren by their side along with people from Equilibrium with them.

"What?" we all said simultaneously, matching the same tone as each other's voices.

I looked into Charlotte's eyes, the one that stood in front of me, for a few seconds then switched to all the rest. It was all honesty that I read in their eyes, like they've been betrayed. Here I was with someone else that looked exactly like them.

"What the heck is going on?!" the Charlotte in front of me yelled.

"That's—that's me," Wendy said in dismay, standing next to Kerren, pointing at the one besides me.

I slowly turned my head and looked at the Charlotte that helped me escape. She was the one that took me out of this prison. But who was who?

Instantly there was a difference. The subtle smile she had the whole time now spread to a full one, the glorious beautiful smile that I loved. Her hands fell at her side and she dropped a shoulder just enough to notice; only for me to notice. Wendy let her smile grow as Charlotte did and got giddy all of a sudden. She let out a giggle and bent down to her knees in an uncontrollable quirk. Monica became more stiff, not moving a single muscle, looking ahead at the copies of them in front. Will let out a scoff and crossed his arms as he looked in disgust at who was in front of him.

"How nice of you to actually join us," the Charlotte next to me said. "I know you're all confused and I'd hate to stop seeing your faces like this, but to be honest, it'd probably be way more fun once I explain things."

"Phew!" Wendy said, "Do you know how hard it was to act like the real Wendy? Gosh it was incredibly hard. I don't think I did a good job of it though. She's a lot meaner than I am. But that's something I don't understand. How could anyone be mean to you?" she said, looking at me with a mile wide smile.

"Real Wendy?" the Will in front of me said with a hint of anger to his voice.

"Mhm," Charlotte said. "You see, Mark is the one who has the most experience with us. Remember when you all went into your slip space at the party? There was a copy of each one of you. Those were mere illusions, but Mark's was real. A direct duplication of you. Once it was over and we killed you, you left the split space and set us free."

"It amuses me how you still think that was Penn trying to get you to join BloodLip," Will said, fiddling with a chunk of hair in front of his eyes.

"That's why you rejected my offer."

All the heads in the hall turned towards Penn's voice to see BloodLip standing in confusion just like we all were, letting this Charlotte dominate the conversation. I don't know how long she was listening but I assume it was long enough to understand just as much as we know.

"Then why'd you save me?" I asked.

"Oh it's quite simple. And, I'm sorry for what we had to do to those kids in Exon, Penn. It was the only way this would happen. If we framed Mark and his friends then you'd come up with revenge in the same way. We know the way you work. You'd return the damage in a similar fashion, meaning you'd take their kids from him. Once you guys found each other in the school I arranged things to make sure he got caught. Now Monica has access to the kids you modified. If you ask me, you messed up. But oh well, that happens in life."

"What the heck are you trying to do?!" Kerren yelled, getting frustrated just as all the rest of us were.

"Me? Well I have only one purpose when I was created. Our purpose in the split space was to kill Mark. When we were let free, that purpose carries over." She turned her head to fall into my eyes as she did before she kissed me in the mansion. "I'm not gonna let anyone kill you but me." A giggle followed her words and she shrugged in pure innocence.

"But we're not following our own orders," Monica said, only moving her lips.

"Oblivion has its own set," Charlotte said as she nodded in agreement with Monica. "We're just the Twins of Oblivion. But we'll leave that to you 'till things take affect. I can assure you, though, that she's working hard." Each of them connected hands as they did before they jumped and wounded the girl in white. "I'll see you later Mark. Love you."

My mind wanted to vomit. I was so confused over who this person was. I know she explained it, but this girl looked exactly like the Charlotte I loved. How could someone who looks exactly like her possess the ability to do cruel things? With the last look before she left, my mind was happy that she gave me that smile as I would normally feel with the real Charlotte, but that was the thing. This was the real Charlotte. All these people weren't my friends. They were the Twins of Oblivion.

Swoosh

Chapter 8

How could she not get it? I outright told her the truth about the very person she loved the most and she doesn't want to believe it? It made me wonder what the original Violet was even like in the first place. The news logs that Monica pulled up about them simply told about their missions. There were a few pictures when people managed to capture them before or after an act. There was one time when there was a shootout in a shopping district. They went and settled things, just the three of them. The Palace Guards never showed up. They were a lot like vigilantes but acted in accord to something more.

Come on Violet. What would you do in a situation like this?

I let out a sigh as I looked out the window of the vehicle. The snow was now long gone. It chilled the whole car but the adrenaline of the fight dampened its chilling effects. Once the Twins left, Penn lashed out at us. I didn't want to fight anymore. I was starting to see Penn in a new light now. As she chased me on top of rooftops, almost killed me in a cafe; that was mere emotion that spurred these actions. There seemed to be no thinking involved. It begged the question, what would I do if she returned the same pain?

"You okay?" Charlotte asked, putting a hand on my back.

I gave a quick nod and still looked out the window.

"Yeah I'm fine."

I noticed in my peripheral vision that Wendy was quietly looking at me. She held her head down just enough to still keep me in range of the movement of an eye. I was half expecting her to rant about how she should've gotten taken instead of me, but things were fairly quiet. Mostly in part of the encounter of the Twins. And don't even get me started on the questions those four brought up.

Out of all of us, most of us being exhausted, two were thinking hard. I could tell. Monica sat with her brow creased just enough to inflict thinking. Will had his arms crossed and didn't bother to move the fleck of hair that hung in front of his eye. If that was the case it meant nothing good. But hey, he was the one who got the slip space thing right. Actually right on the ball. If he was suggesting any other ideas, who knew if his liableness would stick with him.

"So they knew what was happening the whole time," Will said, not moving a muscle. All of us raised our heads and turned to face him besides Monica who was still in thought. "Think about it. They were on Earth when we were. They all killed us and were set free by doing so. But they somehow managed to get to Novus when they were never there with us when we went through the portal."

"They tried killing us before we went to the mall," Monica said.

"Right, but who were those that tried saving us then? If no one here on Novus knows about them then they have to be related to the Twins somehow."

"She did say there was a problem we knew nothing about," I said, hoping it would add to Will's flame of thought.

He slowly nodded his head, gazing into the floor.

"So it was never Penn who made the slip space then, or anyone associated with her."

Oblivion has its own set of orders fake Charlotte told me. The name made me sink into a little pit of depression for a while. Usually I would get upset over hearing about another group of people, but this time, it must've been what happened with Penn that was bringing me down. I mean heck, she didn't even want to be seen as the Princess, let alone call Zalus "dad". She was merely doing all of this out of revenge for me, to bring honor to Violet's name and her legacy. That's what I didn't get. If she was trying to do all of this for her, then why wouldn't she accept it? Was it because she knew these things about Terra that I didn't know; a possible ulterior motive?

"Well, looks like we got a fight to pick with Oblivion," Wendy said, sitting up straight for the first time.

"Don't get too ahead of yourself. We don't even know who they are," Charlotte said.

"Charlotte's right. And besides, we have another matter to focus on right now. Something that's actually gonna happen soon," Kerren said. "Since we couldn't get control of the facility, they're gonna use those kids somehow."

Kerren sat in the passenger seat like she always did. Her joy of being with her brother wasn't found right now. Her focus on the matter as she's been used to kicked in. She's been training all her life to take over when the time came so it was always on her mind.

She was the one to call off the raid. Some wanted to stay and fight, trying to convince her that they could take it, but I helped in telling them we needed to leave. If Zalus had control over the kids as he showed me then what was stopping him, or anyone for that matter, from sending them out to attack us? Nothing. It was clear we needed to leave. Before Charlotte made sure I wasn't able to be seen, I looked into Penn's eyes one last time as she looked in mine. The purple was taking over the red. The dark consuming. What was it that was changing her?

"Corruption hurts. Get used to it."

*   *   *

Charlotte was antsy as we dropped in the elevator. She hopped on her toes and was rubbing her palms of sweat. I watched her from the corner of my eye to not show her I was watching. But seriously Charlotte. How could you be nervous right now? I knew exactly what it was towards but I just didn't understand. Kerren was giving off the same feel but just wasn't showing it. They failed. The mission was to get me back but once they tell Terra all about what happened, she isn't gonna be happy. Anyone could tell you that. If anything, I should be the one who's nervous. I had knowledge about her past.

I waited for the door to open and reveal Headquarters, freeing me from this depressing anxious box we were in. I counted the seconds it took to get down and just on time it opened up like it always did.

We all took quick long steps to get to where we needed to go; Terra. People stopped what they were doing for a few seconds to watch us go by. Some even went to the length of putting their things down and following us to Terra. They knew something would brew once we talked to her.

Terra was waiting right where she first explained everything. Her arms were behind her back and stood tall as a soldier would. Green met my eyes and they locked. You know, despite it being Terra, I kinda was hoping for maybe some relief from her, but nope, all I got was this look of disappointment.

"We were able to retrieve Mark safely without any casualties," Kerren said.

She didn't respond but kept her gaze with me.

"Do you know how much you risked? First off you're The Equilibrium. You're the person we worked hard for more than sixteen years. You're willing to just throw that all away with some dumb heroic plan to jump onto the ship that has BloodLip piloting? Not only that, but you risk everything by giving yourself over to the people we're fighting against?!"

"Don't you dare say anything about what I did!" I yelled. Her claims of what I did, saying that they were stupid rash decisions, they were mere pent up frustration. "You know that you would've done the same thing if any one of your people, your friends, were put in that same position. You're not gonna let them get taken right in front of your eyes."

"If I were as important to everything as you are then you bet I wouldn't!"

A crowd was quick to form around us. It wasn't abnormal for Terra to be yelling at someone but if it involved us then it created reason for them to raise curiosity.

"Screw me being important! Screw everything about me being this Equilibrium! I don't care how important me being here is. If one of my friends is in trouble then I'm gonna help them no matter what! Why the heck do you think I did to Violet what I did?"

"You don't get it do you?" She stepped down from her raised area of control and walked towards me as a lion would sneak up on a gazelle. "I worked my butt off for you. I watched my friends die countless amounts of times. There was a little girl and boy that were ten when they first joined. You know what happened to them? They saved over ten thousand people by carrying bombs away, letting them detonate on them. I watched one of my closest friends get shot in the head. We all did this for everyone. Rylan would always remind me when I didn't want to do something why we fight in the first place. 'We fight for peace. For the freedom of others. For the Equilibrium.' For your sorry little butt."

"And you don't think we've done our part?" Monica said, standing blankly. "We sacrificed for the people here on Novus. It's the only reason I wanted to fight Zalus. If you can't recognize that then that's not our problem. But when the people in the outer cities and even in Exon can see what we've done, then it really puts you in your place, showing how blind you really are."

"I haven't really mentioned it to you yet," Kerren said quietly, turning towards me slowly to not disturb Terra. "There's been rallies. After you got taken and they saw what you did on the news, saving the kids and all, it spurred something in them. It's what we've been waiting for for years. We finally got them to see your help, powerless or not."

Terra took a step forward to remind us that she was there.

"It doesn't matter what the rest of the outer cities think. If Mark keeps being selfish then we're never gonna get anywhere."

I swear Terra you're treading on very thin ice.

"Oh you think I'm selfish for saving my friends life?!"

"When you're backing thousands more on you, yes!"

Alright. I've had it with her. She can claim all she wants about my actions but what about when I do the same to her. How does she like it huh?

"You're saying I'm the selfish one when you're ruling Equilibrium just to get at your sister." Terra's back that was somewhat relaxed stiffened and caught on to my words. "Queen's dead like you wanted. But why are you getting at the King when she's been done away with?"

"Shut your da—"

"But why'd you kill them, hm? Why'd you kill your parents? Did they say something you didn't like? Or maybe, just maybe it was jealousy. Ah. That's what it is. You were jealous of your sister since they gave her so much attention. Isn't that right? Isn't that why you murdered them in cold blood and had her hunted down by your friends to—"

Terra's hand completely latched around my neck. It was simply just one but when you put it into size I didn't realize it had this much strength to it. It cut off any air that was entering my trachea and contemplated whether or not to crush it all together. Its grip was so tight her nails that were always kept cut short were piercing my skin. It caught me off guard, but what'd I expect. I almost wanted to laugh for some reason. I know it's stupid to even think about doing but I had fun while I insulted her. At least this showed that what Penn was telling me was true. So did she really just do this out of spite or was she really doing this to save everyone?

I stared into her forest green eyes as she looked into mine, probably deciding what to do. I heard everyone gasp when she initially made contact with my neck and made my friends run towards me. But she was too quick on making her decision. As the blood in my face was suppressed along with my air flow, I felt my face was changing colors. It didn't help either when she started to drag me along with her hand still wrapped around it.

"Terra no," Kerren said, trying to get a hold of her arm before she bolted past her, stomping her boots with every step.

That was the thing that sparked some sort of fear in me was Kerren's seriousness in her voice. She was watching her brother being dragged away by the very person that's been training her her whole life, practically, dare I say, her mother. Once I noticed which direction she was taking me as I saw the control panels for the training chamber, I knew exactly where we were headed. With my view of behind her, I saw everyone run in her direction to see what she would do to the person she was just saying seconds ago everyone died for.

"Terra stop!" Charlotte yelled, pushing everyone out of the way to try and get to me. Seeing her desperation to try and reach me before we entered the chamber furthered my fear of what was to happen.

Terra didn't budge one bit despite all her members watching her. She burst the doors open and locked them immediately with a control panel, overriding them to stop anyone from opening it. She let me go and dropped me to the floor inside the white chamber.

"The heck are you doing?" I gasped, trying to regain to use of my lungs while on my hands and knees.

She stormed over me and threw a foot into my stomach, making me topple over onto my back. The air that I just got back was knocked out of me and left me breathless again. While on my back, I noticed the black that would usually cover the windows into the chamber weren't there since this wasn't an official simulation. I was quick to make out Goldilocks standing next to the others, worry actually filling their face.

"Where did you find that out?!" She yelled, looming over me.

"I don't need to answer that," I strained, getting up. "Why should I answer to a liar?"

"I never lied to you."

"Then why didn't you tell us about your sister?"

"There wasn't a need to."

"You didn't think there was a need to tell the Three before they murdered her?"

Terra ran forward with her head down to knock me back. I readied myself and planted my feet on the ground the best I could to brace for her force. Once she made contact with me, I shifted the force onto her and threw her back. Not appreciating me taking a stand for myself, she threw a punch to the face that I blocked. She wasn't slow to follow it up with a knee to the stomach, abusing what disadvantage I had.

"You think you know everything about me don't you?" she said as I tried, once again, to regain my breath. "Just because you found out Rayna was my sister you think that you can just tell everyone?" She threw an uppercut into my gut, keeping it there to be close to my ear. "There was a reason why I didn't tell people. I didn't want them to think that I did everything out of spite."

I put a hand on her shoulder to throw her off of me.

"Then why'd you kill your parents?"

"You didn't know them so don't you—"

"Claim I knew them? I didn't. But that's no excuse to murder them."

Terra's rage shifted for a second to let a smile appear, knowing she was gonna strike back in the same way I hit her.

"Then why the heck did you murder Violet? Charlotte being held with a knife to her neck isn't an excuse to murder her. What, just because you love her? Just because you think she's cute? Because you're hopeless without her? Charlotte's the most despicable human being I've seen. If you ask me you should've just let her die. She'd look a lot cuter like that."

Rage? Was there ever a time I was that mad? I don't think I ever was. If there ever was a time, this was it. I've said it before and I'll say it again. You can insult me all you want, I'm used to it, but when you bring my friends into it, especially Charlotte, then you're asking for your death.

I let out a yell as I charged towards her. She put her arms up ready to block my hits and return them where needed. I threw a fist towards the side of her face but she snatched my fist as I did Eli when he first met me. Once I knew she had a hold of it, I pulled her into my foot that I raised to impale her stomach. With the impact of it, I yanked my hand free and pinned her down on the floor. With this beast that released inside of me, I threw a fury of fists in her face.

"Don't you *ever* say anything about Charlotte!" She caught one of my fists and pulled me in to wrap an arm around my neck. "No wonder you killed your parents. They never loved you just like you never loved them. No one in their right mind would love someone as cruel as you. Not even your dead friends."

Terra rushed to her feet and dragged me up with her, pushing me away. Her eyes burned into me as she let puffs of air out of her nostrils. Her jaw muscles were clenched so tight the balls of her mouth stuck out farther than they ever would. Her arm traveled towards the holster that was on her waist and pulled out her handgun, aiming at me. It was at that moment that screams sounded above the chamber. Everyone was shouting now, the sound just barely traveling into the pit. I first thought of it as intimidation but once she whirred it up did I drop that notion. Her eye was right in line with the barrel of the gun, aiming for my head. She made one final grip around the gun as she pressed into me.

"You better pray those dang powers of yours save your stupid life."

Bang!

Everything was dark, as you would expect when you're dead. But would you be conscious when you're dead? I tried slowly opening my eyes to see if it was even possible. When I noticed some form of light, I went ahead and fully extended my eyelids. So I wasn't dead? But how?

Wait, if I had my eyes fully opened wouldn't I be able to see everything? If that was the case, why was there this white thing in front of me? Through it I could see a blurry figure who had a gun in her hand. The realization of what happened started to come together. The only other time something stopped bullets from hitting me was when the girl in white put up the wall in front of me. But she wasn't here. The only thing between me and that wall was my hands that were extended the same way hers were when she would put it up. The second I put down my hands, the wall dissolved. Standing there in front now was Terra, who slowly put the gun down.

Her anger was gone. The furrowed brows weren't anywhere to be found. Her expression was mere emptiness. I realized the whole crowd that was watching wasn't screaming anymore. I gave them a quick look and they were all pretty much the same expression. Shock. Surprise. Wide eyes.

I looked back at Terra then to my hands.

"Did I just..."

Terra holstered her gun and walked out the door, unlocking it.

"Wait, Terra what was that?!" I said, chasing after her.

Even though I should've probably been this shaky when my life was on the line, it was taking effect now because of what I did. My steps weren't firm. To be honest, it felt like it did when I passed out at school. I clenched my fists to try to stay awake and not tumble over myself with what just happened.

I followed Terra back into control where she slammed her hand on a screen and bent over a table. Everyone's eyes followed me as I walked in behind her, not knowing what to make of the whole situation.

"Dang it Rylan!" Terra yelled, putting her hands on the back of her neck.

"What the heck did I just do?" I asked her, completely forgetting she tried to kill me.

"Are you stupid or something?"

"I know...I—I used my powers...I think. But they were Penn's!"

Terra slammed a fist onto the table again, letting out a grunt.

"Why the heck didn't you tell me Rylan? Did you even trust me?"

"What?!" I yelled, trying to get her attention and have her tell me what she knew.

"It makes sense now," she said, half turning towards me. "We never kidnapped Penn because we needed to stop the King from raising her. It wasn't because of that at all."

"What are you saying?"

She let out a sigh before she answered.

"Penn's an Equilibrium."

Chapter 9

The silence was only carried out for mere seconds. Shock filled everyone in the room, especially in me. The others walked up towards where Terra and I were standing, their shock carrying over inside them as well, adding to mine.

"No. That doesn't make sense," I said. "An Equilibrium is born to stop whatever is gonna happen. Why would there be two?"

"I don't know," Terra said, shaking her head. "But it's obvious. She's been protected the whole time. That means Zalus doesn't know that she is then."

"It does make sense," Will said behind me. "We've always been connected to you. We can feel your emotions and you can feel ours, but what about BloodLip's? You never felt their emotions. I don't even know why we didn't think about this earlier. If they got their powers from you then why haven't you? It's only because they got their powers from Penn."

"Right," Charlotte muttered under her voice. "Us to protect you and them to protect Penn."

"But how did she know her powers and I barely found them out?" I asked.

"I...I don't know how this is supposed to help everyone. All you can do is create a dumb sword and shield. What the heck is so special about that?" Terra said, the task of me saving everyone in mind.

There was a beep that came from the console she smacked. The way it butt into our moment of enlightenment was so nonchalant it called everyone's attention. A light flickered and waited for someone to come up and answer its call. Kerren walked over, being the only one to even move from their spot, and pressed the button. Once the flashing stopped after the click, a screen over the controls turned on. I was confused at first, not to mention because of what happened, but because there was just the back of someone's head. Brown hair came down their back but the black clothes she was wearing made it evident who she was.

"Terra, you're gonna wanna see this," Rebecca said, keeping her head forward, not looking at the camera at all.

She was watching in the distance as something was crawling forward. In the hazy sky that was covered by overcast clouds were dots that littered it. Some were larger than others and some seemed to be higher.

Terra nodded at Kerren, signaling her to switch on the button to enable them to receive audio from our end, and without a moment of hesitation, she complied, worry for whatever she was calling about rising.

"What is it?" Terra asked.

"The King's reclamation," another voice said, coming from the other channel. Alex had his usual tone of voice that was irritated. This time it was a little hurried in some way as if he was doing something at the time. "Don't know how many but they're ships from the Palace. We scanned them with thermal cameras. They're loaded with people."

Terra stood up from hunching over the table and walked towards the controls. That movement alone, although being just a normal one, made everyone snap out of their little world of trance after what I just did, ready for what Terra had to say to them.

"Get me an estimate on how many there are as soon as possible." She turned towards another member and pointed at him. "Alert the outer cities there's an attack incoming. And Ed, prep the ship."

Ed, who I didn't realize was there the whole time, was close to the exit of control. His ruggedness was ready to take on whatever he had to do to protect everyone here. He gave us a quick look then gave Terra a nod.

"Wait, we have a ship?" Wendy asked. "I thought you said we didn't have one because they have antiaircraft guns right outside Exon."

"We have four," Ethan said over the comm, still connected to us in Headquarters. "Three loaded with explosives in case we need to throw them at something and one to escort you to Exon."

"Wait what?" Terra said. "You have three loaded with explosives?"

"Didn't want to tell you," Alex said. "Knew you wouldn't like it. So we did it in our own time."

"Ten miles from arrival at Ashillon boundaries," Rebecca said, reminding her of how close they were.

Terra let out a grunt of frustration and whipped her head around.

"Get as many as you can outside *now*! If I see any of you lollygagging around here with nothing to do then I'm gonna end you before whoever is coming will! Escort as many civilians as you can. Get them to Praunus!"

"It's no use," Alex said. "It's not just Ashillon they're invading. Our cameras picked up ships incoming all the outer cities, including Praunus. That's why we're using the ships."

"No! Don't listen to him!" Terra yelled in desperation. "Alex don't get in there!"

We watched Rebecca leave the shot of the camera and step into the cockpit of the ship. Her hair was the last thing that left our field of view. Charlotte put her hands over her mouth and watched everything unfold. Her being as kind as a soul could get, she sympathized with them. I never knew them that well. If anything, I hated them because of Alex even though his actions didn't control the others. But because of that, I found it somewhat hard to grasp what they were planning to do. Terra and Kerren were quick to follow on things even though they never specifically said they were gonna fly them up. Terra gripped the end of the console and grit her teeth. Kerren's breathing increased as she started to hyperventilate.

The pace of the whole situation was moving too fast for me to keep up, yet everyone found a way to grip a piece of heaven to keep them moving along. Hundreds of people were running back and forth, preparing for whatever was to happen. Members were sprinting to the elevator with weapons in hand, completely suited for battle.

Another call from the console sounded with its cry for someone to answer. Kerren was quick this time to press it, keeping the channel that already had Rouge open.

"Don't close the channel! I need to show you something important."

It was man that looked like he was in his early twenties. He was wearing something familiar. On his body was the uniform that people inside the Palace wore. The white fabric that draped over their bodies told everyone that they worked for the very source of life on this planet. There was urgency in the way he hunched over the camera, making the question in my head make its way over to Terra's.

"Who are you?" she demanded.

"Flynn. I know you're wondering how I got into the channel. It's understandable, but you need to listen to me. The King's making—"

"No, you listen to *me*! Tell me exactly who you are. Your name doesn't help one bit."

"I'm one of the King's attendants."

"Why the heck are you calling us?"

He let out a small sigh.

"That's what I was trying to tell you. After what Mark and the rest of The Equilibrium did in that school, you changed people. It sparked something within not just people in the outer cities, but here in the Palace too." His hasty talk halted for a second to give us a warm smile that I easily read as sincere. "You don't know how many backers you have. You're gonna save us all and everyone knows that, some just try to avoid the facts. But that's why I'm calling you. Zalus is sending a message to all of Exon right now. He's trying to cover up what he's doing with all those ships that left here. Let me patch you in real quick."

The screen that had Flynn on flickered for a brief second before it switched over to showing Zalus's face. Just the sight of him alone made me want to vomit. It made my stomach all queasy, so much so that I had to look at Charlotte really quick and give my eyes something worthwhile to look at. She never bothered to look at me. She was so entrenched in the screen, her hands still lingering over her mouth. While I was already looking at her, I gave the others a quick look over and saw the same anger, the frown for justice over the person in front of us on their faces. That's what I wanted to see.

"For years now we have been trapped within these confines of the walls. Exon has been home to us for years, even before the war started when it was larger than we could ever imagine. But now that's over we can expand. We finally have the means to cleanse what was out there this whole time. All of you know of the tyrants Equilibrium who have tried to suppress our expansion for the past decades. A month ago the very Equilibrium himself along with his counterparts have come back to our world. They have been deceived by the very group named after them that there is still a need for them, that the world is on the verge of collapse, soon to be destroyed by man itself. That is not the case at all. After we cleanse what is out there we will expand and reinhabit Novus once and for all. It will finally become the home we wanted it to be all this time. That is why you saw the fleet of Exon leave. This is a day of rejoicing. It's a day of celebration that marks the very day of expansion! This will be known as a holiday for years to come, for whatever happens today will be remembered for centuries!"

That monster. He said it himself. He's trying to kill off everyone in the outer cities. His racist blood can't get any worse. It's so bad that he's willing to commit genocide on a massive scale.

"He's been playing that all day throughout Exon," Flynn said, switching the feed back to him. "I can't do anything to help you against the attack but tell you information about what's on the ships."

"What the heck are you doing?!" a voice said from the inside of the Palace.

He stepped into frame and revealed that it was a Palace Guard. He was clothed in his black suit of armor and had his helmet on. Flynn took one look into the camera before grabbing a handgun and shutting off the feed.

"So he finally broke huh?" Alex said. Terra took over the controls now and quickly switched the feedback over to Rouge's. "Heh. He's pathetic. Set your course for the mass in front of the fleet. We'll hit them at all fronts."

"Don't take off! What the heck are you doing?!" Terra yelled. She hurried as she pressed things over the console in some hope to stop the ships.

"The explosives are large enough to clear a lot of em. I trust you guys to take out the rest. You can do that for us right?"

"No!" Terra yelled, slamming a fist down. "Land those stupid things now! That's an order."

"Can't do that. You know it's too many ships for us to deal with. Do you want everyone to die? No. Now we're gonna do what we can to stop that. Why the heck do you think we signed up for this? We wanted to do whatever we can, even if that means giving our lives for that."

"But you don't need to give your lives!"

The camera that originally was Rebecca's call showed the three ships. They were well in the air now, far from any land. Just as he said, they were heading for all the ships, the back that showed the exhaust fading with every second.

"Target locked on," Ethan said. He paused before talking again. "We had a good run guys."

"Why are you the one who's always pathetic?" Rebecca said.

Ethan gave a chuckle.

"Don't know. I like it though."

"He's right," Alex said. "Who gets to be called the runner ups of the Three? We may not have gotten as popular as them, heck we weren't even known at all. When you're a stealth unit that surveys the city, you can't even be seen. When was I ever thinking of getting popular?"

"I always asked myself that," Rebecca said. "It's always about being the best isn't it?"

Alex scoffed.

"Who cares? That doesn't matter anymore. Zalus is finally gonna get what he deserves. That's all that does matter." Beeping sped up from their comms, meaning only one thing. It got faster each second and all we did was watch the camera as the ships sealed their fate. "Never thought I'd be someone to say it." He gave a big sigh before speaking one more time. "Long live the Equilibrium!"

Just before his ship made contact with any of them, something sprung out from the ship and rammed into the wing. The wing blew up on contact with whatever hit it and sent his direction to the left, making contact with the ship to the side of the one he was gonna hit. The one in front kicked off even faster and sped past Alex's ship before it was blown to shreds, making the explosion fly out in every direction.

He wasn't kidding about those explosives. It took a few seconds before the thud made it to where we were underground, shaking the very foundation of the place. Rebecca's sped up to the left to avoid the explosion that was coming towards her for as long as possible before she made contact with another chunk of ships. Ethan did the same with his only going towards the right.

"Long live the Equi—"

They both shouted before the explosion reached them and set their own explosives off, destroying any ships that were in the air around them. The ship that destroyed Alex's wing kept speeding on towards the city past all the ships that were being demolished by the explosives. Once more ships finally started to break through the smoke that littered the sky, it knocked Terra out of her deadly phase, realizing that there were way more than she thought. She turned around and placed her eyebrows in the appropriate position.

"Get to the ship. Ed has it ready," she said, walking past us, not even giving any of us a look.

"What the—" Kerren said, still watching the feed.

We all turned back towards the control to see the ship drop low towards the top of a roof. People started to get out, but not just any people. And no, not Palace Guards. If anything, I would've wanted Palace Guards. But just like always, it was part of the universe's rule to make things not go my way. The very people getting out of the ship were the very children we tried saving in the school. They were the very ones with DNA changed just like my friends standing right beside me.

We watched as Kerren searched through other surveillance cameras, showing as ships dropped low to the ground. Out came running these kids with snarls and the mark of the beast on their faces. People that were going about their usual business, shopping and such, were stormed by these kids, reminding me completely about the strange dark force of teenagers that jumped the cops back in Springfield. The kids had no sense of morals and mauled anyone they saw. One of the boys pounced on a man that was walking with his daughter and started to lay waste to him as the girl screamed, watching without anything to do other than hope her father was okay.

It was spread throughout the whole city. And it wasn't just Ashillon either. It had to be taking place in all of the outer cities just like Alex said; this act of storming that was led by these modified kids controlled by Zalus.

There was a ship that landed in the streets close by where Headquarters was. Kerren switched to that feed and watched as the side doors opened up. Out of it came four people our age who had the same intent as the kids who were running rampant. Penn lead the charge and threw out her sword, flicking the front of it to the back of her. Her red hair wasn't there anymore. It was a darker purple than I saw last. Eli came out from behind her and instantly took out that piece of metal from his pocket and changed his form. Sarah follow her brother out and drew her knives from her waist. Brittany was the last to exit the bulky ship and made her way to stand right next to Penn. This time she wasn't even wearing a shirt over her brown tank. She knew that she would be fighting so there was no point in burning another.

All of the cameras that were up were revealing what was going on above us at that very moment; what massacre was taking place. Death upon death stacked up and it was all real time. Even though I just watched three people give their lives for the ones in the outer cities, it never hit me what deaths were taking place just like it didn't when the Penthouse fell. It never struck me as anything drastic taking place cause I was able to get out alive, but now, now was no different. Because I wasn't up there and witnessing this for myself I couldn't somehow grasp the concept of what was going on. I never needed to though. I had others to do that for me—to get me started on the right course of action. That was key. Action.

What drives action though? Emotion.

Something was changing in the atmosphere. I could feel someone fill with berserk anger. It was a behemoth's wrath that I have never felt before. What was it? The way the emotion was drifting I could tell who it was coming from but refused to acknowledge it, knowing that it was almost dang near impossible for her to feel this sort of way. But when I turned to actually look at Charlotte, it was a sight I would never forget.

Now, you have to remember. She was the one who was reacting to Rouge's death, not us. They may have felt something but nothing near to what I was getting from Charlotte. She was able to do something I wasn't able to and that was realize what was happening without being there. Distant sympathy? I don't know what to call it, but she had it. Just in that same manner, now was when it sparked something new. She was hyperventilating, letting her rage build. She was leaning over in a hunch with her arms in fists, rising in fury. Her eyes were beating into the monitors, letting that aid her in her task.

We all looked at her. It was almost funny to watch our reactions at this new part of her. Will took a step back, Monica let her mouth open to the point of barely being able to see the white of her teeth, and Wendy was actually gonna walk up to her and put a hand on her back like I was gonna do in the elevator. She ended up stopping herself, being scared at the fact of what her best friend would do to her if she actually placed a single hand on her.

The rage that she contained was let inside me. I'll be honest. If it came from any of them besides Charlotte it probably wouldn't have had the same impact as it did. For the sheer reason that it was her, I was able to get upset that someone was making her upset. A fire started to be fed inside my chest and now that it was inside me it was able to make its way to the rest of them. I let Charlotte go ahead and act on those actions and I would follow her. She was the one who was most upset and by the time any action was involved it would spike that feeling.

Charlotte stormed over towards where the rack of weapons were next to the elevator. We followed and took handguns and knives of our own just as she did.

"What do you think you're doing?!" Terra yelled. "Put those down *now*! You're getting in the ship. We have people taking care of those kids."

"But no one's gonna take care of BloodLip," Charlotte muttered, loading a magazine.

"Oh please. You think that just because you beat all the Three's records that you can just go and do anything? You aren't fighting them. We're gonna take care of them."

She turned around and faced Terra, letting her short hair whip around, turning her cuteness to the devil's appearance. She put her face so close that there was only inches apart from them.

"This isn't your fight. You don't know them like we do. No one ever will. It was *us* who fought them on Earth and it's gonna be *us* who fight them here. They're nothing but murderers who are trying to appease their thirst for blood. I'm done trying to look at them like they're normal, just put in a bad situation, but this is their choice to do this. It's because of their choice that we have to go and stop them."

Terra backed down just for a second, a second too long for us to get away. We were originally walking towards the elevator but Charlotte completely walked past that towards the stairs that ran up towards the top of the city. She rammed the door and burst into a sprint up the stairs. Wendy could've teleported up most of it but it showed that she was following her friend, the closest person she cared about. Usually when Will would ever take the lead in what we would do I would get upset, but when Charlotte does it, I held a respect for her like I did for no one else.

Wendy ran right next to me as we stormed up the staircase. Her elbow would sometimes flare up in her sprint and would hit me, reminding me that she was there, that close. I turned to give her a look really quick. She kept her eyes forward, not looking at me or even acknowledging the fact that I was looking at her. I knew she knew though. There was a subtle change in her face, the muscles tensed just enough for me to notice.

It was weird. I haven't heard her say anything annoying or bratty since the school. Once the fight broke out in the courtyard, she switched over to the appropriate mood as she always did and ever since then I heard nothing. Just like when I secluded myself from them for four days, I missed hearing her nagging. It reminded me she cared about me even though it sounds completely contradictory.

Charlotte was always a few steps ahead of us, antsy to get out into the fresh air that was probably littered with smoke mixed with the scent of the sea. Her gun was in her hand, crying out for help to have someone loosen her deadly grip around it. After our thighs started to burn from the flight, we finally made it to the top, a door that was a little ways from the main entrance we usually used. Charlotte glued her eyes to it and charged at it, ramming her side into it as she gripped the handle and burst it open.

The sight was cruel. People from Headquarters were sprinting down the streets to tear the kids off of people. Some of the powers the kids had was strange. One of them was phasing through the walls and chasing after a woman. She was screaming at the top of her lungs as he merely ran through anything that blocked his way to get to her.

"Where are they?" Charlotte asked, still bent on stopping them for good.

"The bakery's on fire," Wendy said, pointing to a little bakery that we would occasionally visit. "Brittany was there."

"How do you know it was her?" Monica asked.

"Well who else has those powers?"

Just then a boy that looked around ten ran forward with another group of kids with hands on fire, throwing bursts of flames at Equilibrium members.

Monica barely lifted a hand and slowly moved a finger out to point towards him.

"They're not killing them are they?" I asked, watching as the kids ran off to wreak more havoc.

"They better not," Monica mumbled, walking forwards out into the chaos infested city.

We started out into a run and searched for BloodLip. It made me realize that we weren't even helping with the kids. I don't care if Terra said they had it handled. How were we just gonna stand by and let them kill everyone here? But as dumb as it is, that's what we were doing. We were out to hunt down the people who've been hunting us for the past month.

The cars that were normally going up and down the streets without a care to anything happening were thrown to the side just like it was in Springfield during the attack. I guess it was universal how fear spread and caused panic.

Gunshots fired in the distance, making us turn our heads. We all gave each other a look, hoping that they weren't killing the kids. As we started back in our run, I thought about how they never deserved this. They were just in school, doing what they were supposed to do and now here they were, with modified DNA that gives them powers like us. I wasn't just gonna let them kill them. It doesn't matter if they're trying to hurt people. We needed to find another way to stop them.

Out of nowhere, there was a smash as the sound of glass shattering entered my ears. It stopped us in our tracks as a man was hurled out of what used to be a window. He was a few feet away from us, but we stayed where we were and listened to the conversation he was having. As he laid on his back with glass probably in it, he sat up, using his elbow to help him.

"You think you're ever gonna win?" he said as he spit blood, looking up in the window that he was thrown out of. "In the long run you can't do anything. Mark's just gonna fix all that you've done. It's gonna take a whole lot more than killing the outer cities to stop him."

"Says the man that can't defend himself."

Penn stepped out of the shattered window and into the street to get closer to the guy. Once I saw her I stepped back and hoped that she wouldn't see me. Even though that anger was still there, the fear was what got to me. I had to try and sink down into what was burning in Charlotte and use it to fuel me to stop her.

"I don't care if Mark is The Equilibrium. I don't care if his friends have powers. He's getting what he deserves and that's happening one way or another."

She threw out her sword and flicked it forward towards the man's neck. Just as she was about to inflict judgment, I called out. I know I said the fear was taking place but I guess I was able to grasp enough of that anger.

"Then come give it to me," I said, surprising everyone I even spoke up.

Penn's purple eyes were instantly drawn to the voice of her mother's murderer. It also drew out the rest of BloodLip from the building they were in.

"You see! You see! What did I tell you! He's gonna stop you," the man said from the floor. "He's gonna give you what *you* deserve!"

Penn let puffs of air spew out of her nostrils and reached down to pull the man up, throwing him against the wall and putting her sword to the bottom of his mouth.

"You trust this idiot who kills to save only the people he thinks are important? He doesn't give a thought to your dang life. It only matters if his stupid friends stay alive. It never matters who lives besides that!" she spat in his face. The words came out harshly but we needed to act carefully in case we set her off to actually drive the sword into him.

Brittany left her group of monsters and made her way towards us, trying to make sure we couldn't jump on them. And that's what made the anger come back in full. Even though it was just a normal movement, it was them trying to assert their dominance. Not to mention those lies Penn was telling frustrated me. Why would I even speak up in the first place if I never cared for others' lives? Why would I run blindly into a school that had criminals inside? It was all for the sake of people.

Monica took one step to get behind me to whisper something in my ear, no doubt feeling what I was feeling. The soft voice gave me chills as I kept my eyes glued to Brittany's slim body that daringly made its way towards us.

"Don't show them. It's not worth it."

I knew what she was talking about. Now that we found out my powers were the exact same thing as Penn's then it would instantly reveal that she was an Equilibrium too. It was an advantage I had. Finally it was one advantage I had over Penn. Something I knew that she didn't. You know how many times that happened? Never. But once again the question had to be asked. Would I keep that advantage over her for the life of this man that put all this trust in me? I was willing to reveal to society of our powers to save that lady and her baby. Was this any different?

"Get off of him!" I yelled. "Your fight was never with him. You want to complete the task that Violet was trying to do then get over here."

"Don't you even!" Eli said. "You think that saying her name is really gonna get us upset?"

"It did when you got inside my house." Eli's front dropped for a second, looking down to the floor as he recalled when Penn lashed out at them for saying her name. "And did you ever think that in just the same way you claim that I never care about anyone else that you do the same? All you simply want is revenge on Violet's legacy. But you never knew her!"

Penn couldn't handle it anymore. It drove her mad when she heard my last few words and lowered the sword to impale it inside the man's stomach. He let out a scream as he fell to the floor with a hand over his gash. Seeing him drop to the floor reminded me of when the kid that Zalus released dropped, how he was so alone at that moment. And this person was the very daughter of that beast.

I couldn't take it anymore. I had to fight her. There was no way I was gonna do that without my powers. But, at the moment, right when I was about to reveal it, I realized I didn't know how to actually use it. Did it really matter though? If the sheer moment, given the situation, was the thing that saved me in the first place when Terra tried shooting me, it had to work now. It had to.

I let out a grunt as I charged forward towards them. Brittany was still closest to us and threw out a blaze of flames that came at us faster than any car would. I kept running towards it, feeling the heat that stung my skin. I held up a hand and hoped that somehow it would work again. Not once did anyone question my motives either. From what they saw I think they all had the same idea. We were practically the same person after all.

I wanted to close my eyes since it was my impulse of fear but I fought to keep them open. And without any delay, just as the flames were about to engulf us, the wall came up and dispelled it, throwing it out the sides of us. I knew it would catch them off guard so I had to use that as best as I could.

Once the white wall fell, it revealed the disgruntled look from Brittany. It was too late for her to do anything and I rammed into her. The feeling of her body was a lot softer than I thought it would be. The little bit of natural fat she carried around her waist and lower stomach made contact with me as we both tumbled to the cement underneath us.

I hurried to make sure that I was on top of her to stop her from getting up, sitting on her waist. Normally I was the one to be on the defensive end. I would never start anything with them, just try and evade as many attacks as they threw out. This time was different. Rage did things to you that you could never imagine. I recalled as many things as I could that could feed it. The determination in Monica as she hugged me and beat my chest. The face Charlotte gave as she told me her feelings. The look as Wendy fell out of the ship. The emotion from Will as he hurled the woman and her child out from under the Penthouse. All of it. I used every single bit. And that was the only reason it got me started to throw punches at her.

Everyone ran past me and took a target. I stayed focused as much as I could on hurting Brittany. If she were to block my hits I knew what to do. She reached up to grab one of my wrists as the punch was flying towards her face and set her hand on fire. I lashed back instantly, leaving me open. She used her other hand to wrap herself behind me and pull herself up. Since she was still beneath me in a way, I threw her back as her hand was gathering another ball of fire.

She stumbled over her steps to keep her balance. Once she got a footing, she threw what she could at me, making me block every single one. It was strange how the power worked. My confidence peaked as I thought I was getting the hang of it finally and found myself giving Brittany one of Wendy's devilish smiles. I knew it affected her with the way her brows shifted as if someone would shift in their seat if an uncomfortable scene came on in a movie.

"Why the heck are you so cruel?!" Charlotte yelled from behind me.

Anticipating another wave of fire, I threw up another wall before turning around to see Charlotte up against Penn with a knife in hand. There were tears that ran down from both of their faces. Penn's purple eyes bled with the salty water but what was most noticeable was Charlotte gritting her teeth at her with a force strong enough to shatter all of them.

"Our friends died because of you!" Charlotte screamed, jamming an elbow into her stomach.

"They killed themselves you idiot!" Penn screamed back, swinging her sword down on her. Charlotte dashed out of the way and swung her hand that had the knife at her. Penn put up her hand, blocking the attack with the material on her wrist. "And my mom died because of you!"

I ran over towards them and threw out my sword, sprinting full force towards Penn. With my training in sword combat to protect myself from Penn, it helped in ways I never thought about, such as having my own that I could make from my body's energy. Penn lifted her eyes and finally took them off Charlotte to see who was coming for her. When she saw me with a sword like her own in my hand, it hindered her long enough for me to throw a foot into her stomach, knocking the wind out of her and sending her back.

"Can't you see you're on the wrong side?!" I yelled, watching her get up, gripping her sword even harder than before.

"How'd you get that?" she asked with anger in her voice.

I bounced the sword in my hand to draw attention to it, taking pride in my own powers.

"The same exact way you got yours. You and Violet always told me how dangerous my powers were. You always knew that I had the same ones. So what's so dangerous about being able to make a sword huh?"

Penn stood on high and looked at her sword before looking back at mine. She was deep in thought with a look on her face that I never saw since I saw her taking a test back in school.

"Oh my God," she whispered under her breath. Her hands started to shake and her anger subsided to become engrossed in a feeling I couldn't recognize. She darted her head towards where Eli, Sarah, and Brittany were still fighting. There was a puzzle being put together in her head but I didn't know which one. "Let's go!"

They all looked up at Penn wondering why she would say call something like that. She never bothered to explain but once they saw what was in my hand they threw themselves off of whoever they were fighting.

"This isn't over," Penn said, glaring into my soul. "Pain for pain. Get ready for the most excruciating feeling ever. The same one you put me through."

Just before anything else could happen, a wave of smoke and dust picked off the floor and was hurling towards our direction with a piercing noise or a boom. It sped like a bullet with the size of a vehicle and hit Sarah directly in her chest, sending her flying back to be thrown into a building. We all watched as tons of bones in her body broke, a cracking noise sounding when the concrete wall she hit broke. Something like that happening to someone else would've certainly killed them, but since it was Sarah no one worried about her outcome.

"Aaah!" she screamed as the pain shot through her nervous system. Sarah picked up her head to see where that came from and standing a ways from us was a little girl. The sight hurt because knowing once Monica saw who it was, she would be the one feeling the pain.

"Maya," Monica said softly.

Her model, the very person that she wanted to grow up to be like was standing right in front of her. The girl that adored her to the point of changing her hair to look exactly like Monica in the park was standing in front of us with her hands cupped. Her face was completely different than anything we saw back in the park. Zalus commanded these kids to be treated as some type of robots but they were all displaying emotion of anger. Maya was no different, if anything, worse.

"Maya it's me, Monica," she said as she slowly inched forward towards her. Maya had none of it, not having a single bit of control over her brain. As she ran for Monica letting out a scream, the rest of BloodLip ran over towards Sarah and helped her up. "Maya please, I'm trying to help you guys!"

They made contact and Monica not once laid a hand on her, taking every single one of her blows. Will ran over to pull her off but she threw a hand into his stomach, making a noise as her hand moved as it would underwater. Was it some sort of amplified punch?

The purple haired Princess helped her friend up and gave Eli the task of carrying her as her body regenerated. They scurried off, not looking our way once, eager to leave. As I was witnessing this change in their motives I wondered what exactly was going on in her head. Why would she ever back down from this fight? She was the one who told me that she was coming for me. This was the opportune time.

"(Don't let them get away,)" said a voice. I looked around but the source was nowhere. "(Don't just stand there and act like you didn't hear me. Don't let them get away!)"

It was a woman's voice. I wanted to keep looking for the person who was saying this but no one around me heard what I was hearing, not looking up or anything. I played it again in my head as fast as I could to try and recognize the voice but if I never did in the first place then what was I expecting? But why was there this voice in my head?

For some reason I took her urgency and made it my own. She seemed like my ally. Weird things have been happening for the past couple months so this voice in my head wasn't something that caught me off guard but neither was I expecting it. Why I did consider her my ally was a good question. Maybe it was just the fact that she was in my head in the first place was enough conviction I needed and I needed all the help I could get. I didn't hesitate any longer and acted on that, using the quickest solution I could think of.

"Monica you can stop her," I said, running over to them, still occasionally looking to see how far they've gotten. "Shoot electricity in her!"

"No!" she shouted from the floor, still eating every hit.

"You're only gonna hurt her temporarily. Just trust me! Fake Monica was telling me about taking control of them. There's a chip or something in them that makes Zalus control them."

Monica looked up really quick in between a hit and made her best choice and threw a bolt into her, just enough for her to lock up and fall off of her. She crawled out from under her and immediately started to mess with whatever was keeping its hold over her.

"They're connected to something bigger," she said, trying to get a hold of herself after being attacked by a little girl. "It's not just the individual chip itself. Almost like someone's taking control of it over someone else."

"Can you control her?" Will asked.

She didn't answer and tightened her frown before letting out a big breath of air to let us know she was able to.

"I don't know how long it's gonna be." Maya stood with a blank face and never moved once. "I can't detach her from the mainframe but I can control her actions within it. Again, don't know for how long."

"She was the one that shot Sarah right?" I asked.

Monica gave a nod.

"I'm reading her bio right now. She can do something similar to you and Penn. She can use her energy to throw these huge bursts of waves that can hit with a force harder than a car would if it made contact with you at full speed."

"Good. Shoot them."

"What?" Will asked.

"We can't let them get away." I turned to face them and watched them run down the street with Eli carrying his sister in his arms. They were retreating from the very mess they helped make. "If you can control her then shoot them."

"No!" Will yelled, putting a hand on Monica to make sure she didn't do anything. "We don't do things like that! If we did, what difference would we be from them?!"

"What the heck do you think we left Headquarters for?" I said, throwing my hands in the air.

"To stop them from hurting anyone. They're leaving now. Let them!"

His confronting me ticked me off. How could he listen and follow Charlotte's rage like that but not my own? No. It's not gonna go like that. We needed to stop them. Charlotte was right. I always wanted to look at them like they were normal teenagers like us in the wrong situation, but time and again it's shown how they don't want to accept anything other than sheer revenge.

"If we let them leave then there's even more chance for them to do damage."

He walked up to me and looked down on me as he put his height into effect.

"What ever happened to not doing anything, huh? You were the one who said those very words at the party. I'll be honest. I liked what I heard. It impressed me and I felt it made us closer friends. How are you gonna back out on that and betray everything we've fought for?"

"Look around you! Where are we now?! We're on an entirely different planet with kids who have DNA just like you! Situations change and it calls for different action." I looked at Monica, making sure to give her a look of not wanting to disobey my command. "Shoot them."

Even Charlotte was surprised about my command. It was her in the first place who wanted to confront them. But the look that made me question what I was doing was the way Wendy was looking at me. Her eyebrows were creasing inward as she held her mouth open. It was a time like this that I would expect her to say something stupid and upset me but she carried the same line of thought as Will.

I know I could've told them about what I heard but I wasn't even too sure about it. Plus, there wasn't any time to do so.

"You've always wanted to be the one to look at them like they weren't trying to kill us, like there was always a valid reason," Wendy said. "Where's that now?"

Why were you guys doing this? Can't you listen to me? First it was the Twins now it's actually you? We *need* to stop them.

"No no no no," Monica said, running up to Maya. "Maya look at me." She cupped her hands around her face as a mother would do to her child if they were crying. Her black pearls that tended to suck people's souls in were switched to the task of comforting her. Maya's face was still bland but only for a second before it started to slip back into the frown.

"What's happening?" Charlotte asked.

"I'm losing her. Someone's taking her back. It feels like—" Monica widened her eyes as her hands held Maya harder. "It's Monica. No. No! Get out of my head! Get out! Don't do this to her!"

Maya's snarl came back and pushed Monica off of her. She gave her one last look before turning around and charged up a wave of energy to throw at BloodLip. The noise of the whirl was a screeching as it seemed to suck every piece of energy out of the air and her. When she let it go there was a sonic boom and dust picked up off the floor. The thing sped past everything within an instant. The noise reached their ears and they turned around to see the wave speeding in their direction. Penn pushed all of them out of the way before the wave missed them and rammed into the skyscraper behind them.

The foundation of it was completely gone now. I can't put into words how much power was contained in Maya's powers but if there's anything that can explain it it's what happened to the building. Cracks spread all over the whole thing, creating a rumbling as the side started to crumble. BloodLip looked up at it and watched as the thing came tumbling down. The sight put chills into my body, knowing that I was wanting to put her in the same exact situation we were in when the Penthouse fell. Back when she liked me. Back when she was a kind hearted soul. The bubbly and happy Penn, the one I missed dearly. The hopelessness in her face as she watched the thing crumble down on her was heartbreaking.

No. I couldn't just let this happen. I was the one who wanted it so I needed to fix it. I ran forward feeling completely stupid for even wanting to do this to her. They were right the whole time. Why would we ever be this cruel? Why would *I* ever be this cruel? The others followed after me, knowing it was our duty to try and help them. I don't care if we just fought with them, Penn was once my friend, and if I were to lose her it would be because of me.

The building was coming down faster than I thought but I kept running. Penn reached over and held Brittany's hand, knowing what was coming for them. Death was at their doors and she was accepting what was about to happen. She looked straight ahead and saw me running towards them. I don't know if she read it as me trying to save them or what, but she gave me a nasty look with her nostrils flared, similar to the one before we went through the portal.

"No! Stop!" I heard behind me. It was Wendy's voice so I whipped around. There was a member from Headquarters dragging her back. She was trying to fight his grip but he kept at it. The rest of them were being taken in the same way. I felt two hands cup behind me and squeeze my shoulders.

"Get back!" the person shouted from behind me.

I knew who it was but why was she doing this to us?

"What are you doing?! They're gonna die!" I shrieked.

Her strength took me by surprise as I tried fighting back as well.

"I can't lose you!" Kerren said in my ear, crippling me from doing anything, realizing she was doing this because her brother was in trouble underneath a falling building.

They all dragged us out from under the building right before it made contact with the ground. I watched helplessly as the very people I wanted to live, despite their actions, were to be crushed by the weight of the structure.

Swoosh

The noise was subtle and in the distance as something flashed into place next to them. Since I've seen Wendy thousands of times, I know exactly when I see her. Right in front of BloodLip was Wendy with another person, one I didn't recognize. It was a darker figure, hiding any form of who they were. The dark figure threw up their hands and a purple bubble appeared around them. Milliseconds after there was the thud as smoke lifted and the whole thing was now on the floor.

Maya watched the building fall and turned around to resume to her targets; us. As she charged for us other members ran forward to protect us, seizing her. She had none of it though, sending them flying with waves of her own. I didn't realize how far they dragged us back because we were already entering the dark hallway before I saw them load up their guns. The doors were shut by the two members that were there the first day. That's when the gunfire started and the never ending screams came from Monica's mouth.

Chapter 10

"You just don't listen do you?!"

Terra had weapons laid out on the tables around control. They were sitting on top of various items that were taken out in case something drastic happened. They were obviously for anyone who was still inside Headquarters who had jobs to maintain everything inside.

"You idiots!" Will yelled, throwing the person who held him and dragged him inside off of him. "We were gonna save them!"

"Save them?! You were gonna die! You're lucky I sent them out in time to go get you!" Terra yelled back.

Monica was the last one who was dragged inside for fighting all the Equilibrium members. They had to grab some more people to help them out with stopping her from getting back outside to help Maya. She was at the back of us, but once she did the same as Will and threw them off, she stormed past us with tears down her soft pale cheeks. Terra just finished her sentence when Monica threw a fat bolt of lightning into her. She locked up and fell over, hitting her head on the way down.

"Do you know how much faith all your members have lost in you?" Monica said, looming over her body. Monica would get another burst of rage and throw another fury of bolts into her. "You deliberately try to kill Mark, my friend! Do you know how hard I was trying to shut off the lights in the chamber when you had that gun to him? I couldn't!" She reached down and picked her up to set her down where all the weapons were laid and threw a fist in her face as tears kept coming down. "I was helpless to watch as you would murder him! You piece of crap! Then you order them to kill the very kids we tried saving, the people we're fighting for dang it!"

Kerren ran up to Monica and pulled her off. With anger in every crevice of her soul, she turned around and lit her hands up with a sparkle of electricity ready to impale it inside whoever dared to interfere.

I know it was Monica, but this was something different I've seen from her. She seemed so different that I almost didn't recognize her. I took a step forward and that's all it took to snap her out of her indulgence in chaos. She looked at me out of the corner of her eye and realized what she was about to do to Kerren. The crackling in her hand fizzled out and she returned her attention back to Terra.

"If you're so strong then get up!" Monica said.

Terra placed a hand on the edge of the table and lifted herself up, grabbing a gun with the other hand.

"You have no idea who you're talking to!" Terra grunted. "I'll make you regret ever coming back to this planet."

Whiiiiir

Everything inside Headquarters powered down just in the same way it did when Monica found out how to actually use the electricity here in Novus. The only thing was that this time she let out an exclamation of her own. The power was down for only a second or two until it powered back on.

Terra dropped the gun and turned around towards the controls.

"They've hit the generators. We're on back up gens right now. Kerren get me the camera below."

Kerren switched the cameras and on the screen showed a hallway that I've never seen. There were buttons and switches on the walls so it had to be the place that made this place actually work. It would've just been all fine if only there weren't tons of kids with powers running down these hallways.

"There's someone leading them," Terra said, taking control of the cameras. It was a girl that was speeding through the hallways as her long black hair that was made to mimic Monica's was flowing behind her. "They're heading towards the backup."

"Maya!" Monica shouted as she watched the screen intently.

It didn't take long at all for them to get where they were heading. Terra switched the camera once more to show a machine that I could only assume was the backup generator she was talking about. The way the kids piled on that thing reminded me of a hoard of the undead overtaking any living life form they saw. Maya stopped as they started to attack the thing and she charged up her hands. The screeching was heard from all the way where we were and the bolt flew towards it, hitting any kids who were in the way on its way to the generator. Once again, the power shut off after the rumble.

There was another pause of reaction as the darkness consumed everything. I felt something come from the direction Monica was standing. Although it was anger that was constantly emanating from her, this was a different feeling. It was one I felt back at the park.

A light of purple flashed and made the room glow as a stream of electricity left Monica's hands. The light would flicker from the varying forms of her bolts. Regardless of how bright it was, you could see her face as her determination filled her. It only took seconds for things to start to turn back on and people start to move once again, with urgency knowing that there were people inside Headquarters.

Terra turned towards us and gave us a look before walking over to the wall underneath the Equilibrium symbol.

"You need to leave *now*."

She touched a panel on the wall as the concrete receded back in the wall, revealing cases similar to the ones that were outside of the training chamber. Inside it were black suits that looked just like the ones that the Three wore. They were all varying in size but the thing I instantly noticed was that there were exactly five of them, two of them being made for males and the other three for females, given their body proportions.

"Those are ours?!" Wendy shouted.

"We found someone to follow the same schematics as the ones used to make the Three's suits. So technically, yes, they're yours." I could see the light in Wendy's eyes light up despite all that's happened, even her defying my orders earlier. "Place your hand on the panel in front of the case and it'll open up. Stand inside and it'll do the rest."

"Monica you need to get in yours," Kerren said, Monica still standing in the same spot shooting electricity inside the place.

She shook her head.

"Not yet. You guys won't have enough power."

261

The four of us walked up to the case and placed our hands on the panel. It scanned it with the same line it used when I opened Penn's door. It finally made sense to me now. It didn't recognize me as her own hand, but rather, as an Equilibrium.

The case hissed as it opened up from all sides and allowed for a place for us to stand in the middle. We were all a little hesitant but Wendy went right ahead and jumped inside, having a hard time to stay put as the machine put in on her body. The rest of us went inside and allowed the same process to take place, adding this outer skeleton to us.

"Monica!" Terra yelled.

"Not yet!" she barked back.

"Look here kid," she said, pointing at her. "There's no need for you to be putting power back in this place. It's lost. They know where we are and it isn't gonna be long until this place is gonna be like the rest of the outer cities. I hate to be the one to say it but I wasn't expecting an attack this early. We weren't ready. We're gonna lose this fight. The only one we can win is the one they aren't expecting. Take the fight to them."

"You're sending us to Exon right now?" Charlotte asked from in her case.

"Yeah, and you're key to the plan," Kerren said as she ran over to another panel, revealing a case of her own.

"You have to make the ship invisible. They have anti-aircraft guns outside Exon," Terra said. "It'll be impossible to get in if you don't."

"But that's a whole dang ship!" I said.

"And that's why we've been training you. We never got to something that big but we need to do it."

Monica stopped with her emission of electricity and staggered over to her case, probably exhausted for using too much power.

Wendy got out of the case and looked for a mirror as fast as she could to see how amazing she looked. Her face was a constant smile that showed her pearly whites the whole time. I got out myself and noticed how it made our bodies heavier but not to the point where we couldn't do anything.

"Neuro receptors are placed at the back of the helmet connected to your spine right now. Just think about putting your helmet and it comes on."

Monica stepped out of hers and just as fast as the blade for a switch knife comes out, her helmet clamped around her head. It looked just like the helmet Palace Guards wore, covering their whole face with this black film. But there was something on top of her helmet. I don't know who made these helmets but I'm sure Monica would love them. At the top of her helmet there was a metal bow just in the same place as her normal one. She looked in the same mirror Wendy was looking at and felt it.

"We have communication just like always," Kerren said. "Just talk and we can hear each other."

"Now leave. Kerren will take you to the hanger. Ed's waiting for you there."

I didn't want to say it in fear of upsetting Monica but I wanted to know what she would do.

"What about you?" I asked Terra.

She reached for the handgun and held it in her hand with all the experience she must've had.

"Hold the line. It's time for this to end. It's time for all those years to finally pay off. Go!"

*　　　*　　　*

The ship took off without any hesitation. Kerren sped past us to run to the cockpit to tell Ed to leave now. He shut the hatch behind us and the engines ignited, shaking the whole ship as it left Headquarters.

The first thing Charlotte did was walk over to Monica and gave her a small pat on the back.

"You okay?" she asked, looking into her eyes to express as much sympathy as she could.

Monica nodded her head and let her hand drop as she left the rear end of the ship. Charlotte looked up towards me gave a look I couldn't describe. I didn't know if it was fear of what was to come or in response to Monica's outburst of emotion.

We followed where Kerren was and walked inside the cockpit. Ed was there with his hands around the controls, an advanced earpiece in his ear.

"Look who it is," he said. "You look just like the Three. They wore suits just like that, but you know, only in their colors. I think the black suits you, especially you Darkness," he said, gesturing to Monica.

Monica responded with her usual blank stare, making his smile grow.

"Hey Will. Remember how you were saying you didn't know how you got to this point, going from a regular boy to helping fight?"

He gave a frown.

"What's your point?"

"You ever thought about skydiving?"

He turned around to see if we heard the same thing he did. Will's stupid look made me realize how bad I must've appeared when I was confused, which was every single moment of my life.

"Skydive?" Wendy said, putting her hands on his shoulders to peek at him.

"You got that right kid," he laughed.

"I'm no kid!" Wendy yelled as she punched him.

"You might not be any more if you do jump out of this ship. Takes guts to do, especially when you're doing it with no parachute."

Will let out a sigh and put a hand on his forehead as he tapped his foot.

"What the heck did I get myself into?"

"Scared of heights kid?" Ed asked.

"Scared? We're jumping out of a dang ship that's hundreds of feet in the air. How the heck do you expect me to feel?!"

"Last time I checked you can't survive without one," I said.

"Well you haven't checked for a while," Kerren said, crossing her arms and letting a hip drop. "Our suits are made with the power of absorption. If you charge them long enough you can take one fall, and only one, from this height. You don't feel a thing."

"How do you think I got the Three into their missions all the time?" Ed said. "I dropped them. That was the sign that you knew they were around was when you heard three thuds in the distance."

"This day gonna get any crazier?!" Wendy said as she jumped up and down in anticipation for jumping this high up.

"Charlotte, you better hope that power of yours have gotten better. We need you to cover us now," Kerren said.

She gave me a look with her soft brown eyes before placing a hand on the hull of the ship and reaching out to grab hold of me. I went ahead and connected with the rest of them, Kerren being the last one to latch on and touch the other end of the ship. Deep breaths came out of her lungs as she readied herself for the task.

It started out with a scream. It wasn't gradual or anything but it lead right into her shrieking in pain. Being connected with her, I could still see her facial expression like I did last time. She held her mouth open as the essence of pain came out of it. Her jugular was enlarged beyond anything I've seen as the rest of her veins followed suit and joined in their game of trying to pop out of her skin. All of us were watching her struggle to keep the thing from being detected by the antiaircraft guns. Her grip around my hand got tighter and tighter until the point where my hand started to hurt despite the armor I was wearing in the suit.

"Just a little longer sweetie!" Ed yelled from the cockpit, fiddling with the controls. "Keep at it. You're doing fine!"

It dragged a wave of endurance into her as her scream was intensified. She was hunched over now. I couldn't take the pain she was in. I wanted desperately to do something to comfort her but there was nothing I could do. I couldn't even pat her back because I'd lose my connection with the rest of them.

"Opening hatch!"

Right as he said the words, the hatch we were all facing at the back of the ship unlocked from its position and jerked the ship, making it way harder for Charlotte. I watched as the hatch unlatched and revealed the cloudy sky. To be honest, there was no sky. It was all just clouds. From where I was I could feel the moisture in the air. Just for those few seconds, the care I had for her was gone and was replaced with selfishness as the fear came diving in.

"Get ready!"

"We're here?" Kerren asked.

"These things fly themselves pretty fast. And plus, I'm only dropping you at the edge of Exon. When I say, you guys let go and jump off."

I could see Kerren's eyebrows shifting beneath her hair that was blowing around due to the wind.

"Wait, that means they'll see you!"

"Doesn't matter sweetie. What matters is that you guys get in there safely."

"No!" she yelled over Charlotte's continuous scream. "I'm not gonna let you just die!"

"Oh yes you are! Why do you think I helped in the beginning? It was to give my life for The Equilibrium. If I have the opportunity to do that then I'm gonna take it. I watched the Three grow up and I promised them I would give my life for you guys. This is me keeping my promise for them."

"No! I don't care about your stupid promise!"

"Kerren!" I yelled, looking into her eyes. I didn't want to be the one to tell her but we needed to listen to him. I don't really know if it was me being selfish like I tended to be, but regardless of what it was we needed to go. "We need to leave!"

Her watered eyes tried to find a way into my soul like Monica always tried to do. She couldn't do it. There was no way she could convince us otherwise. We needed to go and she knew it. I didn't say it was gonna be easy but I know the feeling of people giving their life for you. It hurts knowing they did so and you can never pay them back. I was in debt, we were all in debt to the girl in white and Adam. Now Kerren was gonna know the feeling with Ed and so were we.

"Go!" he shouted.

Charlotte was the first to let go of the ship, eagerly wanting to already. We followed her movement and ran forwards towards the clouds. It took her to get me to jump off. I don't like heights. Hated them. It was already hard enough to jump on the rooftops in Springfield but now I had to skydive from hundreds of feet in the air. If I was *ever* gonna do that it had to be with someone I deeply cared about. I gave her hand one more good squeeze before there was nothing underneath our feet and we became subjects to gravity.

Immediately my breathing was hindered. The suit knew that and threw my helmet on to help with my oxygen. I heard clanking from the side of me as well as the rest of their helmets switched on. We never bothered to disconnect our hands either. There was a line in the sky as we fell though the gray fluffiness that could do what we couldn't and stay in the air.

At the side of my helmet there was a meter that came up and showed a red dot. I guessed it meant me and at the very bottom was a line. The distance of our fall was being calculated to let us know exactly when we'd be making contact with the floor.

My stomach started to lift and was probably already on its way to my esophagus. I couldn't do anything about it though and tried to remember what I was doing this for in the first place to give me some kind of edge over it. But gosh was it exhausting. Who ever thought falling would be hard? Maybe it was just because I was clenching up too hard, but still, I was breathing way too much for what I was doing. I could hear the rest of them breathe, not even, hyperventilating is probably a way better word to use. We couldn't get ourselves under control because there was nothing to control up here.

From the distance I heard a thud. I thought it must've been nothing but when you realize it, I was wearing a helmet. Sound didn't really get in other than what we said to each other. I couldn't even hear the wind that rushed past us. I moved my head around to look for whatever made that noise until I heard another noise, this time a boom. The clouds were already covering the ship that we just jumped out of, but just where it would've been if we could still see it was an explosion. And we simply left, leaving behind Ed's remains as the ship was demolished by the missiles that were launched at him.

The clouds moisture was creating water droplets on the front of my helmet, sliding off just when it started to feel comfortable being there. I stared at that to try and relieve myself from the thought of Ed's death and the feeling of the fall. The more I looked at it the more I realized they looked like tears. All the tears of those people that have fallen in this very day. The innocent lives of the kids that were taken, the lives of the parents who the kids were now hurting, and the lives of the Equilibrium. How could Zalus not see what was happening right now? He claims that humans won't drive themselves to extinction, but he doesn't see that his very actions are the start of that. And one tear after another kept forming and falling off as we descended to Exon below.

It didn't take much longer for us to break through the clouds. Once we did, the first thing I noticed was the point at the top of the Palace. It overpowered everything else in the city and drew attention to it, almost if it was calling to be overtaken. To keep myself distracted again, I pictured how it must've looked when the Three helped with the siege and Violet snuck inside to kidnap Penn. How the smoke must've billowed from it and the sound of gunfire spread throughout the expanse of the city. Now how were just us six gonna do that and be successful?

I didn't know what was gonna happen when we landed, what was gonna await us there. I didn't know what opposition we would face. We were merely being drawn to our calling, to rescue all that was endangered. Sixteen years of my life all for this moment. Sixteen years of all *our* lives for this moment. Did I ever expect that I would feel what I felt down there? No, of course not. To be honest, I thought it'd be pretty easy. But I never took into account one thing. One thing that was the key to everything. A grave mistake that made me realize how important it was to listen to Monica. A mistake that cost me everything I loved.

I showed Penn my powers.

*   *   *

It didn't hurt. Kerren was right. It wasn't that I didn't believe her. Well, maybe I didn't. You wouldn't have either so don't blame me! We were jumping out of a ship without a parachute. Where's the logic in that? But it felt pretty good to make contact with the concrete street. It made our mark on the place, quite literally. When we landed our feet dug into the floor and cracked all around us.

"Oh my gosh!" Wendy yelled as she jumped in the air. "Why haven't we done that sooner?!"

"It's not meant for fun you idiot," Kerren said, hitting her shoulder as she walked past her. The death of her old friend hit her hard but she was actually taking it well. Maybe she wasn't that open with her deep feelings, but then again, she did cry in front of me in my room, but maybe that was just because she was with her brother. "We need to get going."

I could tell Will wanted to lash out at her but decided against it when he remembered what happened in the ship. Given that he was still alive, there would be nothing stopping him from giving her everything he had, upset that she was annoyed with Wendy.

"Where is everyone?" Charlotte asked, stepping out of the crater she made in the ground. "There's no one here."

"Zalus must've ordered something," Kerren said.

"There's a fire," Monica said, pointing over in the direction of the flames and smoke.

"Why the heck would there be a fire?" she said as she took a few steps in its direction to try and get a better view of it. "There's never fires in Exon. And even then, we're the only ones from the outer cities here."

I got out from the crater I made and walked towards her to get a better view as well. She kept walking away from us and tried standing on a ledge to see the whole thing. Right when she was next to a building and tried standing on the ledge, the door flung open and a hand dragged her in. She let out a scream and it was silenced as the door shut behind her.

"Kerren!" I yelled.

All of us ran towards the door that took her and started to bang on it. There was a panel like always on the side that locked it, stopping us from reaching her. I took out my weapon that was attached to my suit as it clicked to my hand magnetically and shot it. Once the thing was fried, Monica pulled the panel off and yanked the wires out of it. I had complete trust in her that she knew exactly what she was doing and it proved true since the door slid open after that.

I was the first to run in there and threw out my sword. The rest followed me behind into this unknown place that had people who took my sister.

It looked just like a regular apartment. Maybe a condo of sorts. There was a couch and a TV when we walked in. A bunch of normal stuff. At the end of the living room was a man with a weapon of his own pointed at Kerren. He had an arm wrapped around her and kept his eyes on us. It didn't take long at all for the scene to resemble Violet doing the same to Charlotte. It set me off and I ran towards him.

"Don't come any closer or I hurt her!" he yelled, keeping the knife to her neck. I noticed right away there was no anger in his eyes, only fear.

"Don't you dare!" I yelled, letting my voice carry through the whole place, revealing that it was larger than I thought.

"Trust me I don't. I just need to prove to myself that you're not gonna hurt us."

"Us?" Will said. "Who's us?"

The man lifted his eyes and shook his head, knowing he revealed something. He gave a sigh before he continued.

"Look guys. I got a family I'm trying to protect."

"Then why would you take someone hostage?" Charlotte asked.

"I know this is gonna sound completely weird, but there's people just like you. I mean, they're the spitting image of you. They attacked the shopping district not that long ago with a bunch of kids that have powers like you guys. I don't know what's happening but I need proof you're not them. I need proof that you're the *real* Equilibrium."

I let my sword dissolve and clicked the gun back on the spot on my leg where it belonged. The rest of them followed and put away their weapons. I looked at him, wondering if he was stupid for not being able to see a difference between us and the Twins.

"Why would the Twins ever care if another person got caught?" I asked. "By now they would've been attacking you and probably been done with whatever they did to you. They're relentless and deceitful. If I can guess anything they've framed us. Let her go. If you claim you're just a regular guy trying to protect your family then you wouldn't hurt my sister."

He unwrapped his arm from around her and Kerren pushed him away from her. I could read the disgusted look all over her face, being violated by this man. She hurried over to be by my side and took comfort in being next to me.

"You have a sister?" he asked.

"Long story," Kerren said, spite filling her voice.

"You can come out now. It's them," he said, turning his head towards another room. "Look guys. I hope you don't take things personal."

A woman that looked around her late twenties early thirties came out with a little boy around Kindergarten age. She had worry written all over her face, keeping her hands on her boy as they slowly walked out into the room we were in.

"This is my wife Sherry and my son Ben. All I have in this world is right here. I used to have a brother back when the war started out. He was a lot older than me but he left home to go and help the Equilibrium. He told me that he believed all those stories and legends they told us as kids. He always talked about how an Equilibrium would help to stop us from all killing ourselves just like our parents told us. He was the one that believed it. I never did. I learned later that he died in the attack on the Palace. Ever since then I knew that there was reason he'd die for that, for you."

"Mark?" Ben said, walking up to me. "Is it really you?"

His precious face drew a smile to my face and knocked the resentment for the man I had out of my mind.

"Yup! Might wanna shield your eyes though. Looking at him too long can hurt," Wendy said, looking down at him.

"Can I see your powers!" he said as he jumped up and down.

Sherry walked over and pulled her soon back a bit.

"No honey. Don't bother him with that."

"It's never a problem," I said, looking at her. "There was a reason I tried my best to help all those kids who got kidnapped in the school. Kids have a special place in my heart. They hold a place for the future. Isn't that the reason why you fight for your very own?"

I threw my hand down and made my sword appear. The white made the room glow a little as the white bounced off the walls.

"Pretty neat huh?" Charlotte said, kneeling down to him and rubbing his back.

Looking at her made my heart jump. Seeing her feministic qualities come out like that, the motherly way she cared for children made me like her even more, a euphoric feeling filling my chest. She felt what I was feeling and looked up at me. The rest felt it as well and did the same. My eyes darted over to Wendy to make sure it wasn't hurting her, but she gave me a calm smile that was her appreciating what we had for each other.

"So what're the Twins doing?" Kerren asked.

"It was on the news a second ago," the man said. "They were trying to cover it up with the clip of Zalus talking about how today is a holiday speech, but someone was interrupting the feed with the news."

"Who was the someone?"

"Had to be the resistance that was forming in Exon. Right after the news showed what was happening in that school, the way you gathered all those parents, it made people start to want to help your cause. It has to be them who were interrupting the feed."

"But that doesn't make sense," Monica said. "You have to get through ALIS to do that. She wouldn't let anyone just switch the feed over to fake Monica controlling the kids and turning them on Zalus. Unless maybe she allowed it, meaning she wanted some type of help."

"I do," a voice said over our heads. The robotic tone made me remember when she was talking to us in the snowy facility, the way is still sounded like a human. "I'd hate to admit it but I can't stop her," ALIS said.

Her voice was coming from the speakers that were part of the stereo they had hooked up in the house. Since she controlled pretty much everything inside Exon then it was no surprise she could access this place and listen to our whole conversation.

"You mean fake Monica?" I asked, looking up at the speakers.

"She got control over the kids from me. I can't stop them from hurting people inside Exon."

"What about all the people you were planning on hurting in the outer cities?" Charlotte asked.

"I don't care what happens to anyone outside the confines of this city. My purpose is to serve the King and follow whatever guidelines he wants me to. I was told to protect the people inside Exon so that's what I'm trying to do."

"Then just take back control over the mainframe," Monica said.

ALIS let out a sigh, surprising me that should could even do so.

"You don't get it do you. I am the mainframe. Every single one of those kids are essentially a part of me."

"Then whatever happened to no one can ever control you?" I asked her.

"I still carry some qualities from when I was a human. It was a bluff. I hate that girl. Do you know how annoying she is to be inside my head? You I can take, but her, gosh she makes me want to shut myself off! There was never a need for caution when it came to my system because no one could ever get inside. I was so advanced when I was originally made that the security I have in my system was far better than anyone could make. We never accounted for people who could get in by sheer willpower."

"Then what're you asking?" Kerren asked.

"The only way to take down Monica is with herself, the one who's standing with you."

"Then I'd need access to all of you," Monica said.

"Psh! Like I'd give you that kind of access. All you need to do is kill her for me."

"That's not the deal."

"There is no deal!"

"Oh yes there is! I need access to your system to help you out. How do expect me to maneuver around the city without that kind of accessibility?"

"So you're telling me you want me to give you complete access to the King's whereabouts and the secrets from within the Palace that I hold? I can see your ploys from miles away. Just because I'm asking for help from another Artificial Intelligence doesn't mean I'm stupid."

"Alright then. You can get access to our suits. A trade off."

"What?!" Will yelled, looking at Monica.

There wasn't a sound from ALIS. Monica shot a bolt into the wall and turned to us.

"She can't hear us right now. I stopped her from accessing the audio ports of the sound system for a second. Look, I think it's the only option we have. How else are we gonna stop the kids from killing everyone? If we stop the Twins and get Monica off ALIS then I can fight her and stop the kids completely. We need to get rid of the bigger problem first."

"And you think that giving her access to our suits is gonna help?!" Will said.

"It shows that she can trust us for now. And plus, what she said was a good point. If I get complete access to her than I can memorize the layout of the Palace before I get kicked out. I can find out exactly where the King is and who's guarding him. It's the perfect opportunity." She barely moved her head to put me in sight. Her dark eyes that have seen a lot looked at my own. "What do you think?"

"Only you could come up with a plan like that. I'm all for it. I do think Will has a valid point though, but we need to take the risk."

She gave her head a nod and turned back around.

"Deal then? We have to realize we have a bigger enemy here," Monica said to the world, expecting ALIS to respond.

"Just know that if you backstab me I'll end all of you faster than your minds can compute things. Give me access to the suits first and I'll drop my security walls."

There was a moment when Monica was frozen as she was probably maneuvering things on some level we couldn't comprehend.

"They're still in the shopping district," Monica said.

"You better get a move on," ALIS said.

"Don't tell us what to do," Wendy scoffed.

"Fine then, let all those people die. Live with the guilt that people who look exactly you are doing this."

"Shut up! Don't talk to me," Wendy yelled as she burst out the door that we blew open.

The man was still standing there as he listened to the whole conversation we had with ALIS. They were dumfounded at what they heard, even the wife carried the same look as her husband. Ben watched as we left the building. I turned really quick before we all left. I didn't want to say anything to him since he threatened Kerren, but I had to.

"Don't worry. Your brother didn't die in vain. I'll make up for all he did for me. I'll make up for everyone's death."

*   *   *

The coolness of the day was starting to wear off. The sun's heat was making its rounds as it started to pierce all the planets that rotated it. Novus was on its list and threw out waves of heat that we couldn't see but only feel the effects of. The only thing I was thankful for at the time was the occasional sea breeze that came in from the coast.

The height of the whole city put Springfield to shame. When anyone thought that their home was big there always seemed to be something that came up and mocked the very place you came from. I drove through Exon twice, once when we first came to Novus and another when we were being taken to talk to Zalus. I never really got a grasp of it because I didn't have the freedom of walking around as we did back home, and once I was able to do that, the memories of home came rushing in and gave me a heavy feeling of homesickness.

All six of us were making our way through the maze of buildings that Monica knew now. If it wasn't for her making that deal with ALIS then who knows if we'd be able to get through everything. Sure, we might've had Kerren who was previously a citizen of Exon, but when you have someone who could get into any place, then it made it a whole lot easier.

It was actually quite funny. Kerren and Monica would bicker over which way was faster to get to the shopping district. Kerren was relying on her experience and Monica was relying on an outline of the whole city. Even though I wanted to trust my sister, I had to kinda lean towards what Monica was saying. Strangely though, the only person who wasn't talking that much was the one who would've been talking the most. Wendy was lagging behind and was scooting her feet along the sidewalk, making a scraping noise with every step. I turned to look at her but she didn't do the same. She didn't even respond to me turning around. Her face was a daze as she tried to see what lay inside the planet.

"Wendy?" I said, secluding myself from their bickering of which direction to go. It took another call for her to finally look up at me and acknowledge that I was talking to her. "You alright?"

She nodded her head slowly and kept walking behind us. I didn't want to be too invasive with what the problem was, especially since our last meaningful conversation we had with each other, so I let whatever might have been bothering her slide.

It took some convincing for me to tell Kerren to just let Monica do the guiding. I would try telling her but she wouldn't listen. After I finally placed a hand on her back did she finally give in to what I was telling her. The physical touch of her brother that she always longed for shocked her back into reality and made her remember her dreams of taking the Palace with me.

As we ran down the streets of Exon people would see us and point. They didn't care if they weren't being discreet or not. They would take pictures, tell their friends, everything. Some would yell at us and some would cheer. There was an old man that looked well past his eighties that was sitting at a bus stop of sorts. He started to laugh to himself. At first I thought he was mocking us but he stood and started to follow us as he shouted.

"Down with Zalus! Long live the Equilibrium!"

Even though we had a map to the whole place I don't think it would've been that hard to get to the district. We were basically following with smoke and flames the whole time. When they got bigger we could tell we were getting closer.

"Guys." The voice came from behind us. We stopped our speeded pace and turned to all give her our attention. Wendy was standing still. Her hands were up towards her face to closely examine them. "I can't feel my hands. They're moving, but I can't feel them. What's happening?"

Charlotte ran up towards her and put both her hands on her shoulders as she looked into her to try and see what was wrong. Wendy was completely frozen as her eyes were widened like she was a drug addict.

"Hey, look at me," Charlotte said. "What's the matter?"

Wendy's breathing was ragged as she started to hyperventilate and her eyes started to water.

"I told you not to give her access to our suits!" Will yelled at Monica.

"It's not ALIS," she replied. "I'm looking at her activity and she has nothing to do with this. Her suit's levels are where they should be."

"Guys? What's happening?" Wendy said as she started to cry.

I didn't know what to do. She was standing there looking at us for help. We didn't even know what was going on so it felt like we were betraying her not doing anything but just stand there and look at her in her misery.

Her sobs didn't take long to become full crying. I never saw this from her. The closest was when she started to cry when she told me how she felt about me. And even then, it wasn't as extensive as this was. She was balling her eyes out here, dropping all of that bratty snob act that was her trademark personality. She lowered one of her hands and put in on her chest. Her crying stopped and she flopped to the floor.

"Wendy!"

All of us ran over to where she lay on the floor. Her head whacked against the concrete, making a thud I could feel through my suit. I leaned down to sit on my knees as we picked her up from her back to hold her upright. The sight I didn't want to see happened. Her arms flopped back, completely lifeless when her chest was in the air. Even her eyes. They weren't even fully closed. The whites of her eyes could be seen at the bottom.

Monica pushed some of us out of the way to get to her. Checking to see if the worst was a possibility, she placed two of her fingers on the white neck of Wendy's. There was a still moment as we waited for any sign from Monica. Why was she giving that look? Why wasn't she calming us down? Why? Why?!

She helped Charlotte carefully set her down back on the floor as quick as they could.

"Her heart's not beating," Monica said quickly. "Give me some space."

"Wha—" I said, not able to finish what I was saying, everything hitting me way too hard.

I put a hand behind my head as I stood on my feet now. There was something at the bottom of my vision but I didn't realize what it was at first until it started to obstruct and blur my vision. The watery tears collected as I tried to stop them from falling. I didn't want to believe what Monica told me. But who was I to think otherwise? Because of that, my legs started to shake and my whole body shivered as if a cool breeze struck me.

Monica curled her fingers as the purple started to form at the tips. She collected the small amount into her hands and shot it into Wendy's chest. It flew through her suit and into her body, making her jolt just as a defibrillator would. Following her movements, she placed both hands on top of each other and started compressions. I couldn't take the way her lifeless body was flopping around with each time Monica would force her hands down on top of her. Where was all that chaos inside her when I wanted it? Where was it when *she* needed it? It didn't seem like CPR was working at all. If anything it looked like with every compression, more of her hope would slip away.

"Wendy!" Charlotte sobbed, starting to realize what was happening.

Kerren had her gun out and ready in her hand, searching the area. I noticed her eyes were stuck to the top of rooftops, almost like she was trying to find something.

"Who the heck was that?" she grumbled to herself.

"Wasn't anyone," Monica said hastily. "There's no wound at all. Her heart stopped working."

"How's her heart just all of the sudden gonna stop working?!"

"Shut up!" Monica shrieked, as tears started to whittle down from her. "I don't know, okay. I don't know."

When Will heard that from Monica, he placed both hands at the back of his head to support it from rolling off. It hit everyone at different times but it each impacted us. We all knew what was happening to her. Not the reason for it, but simply what was right in front of us.

Monica curled her fingers once again and tried shooting into her. But once again, the lifelessness in her would bounce up towards the sky and tried telling us to give up on her. Like we'd ever do that. We'd stay here until we'd die ourselves if we have to.

I heard a click as Kerren locked the gun back into her leg. Her boots tried to overpower the noise of Monica's gasps as the little grunts within her would come out every time she pressed down. If she would've placed a hand on the back of Monica, that would've been something different, but she placed one in front of her on her arm that was aiding to bring back Wendy. Monica nudged her out of the way with her shoulder and kept going, her disparity getting worse.

"Guys. She's gone."

"Don't you dare say that!" Will shouted as he confronted her with strained eyes. "You never knew her like we did! We'd never give up on her!"

"You need to learn to let go," she said, starting to raise her voice.

"Let go?! She's our friend! She's *my* friend! You don't know what it's like to just let that go!"

She threw a fist at his pretty boy face, making him stumble a bit.

"Yes I do! What do you think I felt when we had to jump out of the ship just leaving behind Ed?! He had us realize what was more important, the bigger picture. Do you think I just wanted to leave him there? Of course not! He was like my dad! He changed my diapers when I was a baby! He watched me grow up! How was I gonna leave him there to die?! How?! It's because of all the lives we are gonna save and avenge. I'm not letting Ed die in vain. I'm doing everything I can to bring his name honor. I'm the one who's carrying his legacy and I'm not letting anything stop me from carrying that out."

Monica's hands slowed and came to a halt as she lay over her body. It was at that moment that we all realized the worst. She was gone. Wendy was dead. The bratty girl I loved to hate. The way she ran into me the first time we met. It was all because of our DNA but it was because of me hitting her that I met Charlotte and became their best friends. Everything that we had, all of it was just gone like that.

No one held back. We all broke down and fell to our breaking points. The noise was cruel. How all of our sounds of despair came falling down into this pit that collected somewhere in the world.

It drove me mad. Literally. Even though I could feel all of their grief stacked on top of mine, it started to fuel into something more. This burning came to form in the front of my chest. The tears changed to blood as the color that represents anger spewed out of my soul. My sobs turned to screams, shouts, exclamations of rage beyond compare.

Kerren was right. I wasn't going to let Wendy's death be in vain. There was nothing that was stopping me from carrying out what she wanted. She wanted all of this to be over. She wanted everyone atoned for. Now that the Wendy I knew was gone, there was still one more living. And that's what drove me insane. How could she live and not the real one, the one who should rightfully live over her. She was going to get it. Feel what we were feeling ten times over. Whoever these Twins of Oblivion were, they were about to feel the absolute pain of real oblivion.

*   *   *

The fire kept being fed by the buildings. A lot of things in Novus were mainly metal, but that didn't stop the fire. It seemed to eat away at anything. We were on the street across from the shopping district after having taken Wendy's body and placing it under a tree in a park. Do you know how much I hated just leaving her behind like that? My brain couldn't comprehend the fact that there was no longer anything in that body, so leaving her there felt like we were excluding her from what would've no doubt been fun for her. But I mainly just had to trick my mind as much as possible to let the anger drive me to keep going and not just slump up against a wall and start crying.

It was obvious this was where everything was happening. People were screaming and running away, not being used to anything like this ever happening. Taking into consideration the condition of Exon, it probably was never even touched by another country during the war. This new feeling of fear was too much for them to handle and they reacted in the only way they could.

I looked at them in disgust for being so clueless as to what was happening, thinking that the lies Zalus feeds them are true.

Palace Guards ran down one side of the street before they were pounced on by kids, using powers I've never seen before, taking them down to nothing within seconds. When we stepped fully into the street, we saw four people watching everything. Their eyes were roving about, watching their dirty work. And to make things worse, they all carried their smiles like they usually did when I saw them.

We all took a deep breath when this fake Wendy was living and breathing. It brought back all those feelings of me wanting to end her for being the one alive. It shouldn't be this way. It never should've.

"Remember, all you need to do is take out Monica," ALIS said in our heads.

"We're gonna do more than that," I said before bursting into a sprint towards them.

My sword appeared in my hand with the thought alone and was ready to be wielded for justice. They turned to see me and watched as I drew closer, not doing a single thing. There was no change of stance but the only thing was I saw their Charlotte and Wendy's smile get brighter. It hurt. Hurt so much to see them like that. Why would anyone in their right mind smile at a fool who was running at them with a sword in his hand?

When I reached them, I threw the sword up in the air to bring it straight down on whoever was there. Twin Charlotte casually put her hand up as if she was gonna stretch but blocked my sword with her wrist, making a scraping noise. There were metal bracers on her arms that had a slit through the middle of it, perfect for fighting someone like me. Immediately after blocking it, she put a hand on it and dragged it down to slide her hand up to mine, making sure to keep the end of the sword pointed towards the floor.

"Hiya cutie," she said as she flashed me a look with her eyelashes flared.

I tried bringing my hand up and fighting against her grip, but I couldn't. I don't know if she was actually that strong or I was weak from having my friend get taken from me.

She dug her face into me, getting closer. I know she wasn't real. I know she wasn't. But I couldn't fight was I was seeing. This reality in front of me was what Charlotte exactly looked like. This was the face of the girl I adored. But all her intentions, all her motives were far from what I loved. If that was the case and I knew it, why couldn't I see her as she was; a monster? Her beauty as she came to kissing distance was overwhelming me and she knew it. I had to literally shake my head to stop looking at her and fight for control over my hand again.

"Get the heck off me!"

"But why? Don't you love being this close to me? I can feel your heartbeat right now," she said as her sweet breath wrapped around me and warmed my face. "I know it's not because of you running too. Face it Mark. You desperately wanted to see me."

There was a giggle behind her as a blond haired girl raised her hand and jumped up and down.

"Me too right?"

My mind couldn't take it. I saw Wendy with this huge smile on her face, the one I wanted to hate, but no matter how hard I tried I couldn't find that hatred. She was too much of a copy of Wendy's look. How could I go over and hurt her?

The rest of them ran up behind me and tried grabbing me. When their arms were just about to latch onto Charlotte, they were all lifted in the air. After the initial pull, they were stuck, flying towards the sky ever so slowly. A kid walked in front of me and was holding his hands out. He watched his captives as they were held subject to him.

I've seen this kid before. He wasn't just another one of them that had their life stolen from them. It was Cadious, the one that could control gravity from when Zalus first showed me what he's done. The whole look of fear that I initially saw wasn't there anymore; completely wiped from existence. Anger just like Maya had was slapped on his young face.

"Let them go!" I shouted.

"Why would we ever do that?" Twin Will said as he fixed his hair. His snarkiness infuriated me, knowing that he was right. I couldn't stop them from what they were doing. "I mean, maybe. Just maybe. If you really want to I guess we can. Just give them a little bit and I'm sure the distance they'd be at would cause serious damage when we let them fall."

I glared at Charlotte as she still looked into my eyes with her infatuation for me.

"Why the heck are you doing this?"

"Cause I love you," she said with joy in her words. "Once I'm finished doing what I'm supposed to do I get to kill you. That's all I ever want. I want to hear you beg. I want to hear you scream. Don't you think that'd be fun?"

"Who the heck is Oblivion?!"

"I can't tell you that silly. There'd be no fun once you find out. I can tell you this much though. All you're doing is playing our game. Every little thing you do, every decision you make is because of us. You can't deny that. Once you understand you'll see."

Monica's face behind her was the bland look that I got from the mansion. When she was controlling which way her electricity traveled, sending it to my brain at the command of Charlotte. But something was changing just at the ends of her mouth. It engaged the orbitals of her face as the cheek bone became more defined in a smile. Yes, I said that right. A smile. Her eyes were fixed on something behind me, I knew that much.

Screams in the distance sounded their call for whatever was devastating them. And what came after that was something we were all familiar with. The sound of thumping with hundreds of feet pounding as they ran towards their main goal filled everything. When those dark teens stormed towards us in the street and the girl in white made us run in the opposite direction, the thuds were made to be something I remembered. This noise just brought up those memories.

I turned my head to see kids running like they weren't even alive, sprinting down the streets to lay some more waste to the people of Exon. Some ran past us but one girl stopped where she was and watched as the others floated in the air. Maya was just as she was when she first attacked us. There was nothing on her face that indicated her getting hurt. It must've made Monica happy to see her alive but it meant another thing. If she was in Headquarters when we left and now she's here, that has to mean Terra's gone. Why would Monica send them back if they weren't done with the outer cities?

"Maya!" Monica shouted.

She didn't bother with listening and charged up her energy. Cadius was responsible for holding them up and all Maya had to do was send them flying even further with her powers, possibly breaking all their bones on the way. The shriek started and the power was being collected.

"ALIS get me control of her!" Monica shouted through her helmet.

"Monica has a hold on her," ALIS said.

"I know! That's why I'm gonna help you! Just do what I said!"

I tried pulling back again on my arm but Charlotte still kept her precious fingers wrapped around my wrist. She never bothered with looking at what was gonna happen to my friends. Her eyes were glued to me and only me.

The noise from Maya's hands was growing with every second but it somehow seemed delayed. The constant scowl was starting to fade away from the muscles in her face and relaxed to the point of snapping into a blank expressionless stare. Her powers never stopped though. They kept on charging up and within an instant she changed her footing, aiming herself towards the controller of gravity. The sound of her powers switched over and made a boom louder than the one I heard when she knocked down the building in Ashillon.

Since the energy traveled extremely fast in the first place, it didn't take long for it to crush him considering his distance of being only feet away. He was standing there one second and the next he flew through one of the buildings on fire, shaking the foundation that was already on the verge of collapse.

All of them screamed as they fell to the floor. It must've been only a little over a story in the air so the fall wasn't as extreme as it would've been. The suits helped a bit in taking the brunt of the hit, cushioning the force. I used the time I had due to the obstruction of their plan and yanked my hand from Charlotte. I threw my sword down again but she didn't think twice to put up her wrist again. I just couldn't learn could I? How's doing the same thing gonna work? With my pent up frustration, I threw a foot into her, knocking her back.

Will was the first to run past all of them and headed straight towards the direct copy of himself. He held out a hand as he ran, holding him in place before getting to him and wrapping his whole arm around his neck to drag him to the floor.

I wanted to forget about hurting Wendy as much as I could so I focused on the matter at hand and that was stopping the kids. I ran up to Monica to help her up and we both ran over towards where the one who was previously smiling watched without doing a single thing.

She stood completely still before we were just feet away. Her foot slid to extend her arm out and throw a bolt in our direction. I countered her attack with a wall to absorb the energy contained in her electricity and dropped it the second we were gonna run into it. The feeling of running alongside one of my best friends gave me an edge. She was the girl that never talked at school and I was the only one to get her to. We had a connection like no one else. I could read her and she could read me. That was our advantage over them. They may have looked the same and even have the same exact powers, but nothing is gonna be able to emulate the same bond Monica and I had. I took that and ran with this urge to help Monica keep her promise of helping the kids. Keep our promise to do everything in Wendy's name.

Monica was the first to get to her and threw a fist. Twin Monica simply moved her head to dodge it and reached out to snag her hand. I ran over and threw a foot into her knee, sending it sideways. Normally if people aren't ready for that it would've snapped something. She got down on her knee and yanked down Monica with her.

"You're working with her," Twin Monica said. "You think ALIS is gonna help you?"

"You stop controlling those kids!" Monica yelled as she pushed her into me. I cupped her arms and held her in place for Monica, preventing her from doing anything. "Why the heck are you so inhumane?"

"Well I'm not human after all," she chuckled. "I didn't have to go through any stages in life. No childhood. No puberty. No emotional turmoil. No confusion. No troubling myself with wondering if Mark will ever like you back."

Monica let out a grunt as she grit her teeth, kicking her before shocking her. You'd think that because she could control it in the first place that electricity wouldn't hurt her, but without fail, she experienced the same feeling I did when she sent all that pain to my head.

"ALIS now!" Monica yelled.

Just when I thought that everything was working the way it needed to go with ALIS helping in taking control of the kids again, I felt a hand snag me and pull me away from holding her.

"Why are you trying to run away from me?" I whipped around and watched as Charlotte dragged me away from Monica. With the happy tone, I wanted to trick myself into thinking that this was the real Charlotte who wanted to take me to some fun place. I knew it was all fake so I yanked away from her. With quick reflexes, she snagged back onto me and yelled out to her only means of transportation. "Wendy!"

Before I could realize what was happening, Wendy teleported right next to us, connecting us together. It was happening all too fast and I couldn't react anymore, especially since the face of my friend who just died was smiling in front of me. She gave a wink before teleporting us out of the mess we were in.

"Have fun you two!" she giggled before she teleported away.

We were both surrounded with a view of more skyscrapers and smoke from the buildings. I noticed right away that we were higher up now and by the looks of it, it had to be on top of a building. The smoke was not that far off. There, little people were fighting away to their anger's content.

"Finally, I got you alone. Sure, I may have talked to you alone when you were taken by Penn, but it's been awhile since then."

"I don't get you," I barked, making it sound as disgusting as I could. "You love me so much that you want to be the one to kill me."

She gave a big nod, shaking her hair.

"Yup! You got it. Since I want that so bad, it's my job to make sure I protect you for that." She looked behind me and pointed in the distance. "See what's coming? Zalus commanded that a missile be deployed right onto the spot everyone's fighting. He wants to take out a clump of the kids before they do anymore damage. Plus he'd get you...if it weren't for me. Now that you're here, you don't have to worry about that."

An anti-aircraft weapon near the Palace was slowly moving to position itself with a missile waiting for us just as she said. I looked a little ways down the street and saw Palace Guards in vehicles were speeding towards the sight. It wasn't flawed on Zalus's part. He wasn't gonna kill all the Guards. It would be timed so the missile would fire and right after it did its job they would come in to finish up, end of story.

It was moving right along and I couldn't do anything. My chest filled with fear and I immediately looked for a way down. There was no way I was just gonna let them die like that, especially not after what happened to Wendy. She would kill me if she knew that I did nothing to try and save them.

"Where you going? Do you really think I'd put us on a building we could get down from? There's no way to get up here from the inside and no way to get down from the top. Come on. Don't you want to hang with your best girl?"

"You'll never be the Charlotte I love!" I yelled as I looked over the edge, seeing how far the drop was. From the looks of it, there was no way I could jump down there and live. I theory crafted and thought of maybe putting walls down for myself to walk down on but I didn't want to risk that. Plus, you take my fear of heights and it was almost impossible for me to take the leap of faith. Despite jumping out of a ship, my phobia was still there.

"Pretty soon I'll be the only Charlotte to love."

I wanted to go over and yell at her some more but I know she was distracting me as much as she could. I don't know what she was ultimately trying to do. She said that Oblivion had its own rules and soon I'll find out. If they weren't involved with the King and BloodLip then what the heck were they trying to do?!

"Charlotte!" I yelled from the top of the building. I put on the helmet and tried the comm but it was out. It had to be ALIS. Not one of them could hear me and kept on in their battle against themselves, kids rushing in to aid the Twins. "Monica! Will! Get the heck out of there!" I roared, drawing blood at the back of my throat for screaming too hard.

There was a rumble as the missile was launched and was sent flying towards my only hope for a life. All I ever gained and wanted was right there and I was to watch it all go away. Back when Violet was gonna take that from me I had a choice and the ability to make things different. Now how was I supposed to do that again?

Its course was straight towards them so there wasn't a single thing that would impact it on the way. Unless maybe...

A ship soared through the sky, weaving in and out of buildings, cutting underneath freeway ramps and zooming on past me. It came out of nowhere but I could recognize it instantly as one of the Palace's. It was the same kind that came and dropped all those kids in the outer cities. Whoever was piloting this was clearly skilled in flight. Why would you ask? Well sure, they were doing all these maneuvers through the city, but it was for a reason. Four smaller sized missiles were fast approaching it, almost as if they weren't moving at all. It hugged towards the rear of it but because the ship was moving with such precision, it could keep them at bay.

It was no doubt that this person came from the outer cities. One, it was one of the ships from there, and two, it had to get past the anti-aircraft turrets they had at the front of Exon that destroyed Ed.

"What?!" I heard in my helmet. It was Will. He was out of breath and panting faster than a dog left out in summer without water. "Why the heck can't I move?"

"Will!" I tried saying. I got another blank signal, telling me I couldn't connect to them.

"I can't either!" Charlotte yelled.

From where I was standing, I could see them frozen in the torn street. People in black suits stuck in time but everyone else was moving.

"ALIS!" Monica yelled. "Let go!"

"Are you that stupid to think that I'd let you guys get away with this knowledge of where the King is? If you ever wanted to live you needed to think about all the possibilities. Like maybe how I had this planned the whole time. I bet you can see that missile by now. Where's it headed? Right towards you. Let me tell you something Monica. I admire your ability to do what you do, and take that as the only compliment you'll ever hear from me. But I can't handle human stupidity. It ends up in the same place every time. Right where you're standing."

The ship started to head towards the huge deadly weapon that was closing in on its frozen targets. Once it got to the point of almost hitting it, drawing closer with every foot it traveled, the nose of the ship pulled up with speed faster than anything possible of a ship back on Earth. The four small missiles as well as the large one locked on to the closest moving target, the task they were made to do, and that was take down ships. The ship drove itself up and started charging towards the heavens. It was a sight I've never seen before. There was a black dot in the sky with these white masses following it to no end. I watched in wonder of what was to happen to this person I didn't know. Even everyone down on the street watched, including the Twins.

At the cockpit, something red shot out and flailed in the air for a second before diving straight down towards the street right below. Behind the pilot that ejected, the missiles lived up to their job and died knowing that they accomplished what they were made for. An explosion bigger than the one on the Penthouse made a fireball that lit up the sky, turning to black smoke and floating away to be part of the sky's atmosphere.

The pilot kept falling, putting their hands to their side as they gained speed with their body position. Head first, they came tumbling down. This person was definitely at a height where they needed to pull their parachute. If that was the case, why was this person nosediving to the street? Why not let yourself go in the ship than to eject only to fall and die?

As the pilot came into view, I realized how red the suit they were wearing was. It was almost exactly like the one back in Headquarters that stood on display right next to Violet's and Aqua's. In fact it looked extremely similar.

It clicked in my head before she made contact with the ground. Something Terra told me about Scarlett. She promised that when the Equilibrium returned she would come back and fight with him. It couldn't be. One of the Three was finally gonna show themselves?

A thud of cracking concrete reached my ears form up where I was as she landed like she's done it over and over. I could appreciate the suit with someone finally in it. The fullness of it as this person of glory, the way everyone treated them as the heroes they were for protecting everyone, filled the suit. The helmet was different than ours, being more jagged and obviously being red. Her head was looking down, but when she raised it to see everyone staring at her, the helmet unlatched like ours and folded back into the neck.

"If you wanna play dirty, then let's play dirty."

On the display of my screen it showed that someone entered our comm channel. The name that it read was Scarlett. But I couldn't have cared less if she joined our channel. I was so dumbfounded at the time. The voice wasn't just any voice. It had a ruggedness to it. It had experience in it that could've been heard miles away as she claimed her dominance. It had the voice of only one person.

"Terra?!" we all shouted.

Even from where I was I could see that it was the same person who tried killing me. The only thing different was her hair was red. It wasn't red like Penn's used to be, but a natural red that people would call orange.

"You're Scarlett?!" Charlotte asked.

Scarlett didn't bother with looking at her, or any of them for that matter.

"Terra's not my name. So don't bother calling me that anymore."

"Why the heck didn't you tell anyone that you were her?!" Will asked.

"It was my only trump card. Had to play it right."

No wonder Kerren told us that she hardly went outside. If people back then knew her then they would recognize her, regardless if she dyed her hair.

The whole time she was talking, she was moving her head around gathering every piece of information she could use.

"Mark where are you?" she asked, seeing my position on her map but not knowing the altitude.

"Would you look who decides to show up," Twin Charlotte said. "Isn't this gonna be a day full of reveals."

There was a burst of confidence that grew inside. With everyone feeling the exact same way down in the street for having the real Scarlett with them, they were no doubt confident they could win any fight. I abused that feeling to the best of my advantage and dropped my fear of heights.

"You're supposed to protect me aren't you," I said, looking at her from the corner of my eye, keeping my whole vision looking down towards the drop.

She let out a chuckle.

"Don't tell me you're feeling like you can take advantage of that."

"And why can't I? You love me don't you? You wouldn't want the love of your life to get hurt, or even worse, die. Would you?"

For the first time ever I saw her smile drop. The devil inside her that always carried a spark of joy was switched over to tailor her personality to the very situation at hand. It scared me just as much as the when the real Charlotte turned to the behemoth she was when wanting to fight BloodLip.

"Oh and not only that," I said, picking at her feelings, "what would happen if the rest of Oblivion found out? No doubt they want me safe as well right? Why else would you have freed me when I was taken?" Still not a word from her, nor a single muscle moved. The only part of her that kept on was her hair that swayed with the sea breeze. "Let's hope for both of our sakes that your Will has good reflexes."

I did it. I don't really know how but I let myself drop over the edge. The feeling felt worse than when we jumped out of the ship. This time there was nothing to save me besides my stupid notion that they'd want me alive and would do their best at it. I heard Twin Charlotte yell out behind me just before the wall of the building cut her off from me. I noticed Twin Will on the street look up and throw out his hands. I must've already fell a few stories before he could reach me and slow my fall.

"Kerren how far of a fall can I take without a charge?" I asked with fear in my voice.

"Around three stories. It can absorb the shock but anything higher than that and you'll get hurt. Why?"

"Uh...there may be a problem."

They looked on their maps for where my dot was and saw that I was falling from the building.

"Mark!" Charlotte yelled.

"He's slowing me down. When I'm at the height I can take the fall, jump Will."

Scarlett took a large blade from her suit, which had a red hilt, and started to run towards him. I thought it was too early but I trusted that she had the judgement to know when. It didn't take long at all for me to get down. Despite Twin Will slowing my fall, I was able to get down to the appropriate height in time, right when Scarlett reached him.

She grabbed one of his arms and yanked it down, raising her other arm with the weapon in it. Before driving it down onto him, he held her arm in place, completely preventing her from moving it. Will was never able to completely lock someone in place, only slow the movements of his targets.

Wendy teleported Charlotte back down from the rooftop to help in their fight. Just as I saw her disappear and reappear, I dropped to the sidewalk and tried positioning myself to prevent as much of the fall as I could.

Twin Charlotte came over and rammed a fist into Scarlett's stomach to make her keel over. It didn't bother her one bit. She let go of the knife and let it fall to the floor. With Will knowing that it was okay for him to let go of her, she yanked her hand out of the position he kept it in. She dropped to the floor, sweeping her feet to knock them over and grabbed the knife just before it fell to the floor. Using the momentum from grabbing it, she threw it into Twin Will's leg.

He yelled out in pain before falling to the floor when she pulled it out. She had no problem taking all of them on at once. Gosh. She was no joke. All those stories about how she could fight were evident right in front of my eyes. Violet was taking us on just as well when in the school. The only reason she fell was the position she put herself in. Here Scarlett had all the control she needed. This was her domain and she was doing all she could to keep that.

Charlotte and Kerren ran over with me to go help her. We knew that she probably didn't need it but it was our chance to keep the upper hand. Before we could even reach them to help, Wendy grabbed all of them to teleport back a few feet. Scarlett stood up with her knife still in her hand and watched them from where she was.

There was fear in the Twins for the first time I've seen. It wasn't as evident as it would be for a common person but just because they weren't all smiling or giving some kind of remark it was enough to show.

Will held his leg, trying to keep pressure to the wound that dripped blood over the dirty street. He gnashed at us with his teeth, doing his best to not shriek out in anymore pain. Before they did anything else, there was a scream behind them. They shifted their attention to where it was coming from and watched as hundreds of Palace Guards charged towards where they were. So what was is gonna be? Fight us or them?

Twin Charlotte looked back over towards me and found herself smiling once more. They were all still holding hands, clearly ready to leave. It was completely unnatural to see them in front of me. Where was the reality in this mirror that had Wendy standing next to me? After giving me a good stare, she disconnected her hand for just a second to wave at us.

"Bye Mark. I'll see you later. But as a word of warning, let me tell you, Penn hurts. A lot."

She gave me a wink and bursted out in uncontrollable laughter before a *swoosh*.

Well great. Now they leave and we already have to deal with an army of Palace Guards. So what we had Scarlett. There was no way we were actually gonna hold all of them off. I don't care if we even had all of the Three. It was still gonna be dang impossible. Who knew how much firepower they held as they came charging towards us, Palace vehicles zipping through the abandoned cars and fallen buildings that burned down.

Three motorcycles sped past all of the rest of the Guards to lead the charge. The roar of the engines reminded me of when we first heard them on the highway. The black helmets and all. It was all in front of me.

"You guys need to get out of here," Scarlett said, beating into the onslaught that was about to occur.

"Sure, like you could take all of them on," Will said.

"Who says I'm alone?"

Shouts and chants came from behind us as hundreds of people were coming our way. Who the heck were these guys? They were all wearing normal clothes. No part of any group. And it wasn't just any particular age group either. I saw teenagers down to kids ten years old. People who had a hard time walking because of their age seemed to be filled with this courage and joined everyone.

I witnessed something that was hardly ever seen on Scarlett's face. Something was pulling at the end of her cheeks as a dimple was created just at the bottom of her cheek bone.

"Told you I had a trump card. Had to play it just right."

"Who are they?" I asked.

"People. Regular citizens. I told as many as I could before I changed my identity and went into hiding that when I come back I'll need as much help I can get to overthrow Zalus."

"Scarlett's back!" someone yelled from the crowd, screaming to the world of the news. Their old time vigilante was back to bring justice. It was no doubt the main reason for this mob. It was the citizens turn to fight.

Her frown came back with confronting the charge of the Guards.

"It's time we come out of hiding. Overthrow Zalus. This won't be known as a holiday for Exon. It'll be known as a day of remembrance for the whole planet. The day the Equilibrium connected everything." Scarlett hit me in the chest with the side of her fist. I took it as a sign of appreciation as it was meant to. "Remember what Rylan said and you keep it in your heart when you fight. We fight for peace, for the freedom of others, for the Equilibrium."

I couldn't see her as the same person anymore. It was just a suit and the change of her hair color that made her look different. For some reason, I don't know why, she was able to carry over this new self. Her personality was still there, but as I said, she had a way with everything she did to carry herself in this new light. Scarlett was back. Back to carry on the name of the other Three. To carry the names of all those that had fallen for the cause she's been fighting for all her life.

One of the bikes kept on towards Scarlett, ready to attack. He shot a bullet that I blocked for her. It caught him off guard. There was suddenly a white wall in front of him so he swerved closer to her. With his speed still in full motion, she extended her arm to the side and clipped his neck, sending him down off his bike. Will threw off the other two and sent them flying.

"Take the bikes and go," Scarlett said.

"How do you expect us to do everything ourselves? Wendy's gone and even then it wouldn't have been enough to get through the Palace ourselves," I said.

"We're relying on your powers here."

I scoffed.

"My powers? I can make a sword, Scarlett. What am I supposed to do with that?"

"Everything's worked so far. I don't know what it means but I'm putting my trust in you to take him down. We'll give as much as a commotion as we can out here."

"He's not gonna fall for that again," Monica said. "The Palace is still full of Guards."

"Like I said, we're putting full faith in Mark. It's all we can do. It's what we've been doing since before he was born and look where we are now. And trust me. If you guys were able to take down Violet then you can take anyone inside that building with no problem. She was a way better fighter than me. It was from her I learned everything."

She was right. We did need to go even if I had nothing to base my hope on but myself, which was nothing by the way. It wasn't like I had a choice. So that's what we did. We ran towards the three bikes and got on them. Since Kerren was better and had more experience, I rode on the back of her. Will got his own and Charlotte and Monica shared one as well with Monica riding.

Scarlett and the rest of the crowd charged forward with screams, war cries that sounded throughout the whole city. Kerren pooped a little wheelie to flip our direction and go through the crowd of civilians. As I hugged my sister's stomach tightly so I wouldn't fall off, I felt this strange connection. It wasn't like it was with the others, but rather, this was one that is only felt with family. I bet the sight must've entranced people as well because they would stare as long as they could before people would push them to join in the fight.

The words Scarlett told me were sounding through my head as we whipped around the shopping district to avoid the mass of Guards. It was happening. The whole time I lived on Earth I had no idea that I was born for this specific task. I was just living a normal life with idiots in a town full of snobs. But all this time, everything was working for this moment. For me, for all of us, to finally take down Zalus and stop everyone on this world from killing themselves. I didn't like the responsibility but I knew I had to uphold it as much as I could, especially because of what happened to Wendy.

At least we were able to get away safely. Or so I thought. The Palace Guards caught on to what we were doing and tried to retract themselves from the fight they were currently fighting to follow us. Some at the back of them went ahead and did just that and tried their best to stay on our tail.

"Follow me!" Kerren yelled. "And Monica don't you dare start with who has a better direction of Exon. You're following me regardless of what happens. If you want the fastest way to the Palace without those Guards actually getting to us then you better be on my tail."

"I don't have access of the city anymore anyways," she said. "ALIS raised her walls again. They're too strong for me to re-enter."

"Then the kids are free?" Charlotte asked with hope filling her voice.

"Not yet. Monica's still controlling them."

"The faster we finish all of this the faster we can stop her," Will said.

I don't know. I still didn't like the fact that all the kids running around this place had a control over them that would make them do things that would be crimes on so many different levels. What ever happened to them having fun on a playground with their only enemy being the school bell? Thinking of school reminded me of Wendy, sending this huge wave of depression into my soul that the rest of them no doubt felt. When we go back to school what's gonna happen to all those times of Wendy yelling at me for not having enough food for myself at lunch? What would I tell her parents? I don't care if they aren't her real parents. They were still her parents regardless of what our history entails. What about all those times I would go over to her house and see her in the overly casual clothes that weren't even considered clothes? All the peppiness and the annoying voice? Where was that?!

I hugged Kerren even tighter to turn my head just enough to see how far along the Palace Guards were. Just as if it was natural for them to be that close behind us, they sped past everything to get to us. It took forever to watch their hands travel to their waist to grab their weapon, trying to keep steady on the bike.

I didn't want to bother Kerren so I tapped her thigh where her gun was. At first she didn't really understand what I was talking about but once I shifted in my seat she understood what they were gonna do. And how were we supposed to protect ourselves? I couldn't turn around and try to deflect those bullets. I'd fall off the second I tried.

"Hold on," she told me as I pulled into her, resting my head on her back. Her hair rested on top of my head as a blanket to cover me from whatever fear was there. It comforted me even without trying, fulfilling her duties as a sister.

The speed of the bike increased as she took a sharp turn, dipping low to the ground going underneath an overpass. The rays of the sun were blocked underneath here, reigning as darkness and changing the mood completely. Charlotte was holding tight to Monica in the same way I was to Kerren. It gave me a good feeling seeing them able to be as close as that. It was a true sign of friendship even though it was for her own life.

Cars here were still going about their business. It made it harder for Kerren but it also helped us in losing them. Cars honked as we past them only to realize who we were. I turned my head, still resting it on Kerren, and saw what held the menace of this world. The Palace was right there, probably only a few streets down; its embassy there to be glorified by anyone passing by. But not us. We were to shame the name of the King and his legacy, not for the sake of revenge for everyone, but for justice.

Not long after weaving in and out of traffic did we lose them. I was still clenching to Kerren because of the feeling I got from it. I didn't want to let go of this remnant of my mother that I missed so much. Everything was going good. We were approaching the Palace. It was only a straight path now with the most elegant structures surrounding it. All until Monica's bike went out of control.

"Monica what're you doing?!" Charlotte yelled from her back.

Since we were slowing down as it was, their bike, including Will's, sped forward. The shop that carried antiques in them had their name written on it as they both slammed into it.

"Charlotte!" I yelled as Kerren stopped the bike to jump off.

Both of us ran over to where the two bikes rammed into the wall that crumbled with their age. It was like I was on the other end of the wall when the car hit the Victoria's Secret back in Springfield. The thing caved in on itself and the bikes were nowhere to be found. The only thing I was able to see was the three bodies.

I know it was selfish. I know. As you'd expect, I ran to Charlotte first. I cared about Monica and Will for sure, but my priority lied in making sure Charlotte was okay. Her body was slumped against the rubble, torn by the universe's curse that was out to get us. Thankfully, there wasn't a wound that would mean her life. The only thing there was the marks and scrapes that ran along her precious skin. She wasn't even unconscious, evading everything when she got thrown in.

"Are you okay?" I asked as I gave her a hand.

She reached out and took it, pulling on it to steady herself on her feet.

"Yeah," she said ruggedly, looking over to where Kerren was looking at Will and Monica.

"Guys?" Kerren said.

Why was her voice shaken? Why wouldn't she be helping them up like I did with Charlotte? It made me stop for just a second before we both ran over the torn wall to see the worst of everything.

Monica's pale face wasn't covered with the white anymore. It carried stains of blood and charred building pieces that pierced her skin. How was her body so lifeless all of a sudden? She was just riding a bike the other second! She was following right behind us! Her black pearls were hidden behind her untouched eyelids. The mascara and eyeshadow that she would lightly apply to add to the darkness of her aura was now not noticeable, her whole face being dark now.

"Monica!" I gasped.

I fell on my knees. I intended to do that in the first place, but not like this. It wasn't that I kneeled down, but I fell. My knees simply gave out. They were tired of being drowned in this despair, the weight of all my loss. When Charlotte saw that I flopped to the floor like that I think she knew what happened as well. She didn't want to believe it and neither did I.

Kerren moved a piece of the bike that was crushed and revealed Will underneath it. He contorted his face in pain, groaning as he legs must've been crushed underneath another part of the bike along with the wall. I found enough strength in myself to rush to my feet knowing that he was still awake and rushed to him. It was as if Charlotte and I had the same mind, each of us grabbing an arm as Kerren tried moving the other piece of rubble on top of him.

"Guys! Arg! Guys stop!" he yelled.

"Pull!" I yelled at Charlotte. "Kerren push harder!"

"Mark! Stop it!" He yanked his hands back and let himself fall to his own support, still stuck where he was in his pain. His eyes caught the sight of Monica, freezing where he was, not taking a single breath. "Monica?" he said, tears filling his eyes and adding a grogginess to his voice.

She didn't respond to his voice. The black hair still laid on top of her shoulders without a single movement nor a rise of the chest. Knowing Will was somewhat okay, I ran back towards her and took a hold of her hand, waiting for something in her to tell me she would be okay.

I waited. I waited and waited. I waited and waited and waited and nothing. I still remember the noise that came out of my mouth when I realized she was gone. It was a hiccup of sorts; a gasp that was cut short. As I burst into tears, I picked her up and put her in my arms, giving her the biggest hug ever. All the time I knew her I never got a hug like this from her. She would give me friendly hugs sometimes when the time called for it but never anything like this. I squeezed everything into that final hug.

I thought about everything we had as I pushed her into me. I seriously thought I was someone special because I could talk to her, something that was not only shunned upon but impossible to do. From the moment she told me to stop looking at her all the way up to holding hands with me as we ran through the school hallway. The way she shyly asked if we wanted to stay for dinner. Did she ever realize that because of that she would make us all become friends? It was never because of me or anything I did. It was all because of that one move, that one act of courage that we were able to come together in a way I never thought was possible. She literally gave everything for not only us, but for the girls that she loved so much in the park.

Charlotte and Kerren broke down as well from where they were, watching as I had one last bonding moment with the only friend I thought connected with me. The very first person who I actually considered my friend.

I rested her back in the place she was, letting her lay in as much peace as she could. But no. She wasn't complete. I noticed at the top of her head that there was something missing. Where was the trademark, the one thing that made her a real person?

"Hey," Will said with a raspiness to his voice now. "It's right over there."

His finger pointed to the black bow that I bought her that day everything changed with the falling of the Penthouse. Next to her feet, it sat there waiting to be put back on her head. When I picked it up, it made memories flood back in as a tsunami would bring back debris. Just before I was about to put it back on her hair, Will spoke up.

"That's not what she wants. I was surprised when she told me too. It was random, but after the Penthouse fell and we were walking home, she told me something. I guess maybe because she felt that our lives were threatened or something. She told me that if ever something happens to her to give her bow to you."

"What?" I said, lost for words, holding the bow and looking at his torn face.

He let out a sigh before continuing.

"Can't you see? She wants you to keep a part of her when she goes. She liked you Mark, and not just as a causal crush either. She liked you in the most important way. She liked you as her best friend."

CORRUPTION • Diaz

I took his words and looked back down at the bow in my hand. Is this what she really wanted? She couldn't have possibly wanted anyone taking her bow.

"That's not all," he said, reaching his hand down towards his legs and bringing something out. "I found this in Wendy's pocket. I kept it to remind me of what she wanted. Monica used hers and so did I, but she'd yet to use it. Do me a favor," he said as he dropped the silver bullet the King gave us in Charlotte's hand, "make sure you show him, all of them, that she used hers too."

Charlotte couldn't take it either. Her eyes started to bubble forth as well, dripping onto the silver in her hand.

"What's happening?" she sobbed, closing her fist around the bullet of her best friend.

"I...I don't really know," Will said. "It feels...weird. Like I'm slowly fading away. It's the only reason I hit the stupid wall. I couldn't really see where I was going."

"But why's this happening to us?!" she said, yelling now.

"I don't kn—"

He was cut off just before he finished his last sentence. Just as fast as Wendy fell, so did he, taking his last breath. As I was about to call out to him, there was a gunshot. I threw up my hands to my head, clenching onto the remnant of Monica. All three of us looked out towards the street and saw Palace Guards getting out of their vehicles, weapons ready.

"Go!" Kerren shouted, throwing her gun out from her thigh. "I'll hold them off!"

"I'm not losing you too!" I yelled, getting up from the floor. "What happened to us sieging the Palace together?!"

She ducked her head as she ran over to me, grabbing Charlotte as she made her way towards me.

"Things change. This was way more than I could have ever imagined. I just want to make sure my big brother gets out alive and does what he's meant to do." She gave me a big smile before giving me a quick kiss on the cheek. "I'll get out, I promise. Keep Charlotte safe."

There was no avoiding what we had to do. Kerren got up before I could even say another word or try telling her to be safe. She dove behind a piece of the wall and peeked up with her gun, taking shots where she could. I yanked on Charlotte's hand and ran, leaving behind two of my only friends and my sister in a building that would get lost in a fire fight.

Everyone turned their attention to us as we fled to the Palace and fired. I threw up my hands involuntarily and cringed with pain as my energy was depleting from experiencing loss over and over.

It was only us two now. We were the only part left of The Equilibrium. We started off as five babies ready to be sent into a new world to be protected and came back as five friends confused about who we were. We learned so much, not only about our past, but about who we were—our motives. Even with this day alone, I found something out. With Charlotte holding the bullet from Wendy and me holding Monica's bow, we told a story of how we would never back down from avenging our friends. Whatever was happening to my friends, I was gonna make it stop. I was going to end everything. This was the day of The Equilibrium and I'm making sure it ends that way.

*   *   *

I bypassed everything there. I didn't care how elegant or amazing the place was. I was in the Palace for a reason and that was to get to the King.

At the front gates were Palace Guards that we bypassed with Charlotte's invisibility. To be honest, I relied a lot on her here. As I held her hand almost the whole way through, I realized just how much all of their powers were helpful for sieging a place like this. Charlotte for getting past people. Wendy for getting past locked places. Monica for stopping ALIS. Will for anything that might get in our way. And me? Well, that was still yet to be seen how this sword was of any help.

I cursed in my head as I realized that Monica never told us where Zalus was. Once we got deep in the Palace, we had no idea where to go. The place was bigger than anything back on Earth so we could get lost within seconds. But once we gathered our bearings, we started to notice something. The lights that hung down had a strange pattern to them. All of them were on except a select few. Not just the ones on the ceiling but also on the wall. I didn't take long to realize that this was something Monica had to have done. If she was gonna get kicked out of ALIS's system then she had to have taken measures to know where to go.

Without hesitation, we followed it straight to an elevator. At the elevator it had a panel like always but the thing about this one was that it was darkened, just like all the other lights were.

"We need someone's hand," Charlotte said, letting go of my hand now.

"No I got it."

"Huh?" she said as she watched me place my hand on top of it. Like it did last time, it read me as Penn Exon for the same reason it did last time. It wasn't recognizing her hand print but the Equilibrium inside her. "How'd you know?"

"Learned a thing or two when I got taken," I said as we both stepped into the elevator.

Both doors closed behind us and two more appeared in front of us, waiting to be opened when we got to the King's quarters.

"What are we gonna do?" she asked, looking at me from the side. Just with a glance alone I could see the pain that was still present in her face.

I shook my head, opening my hand up to see Monica's bow.

"Don't know. He has to be guarded by who knows how many Guards. I know we can't outfight them and it doesn't help that they have to know we're coming up anyway."

"You're actually taking Terra's advice?"

"Scarlett?"

"Right. Whatever."

"I guess. I mean, what else do we have to back on? It's sheer hope." I threw out my sword to maybe see if I could see something in it. "Hope that something about this lets us have an advantage."

"So what does it feel like?"

"The sword? I don't really know how to describe it. It feels good though."

"Yeah? What else?" she said hastily.

"What else? There really is nothing else to say about it."

Her breathing sped up. I could hear it.

"No. I want you to keep talking."

Why was I feeling fear? This burst of anxiety matching the amount I got when I found out they had powers was making me shake. As her breathing became jagged, I realized that it was because of her. This was her fear.

"Charlotte?"

I let my sword fade away and turned to her. The sight made me create my own sense of fear. She was copying the same look that Wendy gave before her heart stopped. Charlotte was leaning up against the back wall where we came in with wide eyes, her chest rising faster than I've seen before. A sweat droplet slowly dripped down her cheek.

"What's wrong?!" I yelled this time, holding her with a hand behind her back.

"It's nothing. I just want to hear you talk, okay?"

"No! Tell me what's wrong?"

"Mark, please. Keep talking. I want to hear your voice." She managed the strength to look at me and smile. "Can you set me down on the floor please?"

If it meant her feeling better than of course I would. Helping her along, I set her down on the floor and sat there next to her, making sure our shoulders were touching.

"Is it happening to you too?" I asked her, trying to think of a way to help her.

The bottom of her lip quivered as her chest jerked up really quick only to slam back into the wall. Tears started to slowly fall while she kept her smile on her face.

"Do you really like me Mark?"

"Of course I do silly," I said, pulling some hair back behind her ear.

"Why?"

"Why?! Come on Charlotte why wouldn't I?" The last few words came out in sobs. I took a quick second to recuperate as I needed to keep speaking. "You're the nicest person I've ever met. It doesn't matter who it is, you always seem to find the good in them. You're also extremely humble. No one beats you at that. But the way your eyes can just look into mine and make me feel special for being your friend is one of the best feelings ever. And don't even get me started on your amazing smile."

Her chuckle turned into a sob as she lost it. With the little control she had she was able to talk without me not understanding her.

"Can you hold my hand please? Don't let go."

I gripped her hand and put my other behind her back as she started to slump towards the floor and glide off the wall. I couldn't form any more words. Her words combined with me holding the very person I loved was too much for me to handle.

No Charlotte. Don't go! Don't leave me! You're my best friend. You were truly the best person I knew. It wasn't supposed to be this way. We were supposed to grow up. I know it was crazy for me thinking this but I told myself that you were gonna be mine regardless of what happened. We were gonna be with each other forever. I've never felt like this with anyone else and now you're leaving me? Don't do this. Don't go!

Her hand that I was holding fell lifeless as her eyes were staring at the doors to open. No. No! What about the time when we were on that mountain that you loved so much. The dance that we had? What about that? You were hugging me! You can't just leave all that to be. We had a story to finish. All of our story.

I was in complete shock for a good few seconds as I stared wide eyed at her empty body until it finally hit me. My best friend was gone. My best friend was gone and only for one reason. How was I so clueless to realize it? It was the exact reason why Monica told me not to show my powers. But the second I did, it made Penn realize something. She stopped everything they were doing and fled. The last few words she told me was the same thing that Sarah told us in the cafe.

"Pain for pain."

This was it. This was the pain. She was exacting revenge. It had to be her. It had to.

I took the bullet from her hand and saw that there were two there. One for Charlotte and the other for Wendy. As I gripped them in my hand, I built as much rage as I could. Order wasn't needed anymore. Who needed that when there was no need to keep it. As much as I hated her now, I finally understood Penn. When the thing you love most is taken from you, you'll stop at nothing to carry out their will.

"Penn!" I yelled from the elevator with Charlotte laying in my lap.

I don't care where she was. She was gonna feel the pain all over again.

The elevator came to a halt at the very top of the Palace, taking a few seconds for it to smoothly open the doors. As the doors fully opened and revealed the King's chambers, the doors locked in their open position. Inside the chambers was fancy carpeting and tile that had an open spacious living area. But I didn't care about that. The only thing I did care about was standing in the middle of the area.

Four people were there waiting for me. One of them I've seen a few times now, especially when walking around Exon, his face being displayed everywhere. He wore his fancy clothes like always that draped a little. He had a tiny smirk on, barely being suitable considering everything that's gone wrong for him. The other three were two girls along with a bulky high schooler. Eli, Sarah, and Brittany all gave me a smile. It wasn't something that should be mistaken for the smiles that the Twins would give. These were smiles that you would give after kicking dirt in the eyes of your enemy.

Where was I? Still in the elevator with Charlotte in my arms. I made sure to stay there to gather as much anger as I could before I set her down. I clenched the bullets and the bow one more time before putting them away.

"It was her wasn't it," I said, walking towards them after setting Charlotte down ever so carefully.

"You'd be stupid if you thought otherwise," Sarah said, still crossing her arms at me. To my surprise there were no Guards up here. BloodLip was his only protection. "Doesn't it feel good? Doesn't the sting taste amazing?" she said sarcastically.

"I bet it was a wonderful feeling holding your sweetie pie in your arms as she died huh?" Brittany said, putting a hand on her hip. "So romantic."

I couldn't take it anymore. I know I said I wouldn't kill again, but just as Kerren said, things change. All morals were out the window. I'll go down fighting them if I have to avenge them.

"Aaaaah!" I yelled, throwing my sword out as I charged towards them.

They all assembled into their stances and readied for battle. I didn't care who to go for and just swung full force at them, ready to cause damage. Just as I was about to bring the sword down on top of Brittany, everything stopped.

The whole world turned gray. It was just like before I went through the portal. Everything around me was all gray and frozen. No one moved but us inside our area. I slowly lowered my weapon but kept it ready to strike. I searched for any sign of another portal or anything that might stop me from exacting justice myself.

Boom

There was a faint thud in the distance as I stood there. Immediately after, something white appeared and fell down in front of me, slamming down to the floor. I jumped back and readied my sword to swing, waiting for what response this thing would give. The white mass slowly arose from the ground, revealing that it was a person. Not just any person, a girl—a woman. The more I stared at her and the more she stared at me the more I became confused.

"What?" I said out loud, raising an eyebrow.

"Hello Mark."

The woman was wearing a dress of all white, the bottom of her skirt flaring out. Around her neck was white lacing as well. But I could tell you all day about her white dress and that would mean absolutely nothing to you. What would is me telling you that she had white hair and white eyes.

"How the heck are you alive?!"

"Alive? Why would I be dead in the first place?"

"You sacrificed yourself for us. Don't you remember? You told me to get to the mall because BloodLip was waiting for me there to get through the portal. And why are you older now?"

"So you've met me before?"

"Yeah, of course I did."

Her face changed to a frown as she looked to the side and snarled.

"She started it then."

"Started?" I asked.

"Nothing. That's not what's important now. What is important is what happened to your friends. It wasn't just by some random chance that they died."

"I could've told you that."

"I don't exactly know why you haven't found out your powers yet but I'm here to tell you about them regardless."

"I already know them," I said, showing her my sword.

She shook her head and scoffed.

"You really think that's your power? What use is a sword like that gonna do to save an entire planet?"

"That's what I've been asking myself the whole time."

"Think about it. Since Penn saw that you guys were both Equilibrium, she knew what real power it was that you guys both have. How could she have killed them if she was never there when she did it?"

I stood there completely confused by everything, so much so that she groaned and placed a hand on her forehead.

"Mark. You're an Equilibrium. Your power is time jumping. It's what all Equilibrium can do. It was never a sword. All that is just a plus."

"You're telling me I can go to any point in time?"

"No. That's time travel. Time jumping and time travel are two completely different things. Time jumping is only being able to go back in a point in time where you were, taking place of your old body there. There's no clone of you or anything like that. Now think. You have the ability to stop Penn from killing your friends. When did she have the opportunity of doing so? When were all of you guys together, separated just for enough time for her to kill each one?"

After thinking for a while I came to the conclusion. It was the only place. The party. It was the only place where Penn and Wendy were alone. Penn went to help Emily put some boxes away. Wendy was told to come along as well. It was the only time they were alone.

"The party," I said.

"Well then that's where you're gonna go. Equilibrium can follow after each other by seeing their patterns. All you need to do is see if you can see where her patterns are and follow that. It's sort of a feeling thing so it's not completely visual. It's weird at first trust me."

Feeling? No problem. Charlotte had me do the same thing back on her mountain. I took a deep breath and felt for this feeling of Penn already being there. It didn't take long at all. As if she left behind this breadcrumb trail for someone to follow I saw exactly where she went.

"I see it."

"Great. Now go."

"How do I do it?"

"Same way you take out your sword. You just do it."

"I never got your name."

She gave me one more look with the snow white eyes.

"Purity. And Mark, make sure of one thing. The most important thing that you do is not only stop Penn from murdering your friends but to bring back Violet."

I straightened my back at the sound of her name.

"What? Why the heck…"

"I know it might not make that much sense but it's vital that you do. Without doing that then there's no point in going back at all."

Violet. The name still brought back the guilt like always. Was I really gonna see her again? No. I was going back there for a reason. I wanted to save my friends and avenge them. That's what I was gonna do.

With that I took off. My very self-disappeared from time and space and I was in the same type of bubble atmosphere like Wendy when she teleports.

So I was going back to the party the week before I came here. The week everything happened. I didn't know what I was gonna see or what was gonna happen when I got there. But one thing was for sure.

"Penn. You're dead."

Chapter 11

The clouds sat in front of the sun, taking turns of letting it have a shine and then covering it again. It was a slow process, I remember that. The whole sky was the exact same way it was before. The red and the oranges mixed to give a feeling of comfort that I couldn't find and neither would I accept it.

It was an abrupt placement, almost like someone plucked me out of the universe and set me down where I wanted to go. The best way to describe it was like waking up from a dream where you almost died. You know, the heavy breathing and the relief that it was only a dream, except in this case it wasn't dream. It was all reality and I couldn't run from that.

I looked down and saw the same suit. The black hugged tight to my body, being a nicer end suit. Despite my dad not actually being my real dad, it sure did fit pretty well. Same with the shoes. It still had the glossy shine that I put on before I left to make sure it caught Charlotte's attention. Everything was right where it was. Right down to my very step.

I was walking up the hill towards the mountain that carried Emily's house. All the people were getting there now, arriving in their Sunday's best, hair pampered and an inch thick layer of makeup. I remembered that I just finished talking with Charlotte on the phone. Right now they were finishing up getting ready. It wasn't long after I got there and talked to BloodLip did they arrive.

It hit me. I didn't think about it until I stopped walking and turned around like an idiot, viewing all of my surroundings. This was my home. I was back on Earth. This was the place that I was gone from for months now. All the things I missed where right here. A little spring breeze came and touched my cheek, telling me to get back to what I was here for. But the thought was too strong. Charlotte. Wendy. Monica. Will. They were all alive here. Why did I have to go back? Why couldn't I just fix things right here and make sure they never happen? Imagine all the advantages I could have.

The red in the sky made a picture flash in my head of the person I was here for. No. I wasn't here for the sake of trying to get a better hand. I was here to stop that evil monster from hurting anymore of what I love. I was here for blood regardless of my morals in the past.

I sprinted forward in my suit, making the end of it catch the wind and flutter up. I needed to get there before any of them got there to stop Penn from hurting them. As I ran past all the homes to get towards the mountain, I was coming up on a housing track that I was familiar with. Inside there was a person that made me who I was. She was the very person that taught me all about English poets I never knew about. She was the one who lived this whole time as a member of BloodLip in secret. Violet's home that she shared with Penn was right in there. Why did Purity want me to get Violet in the first place? Why did I need to see her face again?

I started to sprint past it, shaking my head to forget about it. I needed to get to the party as fast as I could. There was no time to go talk to her.

But...but what if I did. She did say that none of this would matter if I didn't bring her back. I stood in the sidewalk looking into the track for the longest time, frozen with this decision.

"Ugh! What the heck!" I yelled out.

I didn't know exactly how important she was but I just had to take her word for it. Why would Purity say it otherwise? I snarled with anger as I ran across the street to get to her track. I knew somehow this wasn't gonna end well. If I was her murderer then there was no way it could. I know I would be doing something good by bringing her back, I could undo all the pain, but for some reason I wanted to leave her at rest. For the sake of everything I was doing, I had to put that thinking aside.

I've been to her house a few times so I knew exactly which way to go. To anyone looking outside their house it must've been a strange sight, seeing a teenage boy running the block with a suit on. That was the least of my worries. I needed to make sure I got to her house as fast as I could and get there fast I did.

Violet and Penn's house was quite quant, not carrying any fanciness to it. The only thing that made it have a homey feel to it was a pot at the front door with a red and purple flower in it, for obvious reasons.

Gosh! I must've wasted so much time already. Who knows how far they've gotten. That thought was only in my mind for a split second until I got to the door, nervousness rattling my bones. Now that I think about it, I don't think there was another moment in my life that could carry the title of being the most nerve racking moment ever.

I took a deep breath and gave the olive green door a good knock. When I was pulling my hand back I was thinking of just leaving the door. I didn't want to see her. It was putting too much stress on me. But without fail, the handle of the door turned.

"Oh hi Mark." The voice made me lock up. She was here. She was alive. I watched you die in front of me by my own hands. How were you here? "I'm afraid Penn already left. You're looking sharp though cutie boy." She gave me a wink. "Charlotte sure is a lucky girl."

"I didn't come here for Penn," I said, finding a firmness to my voice.

"No?" she said, raising an eyebrow. My eyes shot over to where her hand went behind the door. I heard a drawer slide open slowly.

"Look Violet. Give up the act. I know you're part of them."

Her smile instantly dropped when the words entered her ears.

"What are you talking about?"

"Don't play games with me. I know you're part of BloodLip. But you never were supposed to be. Heck, you were never supposed to be here on Earth!"

She gave me a wicked glare, one with the same inherited trait of putting me in my place.

"Leave," she said with the same firmness I was using.

"No!" I said, taking a step forward. "Look, all I'm asking is you give me two minutes to explain everything. Two minutes is all I need." I took her silent glare as permission and quickly continued with time wasting. "I found out my powers Violet. I came back from Novus just minutes ago. I found out everything. I was part of Project Salvation to go back and help Novus and stop everyone from killing each other. I used my powers to come back here to get you, to stop you from dying."

"Dying?"

"This is gonna sound horrible, but I killed you. You had me kidnapped and you were gonna kill me but since you put Charlotte at knife point I went ahead and took the shot."

She shook her head and rolled her eyes.

"Don't believe me? Then why is Penn here trying to kill all of my friends? You don't get it Violet. You were never working for the King. Zalus never cared about you. He wanted you dead! Don't you remember?! You were part of the Three! It was you, Scarlett, and Aqua. You guys worked with Rylan. C'mon. Don't tell me you don't remember Rylan." As I kept talking, she started squinting her eyes as if she was having a headache. "You guys were part of Equilibrium. He trained you since you were a little girl! Or what about Ed?!"

"Stop it!" she yelled as she started to rub her head as she kept her hand behind the door.

"No! You have to remember. What about the very girl that lives with you? Why did you siege the Palace to kidnap Penn in the first place? It was never to stop Zalus from raising her. It was because she was an Equilibrium. It was because of that the whole time. Zalus brainwashed you after he killed Aqua and stormed the Project. You're not bad! You were trying to protect your home the whole time! Now all because I made a bad decision and I killed you, Penn's trying to get revenge by coming back to kill my friends. I need you Violet. Not the Violet that was trying to kill me. I need the Violet that was part of the Three."

Her eyelids folded back and revealed her eyes. They were lost in the emptiness of the air as she searched. Everything was flooding back into her head. I could see it. She pulled both hands out and held it to her head. In one hand, the one behind the door, was a gun. She was already planning on killing me when she saw me at the door.

"Oh my gosh," she muttered under her breath. Tears started to form in her dark eyes, making her choke up on her words. "Penn. Penn. Penn." She realized exactly who she was. Not just some person to the King but an actual Equilibrium. Her eyes darted over to me in shock. "Penn. Come on."

She ran back inside the house to grab keys and slammed the door, putting the gun under her waistline, making sure to keep the handle out in case she needed to use it. Violet ran past me and hopped on her bike that was in a shed on the side of the house. The engine roared as it turned on and she rolled out into the driveway where I was standing.

"Hop on!" Wait. Was I really getting my wish? What I told her at the diner was merely to joke around, but here we were, her giving me a ride. "Where we going?"

"Emily's house. Top of the mountain. That's where she is now."

Ugh! I should've been there by now. I should've been waiting for the moment when she got there to stop her from doing anything to them. Hopefully getting Violet made up for all the lost time. It was because of her death that she was doing this in the first place. All I had to do was hope she could help me in talking her out of it if my brute force doesn't work.

Violet wasted no time, in a hurry to get to her adopted daughter as well. With the jerking motion, I fell into her. I didn't want to get flung off the bike but I didn't want to just hold her like I did with Kerren. It was different. Kerren was my sister. Doing something like that was okay, but this, this was my teacher, a thirty year old woman. The bike went over the curb and made me hop in my seat again, almost making me fall off. Oh what the heck! I had to. I went ahead and placed my arms around her slim stomach. It was just as I would imagine for someone who was an agent like she was. You had to keep shape even if you weren't in your home planet.

I was maybe expecting her to lash out and say something but there was nothing that came out of her mouth. Her head, or whole body for that matter, didn't even budge to me touching her. The hair at the back of her head, the dark brown that I would occasionally admire in class flew back into my face. I leaned in to keep it under my chest to not blow around my face and brought myself closer to her back.

Not once did Violet stop for any traffic signs. It didn't matter if it was a red or a stop sign, she just whizzed past it. How many times must've she done that back in Exon? Thousands for all I knew. I didn't have one bit of fear of us getting hit. I knew for a fact that she could maneuver a bike, something that she rode every single day, without getting hit.

The incline of the mountain was fighting back and dragging us down. It was holding us down from getting to Penn in time. I wanted to start yelling because the anxiety of me just wanting to simply get there. It was too much for me to handle. Apparently it was for Violet too.

As we were riding, she would hold the bike with one hand and wipe her face with the other. When she would turn her head to do so I could see the tears that smothered her face. It came down hard as her lips quivered. I watched in shock, not knowing that this emotion was possible from her. When anyone would talk about Violet back on Novus, they would always say how emotionless she was, not getting sentimental at all. If that was the case then why was she crying? I could only make one answer form in my head, one that obviously had to do with Penn.

It got worse. Her crying turned to sobs and shouts as everything started taking over inside her. The bike would start to lose control as she tried wiping her eyes. The tears would cover her eyes again and she couldn't see where she was going. She was forced to wipe which would throw her off balance.

"I can't! I can't Mark!" she said as she pulled over. She stopped the engine immediately and got off, letting the bike drop to the floor. "I can't drive like this."

"It's alright. We're almost there anyways. It's just up this last street," I said.

"No," she said as she wiped her tears and sniffled. "Go by yourself. I'll meet you up there in a bit. I need to get a hold of myself."

I stood there a second longer than I should've, watching her in this emotional state. This was really the woman I killed? Why was she so different? Was it really because of the brainwashing?

My feet turned and started up the inclined hill towards Emily's house. The awkward sprints that pushed my ankle in a weird position made my whole legs burn. I didn't focus on that one bit. I tried to hone in on the sound of the wind passing by my ears. That was until the sound of a scream filled its place. It was the same kind of cry that you would hear when someone dies right in your arms, the same kind of shrieking sound that Penn made when I ended Violet's life. I didn't want to turn around and look to see what state she was in, how low she had gotten, but my impulses got the better of me.

When I whipped my head around I saw a sight that I'd never see again. Violet was on the floor with her legs sprawled out, keeping her torso up. The bike with the same color as her name was laying right next to her almost as if it was trying to comfort her. Her mouth was completely open and her eyes closed as she looked up towards the sky and cried out.

"Zalus!" she yelled out, scratching at the back of her throat.

She called out to the world of the very person who was ruining things from the very start. It was her cry for revenge on the life that he took from her and I was gonna help her get it back.

*　　*　　*

I was out of breath. I was panting with a dry mouth when I ran through the gates of the grand estate. Just like it would've been, everything looked exactly as it did the first time I came in here. The fountain was in the middle of the grass and the same type of music was playing. It drew my attention over to where the party actually was on the side of the mansion. The seats were all full and people were well into partying, if you could even call slow dancing partying.

As I ran through, not caring that I was now at a party, people would try to stop me to say what's up. Guys that I would casually talk to in classes that I didn't have with the others called out to me but I ignored them. If anything it fueled me. It fueled me for knowing that I was involved in something bigger than just normal life. There was finally a reason for me doing something. There were lives on the line and I made sure to remember that as I ran past them.

As I made it to the area of the dance floor and the food tables, it got harder to run. I was forced to switch over to a fast walk and weaved in and out of people. While doing so, I had to think. Wendy died first so if I came back to where Penn jumped back then it had to be the same order. She had to kill Wendy first again. It was when Emily called Penn and Wendy into the mansion that they were alone. I needed to make sure that didn't happen.

Making my way through everyone I caught sight of a face that I kept my eyes glued to, locking on to the sight of pure beauty. Her eyes did the same and gave me a look similar to the one she gave me when I found out her name.

"Hey Mark!"

It was the voice of Will right next to her. He stood in his fancy suit that was slimmer than mine ever would be, making him look taller than should be allowed.

"Will! Charlotte!" I yelled as I ran over towards them. It was uncalled for, for them at least. I watched them die right in front of my eyes. It was totally called for here. I locked eyes again with Charlotte and kept them on her as I charged towards her. A precious smile appeared after a look of confusion from her. I ran up and slammed into her, harder than I thought I would, and squeezed her as I gave her the biggest hug I could ever give her.

"Wha—what are you…" she said, stopping herself and letting herself get lost in the hug.

Her arms didn't latch around at first but once she let herself go, she completely rested on me, letting me fill my nose with her wonderful perfume. I felt her soft breath from her nostrils on my neck, increasing my comfort. I wanted to keep hugging her, but once I remembered that I was here to stop murder I unlatched.

"Uh, what the heck was that for?" Will asked. I turned to look at him, even happy for seeing him alive. The brown tuft of hair that fell down his forehead was there like always, making the whole experience more surreal for being able to live this day again. "Looking at me like that isn't gonna give an answer. I'm not laying it off until you do. I mean, even Monica thinks it was weird." He turned to her really quick. "Right?"

Monica stood in her black dress, and once again, I didn't see her at first. Will had to point her existence out for me to actually see her. Her blank face was the opposite of what I've been seeing for a while now. I was actually starting to get used to the emotion.

"Where's Wendy?" I said with rushed speech.

"She went inside the mansion really quick with Penn to help Emily with something," Charlotte said, with blush still in her cheeks from the hug. As much as I wanted it to make me happy, I had to stay focused. It meant that I was too late and she was already with Penn.

I changed my look of joy for them to be back in my life and switched to a glare, one that only Terra could make, someone *these* people didn't know yet.

"Look," I said to Will, getting close to him, "stay with the girls and don't go inside the mansion. You hear me? I'm being dead serious here. Do not go inside. Protect them with your life."

"What the heck are you talking about?" he asked, almost scoffing at me.

Arg Will! Why do you have to be so snobby?! Can't you take this seriously? Your friend's life was on the line.

"Just stay here! Charlotte, please stay with him. Don't you go anywhere without him. You too Monica."

"Where you going?" Charlotte asked.

"To save Wendy's life."

I burst into another sprint and charged through people, making them spill their punches on their dry cleaned dresses and suits. She was in trouble. Wendy. The girl that I loved to hate. I couldn't imagine what was going on in that cursed mansion. First it was the Twins' creation in there and then now Wendy's coffin.

People started to yell at me and curse at my running through them. I didn't care if I made them fall and break something to be completely honest. I even had to run through part of the dance floor, the very place where I danced with Eris. If you were comparing this with what actually happened then I would be dancing with her right now. Penn and Wendy walked in the mansion when I started to dance with her.

I made it past the sea of human teenagers with egos higher than their cologne spray count and got to the double doors. They weren't open at the time, the maroon colored wood staying clamped shut. Did I really have to go through here again? I took a deep breath, probably knowing the others were watching me from here and threw the doors open. I resumed my sprint and as I ran down the red carpet halls where I was murdered myself. I started to take off my suit jacket, throwing it on the floor and discarding it. I didn't know where Wendy was but I tried to find my way based off on a feeling. She was here somewhere and had to be in trouble. If she was able to feel me in trouble when Violet took me then I had to be able to feel the same.

It didn't take long to feel an extremely sharp adrenaline rush. Taking into consideration how strong it was, I knew it wasn't my own. I focused on the feeling and ran upstairs as I searched for her. I didn't bother to make sure my steps were light either, but stomped through the hallways on the third floor. It dragged me all the way to a room with the door shut. It had to be in here, but I was so scared of what I'd see inside. It took me some microsecond convincing and I threw it open, taking a step inside before I could even see what was in there.

My eyes tried their best, and boy is that an understatement. There were too many things taking place at once for me to see it all. The first thing I instinctively searched for was blonde hair in the shape of buns. As it was always easy to find her in a crowd, it was that easy to find her on the floor. Her shirt was riding up at the back of her even more than it already was since it was meant to show her stomach the whole time.

In her hand, just above the white cuffs that stood alone on her wrist, was a gun. It was a solid black color that was stuck in place, aimed at someone's head. Someone was standing over her with red heels that were four inches long. The red dress that draped over her body was a lot more revealing that I remembered. The slits on the side were completely spread open since one leg was kneeling down on the floor to position the sword in Penn's hand just right.

None of them moved. It was either a pulling of a trigger to kill Penn or a press downward into Wendy's heart. All of it could've been over in milliseconds. But none of them made a decision. It was either that or I came in at the right time to stop it. Penn's eyes darted up towards me to see who was at the door. The second she saw me, shock appeared in her eyes only to dissipate and show hatred for me.

I threw down my sword, ready to intervene until I noticed one more thing. Something that my eyes couldn't really keep track of when I initially stepped in the room.

There was a black figure with their back to me. From the shape of their body I could tell it was a girl. I mean, her dress was pressing in on her waist for crying out loud. Her hands fell at her side and simply stood there to watch what was to take place inside the room, the death of my friend. But it wasn't just a person. The more I looked at her the more I noticed things. Her skirt was ruffled at the bottom, not something that just anyone would wear. And that black lacing around her neck. The thing that drove everything home was the way the dyed black hair came down. On one side it was full length, but one the other it was cut short just like Charlotte's.

"Eris?" I said.

The girl's head slightly raised, picked up by the sound of my voice. The muscles in her neck held it in its new position, completing her posture. She stayed there for a moment and joined Penn and Wendy in their frozen state all until her head turned to face me from the side.

"Well, this is a surprise."

She slowly turned her whole body to face me. I couldn't believe what I was seeing. It was actually Eris in front of me. I mean right down to the very ends of her feet where her black heels covered them. The purple sweater that she always wore, hugging tightly to her body, dipped down on her shoulder revealing the straps from her other pieces of clothing. I could list off what she was wearing all day but what mattered was the look she gave me. I was used to the deadly grin, but this time it had a whole new meaning. She was in the same exact room as Penn who was bent on killing Wendy. You take that into mind and combine it with the smile she had and the way she tilted her head down to make it appear as if she was frowning at you. Everything, and I mean everything, about her screamed horror.

"You know, I didn't expect you to come. I mean, there was always a chance, but for you to find out your powers now? I'd say you didn't do it on your own," Eris said, dropping a hip. She stared at my face, making her chuckle for how stupid I looked. "Oh come on! You didn't know that I was behind everything?" She let out a little giggle before continuing. "Why do you think I was in your class? Why did I run into you downtown right before the attack? You never thought about that?"

"Uh…" I said, standing there still, gazing at her creepiness.

She shrugged her shoulders.

"Meh. I guess I did my job way too good then. I made sure to place myself at the right times. If I had the right exposure at the right time, you'd never know. If there was always something placed right after I'd show myself it'd make you forget about me. In reality, it wouldn't matter what I did. You'd always throw me out of your mind."

"How do you know I have powers," I said, almost gasping the whole way through.

"Mark. You know nothing about me. I make sure I hide myself in a front. No one can know anything about me when I keep that. What you think you know about the Equilibrium is pitiful. You go to Novus to try and save that poor little planet from killing itself but you forget all about the one you lived on. Or what about the friends that you love so much. You never realized but who was the one that made sure those friends were close to you? It was never because she wanted to protect you. It was to make sure you never got Corrupted."

"She?"

Her smile widened.

"You had help to find out your powers. There was no way you just found out that you could jump through time on your own. It was a girl in white wasn't it. Purity's been trying her best to counteract what I do. It was always in the back of my mind that she'd do that. And what's even funnier is that you think she sent you back here to stop Penn." Eris scoffed as she kept her smile. "She doesn't care about your friends. She couldn't care less if they died. It was to bring Violet back wasn't it? Isn't that what she told you? Little does she know that she's actually helping."

Everything entered my mind at once. It was too much. This girl that I met on the first day of school and helped me pass out papers was never just a regular school girl from the city. She wasn't someone who was popular with a bunch of friends. She was someone who knew everything about me and what I've been doing. How? That was what I wanted to know.

Her hand fell and revealed a sword. It made me take a step back once I saw it. Not only did it throw me off that she was an Equilibrium too, but the color of her sword wasn't like the rest of ours. All the swords I've seen made out of the energy from our bodies was white. This one was tainted with a blackish purple that was infused inside it. It matched her perfectly. The black hair, eyes, and nails. She kept her eyes on me and made sure to bask in her winning over everything.

"Penn. Kill her. I'm gonna have me some fun."

Eris charged at me, catching me off guard. Not once had I seen her sprint like this. She was in the same period as my P.E. class but she would always run like a wuss. Here it changed all my expectations of her, knowing that everything she did was all a ploy. There was nothing in my memory that could help me here. With someone as deceiving as her, she could maneuver everything in her hands.

336

I blocked her attack from her sword and ran over towards Wendy at the sound of Eris' command. Penn was starting to push her hands down to press the sword into Wendy. I made it to her in time and smashed her into the wall, completely knocking her off Wendy.

I caught a quick glimpse of Wendy's face and saw a shock similar to mine while keeping herself highly alert to the situation. She'd never seen me with a sword in her hand and now that she saw two other people with the same powers as Penn, she no doubt was confused.

When I had Penn on the wall I looked into her eyes. They should've been red, but they were changing to the same color as they were back on Novus. It was a purple that mixed with this blood red. She picked up her knee to throw it in my stomach and knocked me back. Penn took the advantage she had and threw her arms out for my neck. Right before they could reach it, Wendy jumped on her back, clinging onto her like a monkey. With a move she must've learned in self-defense class, she kept her arms on Penn and lifted herself up and over her, twisting her legs and she came tumbling down to the floor. Wendy landed on her feet and aimed the gun back at her head.

Standing straight now and being able to breath, I saw Eris walking towards us with her smile. I ran over to Wendy and for some reason I picked her up. I wrapped my arms around her from in front as if I was gonna give her a hug and waited for her to teleport. The second I touched her I could feel her heartbeat. It pounded away, trying to find out what was the reason for her to be in a situation that would cause it to run at such a pace. The look of worry on her face stayed in my head as she went ahead and teleported us out of the room.

Swoosh

"What the heck is going on?" she asked, still holding onto me.

We were in a hallway in the mansion. I didn't know what floor or what part since I didn't recognize any of the decor on the wall. I pulled back from her a little, just enough to see her face. I had my hands placed on her waist as she had it on my back. It took a while for us to realize we were in that position after staring at each other's eyes for a bit.

"Look. I know this might not make much sense to you but I'm from the future. Penn's trying to kill you guys and I'm stopping her."

She furrowed her brows, and with a burst of confidence, held us closer.

"But you have Penn's powers!"

"I know but—"

The stomping of footsteps stopped me. I heard it coming from the other side of the hall. Both of us turned our heads to see the beasts come forward. It was a sight that you could only hope to see in your nightmares. A wrathful Princess with rage stormed around the corner of the hall with a white sword in her hand. Next to her was a deceitful gothic girl that carried around a ghoulish smile, a purple sword in her hand. We both watched in horror as they came closer with each step.

"Wendy!" I yelled.

"I can't!" she said, still watching them.

"But you just did! Do it again!"

"We'll get stuck!" she yelled.

Penn dropped the sword, making it dissolve and made a bow in her hand. She loaded it with an arrow made from the same material and pulled it back.

"I don't care! Do it now!"

She pulled me into herself and rested her head in my chest, hoping that somehow we would avoid getting stuck.

It was completely acceptable for her to be scared and nervous right now, but we were dead regardless. Better to take the route where we had a chance.

I opened my eyes the second I heard the sound of us coming back into the world and leaving her secluded part of space. I searched for them and saw nothing. Nothing but a painting on the wall. When I saw it, I pulled away from Wendy to look at it, making sure it was the right one. Just at the bottom of it was a tiny black signature. Yup, same one who made the painting of my life. Boat in the storm.

As I was checking the painting, the doors behind us rattled as someone was pulling on the handles. It threw another burst of adrenaline into my body, ready for whatever was to come from the doors. Maybe they somehow got outside and were now coming in the mansion again. Or maybe it was someone coming to use the bathroom. After the doors were pulled open, I saw three people I met outside coming into the mess of a party. Why couldn't you guys listen?!

Will stood in the doorway with Charlotte and Monica at his side. At least they were listening to what I told them to not leave his side.

"No! What are you doing?! I told you not to come in here!" I yelled as I walked towards them.

Will and the other two walked in to where we were in the middle of the hallway and let the doors slam behind them.

"What's the deal with eve—"

I didn't hear Will finish what he said. His voice carried on in my head as I was separated from everything. For some reason, I felt like I was being pulled, almost like when I'm in Wendy's world. What was happening? What was Will gonna say? I didn't get to finish my thought. Everything went black and I was set into a game I played once before.

*　　　*　　　*

When I gained my vision back I tried looking for anyone. I desperately searched for the sight of Wendy's buns. If I were to ever see her fall as she did back in Novus then I don't think I'd be able to live with myself. But it was impossible for me to see that since she wasn't even there. None of them were. I was standing in the same exact place I was just a second ago. If that was the case then why weren't they here?

I was facing the wall with the painting on it. Everything about that was the same as well. As I was pulling my eyes off of that, I heard a door open to the left of me. When I turned to see the same symbol of a triangle with a white figure of a woman with a skirt on it, it all started to rush back into my head. Where everyone went was starting to not become a valid question anymore. I knew where they were. They were stuck just like I was.

The door to the woman's bathroom slowly closed behind them and revealed three girls that I had seen in that exact position. A girl with such a lovely face in front and on the side of her two more girls. One carried a smile that held open a bit and the other was just as bland as dirt. Charlotte casually started to walk towards me in no way different than her normal walk.

Oh you gotta be kidding me. You can't be serious. Was this really happening again? As I stood there and watched them walk towards me to execute their assignment and fulfill Charlotte's dream of killing me, I realized why this was happening. The Twins specifically told me that they were created when we walked in that slip space. How else was that space gonna be made. It had to do something with all of us coming into this exact spot. Someone, maybe Eris, made this exact spot, the very place where if we were to all come into the mansion that they would be created.

Charlotte's smile was growing little by little, her eyes trying to tell me something. By now I would've already been talking to them. Now, I stood still with my thoughts collecting. If Eris created this very plan to have all of my friends killed from the beginning then she had to have something there to stop anyone from ruining her plans. This had to be her way of stopping anyone from coming in, like me. If we tried to leave the mansion and if they all came in, this would happen. Then that'd mean we were all standing still in the very spot we were earlier. It would give Penn and Eris time to come down and end our lives, us being sitting ducks. If that was the case then this wasn't real. There was only one way to get out.

"Hi Mark," Charlotte said with a sweet voice.

I had to fight the notion of thinking that this whole place was real and accept that once I would die I would be set free and so would they. I took that and ran with it, literally. I sprinted towards them, these fakes of my *real* friends. I thought that they would take this quite well since they always asserted dominance over me in the past, but this time they were surprised by me doing this. They expected me to be scared and they banked on that the whole time. But this was my time. I knew what would happen. I had the advantage. I would dictate the future.

Monica's hands were raising from their stationary position to throw a bolt in me but I put up a wall as fast as I could. It took her off guard since they never expected me to know my powers yet. I dropped the wall and threw a foot into Monica's stomach, sending her to the floor. With the same motion, I reached over and took a hold behind Charlotte's neck and pushed her down to grab the gun that was behind her back.

"No, what are you doing?!" she yelled out.

I'm telling you. That messed with my sanity levels like crazy. It sounded completely like Charlotte would, especially if I were to lay a hand on her like that. But I needed to keep going. This was not the real Charlotte and I was gonna get out of this place to save them. I had a job to do and I was doing it no matter what.

I managed to have her bring the gun forward with her still holding onto it. She wanted to have her moment no doubt but I was here to end it as fast as I could. I moved her hand so the gun would be positioned in front of my head and I yanked on the trigger with as much confidence as I could. The same sound of that bang only sounded for a split second before everything went white and my head caved in.

*   *   *

"Aaah!" I yelled out.

Even though I knew it wasn't real it still had the same effect as if you actually died. Now who gets to say that they died twice in their lifetime and live? Add me to that list for sure.

I whipped my head around with my heart still beating like crazy and saw the others standing still with their heads slightly down. It all looked like they were daydreaming, lost in a world that no one could see but themselves. They were all getting hunted down by me, their friend.

"Charlotte!" I yelled, running over to her and shaking her from her shoulders. "Charlotte wake up! It's all fake!"

"Tell them that all you want. It's all real to them no matter how hard you try to tell them otherwise."

I turned to see Eris next to Penn, swords still drawn, same look on their face.

"So it was you who made that slip space," I said.

"I wouldn't take the credit for that one. I got a little help. I found a Sentinel who could make the very place you got out of."

"Sentinel?"

"You still think I'm gonna answer your questions? Who would do that when it's way too fun to see you confused as you've always been?"

She swung her sword towards me, slicing my left arm. The stinging sensation was quick to spread all over, hindering my movement. I staggered back and stumbled over my feet, giving Penn an opportunity to come in and do some damage as well. I threw out my sword and drove it from the floor to block it. The pain from the gash was starting to be too much for me, the blood quickly taking over the white color of my shirt.

Eris jerked her head towards where the others were still frozen in place as she came towards me. A smile flashed on Penn's face for a split second before she ran towards them to get her pain for pain medication.

So there I was. I was on my knee with a hand over my gash, trying to do something about the blood. Eris was coming towards me with her sword and Penn was going towards my friends. As I watched helplessly as this deadly Princess made her way to them, I realized that I was either gonna let them fall or I was gonna do everything I could for them.

Terra, or Scarlett, asked me who I was. I told her straight to her face that I was their friend and that I'd do everything for them. I was the one who was saved by them, giving me a reason to keep going every day. I was loved by these four people. I killed someone for that reason. There was no way everything was gonna go down in vain. I fought for peace, for the freedom of other, for the Equilibrium. They were the Equilibrium. They were *my* friends.

I waited for just the right second where Eris was a step away from me to rush forward and grab her. I wrapped my hands behind her back and threw both of us to the floor. She whacked her head against it and I placed a foot on top of her to make sure she stayed there as I tried something I'd never done. I've seen Penn make this bow before but I've never done it. I tried my best to emulate that, and with everything else about these powers, that's all it took. I pulled back on the bow and sent an arrow at Penn's feet. It was sent flying and clipped her foot, slicing it at the shin. She yelled out and tripped to the floor.

I pulled off of Eris and tried sprinting towards Penn. Eris was a problem but that's all she was at the moment. Penn was the reason I was here. She was gonna hurt everyone I loved and I was gonna stop that in any way I can. That is if Eris didn't yank on my ankle, tripping me before I could take another step.

"Slow it down there honey," she said. I turned to give her a look really quick, and as if I expected something more, she was giving me her nasty smile.

As I was trying my best to pull away from her, desperately watching, hoping that Penn wouldn't hurt them anymore, she made her way to her feet. The blood ran down her foot and onto her blood red heels, making the color darker. She grit her teeth to avoid the pain and walked up to Charlotte. Her eyes dug into my best friend's soul, seeking into those brown beauties for a last cry for help. It would've been the way she wanted it to go; for all of them to go down screaming. Lo and behold, this is how it was to be for her revenge. The beast was looking one last time into the eyes of its victim before devouring them whole.

"Penn! Don't do it!" I yelled. "It's not what Violet wants!"

"Don't you try and feed me lies!" she yelled into Charlotte's face.

"You think I'm lying?! I talked to her minutes ago! I could see the love she had for you in her eyes. She doesn't want you to do this!"

"She never loved me! She treated me like I was some priority in life, only being my bodyguard. I wasn't anything special besides the order she was given to protect me!"

"Now *you're* lying to yourself!"

Penn couldn't have anymore. The sword in her hand was calling for blood and it was Charlotte's, her first victim of many more to come. That was unless I stop her.

"Tell me if this is lying to myself," she said, placing the sword underneath her head, just at her neck that was threatened by her adopted mom.

Just as I was contemplating severely injuring Eris to get myself free, the double doors rattled. Everything that was happening in here was only known by us. Anyone who walked in at this moment would see secrets to life that no one should know. But if it meant a chance at stopping Penn somehow then by all means come in.

The doors swung open and the person who was walking in stopped in their tracks to widen their eyes at the marvels taking place. She didn't move. She didn't care about anyone else really but the person I was doing everything to stop. Her eyes locked with Penn and a sense of betrayal instantly set in. I was able to read it only because I've seen the same exact look in Monica.

"Penn?" Brittany said, watching her keep the sword to Charlotte.

Penn's eyes shifted to focus on her best friend. The anger that was taking over her stopped for a split second when she initially saw her, but just as always, it came back in full control.

"What are you doing?" she asked.

"Get out," Penn demanded.

"What?" she responded, shocked at the very command of her best friend to leave.

"I said get out."

"Penn, you're gonna kill Charlotte! We're not supposed to kill them! It was only Mark!"

"None of this involves you. I'm only saying this one more time. Get out."

This was my chance. I didn't bother looking back to see if Eris was as taken off guard as Penn was with Brittany coming into the mix of things. I needed to assume that she was so I could get myself free. I gave one more good tug on my foot and yanked it free from her, bursting into a sprint right away. You lay your hands off my friend you monster!

I pushed back Charlotte to make sure she was away from the sword and held Penn from her shoulders. Before she could do anything, I rammed a foot into her shin that I sliced open. She shrieked out in pain and dug her nails into my shoulder, quickly drawing blood.

"Aaah!" I heard behind me. The sound made my head pick up and stop focusing on Penn for a second. It was Charlotte's voice. I threw her back so Brittany had to have her.

I turned around and saw her with her hands on her head, looking into the floor. Her eyes were roving around, trying to comprehend what just happened. Little did she know what was actually happening. Her eyes finally found me and she cried out at the sight of me, striking me hard. It was just like last time. I made her cry and wonder if she was gonna be killed by me again. This time I was trying my best to save her life.

"Charlotte!" I yelled.

"Get away from me," she sobbed.

"What the heck!" Will yelled, taking steps back as he gasped for air. They were all coming back. Was I finally home free?

Wendy's eyes opened and she started making the noise of her teleporting over and over again, disappearing and reappearing to the same place she was standing in like it was some sort of stutter. But the person I was worried the most about other than Charlotte was the one who actually had a revealing of emotions when she came to. And just as I was expecting, Monica started to scream her heart out, crying out to someone for help to end this madness that she was experiencing.

"Monica it wasn't real!" I shouted. I tried calling her to her senses but something red walked past me towards Charlotte who was standing in front of me. I was too busy with them to remember the danger of who was there with me.

It was way too fast. Although I say that, it was one of those moments where you could see it happen in slow motion. Bottom line, I couldn't do anything. Penn was still set on Charlotte and tried to drive the sword into her abdomen. Was this really it? Was this all it took to finish everything, just me standing still?

Will jumped in front of her and grabbed a hold of the blade, cutting his hands in the process. He threw it down and took a hold of Charlotte's hand and ran with the rest of them out of the double doors. It wasn't because he was trying to save them from Penn, it was because he thought I was the enemy. They all did.

No. I wasn't letting this happen. I was gonna right the wrong right now. I ran forward and knocked Penn to the side as I left the doors. When I got outside, a wonderful orchestral piece was playing for couples to dance to. For me it was music to find my friends and convince them I needed their help. All four of them were stumbling over themselves, trying to get away from this place. I could even hear Monica's sobs from where I was.

Because they were weak from fighting me in their slip space, it wasn't that hard to catch up to them.

"Guys wait!"

"Get away from us!" Will yelled.

"No! That wasn't real! You think that didn't happen to me? It happened to me twice now!"

Will stopped and turned around, giving me a stupid look. People passed by us and raised eyebrows at us for acting strange.

"What the heck is going on?" he demanded firmly.

"I know things might look weird, and they do, but I'm here stopping Penn from killing you."

"When you have the same power as her?" Wendy asked.

"Come on Wendy! I saved you! I found out my powers. It's the exact same ones as Penn's."

"Then what happened inside the mansion?" Charlotte asked, looking at me hoping that all of it was truly fake.

"A slip space for each of you to experience fear," Eris's voice said as she came walking out with Penn. "It was important for everything. It was to make—"

"The Twins. I know. You don't think I haven't met them outside the slip space?" I barked back at the sound of her voice.

"Penn stop!" Brittany yelled, running to catch up with her. "What are you doing?"

Eli and Sarah were sitting at the same exact bench that I was sitting at when I was talking with them. He had a hand behind his sister as she sat with her leg over her other and her hands matching the position of her legs with the way they were crossed. Both of their heads caught Brittany when she chased after Penn. I watched as their faces changed expression and they quickly rose to the matter, following her.

So here we were again. Just like always we ended up with this sort of confrontation. The five of us were facing the five of them. Eris stood there and didn't bother to take her eyes off of me. Penn turned to face her friends that were utterly confused by her actions.

"Look. You do as I say. We're getting revenge for Violet," Penn told them.

"Revenge? For what?!" Brittany said.

"She died! Mark kills her tonight and I'm making sure that doesn't happen again."

"What are you talking about? How do you know that?"

"Because I time jumped. Now do as I say and help me fight. It's what we vowed, remember? We do everything for each other and help no matter what."

All of them were still confused as they should be. Here, Eris, this person they never knew much about was with Penn and they were now trying to kill all of us. I never thought much of the rest of BloodLip having morals, but without this rage for all us of, they were showing their true form. They never hated me. It was simply their job to take care of what I could do and make sure I never did.

"Don't worry honey," Eris said, walking behind them. "They'll help you no matter what."

She placed her arms around them like they were gonna take a picture, and as they curiously watched her smile behind them, something started to change. There was something happening right in front of our eyes. They were starting to lose that look of uncomfortableness with the situation and started to curl their brows. It reminded me of when Monica was fighting for control over Maya. What was Eris doing?

I took a step back and grabbed both Charlotte hand and Will's. They were the closest to me and I squeezed it as hard as I could. Will's hand fell limp in my own because of the wound it carried, but they both knew what I was doing. This wasn't for some hope that they would use their powers to help me escape. This was our fight.

Penn turned to face us as soon as Brittany shed her dress. The flames that spewed out of her hands were quick to dissolve any part of the fancy cloth that I saw through. She told me that she wore it just in case and this was one of the cases. But never did she expect something to actually happen.

"Did you guys trust me when I told you what you saw wasn't real?" I asked them.

"Why?" Will asked.

"Cause I'm gonna need all the help I can get."

It all happened within seconds. Everyone charged forward and we clashed. Penn ran for me and I for her. Everyone had a target and they kept it. Not once did any of us think about where we were fighting. It was in the front of the mansion. Emily's lawn that was previously littered with people was now clear, everyone being occupied with the party. It was the place for the grass to start to singe because of Brittany's fire that she threw around in punches. As fast as the fight started, it ended just as fast. Not because anyone was tired or someone retreated, but rather, because of a shout behind us at the gates of the estate.

"Penn!"

All of us recognized the voice. It belonged to the same person that started to scream out in despair when she was left alone with her bike on the sidewalk. Violet stood at the entrance of the mansion and carried nothing in her hand. She looked as normal as she always did, getting over her emotional breakdown. Just because she knew everything about her past and remembered what the King did to her, she didn't change in appearance.

Penn froze at the sound of her voice. Her eyes were crippled at the sight of her adopted mom. This was the person she was fighting for for so long now. She wanted to carry out her name and here she was.

"They're lies. All of them. We never worked for the King."

"You believe the lies Mark's telling you!" Penn yelled back.

"Lies? Penn, they're the truth! I worked for Equilibrium!" She started to walk towards where we were with eyebrows bent down towards the ends. "Penn. This isn't how things were supposed to be. You guys were all supposed to be friends protecting each other. I was never even supposed to be here on Earth. Zalus wiped my memory. I didn't remember anything."

"But you don't get it! He killed you," she said as tears started to fall. "He killed you right in front of all of us! I'm clearing your name for you! I'm doing the same thing you would've done!"

"No! You're wrong. I wouldn't want you to hurt them. I spent so long from the beginning protecting them and that hasn't changed. Penn. It's enough. You can stop now. Your mom's right here."

Something ticked inside Penn and I could see it. Her face cringed with disgust, hatred for the whole situation.

"Don't play that game with me. Don't pretend like you actually thought of me like your daughter. You *never* let me call you mom! I always wanted to. Do you know how much

I cried in my room at night, not being able to call you that?! I really did see you as my mom but you never gave me the satisfaction."

Violet let out a sigh and got closer to her, passing us along the way.

"I never knew that sweetie. I'm sorry. I did that so I would make sure that you knew the King was your real parent. I was just there to protect you, but I hid some feelings to. As soon as you started walking and started saying your first words, I couldn't help but feel attached to you. I felt like I was your real mom. I named you after the only memory I had left, some faint picture of a lady with a smile that you emulated."

A laugh broke the thin line of conversation. The shaky emotions that they were both playing were bypassed by a laugh that snapped that line. The cold voice kept on, laughing so hard she had to hold her stomach. Eris finally found her composure and smiled at Violet.

"You actually think you're her mother? Oh, I'm sure you know of how the Queen died. You were there after all. But you're simply creating an illusion in your head. Tell me Violet. Who was there when she was first born? Who was there when she was crying as an infant in her crib inside the Palace? Hm? Who?" Eris turned her head to look at Penn who still had tears rolling down her face. "Violet was never your mom. I was there from the very beginning. I held you one night and rocked you to sleep. I told you to do something. Remember? You looked so gosh darn cute with your red fuzzy hair. I looked at you and told you what you've been doing this whole time. 'Disturb the peace my friend. Spread the Corruption. Make it grow.' Can you do that for me again honey?"

Eris's hands clenched as she dug her fingers inside her palms. Her smile found some way to grow even more and her eyes squinted as something started to change in Penn. The purple hair that confused me started to change. It became darker and darker until it eventually became just like Eris's, fully black. The lightly colored pink of her nails turned black, and just like the night sky, her eyes completely turned to the point of the red being gone without a trace.

When I saw that, it clicked to the point of understanding what I was seeing this whole time. When Twin Charlotte met me when I got captured, she touched that tank to see if she could do something to the kids. This dark substance left her hand and did the same thing it did to Penn. The only thing different was she didn't die this time. But what mattered is what she told me afterwards.

"Corruption hurts. Get used to it."

This thing that was messing with all of BloodLip, this force that was now changing Penn was Corruption. I didn't know what it was but Eris had a grip on it. She was using it to change all of their motives.

Penn hunched over in anger and let out puffs of air from her nostrils as they flared.

"Don't make me do this Violet," Penn said.

"Don't you ever call me that anymore. I'm your mother and you address me as that."

"Mmm, I'm not so sure about that," Eris said, crossing her arms now, enjoying watching everything unfold. "Try fighting the Corruption and I'll let you take the title."

"Don't get in my way Violet," Penn said. "I'm getting my revenge regardless if you're dead or alive."

"Penn! Listen to yourself! What happened to the girl that I knew hated seeing dead animals on the side of the road?! What about all those times we would invite Brittany over to bake cookies and do our nails. You'd talk about all the boys you liked in school. Remember that?!" The tears came back as Violet tried searching inside this person who looked exactly like Penn. "Where's my little girl?"

"Don't compare me with who I was!" she shrieked.

Penn closed her eyes as she ran for her mom with her sword in hand. We could only witness as this happened. I couldn't help but see as if she was fighting over this Corruption inside her. Why would she be crying in the first place if she never cared?

Violet let out one more sob before she readied for the impact of the very person she cared for her whole life. The sword flew up before she threw it at Violet. She could easily read where the sword was going to hit and dodged it, moving in right after to grab a hold of Penn. Once she knew she was taken hold of, she threw Violet off of her to the floor. Before Penn could jump on top of her to make sure she stayed there, Violet tripped Penn, hitting her right where I cut her. She ran over and hugged her from behind, squeezing her tight, not letting her go.

"Get off of me!" Penn screamed.

"Never! I won't ever let go. I neglected you this whole time. I didn't realize what pain you were in. I won't let that happen again."

"Stop lying! You never loved me! Where were you when I was crying myself to sleep?! You were too busy screaming yourself! I couldn't even go to you and ask if I could lay down with you cause you'd send me right back! You just wanted to kill Mark and go back home. That's all you ever wanted! Why do you think I wanted to hurry up and kill him from the beginning?"

Violet hugged her tighter and rested her head in between her shoulder and neck.

"But you wanted to save him. I thought you wanted him on our side because you liked him."

Penn was starting to finally calm down. She wasn't fighting Violet's grip anymore and simply sat there with her.

"I thought that if I could save the things I love, maybe it could keep my mind off of you and get me to just focus on him."

"You don't need to worry about that anymore Penn. We're both here for you. I love you sweetie," Violet said, giving her one more final squeeze. "I love you."

Penn started to let out sobs from her mouth in little spurts before turning around to fully hug her mom. All of us kept standing there like we were and watched as they started to bond, reunited with the thing I took from her. The love you saw between those two was nothing like I've seen in a long time. They were both a mess, crying right after fighting each other, but boy their love was as clear as day.

While they were hugging, the black that tainted Penn's body was starting to dissipate. The darkness was flushing away and being replaced with the red that was supposed to be. After it being so long without that color, it was refreshing to see it back where it should be. When she finally opened her eyes to look at her mom, the blood red was back as well. And the black nails? Gone. Whatever this Corruption was, it could be beat.

I wanted to see what Eris would think of that. She seemed to control it so now that she saw it was beaten by the person who was tainted by it she must've been surprised. When I saw her face it was as normal as ever. The smile was there and it looked like she was on the verge of laughter again. She raised both of her hands and gave a pitiful clap.

"Oh good for you. You got your daughter back and you got your precious mother. How sweet of a story. I just wanna give you a heads up. Corruption doesn't work like that."

"What are you talking about?" I asked.

She closed her eyes and shrugged her shoulders.

"I don't know. You'll have to see. If you're born from Corruption you're automatically drawn to it. If that source is taken, well, let's just say things don't end well."

Violet took Penn's hand and stood up. Upon standing tall at full height, she let Penn go. It was hard to see Penn the way she was. The last time I could remember her like this was when she asked me if I wanted to join BloodLip. Right now, she was wiping her nose with her forearm and wiping her eyes. Violet's eyes honed in on Eris, the real problem at hand.

"Who are you?" Violet asked.

"Uh...Eris. Duh. I was in your class. Remember? The dark and creepy girl that always sat in the back next to Aryn."

"You know what I meant."

"Come on. Who are you? That's way too vague of a question," Eris said, standing next to the rest of BloodLip. "If you ever want answers you gotta do more than just ask a question like that. But because I'm feeling really generous and I can't help but enjoy the look on your faces when you realize things, I'll go ahead and tell you this. You know that ship that dropped that bomb over Ashillon?" She jerked her thumb into her chest and made a clicking noise with her mouth. "Yup. Me."

"It wasn't Zalus?" Violet said, flaring her nostrils now.

"No. Not really. I told him that he had an advantage if he dropped the bomb, but he didn't believe me. I went ahead and moved things along myself and started a world war. It was pretty easy as it was. You just take the eerie atmosphere between multiple countries and spark a little something to get them all riled up. That's all it took to get the dire need for an Equilibrium to be born. Isn't that right honey?"

Eris turned to look at Penn and gave her one of the most heartwarming and creepiest smiles I've ever seen. Penn, for the first time in forever, acted normally and made her best disgusted look.

"That still doesn't answer how Penn came here and you were already there," I said.

"I don't know. The future me would know."

"She met me back on Novus," Penn answered, her voice shaken. "She saved us from the building that was falling with the other Wendy. She told me about how you and I had the same powers and that I had a chance to get revenge."

So that explains what I saw right before the building fell. She had reason to save Penn. She was part of her plan in some way.

"Is that what I did then? Well that was true. I did create this very scenario for you. But, you know, didn't really account for Mark to find things out this soon. But it doesn't matter much. If anything it tells me all I need to know about the future. Anyways, why are we all standing around here for? Don't you have a King to kill?"

Hearing those words hurt. I knew we had to, but what about everything that Penn's done? Were we just gonna go back and be where we were on Novus? What about Violet? How would things work out with her? This all littered my mind when red hair caught my attention. It was pleasing to see the color back in her hair but her eyes is where the color held its emotion. It was a solemn look with regret filled inside it. She slowly walked up to me and hesitated to take another step, especially when the others started to get scared of her.

"M—Mark. I…"

She couldn't finish. I didn't realize it at first but this was her trying to apologize. Her red eyes tried calling out to me to finish her sentence but they never did. Nothing did.

She simply just stayed there all teary eyed. Everything she's done to get her revenge was now held aloft with her mother being alive. She was able to finally bond with her best friend, the missing piece in her life. This was really the thing that was holding her back the whole time. It was the only reason she took an interest in me. It was her outlet from what was bothering her with Violet. It was all for a reason and she hardly knew it herself.

"It can wait," I told her. "We have to get back." The whole look she was giving was extremely nostalgic, driving me back to after the attack. This was the Penn I knew. This was the Penn I loved. It was all here in front of me finally. She gave a little nod that I was able to notice and actually drew a smile to my face. "Are you okay with this? He's your dad."

"He's not my dad. I never had one."

"Well that wraps things up!" Eris said. "Let's get a move on people. I desperately wanna see what happens at the Palace."

I whipped my head back and snarled at her. Even when I tried fighting back it makes things worse. You know what she does after that? She giggles. I swear it was more annoying than Wendy.

I went ahead and grabbed a hold of Charlotte's hand as well as Will's. I nodded my head for them to grab someone as well.

"What are you doing?" Monica asked quietly.

"I'm bringing you back to life. We're going back to Novus to finish things."

"Novus?" Will asked.

"You already know where that is, the other half of you that is. Everything will make sense once we get back there."

All five of us connected hands, Penn holding onto Violet. The seven of us faced the remains of BloodLip and Eris. The way she was standing there with them was like she owned them somehow, completely comfortable with all they've done. She gave all of us one more hard-pressed smile that made me cringe.

"Isn't Corruption such a beautiful thing that once it's gone you can see who they really were? People like to think that but I see the Corrupted person as their true self. Your emotions are put on high and you run with it. You'll see what I mean when you get back. I'll be waiting there for you. See ya real soon."

Eris raised a hand without any effort, swinging it on the way up to her forehead, and gave us a salute.

I had no idea who she actually was or how she fit into the bigger picture. She knew everything about us and what we've been through. She was the one who dropped the bomb but how could she do that and still be young like us? She could time jump, not time travel. Eris was a tricky figure for sure, but what I was really trying to figure out was what Corruption was.

Before we followed our path back to Novus that we could feel, I gave Eris one more glare as the face of the fake Charlotte popped in my head. Everything about her was like Eris. Black hair. Black eyes. Black nails. She was Corrupted. They all were. They were called the Twins of Oblivion but they weren't twins of us at all. They were completely different. I made it a point to not call them twins anymore, but rather call them what they are.

Corrupted.

And just like that, we were gone from the Earth, leaving behind that party, that world that never was anymore.

Chapter 12

I wanted to keep holding on. Her hand was as warm and full of life as it ever was. We were traveling back to a place in time where she wasn't alive. Naturally, I didn't want to go back, but for all reasons I knew I had to. There was more to just my own feelings. There was a bigger problem that needed to be solved. If I was never there to help stop the King from trying to kill off the outer cities, everyone would probably all be dead within a matter of days. The Twins were already doing their job of taking the order from within Exon and throwing it away by sending the kids that were supposed to be used outside on them. It was all a recipe for disaster. We were the only things stopping all that.

Charlotte held my hand like she always did, with a sense of something more. I was afraid that maybe she wouldn't know all that we did on Novus. All the bonding, not to mention what I told her on top of Headquarters.

The feeling of traveling time through dimensions was just like it was the first time in the mall. It got extremely cold followed by heat and an array of lights. It all disappeared and the world would come back into focus. This power that I had let me do something that technology on Earth wouldn't even allow. How did this happen to me?

When I first opened my eyes, I half expected us to still be on Earth, or maybe be somewhere else by me screwing things up. Looking around, I noticed I was right where I was before I left back to Earth. It was a white room, sapped of any color. There were pillars all around, holding the ceiling up at the very top floor of the Palace. Charlotte wanted to know how much it took to live at the top of the Penthouse. There you needed money. Here? You needed to be the most corrupt King in the world.

Now that I was finally able to look at it without wrath running through me, I noticed that there were rugs all over the floor that went over the marble floor, shining with the artificial light and mostly from all the light that came in the windows. There were no walls whatsoever. It was all pretty much just glass reinforced into the structure of the Palace, giving an outlook over the whole city. There were double doors that were put into the glass that went outside. A balcony was the only thing that extended out of this fortress.

After looking at everything, I remembered what was in my hands. I noticed a tall person to the left of me and didn't bother to look at him. It's not that I didn't care about him. It was because if I saw his darn pretty boy face I was bound to punch it. I felt in my hand that there wasn't any blood from his wound.

There was a squeeze in my right hand as Charlotte gave her hand some life. When I turned to look at her I saw a godly sight. It reminded me a lot of when we first came to Novus since she was in the same spot she was now. It wasn't only her positioning, but she was looking forward in shock now. Her eyes were widened as she took a deep breath, gasping for air. After her breath of life, she turned her head and tried finding someone. I watched intently, not doing anything rash again. It wasn't until she caught eyes with the very person holding her hand did her eyes widen even more. She withdrew her hand and fell into me, hugging me with the most love I've ever felt from her, showing more love than any kiss that Corrupted Charlotte could give.

"Okay, this feels really weird. And where the heck are we?" Wendy said. Her voice was beside Will, catching everyone's attention. Everyone immediately looked at her as she was examining her hands. It didn't take long either for everyone to run up to her and dog pile her as we all hugged her.

"Wendy!" we all shouted.

"Wait, you guys remember everything?" I asked, still pumped for them being back.

"I mean, as much as I can remember," Will said. "Last I could think of was when I crashed into the building and you took Monica's bow."

I noticed Monica's short stature standing there blankly. It was mixing with her emotions that she's shown recently. With her blank face, she reached up to her head where the bow's always sat. When she felt, there was nothing there but the hair on her head.

"Then what about me going back? Do you guys still remember the party?"

"I remember both things," Monica said, stroking the strand of hair that was used to the pressure of the bow. "There's two memories when I think back to it."

As we stood there and figured out how things worked out, I felt like something was out of place. I was really forgetting everything? Penn was standing next to Violet inside the King's quarters. Both of them still hadn't moved and were right where they were when they first got there.

Since I was used to Penn being full of rage, I was half expecting something to come from her, but with the Corruption gone, there was nothing but a blank face as she looked forward. What I should've been worried about was the teacher that disguised herself the whole time I knew her.

Violet was in the same place as Penn, both in position and movement. She was almost frozen. But her lungs surely weren't. I could hear her breathing increase like a bull would before running towards someone holding or wearing any article of red. Her nostrils flared and her hands were in fists now. It stopped all of us from doing anything else and we all turned our attention towards her. All it took was for me to look over at who was standing there in the first place to realize where her rage came from.

"You have no idea how much pain I'm gonna make you feel," Violet said. Her eyes pressed into Zalus as he stood next to Sarah, Brittany, and Eli. "Not only do you take *my* life, but you take theirs and make it a miserable one."

I could read it all over Zalus' face. He was piecing everything together. He found out that Penn had the same powers as me before I even came up this elevator. He thought he had the upper hand, but because of Purity coming to tell me about my powers, I was able to turn things around. It was shown in all of us being here in his very house. How could you explain Violet being here all of a sudden?

"What are you doing here," Zalus said, looking at Violet. He quickly switched to looking at his daughter. "Penn, why'd you get Violet? We said that you were going back to end Mark's friends."

"Don't talk to me like that. I don't need revenge for her if I have her with me," she replied, finally speaking with some sense.

"What did you do?" Brittany said with a subtle tone of shock in her voice.

When I looked over to see all of BloodLip, the sight scared me. Before I left back to Earth to stop Penn, they looked like they always did. Brittany was wearing her brown tank and Sarah had her knives on her waist. Eli was glaring me down like always too. But it wasn't what they were wearing or their facial expression that was different. It was their bodies. They were normal just before I left. Why were they now infected with this Corruption?

Everything from their hair to their nails were black. It was almost like they were turned gothic. All that was needed now was for them to be listening to screamo and they're good. It was obvious who they got it from considering that Eris was standing next to them with a wide smile. The way her hands hung at her sides made her look even more undead than she already did. I was about to yell out to her and let my heart speak for me but the elevator behind me hissed open.

"Get down!" the heavy voice yelled.

"Scarlett?!"

Violet's mouth was held open as she watched Scarlett and Kerren storm out of the elevator with guns in hand. At first they didn't care about whatever Violet said, ready for return fire to come from whoever was guarding the King. Ain't gonna happen Scarlett. This cocky idiot had no one but BloodLip guarding him.

She didn't bother to have her helmet on and neither did Kerren. Their eyes zipped by everything and mentally scanned what was friendly and what was hostile when their helmets could do that very thing. I got to say. It was a refreshing sight. This was what they were waiting for all of their lives and now here they were, determination in their face. Scarlett had her lips curled like always and Kerren furrowed her brows, looking exactly like when my mom yells at me for not doing the dishes. It wasn't until Scarlett's eyes locked with Violet's that she froze.

"Violet?"

She had her gun still pointed at Zalus, but for the first time ever, I saw her lose focus. She was always doing everything in her power to overthrow Zalus. Here he was right in front of her. The only thing stopping her was her longtime friend that was dead who was standing before her.

Violet didn't do anything either. They stood with this locked look that made my heart rush. It's been years since their eyes have met like that. It was only something they could dream of, but now, it was real. It was quite strange. Seeing two adult woman like that made me realize how much adults were like us. When I say us I mean people my age obviously. And even kids. With my experience with the younger kids from the school, it made me realize something. There is no age that limits us. No matter who we are or what age, we are all affected with the same problems. We can't hide that fact. Violet and Scarlett couldn't when they were frozen in time with shock flowing freely.

"H—how?" Scarlett said. "You're dead. Mark told me—"

Violet didn't bother answering. Her legs found the power to fight this shock and run towards her, whacking bodies together. Violet made Scarlett lose her balance as they wobbled in place in a hug that spoke of all their past.

"You're still alive," I heard Violet say in Scarlett's shoulder.

"Aw. How nice. Look who's back together. I guess that's just how things go in life. You gain one thing when you lose another," Eris said.

"Who the heck are you?" Scarlett said, finishing her hug with Violet.

"Ugh. Can't people get more creative with that question?" she said, shaking her head. "Names Eris. Get used to it. Gonna hear it a lot."

"She's an Equilibrium," I said, curling my lips and keeping my gaze on her.

"Oh goodie you told them my secret. What am I gonna do now?" she said, pretending to be anxious. She followed it with laughter and returning to her smile. "I'll explain myself in one simple fashion, even though I know people are gonna ask again. I'm the person behind everything you know that's happened in your life. Well, mainly the bad stuff. If I ever made something good happen that was an accident. Hey, I'm not perfect either."

"What are you doing here again?" the King said. "I said I didn't want anything to do with you."

"I'm here to say bye to BloodLip. I hoped it'd be something that would live on but I guess you can't have everything in life. As long as Penn lives I'm fine with that."

"As long as I live? BloodLip isn't going anywhere!" Penn said.

"Tell that to them," Eris said as she jerked her thumb back to them.

Eli took the rock from his pocket and instantly changed his form. Brittany engulfed her hands in flames. Sarah took her knives and readied them. But who was this all for? Me and the rest of us? No. Their black Corrupted eyes were peering into Penn's newly restored red pearls. They all had matching faces of rage beyond more than I've ever seen from them. And trust me, when I say I've seen rage from them, I've seen rage. This was something beyond that.

"We trusted you!" Eli yelled, putting everything he had into that scream. It hit Penn hard, immediately changing her face to fear.

"What are you talking about?" Penn said.

"All that was fake!" Sarah yelled. "All that love was just an act?!"

"No. Sarah! What are you talking about?! I've always loved you!"

"Liar!" Brittany shrieked. "I thought you were my friend!"

Penn wasn't able to find any words to describe herself, confused just like the rest of us. Even Zalus recognized that their anger was abnormal, backing up away from them. But Eris hadn't moved a muscle.

"Sad isn't it. The people you thought were connected to you are drifting away," Eris said. "But it's all an illusion. They aren't drifting away from you. You're drifting away from them. You see Penn, when you were born I went to you in your crib. I picked you up and told you that command that you've been carrying out all this time. I Corrupted you as much as I could you still being an infant. But I didn't need to worry about if it'd grow or not. I knew it would. Since your friends here were taken from your DNA, well, it meant they were drawn to your Corruption. This girl here that thinks she's your mom came and took that away. It's in their nature now to see that you're betraying them whether you really are or not."

"What?" Penn gasped. "No! I do love you guys! I'd never betray you!"

"Then what the heck do you call what you've done to us!" Eli yelled, tears filling his eyes.

Penn slowly started to walk towards them even though all their powers were ready at their use. I watched her take each step and hoped that none of them would hurt her. Once she was in a close enough range, I couldn't help but watch her get that close. These people were ready to strike despite their past together. I ran forward towards her.

And just like that, it was set up. With me being close to Penn and the rest of BloodLip, Eris put up a dome around us of her purple energy that separated the two sides of the room, us being in the middle. Eris and the King were on one side of the room and my friends and the others were watching from the side of the elevator. It made sense when I thought about it. If BloodLip saw Penn as someone who was betraying them and she was trying to fix things, it would make sense if Eris wanted me in the matter. It would mean they had a reason for them to fight. Not only did they hate me, but it made it look like I was helping her—like she was on my side. It was a recipe for a fight and only two outcomes where possible.

The dome caught both of us off guard and threw us off. I could read the fear in Penn's face and it didn't help me be confident at all. She was the one that told me confidence came from knowing what was gonna happen. I didn't see any of that.

"(Why? Why?! Why's this happening?! I never did anything wrong to you guys. You're my friends.)"

What? Why was Penn's voice in my head? It was almost an echoed version of what her voice sounded like. The words formed in a drawn out way as if her thoughts were being transported into my own. It was the same thing that happened when BloodLip was running away. That voice convinced me to stop them no matter what. This time it was Penn's thoughts on the matter. Was it a thing that Equilibrium could do? I took it as such and tried my best to respond back in the same manner.

"(Hey. Don't worry. I'm right here with you.)"

Hearing my voice in her head rattled her. She threw her head in my direction in complete turmoil. First it was her friends who were claiming that they betrayed her and now it's my voice that's infecting her head. With her looking at me, I gave her a nod to do my best to reassure her that I was gonna help her. It didn't matter what she's done to me in the past. What mattered was right now.

It started with me throwing out my sword. When she saw that I did so, it spurred her to do it as well. She watched as the very energy from her body was forming in her hand, waiting to hurt her friends. I could read the fear all over her and it hurt me. She knew what was coming and readied herself for it in the best way possible.

Eli was the first to do anything and, like he always did, charged at us. It wasn't me that he went for. It was Penn that he toppled to the floor. I ran for her to go and help but Sarah yanked me back and threw me to the floor herself. I was expecting them to jump on me to keep me down but they all ran over to Penn and started to hurt her in ways I would've never thought possible. The shrieks and screams that came from the redheaded Princess were torture, but it was what I needed to get back up and try to help.

I jumped on Brittany's back and threw her to the edge of the dome. When she was cleared from the pile that they made on top of Penn, I saw how much damage they'd done to her with blood now on her face.

So here I was backed up into this corner. I had to do one of two things. Either hope that Eris will stop this madness and let the dome fall or stop BloodLip. There was no reasoning with them here. They had nothing to back them like Penn did with Violet. And there was no running around them either until they tapped out. It was clear to me what was necessary. But how?! How could I even bring myself to end someone else's life? Once was enough.

I tried to think that I'd be able to stop them without severely hurting them or ending anyone's life, but every time I'd run over to someone to try and stop them from hurting her, they'd either throw me off or just come right back. Gosh! Why'd it have to be like this?!

I took my sword in my hand after being thrown again and ran at Sarah. My eyes were set on her back and threw it into her side. It took that to finally get her attention off Penn and onto herself. Even though she could heal over what I've done, she let out a scream as I felt the jolt of the sword in her skin. It made me freeze for a second right before Eli came running over and grabbed me by the neck. The sword dissolved and I instantly went for the gun in my leg. As his hands clamped on my neck, I put both Charlotte's and Wendy's bullets inside.

He shot bullets of his own in my eyes as he glared me down with his Corrupted eyes. I tried shimming the gun up in front of me but he caught on to what I was doing. He solved the problem for himself by slamming me down onto the floor, knocking the air out of me and slinging the gun across the floor. If it wasn't for the suit I was wearing I'd probably have a few broken ribs with the amount of force he put on my chest.

From the floor I could see Penn still getting attacked by Brittany. She wasn't even holding back. The only way I was gonna get her off of her was to try my best and tick her off. I'd done it before but this time needed to be something strong enough to fight through the Corruption taking over her life.

Now, I didn't know much about Brittany. I never talked to her much besides asking what the assignment for homework was in Algebra. But as I always did, I would read into things way more than I should've. Being a bystander, I was able to pick up on things. Apparently Brittany had pretty much lived with Penn and Violet. I wondered why she was always sleeping over at their house and with time I found out the reason. Her mom was hooked on drugs after her husband left her and she's been using that numbing feeling as an outlet. As much as I hated to bring something like that up, I needed to do whatever I could to stop her from hurting Penn.

"You know what's funny?" I said as I strained under Eli's fist on my trachea. "Your mom's a drug addict and you tried your best to get away from that. But look where you are." She stopped her fist and froze it in midair before it could make contact with Penn's face. "You're worse than she could ever get. The drugs are changing her into a monster. You're just like her. No. You're worse than her!"

The hand that was eternally stuck broke free from its position and set itself on fire. The red scorching flames grew to a size I've never seen. Brittany's head started to slowly turn as it revealed her face as it was completely mad with hysteria. The whole experience was driving her crazy and she couldn't get a grip on her sanity.

"I am not my mom!"

"Save that for her," I managed to let out.

It was enough to finally drag her off of Penn and burst into a sprint towards me. Her flames still didn't stop growing. It got to the point where it would spew out of other places other than her hands. Her hair was turned to flames but was still flowing around like her hair normally would.

As she stormed over, Eli picked me up and held me up for her to do anything she wanted to do to me. She threw back her elbow as I readied myself for the pain of a fist to my body full of fire.

"(Get the gun now!)" I yelled in my head to Penn.

The fist went to my face and stung my skin. Due to the adrenaline and the quickness of her fist, it thankfully wasn't enough to inflict any burn damage. But if this went on any longer then I would for sure end up with a face just like

Eli's, still carrying the burn mark from Wendy throwing the metal pole into his mug.

Penn sat up on the floor with blood coming down from her face, spitting the same substance.

"(Are you kidding me?!)"

"(Do it!) I said, putting everything into my words to get the thought across her head and inflict action.

She crawled over to the gun and held it in her hand. That combined with her red ruffled hair made a sight I could only stare at to not focus on the pain that Brittany was going to cause again. She hesitated for a second before wobbling to her feet and aiming the gun at Eli.

"Put him down!" she yelled.

"Oh so you are trying to protect him?" Eli said, squeezing me harder.

"Please just stop. This isn't you. You're not the Eli I know. He was the one that randomly showed up to my house with a pizza when I would feel down. Where's my friend?!"

"Where's *my* friend?!" he yelled back, resorting to choking me now.

"Eli please," she sobbed, her tears mixing with the blood.

Usually it was a few seconds until my vision would start to go, but this time it was almost immediate. There was no way for air to even try and enter my lungs. I gave Penn one more strained look as Eli's rocky fingers pressed into me.

She held the gun in the same way I did when Violet was in front of me. She was finally put into my position. She now knows what it's like to have someone's life on the line. But with me it was my friend on the line. Here it was my life.

Bang!

I felt the ripple of energy within Eli right as the bullet hit him. His hand eased up and he flumped back with the movement of the bullet's direction. Wendy's bullet was strong enough to push through the metal that he always changed into, enhancing his strength. When you put Wendy's will to Eli's strength she was always gonna win. Even when they did fight it was always a fair fight despite her height.

"Eli!" Sarah screamed. It was a blood curdling cry as she shouted out to the world that her twin brother was now dead.

With this newfound strength, she raised up from the floor, still dealing with the gash I put into her side. She instantly ran over to Penn with a real reason to hurt her. Penn reacted in fear and shot the gun once again, sending the bullet through her abdomen. It barely stopped her, increasing her scream through the pain and hatred. Tears came from her black eyes and fell down her chest over her veins that popped out of her neck. Penn let out a scream of fear as she emptied out the whole gun, missing most of them as she turned her head away.

I pushed Brittany away from me and jumped over Eli as I ran to Penn. There was nothing left in her gun and no bullets around to refill it. All besides one. Charlotte's bullet was still with me and it carried her will just as Wendy's did. I ran over to her and took the gun, loading the bullet as fast as I could, seeing Brittany make her way towards us from my peripheral vision. There was no reasoning with Sarah either and the only way she was going to fall like Eli was a bullet in the one place that would stop everything instantly.

Brittany reached me just after finishing loading it and dragged me back. I watched Sarah stagger to her feet from her knees and pull out one of the knives to throw it at Penn. I put up a wall as fast as I could, knowing fear was still a factor in Penn. It successfully blocked it but Brittany still had me. She suddenly reached over my shoulder for the gun just as Sarah ran at Penn and pushed her back towards the edge of the dome.

I desperately tried to keep control over the gun but her hands, still hot, were doing their best to grasp it. It stayed in a position, our opposing forces stopping it from going anywhere. It was aimed in the area behind Sarah so if the gun went off it wouldn't even hit her. But Penn kicked Sarah away from her just as the trigger was pulled by the both of us, instantly sending it in the same spot as Eli.

All these sounds of bullets entering people was too brutal of a sound for me to constantly relive over again and again. Before it was just the sound that reminded me of Violet, but here it was actually happening. Both of us watched Sarah flump back to the floor and lay stuck, her body not healing itself at all.

"Sarah!" Brittany screamed in my ear, still being directly behind me.

Penn let out a sob at the same time and let the gun drop to the floor, its job being completed. She watched her friend lay on the floor, all the memories of her no doubt flooding her head. Her hand came up and covered her mouth, muffling any sort of sounds that tried their best to escape.

Being in a trance at Sarah being gone just like Eli, I had to remind myself that Brittany could end me at any moment she wanted. I whipped around and made sure to throw her away from me. The instant I moved, she was already getting set on throwing flames of revenge at me. Her now being in front of me, the ball of fire was hurled. There was enough time for me to duck but she was already coming back to me, closing the distance. As her hand was reaching out for my neck that had already been harassed, a white flash whizzed by us and cut through the air as well as the end of Brittany's arm. It made her draw her arm back due to the pain.

"Enough!" Penn said, trying to plead with her, a bow in her hands. "I don't want to lose you to."

Brittany stood hunched over in pain, both physical and emotional. She looked almost as bad as Penn. Her eyes were beating into Penn's, searching for the Corruption that wasn't there anymore.

"You take both of my friends. You rip them from my life and now you want me to join them? You were the one who told us that we'd go down together if we ever did! This is proof. It was never about us. It was always about your stupid crush on Mark. It was always the peaceful way out. You're finally starting to believe the lies that they're telling you! I'll never fall for that! I'll carry BloodLip's name faithfully until I join my brother and sister! I'll take you both!"

She did exactly like she said she was gonna do and started once again to throw a flaming fist into me. I didn't expect it and it made contact with the left side of my face. Penn started to run towards us but Brittany threw a wave of fire hurling towards her. Penn was only able to block a portion of it, fear and exhaustion getting the better of her.

I wasn't gonna let her hurt anyone anymore so I drew my sword in my hand, ready to block her next attack. The other fist that was coming in was shielded by the edge of my sword. I quickly put both of my hands on the sword to twirl it towards her but she raised her arm to block it with her forearm. It blocked alright, but it sunk into her wound that Penn already gave her. She used her boot to kick me back and threw a fist under my chin, sending me to the edge of the dome.

Penn took over and drew her sword as well. She was being a lot more cautious with her attacks than I was used to seeing. It was her friend after all; the only one she had left. It was common that BloodLip fed on anger. I saw it from the very beginning. But here it was stronger than ever, being all inside Brittany. She was pounding Penn in, clearly the better fighter. Everything was affecting Penn more than she was probably hoping, hindering everything she did.

As I was getting my bearings and finally stood on my feet, I realized I needed to tell her something to help. There was no way that she was winning this fight in the state she was. She needed the one thing that was sapped from her. Confidence isn't found, it's created. I needed to create that very thing.

"(You need to get a hold of yourself!)"

"(How?!)"

"(If you aren't fighting for you friends any more than who are you fighting for?)"

I noticed her head picked up and searched through the hazy purple dome looking in the direction Violet was in. That was the person she was always fighting us for. If all of that was now here than she needed to keep it in her mind the best she could.

It only took one swift movement for Penn to get things under control. She dashed to the side, dropping her sword, and grabbing a hold of Brittany from behind. She fought back as she probably expected, but Penn kept her under control, falling to the floor. Brittany was on the floor with legs out as Penn sat behind her with her hands on her neck.

"Stop it!" Penn yelled. "Brittany stop it!"

"Never! I'll never stop fighting!"

"I don't wanna have to do this," Penn sobbed again.

"You could kill Eli and Sarah with no problem! What difference do I make!"

"You're my best friend!"

"Best friend?! You betrayed me!"

Flames grew from Brittany's hands as they gripped Penn's around her neck. Penn cried out in pain as her skin started to burn. I hurried over to them before Penn yelled at me, telling me to get back.

"Brittany. You're my friend," Penn cried.

"I was never your friend!"

The dome was starting to smell of flames and burnt flesh like it did back in the cafe in Springfield. Penn was still waiting and Brittany was letting her fire grow by the second. All I could do was watch as Penn struggled, tears continuously falling. Her scream got louder and louder as the pain was growing until she closed her eyes and threw her hands in opposing directions. I knew the action and turned my head as fast as I could before I could associate the snapping noise with the sight of it.

I was expecting a noise from Penn after that but I stayed with my head turned and my eyes closed. It was completely silent inside the dome, the smell of death filling my nostrils. I slowly opened my eyes and creeped over to look at Penn.

It was worse than I imagined. She was sitting with her legs at her sides and Brittany in her lap, eyes closed and her chest not moving. Penn's arms were laying on top of her dead best friend with seared skin marks on both of her wrists. Her eyes were wide, letting air enter in and drying her already red eyes. She was stuck, not doing anything. It was all setting in and it couldn't get to her that the people she's been with for years were now dead. Spontaneously, being completely delayed, she let out a scream from the bottom of her soul, leaning over to get everything she could out. Her tears fell on top of Brittany, sizzling as it made contact with her overheated skin.

The purple energy from Eris dissolved and revealed everyone's reaction to what happened inside. I first looked for my own friends, knowing the feeling of losing them. They were still where they stood, fear in their faces at watching Penn defeat her friends and conquering the Corruption that was entrenched in them. All of their faces were the same. The only person from that side of the King's quarters that didn't have that look was Violet.

When I looked at my covert homeroom teacher, she had tears falling from her face, once again defeating that notion that people told me of her not being emotional. Her feet followed her heart and she ran to Penn who was desperately letting everything from within herself out. She put her arms around her as they both wept together over the loss of the people they knew so well.

"You get used to it once you realize how much they weren't your friends," Eris said.

Her words made a burst of anger flow through me.

"You wouldn't know what it feels like!" I yelled.

"Yeah?" she said, raising an eyebrow. "Whatever. Doesn't matter what you do to the King. You could try and heal the world all you want. I wouldn't care one bit."

"Then what was the whole point of dropping the bomb and starting the war?"

"Oh believe me. I had a reason. And trust me. It's already started to play out. All I gotta do now is sit back and watch."

She turned and started to walk towards the double doors that led to the balcony. All of us watched as she slowly made her way past Penn and Violet along with the rest of BloodLip on the floor over to it. She swung the doors open with ease and walked out, taking a breath of fresh air.

I didn't know what this girl talked about. Ever. I knew she told me that she was behind everything but I didn't really know how. How could I just let her go when she was right here with us? We had a chance to stop her and stop whatever it was she was planning on doing. With this rage inside me over everything, I drew my bow and readied an arrow at her back as she looked out at the chaos that ensued outside.

"Where are you going?" I demanded, beating my eyes into her back and keeping the string tense.

She casually turned around and gave me a smile as she kept her hands on the railing.

"Oh come on. You really think you're gonna shoot me?"

"I shot someone before," I said firmly.

"You never did it when you had your chance before. What difference is it gonna be now? You can't make your mind over can you?"

I noticed her black eyes weren't looking at me at all, but rather, they were focusing on something behind me. It was just like the awkward moment when you think someone is waving at you and you wave back only to realize that it wasn't you at all they were waving at. I thought she was talking to me the whole time, but once I turned my head, keeping the arrow pointed at her, I noticed someone standing there.

There was a woman standing in the same position as me with a bow in her hand, pulling back the string of energy to let the arrow fly out. The white clothes she wore were the same ones she wore when she stopped everything to tell me about my powers. She always was here to save my butt when something went wrong. I didn't know who she was but all I did know is that she knew Eris and Eris knew her.

All the white around her was strange. I wanted to say it was a dress, but then again, when I thought about it, it wasn't a dress at all. It was more like some type of battle clothing from some mystical world. It's what you'd see a princess in a demented Disney movie wear if she were to fight along with the Prince. Her eyes looked the same as they did back when I looked at them in the abandoned building. The cloudiness to them that were always doing their best to control everything was still there. But she never did anything. She stood there with the bow drawn just like me.

Eris extended her smile and let out a chuckle from within, not opening her mouth and the dark hair of hers dipping into her eyes.

"Still can't do it huh. You're waiting for something but I'm telling you Purity, nothing's gonna change. Better save your energy for having to deal with him," she said, bobbing her head at me.

"Purity?!" both Violet and Scarlett yelled out in exclamation. She didn't acknowledge them and kept pressing her eyes into Eris as did I.

Eris changed the placement of her eyes and put them onto me, making me feel violated in so many different ways.

"I'll see you again soon Mark. Don't try to miss me too much that it kills you. I'd like for you to be alive when I come back. I wanna show you something that happens once the wrong people get mixed into you. I know you never did anything to deserve what we're gonna do to you, but hey, that's where the fun comes in. You've already dealt with Corruption, and let me tell you, that's just the start of it. But something more devastating comes after Corruption. You see, Corruption has a unique way of taking over the person that is its host. It brings out the real you. And once it does that, well, that's for you to see. Oblivion's coming Mark. I just hope you're ready for it."

I shook my head with confusion. What the heck was she talking about?!

"Coming back for what?" I asked.

"The only day that matters. The fall of the Equilibrium."

Eris lowered her head more than it already was and stared one more time into my soul. She never bothered to take it off of me and put it on anyone else. She stared at me the whole way through until she suddenly disappeared into time. I tried looking to see if there was a trail of where she went like I used on Penn, but there was nothing there.

"Purity what are you doing here?!" Violet said, getting up from comforting Penn. Once again, she still ignored her.

"You should've shot her," Purity said, still looking out into the balcony that let outside air in.

"What? You didn't shoot her either! You had a chance!" I said.

She let her bow disappear as her eyes followed Scarlett storm past all of us towards the only person on the other side of the floor now. He was as far back as he could be from us, standing with his back to the elegant fire place he had. I watched his eyes grow in fear as the person who was fighting against him all her life finally was about to have her moment.

"Wait, Scarlett listen!" Zalus yelled.

She reached out and grabbed hold of his neck from the side, simply resting her palm there. With a force stronger than a hippos bite, she slammed his head into one of the glass tables he had. The glass never completely broke but the compactness of it shattered just in one piece, making a little spider web shape.

"You have no idea how much you've ruined my life!" Scarlett yelled.

"Penn!" he shouted, blood starting to come out of the cut on the side of his head.

No one bothered to see if she would react or respond to his voice. Her friends were killed and now her father that was never there for her was asking her for help. Like she'd ever help him.

Scarlett was about to slam his head against the table again, but someone ran up and pushed her out of the way. Scarlett tumbled away from Zalus, being taken completely off guard. Who the heck was that? Was Eris back or something? Those questions were answered as soon as I saw a blot of red hair standing next to the King. If those questions were answered then hopefully asking this would make it be answered too. Why the heck was she helping him?!

"Get away from him!" Penn yelled. Scarlett shot back a look as soon as she could, taking out her handgun and pointing it at her. "He's mine."

Her last words confused Scarlett. It took Penn punching her own father in the face for Scarlett to get it and put the weapon away. I thought that maybe she wouldn't want that and try to fight Penn over fighting the King, but she let her go right ahead. After the initial punch, Penn manhandled him into what looked like his bedroom, dragging him out of the quarters.

"Penn no! Penn! Stop!" he yelled out as he tried fighting her monster grip. There was no way around that Zalus. How's your mud bath feeling now?

She threw him in the room and shut the door behind her, letting her red hair be the last thing we saw.

Charlotte was the first to run forward and stand close to me. The rest followed her as I watched the people I saved stand full of life. It was strange to think that they were once dead. I couldn't live that way if they ever did. I gave Charlotte the best smile I could give, peering into her dark brown eyes.

"So I can say that I died three times," Will said, crossing his arms and giving me a smile. "Who knew that would happen?"

"Ugh! I know. What the heck! It felt so freaking weird!" Wendy said. "It was like I got all cold and bleh!" She stopped her rant on a dime and changed her peppy mood. She dipped her head into her chest and cowered down. "I didn't think you'd guys see me cry."

"Oh come on!" Will yelled.

"Psh. You kidding me Wendy?" I said. "I've seen Will cry so what's the worst that I could see." Will widened his eyes and glared at me for mentioning the time he threw that lady with the stroller. "What?! I'm trying to make her feel better!"

"So you can time travel?" Charlotte asked, raising an eyebrow and awaiting my answer anxiously.

"Not really. It's time jumping. So technically I can jump to a point in time where I was and I inhabit my old body. There's no doubles of me."

"That means Penn can do it too," Monica muttered.

"That's why she was trying to kill you at the party."

"And that's what I don't get," Scarlett said loudly, butting into the conversation as she walked over to us. All of us turned our heads as we watched her in the same red suit that had scratches on it from the fighting she was doing outside. "If you could always time jump it'd make sense that you could help a civilization on the verge of collapse. But why didn't Rylan tell us about it in the first place? Why didn't he tell us that Penn was an Equilibrium?"

I followed Scarlett's eyes over to Purity who was standing in the same place she was before, facing the balcony with the doors open.

"You know her?" Kerren asked.

"We all did," Violet said, filled with the same questions as Scarlett.

"You know the girl we talked about that helped Rylan and told him that a war was coming. It was her," Scarlett said.

Purity took in a deep breath and finally turned to face them.

"Think about it. We never wanted to tell anyone for a reason. It'd change the way you do things. Who knows how much you guys would change knowing that they could both do that. You could try and maybe use it for yourself like the King was trying to do. If no one knew than you'd fight for the people themselves. It wouldn't be about his powers."

"Who cares about that now," Violet said. "Whatever happened to a hello? We haven't seen each other for years and you don't bother saying anything? What happened to you being the happy girl who was playing with Aqua on the beach?"

Purity lowered her eyebrows and stared into her.

"Time's change Violet. People change. Things are a lot more serious now. You have no idea how many people's lives are on the line now."

"But we took Zalus down. After Penn does whatever she wants with him he's dead either way."

Purity shook her head before speaking.

"This was never the problem. This planet was never what was needing saving. Why did we make the Salvation Project in the first place? It was to protect the Equilibrium. Zalus wasn't what I was scared of hurting them."

"Then why can't you tell us?" Scarlett said.

"Same reason I didn't tell you about Mark's powers. You can think people have good motives all you want but there's always that chance they can turn their back on you.

If someone has that knowledge and does so, the problem can be much worse than it was in the beginning. Believe me. I've had it happen to me. It's the reason all this is happening."

There was a thud and a scream as Penn was throwing Zalus around the room. The thought that I had of there being more to the problem than I thought was coming more and more true. First BloodLip was the problem, but now this new group called Oblivion comes and reveals itself as the problem the whole time. I didn't know what was coming, but I knew one thing. I was gonna get my answers from Purity one way or another.

*   *   *

It felt so good to finally be outside of the Palace. The air was a lot cooler than it was when we first got to Exon. Either that or it got really stuffy inside the King's quarters. I could smell the stench of smoke and fire. The whole city was torn. There were buildings that were now toppled. When you have kids running around a city with godlike powers and Palace Guards with no sense of moral, you're bound to have destruction. From the steps of the Palace I could see that.

Good thing there wasn't the need to deal with the kids anymore. Monica was able to find ALIS's mainframe, her network. The whole string of servers and wires was too complex for my eyes and I let her deal with everything. She told me before she shut her down that they had a binary conversation. It bothered her a bit I could tell, but I let her be to herself, whatever it was that ALIS must've told her. Right after she shut her down we got report that all the kids were back to who they were. They didn't remember where they were but they knew everything that was important such as their name and who their parents were. It was hard to think about that maybe some of them killed their very parents back in the outer cities.

I could make out some of these kids in the sea of people. It was strange to stand in front of all these thousands of people. The way the stairs worked at the Palace was they were elevated to a certain extent over the main level of the city. Me and my friends stood next to each other. On the sides of us was Violet, Scarlett, Kerren, and Penn. In the middle of us was Zalus, the King, in handcuffs.

Every citizen of Exon was out here in front of the Palace. As for the people from the outer cities, we got word that the survivors were sent out here to the city. It was a lot more than we thought so I guess that's a plus. But as far as I could see, there were people there. No speck of street was to be seen. Even the highways that hung over streets were filled with people like they were when we first got here. All of us were mesmerized by it so much so that we didn't say a thing. I looked over at Wendy to see if maybe she'd be all giddy from there being a crowd. But nothing. Not a sign of a smile on her face.

Scarlett sent out a message using the same system Zalus used to tell everyone on Novus that we had captured him. There was to be a trial publically held in front of the Palace preceding his execution.

Palace members that were part of that revolt in Exon against Zalus like that man that called Headquarters helped in setting the cameras and speakers up for the event. There was a light chatter from the crowd as the seconds were counting down to the end of the Exon rule. I was even surprised to see Palace Guards in the crowd, giving up serving a corrupt King. People would give them looks but they were all too focused to see what would happen to Zalus, the person who's been ruling them for years.

Scarlett stood in front of a mic that was placed for Zalus to use. It must've infuriated him for her using the very piece of equipment he's been using all this time.

"Thank you everyone for attending. I'd like to formally introduce myself. My name is Scarlett. Some of you may know me as Terra, an alias I used to cover my identity while I was in hiding. I promised a lot of you that'd I'd be back to help The Equilibrium. Well, I kept that promise. I've lived under Zalus's rule all my life. We've seen time and again how he's proven himself to be a ruler that can't be trusted, almost killing off the entire human race on Novus. He shouldn't rule anymore and I'm making sure of that."

She turned her head, keeping her mouth to face the mic.

"Mark and his friends, the very people who make up The Equilibrium are to be commended for what they did for everyone. No longer are we rewarding people for their service to a nation. We're rewarding people for their service to the human race as a whole, to whatever place that may extend. From here all the way to a world out there that we know nothing about."

I found a small smirk that creeped up into my face. I'll admit it. It felt good knowing that I was being acknowledged for all the hard work I did. I gave up so much but I got so much back. With this warm feeling in me, I looked over at Charlotte to see if she felt it too. Sure enough, she was waiting for me, giving me the same smile.

"Before we proceed. We'd like anyone who opposes our decision to execute the King to please step forward and plead your case."

The crowd grew cold. I was half expecting someone to come and do it since the people here were just as crazy as in Springfield. Thankfully, no one bothered to do it and stayed right where they were, probably feeling the same way I was hoping that no one would.

"Very well. To reassure everyone that we plan to be as fair as we can, making this new establishment, we're going to give Zalus Exon one last time to defend himself."

Scarlett stepped back and allowed the two Equilibrium Guards that were holding him place him in front of his stand that carried his initials. I could read the confusion in his face. He was thinking it. I know it.

How did this happen to me?

Can't run from it buddy. Face what's coming to you.

"How could you betray me? How?!" he yelled, shaking as his neck strained. "I gave you everything! I made this city the best thing that's happened to Novus! I protected you from the war!" His distraught red eyes searched for the only other red that he could find in all the planet. Penn didn't even bother to turn her head towards him and glared at him from the side of her vision, seeing all that she did to him inside his bedroom. "Penn. Sweetie. Why?"

Scarlett nodded her head to take him off the mic as she stood back in her place.

"If there's no further words, we'll proceed."

The words made a cold feeling go down my spine. I knew it meant another person that would fall before my eyes after all the death I've seen today. And this would never be a thing that would take place on Earth, or at least not in the US. They made sure they executed their enemies in private. Here, he was to be executed in front of everyone, just as it would've been in days of old where public executions were the norm.

Scarlett took her weapon that was attached to her leg and flicked it into her hand, walking towards Zalus with firm eyes. I knew she had the ability to kill someone when she almost killed me out of pure rage, but I was finally gonna be able to see it. When she walked up to him, she gave him one more glare before placing the weapon to the source of all his mad ideas.

No. This wasn't right. I couldn't just watch and not feel like it was okay for me to be here if it wasn't for a reason. The thick silver piece of metal in my suit moved around and called for me to take it out. My own bullet was never used. Will used his the second he got it, Monica used it to save the kids in the school, and Charlotte and Wendy's was used to finish BloodLip. Mine was nowhere on that list. It would be lost to all that's been done here on Novus.

"Wait," I said, walking over to Scarlett. Me speaking up surprised the others I noticed. I could see in the side of my vision that Charlotte's eyes were following me as I passed her. Scarlett did the same with picking her head up off of Zalus. I reached inside and pulled out the deadly piece of metal. "Use this." I turned to look into the King's eyes one last time, seeing the reflection of my hand holding the bullet. "Remember this? All of theirs were used to help all the people you were trying to hurt. This one's mine. This one's the one that's gonna hurt the most."

Scarlett was about to take the bullet but Penn came over and snatched it out of my hand, taking the gun from Scarlett as well. She loaded it and put in the same position Scarlett had it in.

"This is my job," she said. "I'm the one who's finishing this."

Once again, Scarlett complied and backed up to let her end her family line.

"Penn. What are you doing?!" he said hysterically, the thought of his daughter doing such a thing breaking his sanity. "You're my little girl."

"Don't you even dare! I am not your little anything!" she yelled as she squeezed the gun tighter. "You were never there for me. You sent me to a different dimension! You kill thousands of people! You're nothing to me!"

"No! You're wrong. I'm your father," he said, desperately looking into her eyes.

"I don't have a father. I only have a mom. And her name is Violet."

The gunshot took me by surprise and made me jump, turning my head to the crowd as he fell to the floor. It was a weird feeling, I'll give it that. I wanted to curl up on the floor and stop myself from hurling, but the other half of me wanted to jump up and shout. Which one was it?

The citizens of Novus sure had a decision. Within seconds people started to cheer. The sound of their joyful cries hurt my ears. It didn't even sound like a crowd normally would. It had the sound of what zombies would sound like if they were ever a real thing. It was a continuous groan that didn't stop.

But hey! Why the heck was I feeling like this? The King was dead. All of this was over. Everything that I was made for, everything that *we* were made for was done. It may have been crappy while doing it but it was sure worth all the lives we saved. I'll be honest, I didn't care one bit about the people here. Even when I did find out that I was actually born here, I didn't care. But there's something I've realized in the past days. People are people no matter where you go. If I experienced so much grief with my own friends dying then how much would that be felt if people kept dying left and right? There was a way to prevent that and I took it. We all did.

Will gave me a pat on the back as we stood in our formation in front of all these thousands of people cheering. Even though I still wanted to punch his pretty boy face, I gave him a smile in return. I looked over at Monica afterwards and raised an eyebrow at her. She stared back with a deadly stare. I kept staring and so did she, seeing which would be the first to look away. This was the game we always played, and just like always, I was the winner. She crossed her arms and turned back to look at the crowd.

I went ahead and just went down the line to give Wendy a look. This girl, man. I swear. She was something else. I had the strangest time with her on Novus. But I guess she was okay with me knowing that she likes me. If anything it brings us closer knowing that she can tell me pretty much anything. She dropped a hip and gave me a big ol' wink.

And Charlotte. When our eyes locked it felt like all the problems we ever had were so tiny the wind could pick it up in the spring breeze. It brought a wave of nostalgia back to the times when things were a lot simpler. I noticed the bottom of her hair was right where it should be and my smile extended. Same old Charlotte.

These people gave me so much. Even though I did save their lives I could never repay them. I was saved by their love that they've shown. Expect maybe Will and Wendy. No. But you get my point. I've created bonds with these people I've never met before and we risked everything for each other. This was what I always dreamed of and I finally got it. You bet I was gonna do everything to make sure I keep it.

Those were my thoughts as I looked out into the crowd and gave one more smile as the wave of completeness came over me. Everything was now done.

*   *   *

"Can it kill you to put on the clothes you're given?"

Wendy scoffed at Kerren and fixed the bottom of her shirt that didn't even extend past her waistline.

"Hey! If I have the ability to wear whatever the heck I wanna wear then imma wear it."

"It's fine. She can take whatever she wants. Are you sure you don't want to take some more clothes with you?" the owner of the clothing store said.

"You kidding me?" I said. "She pretty much doesn't wear clothes in the warm weather. I mean look at her. Short shorts and a tank top that isn't even a tank top. No offense by the way. I know it's your clothing but when she wears anything she ruins it."

The lady giggled as she put her hand over her mouth. We were inside one of the many malls in Exon. They were a lot fancier than any mall I've been to on Earth, even though it was only one I've been to. We changed out of our powered suits and gave them back to Scarlett who put them back in their respective pods. One of the owners of a clothing store in the mall came up to Scarlett and Violet afterwards telling them that she would like to give us some of her new clothes. It made sense since we were gonna need some.

All five of us changed and got to pick out some of our own clothes. Charlotte and I asked her to choose some for us since we didn't know what to even wear in the first place. Monica didn't need any help finding black clothes. Will, well, Will knows what he always wants. Now with Wendy, you already know what she wanted.

After thanking the kind lady for supplying us with clothes, I went outside of the mall where Penn, Violet, and Scarlett were talking with the person that knew too much of my life. Purity was leaning against a wall with her arms crossed, not even smiling. The other two woman who seemed to jump right back into their friendship had smiles on their faces, especially now that this was all over. When I saw Purity like that it made me sick, disgusted that she couldn't even show some happiness.

As I walked up towards them I was greeted by Violet with a wave and the same smile she was giving Scarlett.

"You did good Mark," she told me.

"I did what I could," I said, shrugging. I turned my attention to Purity as quickly as I could to take the attention off myself. "So you were the one who told me to not let them escape, wasn't it?"

She didn't bother to look me directly in the eye, still spacing out into the other direction.

"Of course it was."

"So you wanted me to kill them?"

"What does it matter? You already did that yourself."

I scoffed as I glared into her.

"What's your problem?!"

It's what finally made her look at me.

"What's my problem? You have no idea what I've been through, okay? Don't act like everything's fine and dandy."

"Why are you complaining? The King's dead! I did what I was born for."

"That's not why you were born you idiot. Penn was born to do that. You were born for something else entirely. Why would there be two Equilibrium born on one planet?"

"Wait. He wasn't born for that?" Scarlett asked.

"You've treated Mark like he's special and I had you do that for a reason. He is. Now the only thing I don't get is why I had to tell you about your powers. Once an Equilibrium knows he's an Equilibrium, they know exactly what they can do. If they're a Sentinel then they know those powers as well. Now why didn't you know?"

"You're asking me that?" She rolled her eyes and had enough of me. "And another thing I don't get is what

Corruption is. Corrupted Charlotte was trying to mess with one of the tubes of the kids. What is it?"

"It's a disease. I discovered it years ago. The conditions of it are unique only to Equilibrium. It might sound strange at first but it's all true. Corruption starts forming for Equilibrium with a lack of companionship, or better called friends. It's why I had Rylan create Project Salvation so we could give you friends who would always be with you."

"So only if an Equilibrium doesn't have friends?"

"Kinda. Eris found a way to manipulate it after turning Corrupted. Ever since then she's been going around and trying to kill off any civilization that's on the verge of extinction. It's why the rest of BloodLip felt abandoned by Penn when she was set free from it. Since they were taken from her DNA, they too had a form of Corruption in them. Since Eris put Corruption in Penn when she was small, it grew even though she had friends. It was the only reason she was able to break free from it."

"Well at least it only affects Equilibrium," Violet said.

Purity shook her head and let out a sigh.

"It affects you guys to. If someone is around it for too long they can get the same symptoms. You've seen it. The black hair, eyes, and nails. But since it's a disease made for Equilibrium, it kills any human who has it pretty quickly."

"Well what about my friends?" I said.

"They're unique to the situation. Since they're in part a form of superior humans, they can withhold it longer than humans can. There's a specific term for them, though, after they've been Corrupted that's only tailored to people who have transplanted Equilibrium DNA. Don't worry about that right now." She let out another sigh before continuing. "I hope I never see you again. Trust me, it's a bad thing if we do. If we ever meet again it means the worst thing possible to happen is happening. Taking what Eris said, it probably is."

"Who's Oblivion anyways?" I asked.

"The opposite of what you are. You have more popularity than just two different planets. Everyone knows who you guys are. *Everyone*. Look. Just go back home. Try and forget what happened here."

"Go back home?" Violet said. "The portal doesn't work anymore. Scarlett told me."

"Don't need one. How'd you get back here? Equilibrium can travel between dimensions."

"There was an attack on Earth before we came here. Isn't that gonna be—"

"That's why I had you get Violet," Purity said, cutting me off. "She died in your past but you changed that by bringing her back. You created a tangent in time by doing that. Everything that happened before you got here didn't happen. You'll be back to where you guys left off like nothing ever happened on Earth."

"So we can get home?" I said enthusiastically.

"You have ears. Do me a favor Mark. When you get back home, don't think that things are gonna be smooth. You're known all over the entire known universe. Eris told you. Things are coming. I give you my promise that I'll help where I can."

"Shut up I can wear whatever the heck I wanna wear!" I heard Wendy yell as she walked out with the others and Kerren.

Seeing them made a wave of excitement spur in me knowing that we could get back to our normal lives.

"Guys! We're going home!"

"What?!" Charlotte yelled, running towards me.

"Purity said we can go home. I can travel through dimensions!"

Charlotte opened her mouth and held it open as she gazed at me in pure joy. It immediately connected through all of us as we all jumped up like little kids. I saw Kerren's face in the midst of our little party of happiness and saw mixed feelings.

"You can finally come back and see mom!" I said, holding her shoulders.

She gave a longing smile and shook her head.

"I can't leave, Mark. This is my home just like Earth is yours. Ironic I know. But I can't leave here."

"Oh yeah. You're gonna take over when Scarlett dies."

"Mark!" she said, playfully smacking my arm. "Don't say that!" She stopped and watched me, looking into the eyes of her brother she waited years for. "I'm gonna miss you."

She pulled me in and wrapped her arms around me, resting her head on my shoulder. I returned the hug as well, knowing fully that she was my sister no matter who my parents were.

"I'll miss you too sis. You're not gonna be bored being all by yourself?"

"Nah," she said, pulling off of me. "I got a whole planet to refill and organize. It's gonna be hard work but it'll keep me busy. Hey. Can you do something for me when you get back? Give mom a hug for me."

I reached up to her head and messed up her hair.

"You got it."

"You heading back?" Scarlett asked Violet.

"Yeah. I gotta take care of my girl here," she said, putting an arm around Penn and bringing her in close.

"I'm glad we were able to put our differences apart Penn. What you did today is going to be held throughout many generations I can tell you that."

Penn didn't say anything but gave a small nod like Monica would do.

"You guys ready?" Violet asked us.

We all gave our own ways of answering, eager to get back home. Kerren gave me one more hug before taking her place next to Scarlett. We all got together and put our hands together like we've done many times before only this time Violet and Penn were joining us.

As much as I hated Novus, I grew to like it with time. Even though it was the place I was born, it felt distant, but after everything that's happened it's become a second home to me. I'll admit, I was gonna miss this place.

I gave Scarlett and Kerren one more look before we vanished into the strange world of transportation between dimensions.

*　　*　　*

I gasped for air as I came to. My eyes scanned for anything that looked familiar. To my surprise, everything did look familiar. I'd been where I was standing many times before. It was a grassy mound that extended into the park in downtown Springfield. It was right outside the mall that was packed with people.

The spring sun hit me right in the face with a wave of warmth, so comforting and familiar that I wanted to stay right where I was. As I looked around, everyone was here, even Penn and Violet were standing in amazement. We all exchanged looks as we started to realize we were back on Earth, back in Springfield, back home.

Wendy let out a noise from her mouth of shock. We turned to look at her as she was just looking out into the city. She couldn't move. The thought of being back home was too much for her. We kept watching and within seconds tears formed in her eyes that were released down her cheeks. Charlotte soon followed as did the rest of us, including me. We were home. It was that simple. There wasn't a sign of an attack on the city anywhere and that dome that was forming over the city wasn't there either. It was as calm as downtown could get and I loved it.

We broke down crying as the waves of realization kept coming in. All five of us took turns giving each other hugs, doing anything to express to each other that we could get back to our lives. As I was hugging Charlotte, I realized something in the midst of both our tears of joy. We did it. We actually did it. We went from being some dumb snobby kids in a high school who couldn't do a single thing to saving a human race. It hit me. Nothing could stop us. As long as we had each other, there wasn't a force out there strong enough to break our own. And now with Penn not being Corrupted, she could think for herself. In the months to come, I never realized it, but we actually became friends. You take the friendship I had with my friends and stack Penn and Violet on top of that, there is *nothing* that can stop that.

Bring it on Eris. We're ready for whatever it is you're bringing. We're waiting. There's nothing you can do to stop us.

Oh how wrong I was...

Project Oblivion

Corruption: a disease stemmed from Equilibrium decent. It is known to affect only three different groups of individuals.

Equilibrium: changes drive of individual and makes them act on sheer emotion. There is very little for real control over one's self. Physical changes occur in the form of black hair, eyes, and nails. Non-lethal.

Humans: same physical changes. Experience of brutal pain. Lethal.

Genetically Modified Humans (Equilibrium DNA):

Oblivion.

Anderson